Trained ... assisted with m... ape and homicide. win... ...olden Gateway, Readers' Choice, and Daphne du Maurier awards, her short story 'Scutwork' was selected to appear in *First* ...the ...tars

...ge'

BLIND
FAITH

C.J.LYONS

sphere

SPHERE

First published in the United States by St. Martin's Press in 2012
First published in Great Britain as an ebook in 2012
This paperback published in 2013 by Sphere

A CIP catalogue record for this book
is available from the British Library.

ISBN 978-0-7515-5027-6

Printed and bound in Great Britain by Clays Ltd, St Ives plc

Papers used by Sphere are from well-managed forests
and other responsible sources.

MIX
Paper from
responsible sources
FSC® C104740

Sphere
An imprint of
Little, Brown Book Group
100 Victoria Embankment
London EC4Y 0DY

An Hachette UK Company
www.hachette.co.uk

www.littlebrown.co.uk

Without my loyal readers this book would never have happened.

This one is for you guys!

ACKNOWLEDGMENTS

My thanks to the law enforcement officers and FBI agents who assisted in the creation of *Blind Faith* as well as the members of the Crimescene Writers' Group including Steve Brown, Robin Burcell, Wally Lind, and Lee Lofland. I'd also like to thank the wonderful folks at the FBI's Washington Field Office and their training academy at Quantico for allowing me to tour their facilities, shoot their guns, and ask tons of questions.

Joe Collins provided explosives expertise, while my critique partners: Toni McGee Causey, Kendel Flaum, Carolyn Males, and Debra Webb, kept me mostly sane. My fantastic agent, Barbara Poelle; foreign rights agents, Heather Baror-Shapiro and Danny Baror; and the entire team of amazing professionals at St. Martin's, including Kelley Ragland, Andy Martin, Matthew Shear, Elizabeth Lacks, and Sarah Melnyk, among others, worked their magic behind the scenes to take *Blind Faith* to the next level. Without their expertise and guidance, I'd be lost.

ACKNOWLEDGMENTS

While I've tried to keep things as "real" as possible, obviously this is a work of fiction and my job is to entertain, so any deviation from actual police procedure is my doing, not the fault of my advisors. As always, all characters are totally fictional and solely the invention of a thriller writer's mind warped by seventeen years of working in the ER and with victims of violent crimes.

Thanks for reading!
CJ

PS: For more of the behind-the-scenes story of *Blind Faith*, feel free to check out my website at www.CJLyons .net.

BLIND
FAITH

June 6, 2007:

WALLS PRISON UNIT, HUNTSVILLE, TEXAS

CHAPTER ONE

Sarah Durandt flinched as faded blue-checked gingham curtains rattled open to reveal the prisoner strapped to a gurney.

One of the women behind her gasped. Sarah leaned forward, one hand flattened against the glass that separated them from a monster. She breathed through her mouth. It was the only way to choke down the heavy air trapped inside the tiny cement-walled room.

She and the other witnesses were gathered behind glass so thick halos circled the objects in the white-tiled execution chamber on the other side. Bulletproof glass. Who did they think would be doing the shooting? The condemned man already woozy from sedatives or those who came to watch him die?

Sarah curled her hands one into the other and held them still on her lap, shivering as the air-conditioning blew a frosty stream down on her. Eleven others were crowded into the room with her, families representing the other victims. She barely noticed them. They were here for closure. She needed answers.

Her gaze narrowed to a laser-sharp focus aimed at the prisoner beyond the glass. His arms were extended, needles inserted into veins on both sides of his body. Seven leather straps crossed his body and limbs, holding him in a position eerily reminiscent of a crucifixion. But this man was no Messiah.

This man was the devil incarnate.

Damian Wright was medium sized, someone who would not stand out in a crowd with his bland face, blander features.

Sarah knew better. She knew his cunning. Hidden behind his façade of normalcy smoldered a sick desire to torture and maim. Even here, on his deathbed, he persisted in tormenting her. Denying her the slightest measure of comfort or peace.

She wasn't sure why, of all the victims, Damian had focused his sick power plays on her. She wasn't anyone special, just a schoolteacher from upstate New York who lived in a village of less than five hundred souls. Her brown hair was usually pulled back into a ponytail and forgotten about, leaving it free to fall around her shoulders on special occasions like today—the execution of a serial killer.

Damian's sweat-beaded skin glistened as he lay beneath a large, round surgical light. His eyes were squeezed shut against its unflinching illumination. The warden nodded to a black-suited man with a small silver cross on his lapel. The man stretched out his hand, his wedding ring shimmering as it passed through the beam of light, and pulled a black microphone down. Sarah rubbed her own ring finger, tracing the plain band Sam placed there six years ago.

Uncoiling like a cobra, the microphone bobbed hypnotically above Damian's lips. A click, like a muffled gunshot, echoed through the witness room as the warden switched on the intercom. The scratchy sound of Damian's breathing filled the room.

Sarah found herself inhaling in time with Damian, could almost smell the antiseptic and surgical tape and the stench of sweat and nerves emanating from beyond the window. Alan Easton, who sat beside her, gave her hand a comforting squeeze.

"You okay?" he asked, his tone that of a friend rather than her lawyer. She was the only family here to bear witness for Sam and Josh. The only family Sam had left. And Josh, how could she not be here for her son?

She nodded, her attention focused on the events in front of her. The execution chamber held only three men: the warden in his navy suit, bleached white shirt, and narrow tie; the black-suited minister; and Damian Wright, the man who had destroyed her life.

If Sarah were to describe the Death House to her sixth-grade students back home, she would have said the theme of the room, of the entire building set far apart from normal prison housing, was containment.

Nothing was meant to ever escape this tiny building with its cement walls painted an institutional green. The utilitarian execution chamber beyond the viewing window made no efforts to soften or hide its purpose. A flat surgical table, arms splayed wide, bolted to the floor was its only piece of furniture.

"Any last words?" the warden asked the condemned man.

Sarah came to attention. A fly trespassed into the profane proceedings and beat its wings against the cage shielding two flickering fluorescent lightbulbs, its buzzing deafening. Damian Wright, convicted murderer and child rapist, opened his rheumy eyes and stared directly at her. She pulled her hand free from Alan's, fisted it tight.

Tell me. Say something. Give me a clue.

Her prayers went unheard. Damian remained silent, muscles slack, not fighting his restraints. Only his chest moved, rising and falling as he counted down to his last breath. Sarah's lungs squeezed tight, ready to burst from pressure. Damian stared at her, a smile creasing his eyes.

She blinked first, not ashamed to surrender; she'd do anything if it helped her to find Sam and Josh.

Damian's smile widened. But he remained silent.

Fury knotted her gut. Did he torment her, refuse her the closure she so desperately yearned for, because she'd been away at that damn mandatory in-service on the day he took Josh? Or was it because of all the boys he'd killed, only Josh had a father willing to fight, to die for him?

Alan said it was probably because Sam interrupted his ritual with Josh. Forced him to deviate from his sick, twisted fantasy to kill Sam before he could return to Josh.

The minister intoned from his Bible, his eyes never rising from the written word to gaze upon the lost soul he prayed over.

The words of the Psalm, words that twenty-two months ago would have brought Sarah comfort and solace, were now reduced to meaningless noise with less significance than the buzzing of the fly. She pressed her palm flat against the cold glass, more intent on gleaning the answers she needed from Damian than listening to the word of God.

She'd spent her entire life listening. Where was God when she'd needed him most? Where was he when her husband and son needed him?

"I'm sorry we couldn't stay the execution," Alan whispered. "I know how much you hoped—"

She shrugged his words away, her entire universe consisting of the gaze of a killer. The man who had confessed to killing Sam and Josh—but who refused to tell her where they were buried.

For a year and a half she had fought. Fought Damian Wright's silence, his refusal to see her. Fought the new Texas law that allowed executions to be "fast-tracked" with an unprecedented efficiency. Fought her own desire to see Damian die. A desire superseded only by her need to find her husband and son.

The warden strode forward, reading from a document in a monotone that floated just beyond the periphery of Sarah's awareness.

Where are they, you sonofabitch? Sarah tried to broadcast all her loathing and hatred into her glare, hoping to loosen Damian's tongue in these, his last seconds on this Earth. Her fist pounded against the thick glass, creating only the smallest of muffled thuds.

The killer didn't flinch or look away from her. Nor did he speak. Instead his expression turned to one approaching pity. As if she were the one condemned, not him.

The warden finished and removed his glasses, aiming a small nod in the direction of the executioner's booth. Sarah had researched the procedure. Behind the one-way mirrored glass, an unseen man flipped a switch. Medication flowed into Damian's veins. First more sedatives, then a paralytic, finally the potassium chloride to stop his heart.

Time stopped. Sarah didn't blink. Damian didn't blink.

Three minutes later, the minister stood aside as a man clad in a white coat stepped forward and listened with a stethoscope. He straightened, reached a hand out to Damian's face, and closed the killer's eyes.

The blinds snapped shut.

A collective sigh swirled through the room as the other

witnesses shifted in their seats. Through the haze filling Sarah's vision she heard several women and a man sobbing, felt the rustle of their movements as the room emptied. She remained frozen, not blinking, eyes burning.

Alan touched her elbow, pulled her fist away from the glass, and drew her up onto unsteady feet. "We have to go now," he murmured.

She kept her face craned toward the darkened window until the last possible moment. Finally, Alan led her out into bright sunshine, Texas heat and humidity bearing down on her with the intensity of a ten-ton truck.

For a moment she was the one suffocating under the weight of paralyzed lungs. Her chest tightened. For an instant it was her heart that stopped.

She blinked and pain returned. An ice-pick stabbing behind her eyes, her constant companion for twenty-two months, unmitigated by any sedatives or hope of release. Unlike Damian Wright's pain.

And she knew she was alive. At least her body was. Her mind was. Her soul—that was buried in some unmarked grave back home, up on Snakehead Mountain.

Alongside Sam and Josh.

It's over, it's over, it's over . . . The words threaded themselves through Sarah's mind, spinning a cocoon that blocked out all feeling, providing a soft, safe place to hide. A place where there was no need to think, to do, to react. To be. *It's over, it's over, it's over* . . .

Sarah hugged herself tighter and leaned against the car window, her back to Alan as he drove them away from the prison. She'd promised herself no matter what, she wouldn't break down, at least not in front of anyone.

But Alan wasn't anyone. Alan understood—he'd been through it himself. His wife had been killed by a drug addict who stormed their house looking for cash. That was why he'd left his corporate law practice to focus on victims' rights, to help people like Sarah.

How could she have survived the past two years without Alan?

The tires spinning against the highway carried her away from Damian Wright, away from her last chance to find Sam and Josh. *It's over, it's over, it's over . . .*

Her body sagged against the door frame, her right hand automatically reaching for the single ring on her left. She had no engagement ring. Instead, Sam had given her his most valuable possession, a guitar pick used by the legendary Stevie Ray Vaughan, and promised that when he sold his first song he'd replace it with a diamond. Seven years later, the pick still sat in its black velvet jewelry case on her dresser.

Her hand felt cold, but her wedding band radiated warmth, as if she touched Sam. She spun the ring in time with the words weaving their way into her soul, inviting her to surrender. *It's over, it's over, it's over . . .*

No! It can't be. Not like this.

Tears pressed against her closed eyelids, burned as they fought to escape. Sarah's grip on the plain gold band tightened. Her last link to Sam and, through him, Josh. She was tired, so very tired. She should give up. What more could she do?

After all, she had a life to live. Sam would want her to be happy. Someday. A ragged breath tore through her and she felt Alan stir beside her. Alan—could she imagine a future with a man like him? A man who'd devoted almost two years of his life to guiding her through this morass of pain and grief, who'd brought her back into the light, had given her this one last chance.

Last chance, last hope, last rites.

It's over, it's over, it's over.

Sarah straightened, opened her eyes, and blinked against the harsh Texas sun. She uncurled her legs, smoothed out the soft cotton of her navy blue dress. She refused to wear black, not until Josh and Sam were laid to rest. The dark highway stretched hypnotically into the future.

"You all right?" Alan's gaze left the road to stare at her for a long moment.

A sad smile curled Sarah's lips. "Yes. I'm fine."

It's over, it's over, it's over . . . the words sang through her mind, pounding insistently like a toddler throwing a tantrum, banging his head against the floor when he didn't get what he wanted. Josh had thrown a few of those in his day. Until he learned that when he did, he never got what he wanted.

It's over, it's over, it's over!

Sarah gave a small shake of her head—the only warning Josh needed now. She'd shake her head, smile, and he'd leave his whining behind, take her hand, and snuggle against her. *Sorry, Mommy. I forgot.*

But I haven't.

It's over, it's over, it's over . . . *No. It's not.*

It's just begun.

Wednesday, June 20

Two weeks later

CHAPTER TWO

Supervisory Special Agent Caitlyn Tierney didn't look up at the tentative knock on her open door. Instead she raised a hand in the universal palm forward gesture of "wait" and kept reading the report on her computer screen. Her latest group of New Agents in Training was in their final week of training before graduating from Quantico. Nerves were frayed as they waited to learn their field assignments, so this hadn't been the first interruption of Caitlyn's morning.

She finished reading her NAT's scores on their critical incident projects and nodded with satisfaction. They'd done as well as she'd hoped. Even Santos, the diffident, intense twenty-six-year-old with a background in particle physics, had managed to integrate himself as part of the team. Caitlyn shut the lid to her laptop and looked up at her visitor, half-expecting to see Santos himself.

Instead, it was one of the lab geeks. Ah, man, she knew his name; he worked in DNA. Not Rogers, no, something close. She smiled, keeping her face blandly genial as she forced her brain along its circuitous route to match the face of the man before her with his name.

Finally, it clicked. But it took at least twice as long as it would have two years ago, before her accident. Something she'd never admit to anyone.

"Hi, Clemens," she said heartily, gesturing the tech to one of the two wooden chairs beside her overflowing bookcase. "What brings you over here to Jefferson? Teaching a class?"

He shook his head. "Thought it would be easier than asking you to make the trip to the lab building." He was right; the forensic analysis center had more security than Fort Knox. Even FBI staff like Caitlyn needed a special invite and authorization for a pass to enter. Clemens glanced at the open door and shifted his weight in his chair.

She might not be as good with names as she used to be, but Caitlyn was still a pro when it came to nonverbal communication. She rose to her feet, folded her reading glasses, and nonchalantly closed the door as she crossed over to sit beside him.

"What's up?" she asked, leaning forward and engaging him in direct eye contact.

He fumbled a file folder from his briefcase. It wasn't marked "top secret" or even "sensitive," so she wondered what all the cloak-and-dagger was about. Then she saw the name on the file. Damian Wright.

Her first assignment two years ago after she'd returned to work. She'd hated everything about that case: the crimes, the travel, the blinding migraines that blurred her thoughts and almost crippled her with their unrelenting pain and nausea, and most of all she'd hated her fatuous asshole of a boss, Assistant Special Agent in Charge Jack Logan. Logan had swooped in and taken over the case without any warnings or explanations, something unheard of. ASACs led from behind their desks via memos and directives; they never ventured into the field.

"You know Damian Wright's dead?" she asked the lab tech. "Executed in Texas." She glanced at the calendar. "Two weeks ago."

"I know." Clemens' voice was mournful. "I'm sorry."

Caitlyn's spine went rigid. Bright flashes of light sparked at the periphery of her vision. "Sorry? You can't be saying you found anything exculpatory?"

Caitlyn agreed with most law enforcement officers that death was too good for a lot of these sickos—but it was the best punishment they had. That didn't mean that she, like other LEOs, didn't also live in fear of putting an innocent man on death row.

Which was why she'd reviewed the Texas evidence against Wright herself, even though by the time Texas took over she was off the case. Their case had been rock solid. Not only had he been caught with the still-warm body of his last victim, butchering the boy, but Wright confessed to everything, refused to allow any appeals on his behalf, and became the first person under Texas' new law to be fast-tracked to execution. Twenty-one months from arrest to death, a new record.

Clemens shook his head. "No, Wright killed those boys in Texas, Vermont, Tennessee, and Oklahoma." He paused. Caitlyn took a deep breath, forcing the flashing lights to fade into the distance. "It's the ones in New York I'm not too sure about."

"Hopewell, New York. Josh Durandt and his father. Right before Katrina hit." Caitlyn remembered. No bodies recovered in that one. The crime scene had been halfway up a mountain; she'd been wearing a skirt after being whisked away from a memorial service for the second

Vermont boy. Logan had laughed, giving her no time to change into more appropriate attire and cutting her no slack when her migraine made her sick during the drive down. After she puked her guts out on the side of the road, he'd joked, asked if she was pregnant, adding that was the problem with "today's FBI." He never had to worry about any of the guys letting him down because they went "hormonal" on him.

"See, I was clearing the backlog and I found these samples in the pile to be disposed of," Clemens said, his tone hesitant as he shifted in his seat, obviously having second thoughts. "You know the new director's protocols. All evidence reviewed prior to disposal, even in closed cases. Turns out the results from Hopewell were never recorded. Not anywhere. Case like that, they should have been top priority. Instead they were almost trashed. If it wasn't for the new rules—"

"What do you have?" she asked, sliding the folder from his hand and spreading it open on her lap. The familiar dark lines of a DNA analysis filled the first page.

"The DNA from the Hopewell crime scene—it wasn't Wright's."

"There were two blood samples found, right? The dad's and one other. We assumed it was Wright's since the field kit said it was his blood type and we had his prints on the memory card found there."

"Yeah, it was his print and the card came from his camera. Wright's reflection can be seen in some of the photos. He definitely took them."

"Who was at the crime scene with him? Are you saying he had an accomplice? There was no evidence of that at any of the other scenes." She ran her hand through her shoulder-length hair, absently rubbing at the puckered skin above her right ear. Her hair hadn't even grown out when she was in Hopewell. Back then it had been so short it barely covered the surgical scar.

Clemens blew his breath out. "That's where it gets a bit weird."

Caitlyn straightened. It never boded well when a lab geek called evidence weird. "How weird?"

"Conspiracy theory, cover-up, Area Fifty-One, political and career suicide kind of weird." He grimaced. "I've gone over everything a dozen times. The data is correct. It's the facts surrounding it that are wrong."

"You mean *my* facts, *my* investigation?"

He looked down at his scuffed Adidas and nodded. "Yeah." He looked up again, pushed his hair back when it fell across his forehead. "Well, yours and Assistant Special Agent in Charge Logan's. He was the agent of record. His name was on all the paperwork. But since he's retired, I thought I better come to you." He gave her a hesitant smile. "Maybe you could tell me what to do with it."

Caitlyn stared past him, through her small window that looked out over the expanse of forest home to the Yellow Brick Road, the academy's famed obstacle course. Sunlight streamed in, reawakening her headache. She'd always suspected Logan of hiding something. He'd hustled her off the Wright case as fast as he could, claiming she was needed to help with the Katrina cleanup efforts. She'd spent weeks working with the National Center for Missing & Exploited Children, identifying over forty-eight hundred kids and reuniting them with their families. An area more suited to a woman's talents, in Logan's words. Since they'd had Wright cold on the other murders, she'd let it go.

She turned to Clemens. "Tell me everything."

CHAPTER THREE

September 6, 2005

Dear Sam,

The news is filled with death and destruction. The search for you has pretty much ended as all eyes turn south to Katrina's destruction and chaos. All eyes except mine, of course.

God, I sound like some kind of CNN commentator. I have no idea how to do this. All I know is that I need you—need to talk to you. It's the only way for me to make sense of anything.

The Colonel's wife comes every day. She says talking about you, keeping this journal, is the best way for me to heal, to understand that our Lord has a plan beyond my mortal comprehension and that I must let go of you and Josh and accept you are in a better place and soldier on. You know how she gets.

Today for the first time, I spoke to her. I told her the truth about how I felt. I told her that she and her good Lord could go to hell.

The Colonel hustled her out faster than a lightning bolt, her still sputtering about how I should respect her as my stepmother if not as a Christian woman.

Sometimes I swear the Colonel only married her after Mom died because she bakes the best caramel apple pie in the county and knows how to make a bed with hospital corners. What the hell was he thinking? Don't say it—I can almost hear you humming that stupid song you wrote about her, "Requiem for the Morally Superior and Personality Challenged." Anyway, she's out of my hair and my house, so more's the better.

Dr. Hedeger says pretty much the same thing as the Colonel's wife, only he feeds me Xanax with his tepid platitudes. Tells me that letting my grief and anger out is the best way to "defuse my trauma."

Defuse. As if I'm a ticking bomb ready to explode at the slightest jar or rustle. Tick, tick . . . boom!

Exactly how I feel. A constant coil of incendiary fury curling inside me like a viper ready to strike. Surrounded by a hard lead, dead-numb casing. They tell me to let it out, but they don't really want me to. Lord knows, I don't want to. If I did, I might never stop screaming . . .

So, that's basically how I am. How's everything there? Are you keeping an eye on Josh? I know you are—hell, even Damian Wright knew that. That's why he followed you into the woods. He knew he'd never get a better chance to catch you by surprise and get Josh.

Did I tell you the police found one of his camera cards? While I was sitting in Albany with a bunch of other teachers, being preached to about "no child left behind," that monster was spying on Josh. The card is filled with picture after picture of you and Josh at the park, you two walking home, even a glimpse of Josh and you wrestling on the living room floor. Oh, there are other little boys he'd spied on, but they quickly give way to focus solely on Josh.

Our beautiful little boy. I'm not blaming you. The police said from the amount of blood they found on the trail you put up quite a fight. Heroic, Chief Waverly called it.

They found some blood that must have belonged to Damian as well. As long as it wasn't Josh's blood, I was happy—what a stupid thing to think! But at the time I could only grasp at straws, was hanging on to any thread of hope I could find.

I'm so damned angry. That I wasn't here, as if I could have somehow stopped what happened. Angry at the stupid government wasting time and money on a stupid law with a catchy name that has condemned our children to a level of mediocrity—sorry, you've heard that rant before, haven't you?

Mostly I'm angry at God. How could he have allowed this to happen? To those two boys in Vermont? To the other one they found in Tennessee after they lost Damian here.

Then the woman from the FBI—you would have laughed at her, a redhead with a butch haircut, badly fitting skirt, clunky shoes, hand always on her hip as if she couldn't decide if she was a woman or one of the boys. I overheard her telling Chief Waverly that Damian's signature was to snatch and grab his prey. That he killed them quickly, brutally, with his bare hands, it makes him feel like God, us-

ing his hands, feeling his flesh against theirs while they die—how the hell can she know that?

That's when Hal Waverly saw me and shut her up. He took me by the shoulders and steered me out to his squad, found me something hot to drink that stopped my teeth from chattering. Then he told me about the blood in the clearing off the trail. About finding Josh's Tigger, ripped to pieces. That they'd called off the search because of the hurricane arriving. That once the weather cleared, they'd get the cadaver dogs out there.

Said I needed to accept the worst. Idiot. Like I could ever accept that. Not without seeing you and Josh. How could I give you up so easily?

Last week. Seems like another life. The search and rescue and cadaver dogs from Saranac are all down in Mississippi and New Orleans now. The FBI has come and gone, but crime scene tape still blocks the room at the Locust Inn down in Merrill where Damian Wright stayed. They just missed him in Tennessee, the news said—hot on the trail of a killer.

If I was Damian, I'd head down to Texas, blend in with the refugees there, get lost in the crowd. I wonder if the police have thought of that, if they're looking for him there? Seems like he was headed south. The mom in Tennessee at least has a body to bury—a pair of hunters interrupted Damian before he could finish hiding that boy. Nelson was his name. Cute kid from the photo in the papers. Black curls, big dark eyes, wide grin.

Just like you and Josh. I know Josh must be with you. He has to be. That hope is the only thing keeping me sane. Knowing you two are together.

I will find you. Soon. I promise. Maybe the rain will wash you free. If Damian didn't bury you too deep. But then the animals—I can't stop thinking about what they might be doing, teeth and claws. The pictures going through my mind—what Damian did to Josh after he finished with you. . . .

Sorry, I'm back now. Sometimes I just have to go shut myself in the bathroom, all the faucets running as hard as they can go, and I scream and scream until my voice has run out and the room is filled with steam and I imagine you're there in the mirror and Josh is sleeping just beyond the closed door. I hold my breath until the fog clears and it becomes all too obvious to anyone sane that I'm alone. Alone with my thoughts and fears and anger and despair—I miss you both so much I can't even imagine words equal to the task.

Hal Waverly's been a rock. Course, as Chief of Police he's seen bad things before—and he's lost someone himself, so he understands better than anyone. He keeps to himself, kind of hovers in the background, checks on me between calls, making sure there's food in the house, that I don't wear the same clothes three days running. Most of all, he doesn't judge me when I need to escape—usually out into the rain and fog that's trying to drown us this past week.

Everyone else puckers their lips, wondering if I'm gone round the bend—or if that ticking time bomb has finally exploded. Not Hal.

I hate to admit it, but even the Colonel's wife has been a help. She shoos everyone away, cleans the house, and sends me to bed after a hot bath and cup of her herbal tea that tastes like a grandmother's hug, all warmth and cinnamon. I keep kicking her out, but she sees me as her project—as if she's the only one who can redeem me. Hate to tell her it's a waste of time.

My brain feels fuzzy. The Colonel must have slipped more Xanax into my tea. Or maybe Prozac. Or both. He hovers over me like fog on the mountain. They're all watching me—the Colonel, his wife, Hal Waverly, Dr. Hedeger, everyone from school. The whole town holding its breath, waiting for me to explode. Tick, tick, boom.

They think I'll kill myself or at least hurt myself. But I could never do that. Not until I find you.

Then, we'll see. I can't imagine past that.

For now, hold Josh tight, tell him not to be scared, tell him Mommy loves him soooo much. Tell him I'll find you. I will find you both. Somehow, someway, someday.

I love you. God how I love you—why couldn't I have been here? Why couldn't it have been me?

I sleep with the curtains open so I can see the mountain above the fog. It makes me feel like you're watching over me from somewhere up there in the darkness. And if I leave the light on, maybe then you and Josh can find your way home . . .

CHAPTER FOUR

Bracing herself, Sarah pulled open the Rockslide Café's door, releasing a buzz of conversation mingled with the fragrant scent of fresh-brewed coffee and cinnamon buns. The Colonel was behind the counter, manning the morning rush as usual, slinging hash and flipping pancakes while never missing a beat in his conversation. He wasn't going to like her plans for her summer vacation. But she was used to his disapproval.

She stood in the doorway for a moment. The fifties-era diner was all chrome and red vinyl, the decor consisting of photos deemed noteworthy by the Colonel. Including one of Sarah, mouthful of braces, graduating from high school and another of her, sans braces, accepting her college diploma. One day last year, without warning, the Colonel had added one of Sam and Josh in a place of honor. Josh held aloft a northern pike, the fish almost as tall as the three-year-old, while Sam had his arms wrapped around him, steadying him. Sam's smile was even wider than Josh's, his eyes gleaming with pride.

Hanging that photo among the pictures of the Colonel's military career highlights, the prize bucks bagged by family, and the Colonel's lodge brothers was probably the most sensitive thing Sarah had ever seen her father do. She'd started coming in more often after that. Not that they spoke much—but sometimes words didn't really say what you needed them to anyway.

"Hey, kiddo," he bellowed, swiping a clean spot for her at the counter. "George here thinks the Martians are landing."

"I didn't say they were aliens from outer space," George Dolan protested, sloshing coffee out of his cup as he dunked his cinnamon bun. He took a bite, sopped up the coffee running down his chin, and continued. "I said them lights could mean aliens, like *illegal* aliens."

With a measured hand, the Colonel poured batter onto the griddle, forming perfectly symmetrical pancakes, each a regulation three inches in diameter. "What the hell would illegal aliens want here?"

"They could hide out in the caves up on Snakehead. Just like in Nam."

Silence descended as the Colonel turned and stared at George for a long moment. George had the good grace to blush and look down into his coffee cup.

"You don't know nothing about nothing. Been watching the History channel too much is all." The Colonel turned back to finish Sarah's pancakes, flipping them onto a plate and sliding the plate in front of her in one fluid motion.

"Yeah, mebbee. But you didn't see those lights. Moving up and down, across the dam, vanishing into thin air."

"You sure it was a person? Maybe it was some kind of natural phenomena." Sarah doused her short stack with maple syrup collected from the forest behind her house. "Snakehead's known for its fog and mists, especially this time of year."

Hal Waverly came in and sat down beside her, unfolding his paper and nodding as the Colonel poured him coffee. He and Sarah had grown up here in Hopewell together, been friends since they were eight, but these past two years, since Sam and Josh died, she felt like she'd lost track of Hal. He was always there, always helping, yet she'd never before noticed the creases that had dug their way into the corners of his eyes or the dark circles hanging beneath them.

Guilt made her look away. How much else going on around her in the past two years had she been blind to?

"You mean like swamp gas or them northern lights we saw last year?" George said, still going on about his mysterious lights. "No, sir, this was near to the ground. And it moved. Hal, when you gonna get someone out there to check? What do we pay you good money for anyway?"

Hal snapped his newspaper. "Ask the Colonel. He's president of the village council. When are you going to give me enough money to hire another man? As it is—"

"Now Hal, don't you get started on that again. We got you the new government center, didn't we?" The Colonel's voice had a bite to it, one that in his past life would have had men snapping to attention.

George and Sarah both leaned back, staying out of the line of fire. The new government center was the latest controversy rocking Hopewell. Somehow the Colonel's wife had convinced the government that not only did Hopewell, New York, population 468, deserve its zip code reinstated, but since the Snakehead dam was a prime terrorist target, it deserved funding for a new post office/police station after the floods of 2005 destroyed the old police station.

"Fat lot of good it does with no one to man it. Me and my men are on patrol full-time. If it wasn't for the county dispatcher handling calls and the mutual aid pact with Merrill, we wouldn't even have time to do that." A familiar edge of frustration lingered in Hal's voice. For years he'd been fighting a losing battle with the village council and his budget constraints. Sarah felt sorry for him. Hal worked hard and only wanted what was best for Hopewell. With an air of defeat, he took a drink of his coffee and buried himself in his paper.

"What are you doing today, Sarah?" the Colonel asked.

"I'm going up on Snakehead for a few days, get some hiking in."

Her announcement was met with silence. Even Hal lowered his paper, giving her an appraising look.

"I don't think that's a good idea. Why don't you head over to Lake Placid?" the Colonel said, aligning the salt and pepper and sugar shakers into a perfect parade formation.

"Yeah. Or I hear there's a great art exhibit over in Montreal."

Sarah swiveled on her stool to stare at George. The truck driver wasn't known for his love of fine culture.

"How would you know?" the Colonel asked.

George colored but didn't back down. "Because I been there. Took Mary. It was one of them Impressionist French guys—lots of swirls and color. Kind of pretty." He brightened and smiled at Sarah. "Perfect for a relaxing holiday. Better than tramping up there." He indicated the mountain above them with a jerk of his chin.

Sarah opened her mouth, reconsidered, and jammed a forkful of pancakes in before she could say something she'd regret. It wasn't that the men were afraid for her physical safety—she'd hunted or worked search and rescue with all of them at one time or another. They were worried about her mental safety. As if after almost two years there was still something she could find on Snake-head that could push her over the edge.

It was sweet, really. But she had to do this. Find Sam and Josh. Or somehow finally move on. Facing the mountain was the best way she knew to do that.

"The weather's supposed to be gorgeous. Why would I want to be stuck inside with a bunch of old paintings?"

"No. It's too dangerous. What about these weird people prowling the mountain at night?" the Colonel said.

Sarah swallowed her anger and forced herself to remain calm and logical. She'd spent plenty of nights alone on the mountain, although none since Sam and Josh. "Your aliens? Don't worry, I won't be anywhere near the dam."

"Where are you planning to be?" Hal folded his newspaper and regarded her with a serious expression. "You ought not go alone."

"I'll be fine. But I wouldn't mind borrowing one of your two-ways, just in case."

"No problem. Radios are one thing we've plenty of. You going over to the west face?"

"Thought I'd start up near the Colonel's cabin and kind of meander down. It's been a while since I've spent a night on the mountain." Two years to be precise. The last time she and Sam had taken Josh up to the cabin. The men busied themselves with their food. Sarah's smile wilted. "Anyway, it will be a nice change of pace."

The Colonel twisted his lips. She knew he was ready to bark an order at her to cease and desist, so she arched an eyebrow in a preemptive strike. He put up a hand in surrender, backed off to brew a fresh pot of coffee.

"You just watch out for those aliens," George said. "Who knows what they want."

CHAPTER FIVE

Caitlyn and Clemens moved to the one area on base even more secure than the lab building: the picnic tables in front of the Hogan's Alley Deli. Just a block away from the most frequently robbed bank in the world (courtesy of the weekly training exercises), they sat surrounded by trees with a view of anyone approaching and no chance of being overheard except by the tame deer and squirrels that populated the forest. The only interruption was the occasional bark of an order from an instructor leading a car-stop drill along the street past the bank.

As they walked over to the deli, talking about anything except the incendiary contents of the folders Clemens carried in his briefcase, Caitlyn had taken measure of the lab tech. He'd enthusiastically informed her that he came from Pittsburgh with a master's from Carnegie Mellon and a PhD from Pitt, that he loved working at Quantico, and that his fiancée managed a clothing store in Fairfax. Nothing to set off warning bells, his face had been open; he'd even blushed when mentioning his fiancée and their upcoming wedding and honeymoon.

She waited until he finished eating before prodding him back onto the topic of the Hopewell case. Not wanting to tempt her impending migraine prematurely into life, she'd barely touched her food. Clemens didn't seem to notice.

The headaches were just another part of her new reality—one she'd learned to manage. When she returned to the office, she would gobble down a few naproxen. If those didn't do the trick, she'd deal with it when she got home tonight: shoot up with her Imitrex, swallow a few Fiorcet, and curl up in the dark.

Tonight, she promised her silent but almost constant companion, *tonight I'm all yours.*

Post-concussive syndrome, the docs at Hopkins called it. Traumatic brain injury. TBI. Caitlyn called it hell on earth.

Since she'd sustained her original head injury—a skull fracture and a blood clot in her brain—in the line of duty, she could have applied for disability. But Caitlyn refused to admit she was in any way disabled. Not to herself and certainly not to the Bureau. She could just imagine what Jack Logan and others like him would say if she did. *What's next?* they'd laugh. *Medical leave for PMS?*

No, she wasn't disabled. Just disadvantaged. After the operation to remove the clot and repair the torn blood vessels in her brain, she'd learned how to do almost everything again. How to associate names and faces rather than simply memorizing them; how to read even though some of the letters still seemed jumbled, especially if they were on a computer screen; how to handle her migraines and the symptoms that accompanied them.

None of which kept her from doing her job—and never would.

"Whose DNA was up on that mountain?" she asked Clemens as he wiped chocolate chip smears from his lips.

"That's the problem." He pulled out a stack of folders, shoved their paper plates to one side, and lined up two DNA samples. Even she could see they didn't match. "This is Wright's. And this is Durandt's exemplar collected from his home." He slid another photostat of DNA bands from the folder. It matched Durandt's. "This is the first sample from the crime scene. I found it with the others in the batch scheduled to be destroyed."

He stared at the three DNA samples for a moment, then cleared his throat before adding a fourth. "This is DNA from the second blood sample found at the crime scene."

Caitlyn leaned forward, scanning the gray lines. The final DNA sample didn't match Durandt's, which made sense because it was a different blood type. But it also didn't match Wright. "You're saying it wasn't Wright's DNA at the crime scene?"

He gave a halfhearted shrug. Not committing to anything. "When Wright's DNA didn't match, I ran Durandt's through the system again, thought maybe the sample numbers had gotten mixed up or some clerical error. But I got nothing."

"What do you mean? He's a victim. His DNA had to be in the database."

He shook his head. "See what I mean? This case is freaky weird. Samuel Durandt wasn't in *any* of our records. Like someone wiped him clean. If I hadn't looked at these samples before they were destroyed, he would have been erased, like he never even existed."

"Who would do that?"

"You tell me. But," another hesitation before he slid one more DNA result from his folder, "I did find this."

She frowned, took the DNA sample from his hand, and laid it beside the others. Now there were three identical DNA patterns. "So where's the problem? You must have found his file somewhere—Durandt matches Durandt matches Durandt."

"Except this one *isn't* Sam Durandt. And you can't use it as evidence. I got it from a bone marrow donor database."

"Excuse me?"

"I know, I know. I didn't have a court order. But you have to understand, this kind of thing just isn't supposed to happen. Not ever. There are safeguards and checks and double checks . . ." He paused, one finger tapping the last DNA sample. "Besides, when I start working on a problem, I just can't—"

"Stop until you unravel it," she supplied. She knew because she was the same way. Tenacious, her father called her, usually with a smile. Stubborn, the rest of the family said, never smiling. Her chief strength—and greatest weakness. Not letting go of something once her curiosity was aroused.

"So whom does this illegally obtained, inadmissible DNA belong to?" she asked.

"Someone named Stanley Diamontes."

"And who the hell is Stanley Diamontes?" she asked, one hand massaging the pressure point at the base of her thumb, certain she wouldn't like the answer.

"Well, unless Sam Durandt has an identical twin brother, Stanley *is* Sam. Wait. It gets worse." He slid another DNA sample and laid it on top of the second DNA sample from the crime scene. The sample they'd thought belonged to the killer, Damian Wright. It was a match.

"Our unknown subject has a name. Do I want to know who he is?"

"No, but I'll tell you anyway. Leo Richland. Deputy, United States Marshals Service. Richland has been missing for two years. Last seen in Fairfax, Virginia, the day before Josh and Sam—or Stan—Durandt were presumed murdered by Damian Wright."

Caitlyn sucked in her breath as the flashing bright lights returned with a vengeance and nausea twisted her gut. The gray and black lines on the DNA evidence blurred before her.

"That's all I've got. I figured since Logan is retired, the case belongs to you, so . . ." His voice trailed off. He closed the folder and slid it across the wooden picnic table to her.

Sam Durandt wasn't Sam Durandt? And instead of Damian Wright killing him and his son, a U.S. Marshal had? A U.S. Marshal who'd gone missing under mysterious circumstances and who had no earthly reason for being anywhere near Hopewell, New York, on the day Sam and Josh were murdered.

She blinked as sunlight blared off the glossy white folder. Reached for her sunglasses and somehow fumbled them on without poking an eye out. She never allowed her migraines to hit her at work, could always block them, keep them at bay. But this one had snuck beneath her guard.

"Thanks, Clemens." She tried to keep her voice clear of the vise of pain tightening behind her eyes.

"Don't thank me," he said. "I'm thinking I just gave you the equivalent of a ticking bomb." He brushed the crumbs from his lap and stood, grabbing his briefcase. "Good luck, Caitlyn."

She stared at the closed folder with its FBI crest emblazoned on the front. A crisp breeze scattered the paper plates with the remnants of their lunch, blowing the trash into the grass. Caitlyn ignored it, allowing Clemens to rush after them as she struggled to contain the migraine before it totally crippled her. She focused on her breathing, using the FBI crest as her focal point. *Fidelity, Bravery, Integrity,* the words beneath it read.

Finally, she forced the blasts of pain to recede enough so she could stand without wavering. The glossy folder clenched in her hand, she walked back toward Jefferson Hall.

Jesus, Logan, what the hell have you gotten me into?

CHAPTER SIX

They caught him. Oh my lord, my hand is shaking so badly I can barely write.

They caught him! Damian Wright. He was in Texas. Hiding in a group shelter for Katrina refugees. All those little boys—he must have felt as if Katrina and the despair of a million people fleeing for their lives was a godsend, an unholy offering to his sick perversions.

A National Guardsman caught him with a boy. Felix Martinique. The body was still warm, Damian was covered in his blood. All I could think about was Josh. I spent the rest of the day locked in the bathroom, screaming where no one could hear or see me, visions of that monster and our little boy . . .

He confessed to the two boys in Vermont, the one in Tennessee, another in Oklahoma. But not to you or Josh. Why? I don't know this man—why is he trying to destroy what little life I have left? Why can't he give me any peace of mind?

Why can't he give you back to me?

Dr. Hedeger says he'll put me in a hospital if I don't start eating or sleeping. He has everyone watching over me like I'm a prisoner in my own house. It's only because there was an accident at the Rockslide today—the Colonel started a grease fire while trying to sneak a fried bologna sandwich— that the Colonel's wife is gone, I have the house to myself.

No one seems to understand that it's only when I'm on the mountain, on the same path you and Josh took, following in your footsteps, the sound of Josh's laughter just out of sight, beyond the next bend, beckoning to me—it's the only time I'm alive.

The rest of the time I'm dead, numb, leaden, too heavy to move even to close my eyes and sleep.

If I could only find you . . . are you looking for me too? Does Josh cry for his mommy?

I hope not. I want to think of him happy, not remembering the horror. . . .

A lawyer came to see me today after the Colonel's wife left. Nice guy. Works for a victims' advocacy project. He heard about us and he's willing to help any way he can.

I almost slammed the door in his face. Almost told him the only help I needed was my husband and son back at home where they should be. But he didn't look at me like he was afraid of any sudden moves I might make. He didn't stare, waiting for me to fall apart, to shatter into bits and pieces, tick, tick, boom.

He sat and listened. For the first time since you

left, I was able to force words past this knot in my throat that's been strangling me. I talked. And talked and talked.

Poor guy, probably thought I was nuts. But he didn't run. He listened.

I even showed him Josh's room, your piano, the songs you were working on. I told him how we met, showed him pictures. You holding Josh after the doctor handed him to you, looking scared and unsure and surprised and delighted all at once. The one of Josh sleeping naked except for his diaper on your bare chest when we were both too exhausted to do laundry. Josh's first birthday, all of us wearing enough birthday cake that we needed to be hosed off afterward.

Alan, that's his name, Alan Easton. He smiled and even laughed. Like no one has in sixteen days—as if it was against the law to laugh in front of a grief-stricken mother and wife.

I think you'd like him. You know why? Because once his laughter shattered the awful silence shrouding our house I found myself smiling. And babbling. He sat at your piano and my heart squeezed so tight I thought it would burst with pain, but then he began picking out your latest masterpiece.

You remember: "Your eyes remind me of the sky at night, your lips promise me a chance at life." That one.

Alan tried singing it and, believe it or not, he sounded worse than you! I couldn't help myself. The laughter sparked through me, fizzing up like a bottle of beer shook too hard and I couldn't stop it spurting out.

I laughed so hard I cried. And once the tears started—remember how I was early on when I was pregnant with Josh? Like that, only worse.

Alan didn't get that wide-eyed look of horror everyone else gets when they're with me. He stayed, held my hand while I cried enough water to flood the Sahara. Then he left, promised to look into things and come back tomorrow.

I sat there alone in the living room, the first time I've been alone in our house in sixteen days. It felt crowded yet empty all at once. Now I know what they mean by the term: silence is deafening.

Our house, always so filled with noise and love. Your music, your godawful caterwauling when the spirit moved you—you're the only songwriter I've heard of who couldn't carry a tune in a bucket— Josh's running feet, the dryer clanking off balance, Josh's laughter, your laughter, there was none of that.

Just the creaking of frogs outside and the groans and hums of an old, empty house.

I sat there awhile, not sure what I was feeling. But it was something.

I even ate some chicken the Colonel's wife brought last night. For the first time in weeks, I could actually taste it.

I took a shower and then a long, hot bath. It's not even five yet, but I feel so very tired. I borrowed one of your T-shirts to wear to bed. One from the dirty laundry, the better to smell you, to be with you tonight. I had to empty the hamper of yours and Josh's clothes and hide them in a bag under my bed before the Colonel's wife did the laundry and sanitized you out of existence.

I'm going to sleep now, but I'll leave the window open and the light on for you. As soon as Damian Wright tells me where to find you, we'll be together again. I promise.

Kiss Josh for me. Good night, my loves . . .

CHAPTER SEVEN

Sarah organized her plan of attack more carefully than a general facing a superior opposition. She'd promised herself she'd give this everything she had—devote her entire summer to finding Sam and Josh if need be.

And then . . . She paused as her fingers danced over her freshly copied satellite imagery maps of Snakehead Mountain. If she found them, maybe then, maybe finally, she could say good-bye.

She used Sam's office as her campaign headquarters. It was a bright and cheery room in the rear of the house, although to be honest, Sam had written more music here than insurance policies. Her topo maps and satellite images were taped over posters of his heroes: John Lee Hooker, Stevie Ray Vaughan, Bob Dylan, Eric Clapton. She'd never understood why he'd come to Hopewell to set up his independent insurance agency; he never spoke of his life before moving here except to say that his family was gone and there was nothing left to tie him to his hometown. He always got a sad look when he spoke of his past, even though he never actually told her much in the way of details. She'd learned not to pry, figured he would tell her when he was ready.

A cough at the door interrupted her. She looked up to see Hal standing in the hallway, a small Motorola in his hand. "I knocked—"

"Sorry, I was running the copy machine. Thanks for bringing the radio."

"No problem." He joined her at the drafting table Sam had used as a desk. Leaning forward, he examined the topo map she'd laid out. Neon orange highlighted the areas on the map where Sam's blood was found, the spot half a mile away where Josh's Tigger was abandoned, the areas searched two years ago. A breathy whistle escaped him. "Helluva lot of territory to cover. With no guarantees. These mountains don't give up their secrets easily."

She stood beside him, her hand clenching and unclenching as she stared at the vast wilderness depicted on the map. "I know."

"I just don't want you to be getting your hopes up. Again." Silence. They both knew how Sarah had spent last summer. Down in Texas, living out of a Huntsville motel room while Alan tried unsuccessfully to get her an audience with Damian Wright. The man had finally confessed to killing Sam and Josh, but still refused to tell her what she needed to know. Then, once she'd come home . . .

Hal squeezed her arm, seemed to follow her thoughts effortlessly. Why not? He knew better than anyone what she was going through. He was still beating himself up for not being there the night his wife killed herself. He tilted his head, met her gaze. "Sure you know what you're doing, Sarah? Sometimes it's best to leave well enough alone."

"I need to do this, Hal." She forced herself to smile, patted his hand reassuringly. "Don't worry, I'm not about to go off the deep end again. That's behind me."

"Some things you never put behind you," he said in a low tone, his gaze drifting to the only corner of Sam's desk empty of photos of her and Josh. "Some things you just learn how to live with." He paused. "You need to find a reason, Sarah. Something—someone—to live for."

They were the same age, had grown up together, best friends for decades, but suddenly he seemed much older and wiser. As if losing Lily had shown him a truth that still eluded Sarah. She stepped back, turning to gather the enlargements she'd just made on the copier. Lately, Sam's ancient Xerox was really getting a workout.

Hal took the top sheet from her. "This where you're looking?" He traced a finger along the ridgeline between the mountain summit and the Upper Falls. "Rugged territory—especially after the freeze-thaw cycle this spring. Been a couple rockslides off the eastern face near Snakebelly and the Devil's Elbow."

The Devil's Elbow was where the river and the mountain gorge took a sharp ninety-degree turn, then dropped precipitously, creating the Upper Falls. Several deep crevasses broke through the gorge wall near there, including the infamous Snakebelly—so named because it was the river's graveyard. Any large pieces of flotsam from upstream would invariably get caught in the current and directed into the chasm, usually undetected until a rockslide or avalanche loosened the debris and freed what lay hidden beneath.

"I'll be fine. I've climbed around there all my life."

Hal nodded, his gaze still following his finger as it traced the closely stacked lines on the topo map. "Maybe you shouldn't go alone."

The light reflected from the pale ring of flesh where he used to wear his wedding band. When had he stopped wearing it? she wondered, twisting Sam's band on her own finger. Lily had died a short time before Sam. If Hal was ready to move on, did he think she should as well?

No. Not until she had the answers she needed.

His arm brushed against hers and she stiffened. Surely he wasn't—he didn't—no. They were friends. Had been friends far too long for him to feel *that* way about her. After all, they weren't kids anymore.

"Remember senior prom?" He surprised her by following her thoughts again. "Took me forever to work up the courage to ask you and by then it was too late. You went with Tommy Hopkins instead."

Sarah snatched the map away from him and began to fold it, her fingers mercilessly pressing creases into the paper. Hal's hand hung in the air, his expression wounded. She tried to spin her abrupt reaction into a joke. "Hal Waverly, are you trying to come on to me?"

He jerked back, both hands raised. "Not me. Alan."

"Alan?" She focused on the map in her hand, confused. It was as if her mind was wrapped in a cocoon and she was slowly pushing free, shaking off two years' worth of grief-induced numbness. Finally seeing things as they were but struggling to fumble them into context.

Wake up and smell the coffee, Sam's voice sang through her mind, another one of his corny jingles that he was never able to sell.

Thankfully Hal ignored the sudden awkwardness and brushed the back of his jeans with his palms, as if brushing away the tension between them. "The man's crazy about you, Sarah. Any fool can see that. Giving up his practice in the city to move up here—"

"It was only because of the case, Damian Wright. Alan was trying to set a precedent for victims' rights with my appeals. It had nothing to do with me."

"Oh really? Then why is he still here? Hanging around like a kid too shy to ask a girl to dance."

She waved her hand to shut him up. He ignored her, propping his butt on the desk's edge. "He seems good for you. When you're around him, you seem, well, happy."

"Hal. Please. You make me sound like I'm some weepy widow trailing around in black veils. It's been a rough two years, but I'm doing all right."

"You are. And I think Alan has something to do with that. He's not the only one who wants to see you happy, Sarah. I heard the Colonel asking him his intentions."

She straightened and pivoted, the blood rushing to her face in embarrassment. "He has no right—it's my life and I'll live it the way I want!"

"That's the point, isn't it?" Hal gave her a half smile. "Sarah, you didn't die on that mountain. Don't waste your life just because some madman killed Josh and Sam."

If anyone else had spoken those words she would have snapped, exploded in rage, and ordered them from her house. But this wasn't anyone. This was Hal. Who said what Sarah knew in her heart was the truth.

After Lily died, Hal had faced that difficult truth. Only it wasn't a truth Sarah was prepared to face. Not yet. Maybe not ever.

"I need a little more time." She shoved the map into the pocket of her Gore-Tex jacket. "If Alan understands, he'll wait." She finally raised her head, met his gaze. "Just a little longer."

"You have to tell him how you feel one way or the other, put the poor guy out of his misery at least."

"All right, you made your point. Now don't you have some crooks to lock up or something?"

"Just finished a twelve, I'm not officially back on the clock until tomorrow morning. Of course," he gestured to the cell phone, pager, and radio weighing down his belt, "that doesn't mean they won't call me back sooner." He blew out his breath. Dark circles shadowed his eyes. New wrinkles lined his face and his jaw muscle kept twitching. "Guess I should go home, get myself some rest."

Sounded like a good idea. He appeared close to exhaustion or a breakdown and the tourist season, Hal's busy time of year, had only just begun. Once again she chided herself for not paying more attention to her friends. How much had she missed during the past two years, so focused on her own sorrows? "Why don't you take some time for yourself? You haven't taken a day off in ages. Take a vacation, go someplace far away, find a cute girl, and break her heart like you did mine in high school."

That made him smile. "I'm thirty-two, if I start chasing after girls I'll have to arrest myself. Besides," his gaze speared past her to fix on the mountains framed in the view from the window, "guess we're both tied to this place."

He handed her the radio and a spare battery pack. She walked with him to the door. Together they stood on the front porch, Snakehead towering over them, casting the house in shadows.

"How long are you planning to stay up there?" he asked.

"A few days. Then I'll come back, resupply."

A frown tightened his forehead. "How about if you give me a firm return time so I don't have to send people out looking for you? You be back here by Friday afternoon, all right? Then you let Alan take you up to that Montreal art exhibit for the weekend. See how it feels, life away from all this."

Hal wore his stubborn look, the one that wouldn't take no for an answer. Seemed like the town had formed a conspiracy trying to get her and Alan together. But a weekend away, without murder as the main topic of conversation, did sound nice.

She surrendered. "All right. On one condition. That you take a vacation as well. Go, have some fun, let Hopewell take care of itself for a day or two."

His smile crossed his face without making it to his eyes. "Deal. Come Friday, you and Alan go to Montreal and I'll officially take off for parts unknown."

"Just don't get yourself arrested, Chief." That earned her a wry smile as if Hal had a private joke he wasn't about to share.

"Good luck, Sarah. And have a care." He sauntered down the path to where his GMC was parked. "Call me if you need anything."

"I won't be needing you. Go home, get some rest."

He gave her a wave as he climbed into the SUV, honked once, and did a rapid three-point turn, spinning gravel. The hemlocks lining her lane swayed in the wind, seeming to close in behind him. Silence fell as the dust settled.

Sarah took a deep breath, filling her lungs as if preparing for a long underwater siege. Nodding to Snakehead, accepting its silent challenge, she went back inside to collect the rest of her gear.

The Colonel's hunting cabin was near the top of the mountain, the last shelter accessible by the dirt track that passed for a road. Her plan was to drive up, park, then work her way down. No need for a tent, the weather was mild. All she needed was her sleeping bag and a ground cloth. If the weather turned, as it was prone to near the summit, she could always bivouac in the single-room cabin.

Of course, the Colonel's wife would heartily disapprove of a woman staying alone in a cabin lacking plumbing or electricity—much less sleeping out under the stars. The thought made Sarah smile.

It wasn't that she disliked the Colonel's wife or felt no one could ever replace her mother. All right, it wasn't *just* that she disliked the Colonel's wife. It was the fact that Victoria had never given Sarah a chance to know her, much less like her, before she moved in and began to run the Colonel's life for him.

The man was in charge of two hundred men during the Vietnam war, so it was surprising to Sarah that he seemed to enjoy his newfound captivity. Or at least his warden.

Sarah's head bobbed in time with a tune she hummed as she arranged her gear. One of Sam's ditties, from his country-western phase. He'd called it the "No Sunshine, Stuck in the Mud, Rainy Day Blues."

I'm coming, guys. Don't worry, I'll find you.

JD Dolan pedaled his Diamondback furiously, straining to gain the momentum necessary to conquer the last hill standing between him and Main Street. Doc Hedeger's purple Victorian became a fuzzy blur on his left side as he rounded the corner. Brakes squealed, a horn honked, but JD didn't care. He sped past the squat orange brick post office, a building so ugly it almost caused a civil war. Well, the closest thing Hopewell ever had to a civil war. Or any excitement at all.

JD had covered the protests for the Hopewell school newspaper. Mrs. Durandt, the faculty adviser, submitted one of his stories to a statewide competition and it won second place. Mrs. Durandt had been so impressed she agreed to help JD apply for an internship at a TV station in D.C. If the documentary he produced this summer was good enough, he might get paid to go to D.C. and learn all about journalism next summer instead of delivering appliances with his dad.

"Slow down, you hooligan, you!" Victoria, the Colonel's wife, shouted as JD's bike skidded through the post office's gravel drive, spraying her freshly swept sidewalk with stones. "I'll call Chief Waverly on you, I will!"

JD's only response was a smile as he leaned farther over his handlebars. Almost to the top, a new world speed record about to be broken, Lance Armstrong, eat your heart out! He wasn't afraid of Hal Waverly. The chief would be out on patrol, probably helping lost tourists change a flat tire. Hal was always helping someone somewhere, spent even less time at home than he did at his ugly new office.

That was the thing about growing up in a small town at the end of a road going nowhere. JD knew everything about everyone—and they knew everything about him.

Or at least they thought they did. His smile widened into a grin as he crested the hill and raised his hands in victory. He coasted down the other side, along Main Street, passing houses where he could name every inhabitant, including dogs, cats, canaries, plus assorted gerbils and hamsters. He dodged the bakery's van just as Mr. Harris pulled out, right on time as St. Andrew's bell chimed the hour.

Predictable. Boring. That was Hopewell.

This was JD's last summer of freedom. He tasted the words. They felt good. Next year he'd be sixteen and would spend the rest of his summers working. He hoped he'd make enough to be able to go to college. After college, more work. But the next seventy-two days were his.

A familiar figure leaned against the lamppost outside of the Rockslide. JD sucked his breath in like he needed extra oxygen and jammed on his brakes. He screeched to a stop, feigning nonchalance despite the fact he was huffing, finding it hard to breathe.

"Hi, JD," Julia Petrino said with a smile that made his chest tighten. She was dressed in cutoff jean shorts, two spaghetti strap camisoles overlapping, one red and one purple, but somehow they didn't clash—not clinging to Julia's perfect body. Her long, blond-brown hair stirred in the breeze, and he watched as her nipples rose beneath the layers she wore.

Oh yeah. This was going to be a summer to remember. For the rest of his life.

"I thought maybe you'd forgotten our date," Julia went on, oblivious to his inability to force his gaze away from her breasts. She swung her leg over her bike, offering him an even more mesmerizing sight of her rear, pale strings of frayed denim brushing the backs of her smooth, tanned thighs.

"Uh, no." The words emerged in a croak. JD cleared his throat and tried again, gripping the handlebars tighter to disguise his sweaty palms. "Where did you want to start?"

She shrugged, an elegant motion that set her hair swaying and made JD's mouth go dry. "We've got all day. I picked up some fried chicken from the Rockslide." He noticed the daypack she'd strapped to the bike's rear fender. "Want to go up the eastern face? Maybe to the Lower Falls?"

He arched an eyebrow at her, balancing on both pedals of his bike. "That's a mighty steep trail. Sure you can make it all the way?"

Her smile radiated confidence. "I can if you can. Race you."

She pushed off, standing on her pedals, gliding along the short downhill stretch. Then she began to pump hard as she turned right, heading up Rattlesnake Pike. He let her get a head start, admiring the view and certain he could catch up.

JD licked his lips and followed after her, inhaling the intoxicating perfume of his last summer of freedom.

CHAPTER EIGHT

A short time after Hal left, Sarah hoisted her pack on her shoulder and let the back door slam shut behind her. No need to lock it. She had nothing left for anyone to steal.

She craned her neck to look up at the mountain towering above her. The summit wasn't visible, not from here. A crowd of trees, just coming into their foliage, waved in the wind, inviting her to join them. Two hawks spiraled overhead, then vanished as small black dots against the afternoon sun.

She shrugged her pack into place and began hiking up the trail. It would be a longer trip up, but this felt better than driving. As if she truly was following the footsteps her heart heard every night—at least on the nights when she could sleep.

The trail curved along the side of Snakehead, coming to a clearing where the Lower Falls could be seen in the distance. It'd been a year since she'd come here and her instincts were to race past this spot, try to outrun her memories.

Sarah forced herself to stop. Trees and brush crowded

together as if preparing for an ambush. Her heart sped up as the clearing closed around her. This was it. This was where Damian Wright had caught up with them. This was where she'd lost everything.

Her heart pounded so hard she had to close her eyes for a moment, take a deep breath. When she opened them, she turned her back on the clearing, unable to face her emotions. The familiar view comforted her. From the edge of the gorge she could see upriver to the Lower Falls and Hal's house and downstream to the dam, the reservoir, and Hopewell: a hodgepodge of whitewashed siding, asphalt shingles, and brick poking through the trees. The only distinct landmark was St. Andrew's bell tower reaching heavenward.

Silence reigned here. The buzz of gnats and mosquitoes vanished. Soft evergreen needles muffled her footsteps and filled the air with the damp, sweet scent of pine. All she could hear was the sound of her own breathing; even the roar of the waterfall was subdued. As if this was a holy place, a sacred place.

Gathering her courage, she turned in a full circle, her mind filling in physical details two years had erased. The clump of mountain laurel spattered with Sam's blood; the dirt beneath the red oak turned into a small lake of crimson where he must have fallen; the churned-up leaves where he'd tried to fight Wright, spilling a small amount of the killer's blood; the hemlock tree where the camera card had been found . . .

She blinked and the sun-dappled clearing transformed into crime scene photos. Blinked again and reality returned. Sarah swallowed hard, found herself breathing through her mouth as if trying to avoid the scent of death.

Her hands gripped her pack straps so tightly the nylon webbing bit into her skin. Many times, swaddled in the mountain's mist, she'd fled here in the middle of the night, trying her best to cross over, commune with the shadows.

One night last year, she'd almost made it. The night she'd given up, when she'd decided to break with this world and surrender to the next.

August 30, 2006

This will probably be my last entry—who needs words when we'll be together soon? Sorry if it's hard to read, I'm sitting under an oak in the clearing above the dam. You know the place. You died here.

At least that's what the experts finally decided. The rain came too soon for them to do a complete analysis, but based on the photos Hal took, they figured you tried to save Josh, fought Damian Wright, managed to hurt him a little before he killed you. They found a few tracks from a man moving slowly, possibly carrying a heavy object, and decided that, for whatever reason, Wright carried you away before returning to take Josh.

Hal doesn't know I've read the forensic reports. He keeps his copies locked up, refuses to let me see them. But Alan was finally able to get a copy of the FBI report—Freedom of Information Act, they call it.

It sure as hell freed me. Even if Damian won't talk to me, won't look me in the eyes or give you and Josh back to me, even so . . . now I know.

One year today. 365 days—and nights, God, how I've come to despise those wretched lonely nights, crawling between cold sheets, my feet sliding across to your side of the bed, searching for warmth and never finding any.

Nights that stretch out too long and too empty for any human heart to bear. Nights that too soon give way to a new day, waking up with my stomach tight and the house too silent, too quiet, knowing I have to face one more day pretending to be alive when really I feel already dead.

It was easier when school was in session. I stayed late, volunteered for any extracurricular activity I could, avoided the hallway where the kindergarten and preschool classrooms are at all costs, planning my route to evade the sound of laughter coming from the kids Josh's age like I was crossing a mine-field. And this summer has been spent in and out of hot cars, too-cold courtrooms, moldy motel rooms. For a while I thought I might find you down there in that Texas heat where I spent every moment searching for the courage to face Damian.

But I failed. Now here I am. Buried in the night-time mist Snakehead is famous for, fog so thick you need a machete to cut through it—that's what you used to say. Now I embrace the fog. If I can't see clearly what's moving beyond it, who's to say it can't bring me you and Josh?

That's the wine talking. You know me—one glass and I'm whistling Dixie. Tonight I've almost finished an entire bottle, saving just enough to take my medicine.

One year. That's how long mourning is meant to last. One year is all they give you. They. Who the hell are they, anyway? Damn them to Hell.

I seemed to have squandered my year with little to show for it. It hurts just as much today as it did that first night—maybe more. Then I was numb, in denial, shock. Now I'm awake, aware . . . alone.

Even Alan seems to think I'm over losing you and Josh. I feel like a secret addict, hiding my drug of choice. Melancholia they called it when the great writers, Poe, Joyce, Hemingway, Browning, Faulkner, suffered it. They used their despair to create art. What have I created?

Worse, if I give it up, if I give you up, allow myself to "move on"—what do I have left?

You wouldn't believe how popular I was today. Everyone in town asking me how I was doing, did I have plans for tonight? Even the Colonel's wife invited me over to dinner, her face all screwed up in a fake smile filled with pity. I told them all that I had plans with Alan. Told Alan I had plans with the Colonel.

When really, I have plans with you and Josh.

That's the last of the pills. See you soon, my loves . . .

CHAPTER NINE

Brilliant shafts of sunlight lanced through the trees, dancing on the path before her. Sarah allowed them to lull her into a mindless rhythm as she crossed the clearing. This area had already been searched multiple times; she wouldn't find anything new here.

The last time she'd been up here, she woke in the back of an ambulance. Shivering, her clothes cut open, wet with vomit, an oxygen mask smelling like an old rubber tire secured around her face, a needle pinching her as the EMT started an IV. Alan beside her, holding her hand. Flashing lights filled the rear of the ambulance from the GMC that carried Hal and the Colonel, following close behind.

Alan had squeezed her hand, his face tight with pain, skin pale in the bright lights. He told her how he'd called the Colonel and they drove to her house, found it empty, and got Hal out of bed to help them search. That when he'd found her she'd been cold, barely breathing, but had apparently had thrown up most of the pills she'd taken.

His words passed through her like the mountain mist,

without her comprehending anything except that she wasn't with Sam and Josh. She had failed.

The next two days were a blur of IVs, charcoal being forced down her only to be thrown up in a black slurry all over her hospital sheets; social workers and counselors and the Colonel—but not the Colonel's wife, thank God for small favors—and Dr. Hedeger, Hal, Alan, and more people poking and prodding her body and her psyche.

The third day she'd been transferred to the psych ward. The psychiatrist who met with her seemed too young to know anything about the secrets of the human soul. He sat back, fingers absently stroking the fashionably narrow strip of hair on his chin, and smiled at her.

"You won't be here long," he said with confidence, before she said a word to him. "I've read your file. This wasn't really a suicide attempt at all, was it, Sarah? It was what we call a gesture. A symbolic cry for help. For attention."

She curled herself up tighter in her chair, knees drawn up under her chin, and stared at him. He was in his late twenties, only a few years younger than she was, yet she felt ancient in comparison. He must have been fresh out of residency, still full of book learning and the unique form of paternalism fostered by the medical training system.

The room was small, silent, all noise deadened by the soundproofing tile that covered the walls and ceiling. He sat in a tweed chair meant to be comfortable yet too heavy to use as a weapon—a twin to the one she was curled up in, her hand stroking the scratchy upholstery as she tried to remember why she was still alive and why it mattered at all.

She breathed in reconditioned air scrubbed clean of anything living and artificially flavored with vanilla and stared at the man who was so eager to heal her, to send her back out into the world. He knew nothing of her, nothing of the real world.

"After all," he continued when she didn't respond, "a smart young lady such as yourself would have researched the drugs she was taking—if she really wanted to kill herself. She would have known drinking that much alcohol on an empty stomach would induce emesis before any of the medication could take effect. And she would realize the clearing where her husband and son died would be the first place any would-be rescuers would look for her."

He smiled at her, smug and superior and satisfied he knew everything there was to know. That he had all the answers.

"Tell me what's really bothering you, what you want," he said, flipping a small notepad open and resting it expectantly on his knee. He seemed satisfied he could already count her as a success, as if some unseen force kept score. "We'll work it through, get you out of here and back to your life."

Realizing it was her key to freedom, Sarah answered his questions, fabricating and agreeing with his self-important theories when need be. Anything to get out of there.

But she learned three important lessons from the young Dr. Freud wannabe.

First: research, research, research.

Second: drugs first, alcohol last.

Finally: go deeper into the woods. Go where no one can find you until it's too late.

CHAPTER TEN

Even though it was almost dark by the time Caitlyn drove home to her apartment in Manassas, she kept her sunglasses on. The migraine pounded furiously, snarling like a beast that refused to be kept from its prey.

She wrenched the steering wheel of her Subaru, parked it haphazardly in her space, grabbed her bag, and almost passed out at the noise of the car door slamming. *Breathe, just breathe,* she told herself as she doubled over, braced against the still-warm and ticking engine compartment.

She pushed away from the car, refusing to fall apart out here where her landlady could see her, and stumbled to the stairs leading up to her apartment on the second floor of the lovingly restored Victorian. Hauling herself up the twelve steps, her bag banging against her hip because she needed both hands on the railing, chips of paint splintering away in her grip, she finally made it to her door.

The key trembled in her hand. Her vision had almost completely gone black. The pounding in her head drove out any other sound. If she had screamed, she never would have heard it.

Finally the key turned and she shoved the door open. Rushing inside, dropping her bag, kicking the door shut, she ran to the bathroom, barely made it before she vomited. The stench of burning flesh overwhelmed her—a sure sign this migraine was going to be a bad one. As if she needed more proof.

Her best-laid plans ruined. After spending the afternoon reviewing the Hopewell case, she'd thought she could out-smart the headache by using some Imitrex at her office. The powerful, injected medicine never failed her. Never.

Until now. She slid to the floor, her cheek resting on the tiles beside the foot of the toilet, one arm still draped over the seat, and surrendered. The pain overtook her like HRT storming a building: shok-rounds powerful enough to blow steel doors apart, stun grenades with blinding explosions of light so intense they shook your body, the thunder of shotgun fire.

Unlike a quick-response raid, the migraine continued its close-quarter combat, taking its time as it stampeded through her brain, her body, her mind.

Caitlyn lay there, her body shuddering, twitching, out of her control. Nausea twisted her gut; acid burned her throat. The arm resting on the toilet screamed with pins and needles. She let it slip to the ground. That small move-ment was like pulling the pin from a grenade, setting off another explosion of pain.

Her Imitrex and Fiorcet were in the medicine cabinet above the sink. Light-years away. Alongside it was the Phenergan the doctor prescribed for when the nausea got really bad—too late for that as well.

Her arsenal. All out of reach and useless to her now.

She cried out, the sound echoing from the tile walls, reverberating through her mind. In the darkness, she inched her hand forward along the floor. She closed her eyes against the pain and the vision of her hand holding her Glock, squeezing the trigger, the bullet spiraling in slow motion toward her head.

Not even the migraine from hell would survive a .40-caliber round at point-blank range, she thought with satisfaction, glad to have devised a strategy to outwit her opponent. Like father, like daughter.

Why not? The doctors had told her if the headaches grew worse it meant one of two things. Rarely, it meant the brain was healing, the headaches escalating before burning themselves out. More commonly, it meant the scar tissue in her brain was causing more destruction, permanent damage, and things would only get worse. If the scarring weakened a blood vessel and it burst, she could die.

No. She wasn't giving up. It was only one headache. One did not a pattern make. Another strangled cry forced its way past her clenched jaws as her fingers found their target.

Not her Glock. That was in the living room in her bag, thankfully out of reach. Instead her fingers closed on the still-damp washcloth she'd left on the tub's edge this morning. Greedily she raked it in, mopping her face, inhaling the scent of lavender—anything was better than the acid stench of her vomit.

The headache pulled back, momentarily, then hit again with a sucker punch of pain. Caitlyn wadded the cloth in her mouth and bit down against her scream.

She was helpless, at its mercy, nothing to fight back with except her own stubborn will.

Think, focus, concentrate. Drive it back.

A woman's face appeared in her mind. Sarah Durandt, an expression of outraged disbelief twisting her features. Denial, anger that no one was searching for her lost boy and husband, and finally whimpers of pain when they showed her the proof that Wright had taken her son, killed her husband. She had crumbled, leaning heavily on the local police chief's arm, but Sarah Durandt had not fallen.

Instead, she had raised her head, eyes blazing out at Caitlyn, and said, *You find my son. You find Josh and Sam. I will not let that monster keep them. I don't care what it takes, you find them.*

At the time, Caitlyn both admired and pitied the mother for her fortitude. She knew from experience the grief following an act of violence often destroyed the loved ones left behind.

Although Sarah had spoken to her, her words weren't for Caitlyn. They were for herself. Caitlyn couldn't have done anything to help the lady anyway. Her job was to catch a killer before he struck again, not body recovery. In any case, events quickly swept her away from Snakehead Mountain, the town of Hopewell, and Sarah Durandt's public tragedy.

Now, somehow, they had brought her back.

The migraine's grip slipped a bit. She kept her thoughts focused on the new puzzles Clemens had delivered today. A missing U.S. Marshal, a missing man and his missing son, a helluva lot of blood from both men at a crime scene. What did it add up to?

To find the answer, she'd gone to Durandt's previous identity, Stanley Diamontes. His records, like Durandt's, had been totally erased from the system. It was only through doing a LexisNexis search that she'd been able to find enough to piece together a scenario. Thank God for the Internet.

Seemed Stan was involved in a money-laundering scheme for a Russian named Korsakov. Stan, seeing the errors of his ways—or more likely to cover his ass and avoid prison—had come to the FBI with enough information to convict Korsakov. Then Stan had promptly vanished.

Which translated to witness protection. And where better to stash a Malibu surfer boy than the mountains of the Adirondacks? That might explain Richland's involvement.

If not for the fact that Richland never worked WITSEC. His short, undistinguished career with the Marshals had been limited to fugitive apprehension and security details.

Her fingers and toes finally unclenched as feeling returned. She spit out her makeshift gag.

If Durandt was in the Witness Protection Program, someone had concealed all record of it. Caitlyn had been unable to find any record of Stan Diamontes except for the single DNA sample Clemens stumbled across, collected fifteen years ago during a Stanford bone marrow donor drive. Every other trace of Diamontes had been erased. Even the guy's prints had been removed from AFIS.

She rolled over on her back, able to breathe, the headache now a mere pounding. As she opened her eyes and stared into the darkness, she thought about the men who would have the power and ability to erase classified DOJ records.

Could be some kind of intelligence thing. NSA, CIA, somewhere in alphabet land? Nah, they wouldn't have any need for a second-rate bean counter like Diamontes. And why would Richland be involved?

Maybe Richland wasn't one of the good guys? Her research had revealed a mediocre record. Less than mediocre if you knew how to read between the lines of the bureaucratese wording of his fit-reps. And one curious item—he'd worked the Korsakov task force with her old boss, Jack Logan, back when they were both field agents.

Caitlyn blinked and it barely hurt at all. Nothing a fist-ful of Toradol couldn't handle.

She sat up, breathed out against the head rush until her vision cleared, then braced herself on the toilet and slowly climbed to her feet. She kept the lights off, feeling her way through the boxes of syringes and bottles of medicine un-til she had the right ones. Despite the doctor's warnings about using it too frequently, she'd shoot up with Imitrex again—couldn't risk the migraine returning.

Not now, not when she had work to do.

She used the auto-injector, the pain of the needle in her thigh nothing compared to the remnants of the headache. Or the thought that this might be her last case for the Bu-reau. If the headaches persisted like this, there was no way she could remain on active duty or carry a gun. She winced and turned on the cold water. The sound of rushing water was soothing, a happy sound, bringing with it a quick flash of memory: her father and her standing at the edge of the river, his arms around her, guiding her fishing rod as she cast.

A little water splashed on her face, mouthwash rinsed and spit, and the nausea was still under control, so she swallowed a few Toradol. If she didn't take them with food, they'd eventually burn a hole in her stomach, but the thought of anything to eat made her break out in a cold sweat.

She focused on the Hopewell case again before the nausea had a chance to grow. One thing was for certain; whoever wanted Diamontes erased from the known record had money. Lots of it. Because the only person with access to the files and the security clearance necessary to make them vanish was Jack Logan.

And Jack Logan worshiped two things and two things only: money and power.

Her fingers still shook, felt numb as she stripped free of her sweat-soaked clothes. She held on to the sink for balance, kicking off her leather flats and struggling out of her khaki slacks, sleeveless cotton sweater, and underwear. Barefoot and naked, she crossed the hall into her bedroom and fell into her bed, pulling the covers tight over her, blocking out the world.

Sarah Durandt, her face filled with pain and yearning, was the last thing Caitlyn saw before she finally escaped into sleep.

CHAPTER ELEVEN

JD was hot, sweaty, and totally starving by the time they reached the overlook across the road from Hal Waverly's house at the top of the Lower Falls. The flat viewing area was empty of any cars, all the day tourists long gone. They were missing the best part, JD thought. Being here, the earth beneath his feet trembling from the force of the water roaring below him, the sun setting over the mountains beside them, streaking the sky red and gold, and, best of all, a beautiful girl at his side.

Julia set up the tripod for her father's high-powered digital SLR camera while JD used his inexpensive hand-held to film her. As she unfolded a towel and set out napkins, he unpacked the food, sneaking a chicken leg to munch on.

"Where was the last sighting?" she asked.

He wiped his greasy fingers on his jeans and unfolded his map. They'd tried to record every sighting of the mysterious lights over the past month, and now that school was out, they finally had the chance to record the phenomena firsthand.

"My dad saw them last night. At the dam and along the east side of the reservoir. Said he saw them at nine forty-five and again about an hour later."

"And two nights before was when Mrs. Patterson saw them along Rattlesnake Pike, just below here."

"Right. And we have that bus of church kids from Merrill who e-mailed me that they saw some around the Devil's Elbow as well, beside the Upper Falls, but no one could give me any specifics, so I'm not sure if we should count those."

He looked up from his spot on the ground. God, he loved the way she pursed her lips together, a small dimple digging into her chin when she really thought hard about something. Julia was the only person who took his project seriously. Even his dad, who had actually seen the lights, didn't think they were worth his spending his summer trying to investigate them, much less create a documentary out of the mysterious phenomenon.

Julia sat cross-legged in front of him. How the heck did she do that? One second she was standing, the next she seemed to float through space, her legs effortlessly folding beneath her. Her knee brushed his as she leaned across him for a piece of chicken. She tore into it, her teeth bared, totally unladylike and absolutely mesmerizing.

"I think," she said, swiping her mouth with a napkin, "we should try to get one of those timers or motion sensors. We can't keep spending all our time watching when the sightings are coming from all over."

Sure he could—if it meant spending long summer nights huddled at the camera beside Julia. But she had a point. So far they'd tried for hours on end to spot the mystery lights, without success. His documentary was doomed if they couldn't get actual footage.

"Seems like we're always one step behind," he said.

He munched on another piece of chicken as he scrutinized the map of sightings. "They're all along this side of the gorge, but there just aren't any good vantage points. Maybe tomorrow we should go over to the other side? There's a scenic overlook there."

Julia lay flat on her back, staring up at Snakehead's summit above and to the north of them. "It would take all day to get up there on our bikes." She scrunched her face in thought and JD wanted nothing more than to smooth his fingers across her skin, erase all the frown lines. "Why don't we camp out at the old caretaker's cabin down by the dam, instead?"

"All the fog gathers down there below the dam, but we might see something. And there have been more sightings near the dam than anywhere else." He thought about it, liking her idea. "Maybe the dam is the target."

JD lost himself momentarily in the fantasy: him stopping a band of wild-eyed terrorists, the gleam of pride in his father's eyes, the whole town cheering as they gave him a medal, Julia at his side.

"More likely it's kids skinny-dipping in the reservoir." Julia sprang to her feet, brushing stray strands of grass from her shorts. "It's getting dark, I'll take the first shift."

JD couldn't argue as he watched her lean over, focused on the camera's viewfinder. Darkness gathered around them, but the night was warm, the stars bright. They both had headlights on their bikes and midnight curfews, and the ride down the mountain road was a lot easier than the ride up. Besides, no one ever drove Rattlesnake Pike at night. The dirt road was tricky enough in the daytime and the only person who lived this high up on the mountain was Hal Waverly, who'd be at work, like always.

Until then, it was just JD, Julia, and the mountain. A smile stretched his face, accompanied by a warm stirring below his waist. So far he hadn't even found the courage to kiss her. She was special. He had to work his way up to it, do it right. That was okay. He had all summer.

"Hey!" Her voice rang out through the night clearer than a church bell. "I think I see them!"

It was dark by the time Sarah stopped. She didn't mind hiking at night, not with the full moon to guide her. But her body rebelled, near to collapse. She'd marched up the mountain like a zombie, not stopping for food or drink or rest. She looked around, recognized where her feet had unerringly led her.

The top of Snakebelly. The first time she'd taken Sam camping, she brought him here. The first time they had made love was here, beneath the shimmering night sky filled with the cascading stars of the Milky Way. She remembered how frightened Sam had been when she jumped off the cliff, rappeled down into the gorge. His face had been whiter than snow, covered with sweat as he forced himself to peer over the edge.

That had taken him more courage than she understood at the time. She'd played along the cliffs of this mountain since she was a child, had never known any fear, or met anyone afraid of heights. But then, Sam wasn't like anyone she had ever known before.

When she realized what it had cost him to watch her blissfully teeter on the edge of the crevasse, ropes or no ropes, she discovered she had found someone who meant more to her than her first love, the mountain. She hung up her climbing gear, using it only when needed during search and rescue missions.

Below this granite ledge was Snakebelly, the crevasse where the last body on Snakehead had been found. Lily Waverly, Hal's wife.

Snakebelly was where the river deposited all of its dead, although it often sequestered them for a time, sometimes years, decades, or even centuries. When Sarah was ten, hunters had found the remains of what researchers from the Smithsonian eventually decided were two Native Americans dating from the twelfth century.

A man and a woman. Suicide pact? The researchers had argued. Native Romeo and Juliet? Or the real-life inspiration for the Iroquois myth of Ahweyoh and the Thundergod she had sacrificed her life for?

Sarah told Sam about the ancient bones the first night they spent up here. A crisp summer night, it was just cold enough to require a fire and someone's arms around you to keep warm.

Even Sam had to admit this wind-scoured ledge with its canopy of trees and front-row seat to the heavens was one of the most romantic places on earth. As long as you didn't look down.

The sound of the water had been bright and cheerful, splashing in the gorge below, a playful accompaniment to their mutual exploration. They were in love already—even though they had only known each other a few weeks—but neither was quite ready to admit it. Yet.

"So tell me about this Indian princess," Sam had asked after he put his guitar aside.

Sarah leaned back into his arms, enjoying it as his fingers strummed the skin inside her wrist as if coaxing a melody from his guitar.

"You sure you want to hear? Most versions don't have a happy ending."

"Maybe I'll write a song about her. Make up a happy ending."

"She wasn't a princess. Just a young girl who lived among the river people. But she refused to marry, despite her family's commands. Instead Ahweyoh took a lover. He was a stranger, frightening to Ahweyoh's people with his broad shoulders and booming voice that stirred ancient memories of the wars between the gods and the evil ones. They wanted no part of those ancient legends, even though the stories were their legacy, ran in their blood. No, all they wanted was peace and quiet, to live beside their river, catch the fish it provided, grow their crops."

"Hah," Sam had said with a chuckle. "I'll bet that didn't stop two horny kids in love."

Sarah nudged him with her elbow and continued. "Shunned by the river people for her affair, Ahweyoh was exiled. She packed her canoe and traveled farther than any of her people had ever journeyed before. A great fog enveloped her, storm winds buffeted her, but she followed the current and remained true to her course. When the clouds lifted, He-noh, her lover, was waiting. He revealed his true form to her—he was a Thundergod. He invited her to marry him and join him in his house in the clouds."

"And they lived happily ever after," Sam put in, nuzzling her neck as his hands began to roam beneath her shirt.

"Not so fast, Music Man. He-noh told Ahweyoh of an ancient prophecy. An evil serpent demon would attack and kill the river people. She renounced immortality to journey back to her homeland and warn them.

"They scoffed and laughed, assuming the god had cast her aside once he was finished with her. Then the water demon attacked. Ahweyoh called upon her Thundergod's help and together they battled the serpent. She paddled her canoe on the river, serving as a diversion, while He-noh lanced a thunderbolt through the demon's eye."

Sam squirmed, tightening his arms around her, and Sarah knew that he was now fully engaged in her story.

Typical guy—didn't care until there were blood and guts and gore.

"The writhing serpent's body carved out the gorge, rerouting the once peaceful river into a treacherous length of rapids and waterfalls. As the serpent coiled its body, ready to spring on Ahweyoh, the Thundergod emerged from the mist and severed its head from its body, flinging it to one side. Thus Snakehead Mountain was born. The snake's body formed the other mountains to the east and south."

Sarah had spread her arms wide, indicating the sinuous curves of the mountains hidden in the darkness. Sam ducked beneath her arm, rolling her onto her back as he kissed her thoroughly. "See, a happy ending," he said when he came up for air.

Sarah let it go at that, releasing herself to Sam's passion. But she knew the truth: most of the legends had no happy ending for either of the lovers.

The ancient myth played through Sarah's mind now as she spread out her tarp and drank some water. Her mouth was parched, her muscles shaking as she sat on the ledge, looking south over the gorge. Hopewell's lights were out of sight, beyond a fold in the mountain ridge and too far to the west of where she sat.

Her only companions were an owl whose hunting silhouette flitted across the moon, the granite boulders lining the ledge, a few hardy oak and hemlock trees that dared to bury roots into the rock face, and the legend of a dead Iroquois maiden.

Like many heroes, Ahweyoh had not been well received after saving her people's lives. Their village, their homes were destroyed and they blamed her. After all, their lives had been peaceful before she involved them in the battles between gods and monsters.

Caught between two worlds, unable to return to her lover after refusing the gods' gift of immortality, Ahweyoh placed all her hope in one thing: her love for Henoh.

Late one night, under a full moon, she paddled her canoe through the rapids that now churned her once peaceful river. Then she calmly set her paddle aside, raising her arms out as the powerful current carried her over the Upper Falls. She called out her lover's name, certain he would descend from the mists and carry her to safety. There, in the mist that came nightly to the mountain, they could live forever, between the cloud world of the gods and the rocks and soil of the mortals.

Sarah stretched out, allowing the tendrils of fog that spread out from the forest behind her to engulf her, wishing they were as warm and solid as Sam's arms had been. The moon winked in and out. The owl called out in victory, a whoosh of wings humming through the air over the gorge. Her body went still, the hard earth and cool night air disappearing into the mist. As if she were leaving her body behind, entering the in-between world, the limbo that was the only place where Ahweyoh and Henoh could be together.

There were several versions of the legend. One ended with the two lovers together, their spirits destined for immortality, coming to life nightly through the mountain mists even though their bodies died a mortal death, crushed by the rocks below the falls. That one emphasized the Thundergod's sacrifice of his own immortality to be with his one true love.

Another ended with the Thundergod being trapped by his brother gods before he could reach Ahweyoh. They captured him, chained him to the clouds, refusing to allow him to steal away to Earth, leaving them without his strength and protection. His cries echoing through the gorge, deafening all creatures who heard him, he watched in horror as Ahweyoh and her canoe flew through the air only to crash to Earth again, battered and beaten by the rapids and rocks.

A shiver ran through Sarah's body, reminding her that she was only human. She blinked, stretched, and reached for her pack. She wouldn't bother with a fire, not tonight. Instead she munched on a PowerBar and wrapped herself in her fleece jacket.

While she taught all the versions of the ancient legend to her students, Sarah much preferred the third ending, had ever since she'd first heard it as a little girl.

In this one, the gods recognized Ahweyoh's courage in helping them defeat the serpent demon. When she launched herself off the Upper Falls, the mist parted and a shaft of moonlight shimmered through the night, creating a path back up to the cloud world and her Thundergod. He waited for her on the moonbeam, reaching a hand out to catch her when she faltered and would fall.

And of course, together they lived happily ever after.

Sarah wadded up the wrapper from her makeshift dinner and shoved it back into her pack. She rolled herself up in her tarp so that she wouldn't wake up covered with dew and closed her eyes on the mystical world swirling around her.

She was too old to believe in fairy tales. Especially ones with happy endings.

Thursday, June 21

CHAPTER TWELVE

Sarah woke feeling groggy, punch-drunk. She sat up, head reeling, eyes gritty. Dehydrated. Idiot, she knew better, should have drunk more during her climb up here yesterday.

She wiped her face, forced herself to down a liter of water followed by another energy bar. As she combed her fingers through her hair and tied it back, she felt more human.

The only human. The granite ledge jutting out over Snakebelly felt suspended in both time and space. Across the gorge the rolling ridges of the mountains to the south spread out like ripples on an ocean of gray-blue fog. Overhead, several hawks swirled, disappearing into the sun that crowned the eastern slope of Snakehead. The only sounds were the rustling of the wind through the branches and the distant rumble of water from the gorge.

Crisp air sliced through her lungs, rejuvenating her. Yesterday felt like a blur, but today had dawned clear and brilliant.

She tidied her simple camp and pulled her binoculars

from her pack. After taking a moment to enjoy the antics of the hawks, she stepped to the edge of the ledge and shimmied belly down on it. She focused into the shadows that clung to the granite boulders fifty yards below. Sunlight gleamed off eddies in the river's current as it twisted around the rocks. The river had carved out a niche over the millennia, a hidden trap for the unwary. Not that anything or anyone could survive the falls half a mile upstream.

Sarah scanned the treacherous inlet. Tangled tree limbs sprouted here and there like a skeleton forest. Something bright and white and gleaming caught her eye.

Correction. A forest of skeletons.

Well, at least part of one. She zoomed in, trying to tell if the bone was attached to anything human. Hal was right, there had been some recent rockslides. The ground was littered with newly fallen bits of the mountain.

Maybe it was a deer. Animal carcasses could just as easily find their way to the surface here at Snakebelly. She felt her throat go dry. Could she have found Sam? After all this time?

Her fingers slipped on the focus wheel, her palms damp with sweat as they gripped the binoculars. The bones, there were two of them she saw now, were long and slender. They disappeared beneath a tangle of tree branches caught in the river's current.

Probably was a deer after all. She released her breath, unaware she'd been holding it.

A gleam of silver sparked in the sunlight.

Deer didn't wear wristwatches.

CHAPTER THIRTEEN

Now that she was past D.C. and the snarled wasteland of freeway surrounding it, Caitlyn had room to maneuver the Subaru. Cruising along the left-hand lane, she not so subtly encouraged anyone dawdling at less than eighty miles an hour to get the hell out of her way.

One of her favorite perks of carrying a badge. Since she wasn't on official business, she had to use her own vehicle, but that was all right. So far the cops she'd passed seemed more interested in keeping traffic flowing smoothly than spending time writing tickets.

She'd just passed East Brunswick when her cell phone sang out. She hit the hands-free button. "Tierney here."

"Caitlyn," came a voice mellow with California sunshine, "how ya doing, girl?"

"Hey, Royal, thanks for getting back to me." Royal Hassam, an assistant U.S. attorney based in L.A., was an old friend and the one person she trusted to help her get the inside scoop on Stan Diamontes' involvement with the Korsakov case.

"When you going to come out here, spend a week on

the beach with me? We could drive up to Big Sur, fresh air, sunshine, ocean, and no office politics."

"You make it sound tempting, but I need to finish this case first. Were you able to find anything on Korsakov or Diamontes?"

"Yes, ma'am. Funny thing that. Korsakov is due in court today. Has my boss about stroking out."

"Why's that?" Caitlyn spied a rest area approaching and swerved into the exit lane. She cruised to a stop, all attention fixed on the phone.

"His conviction is getting overturned on a technicality. We can't retry him without Diamontes' testimony. And of course, we don't have that, seeing as Diamontes is dead."

"So Diamontes really is Sam Durandt."

"Sweetheart, of course he is. You ought to know— your old boss, Jack Logan, is the one who worked that end of the case, got Diamontes into WITSEC seven years ago."

Caitlyn pursed her lips in a silent whistle. She'd tried contacting Logan, but he was either unavailable or ducking her calls. She suspected the latter. "Guess he forgot to mention that when we worked the Durandt case."

"And I thought our office politics were bad. At least we only mess with the state and local prosecutors; we don't go around screwing ourselves."

"Keep it clean, Royal." Never knew who might be listening in. She didn't need Royal to get his ass in a sling because of her—or news of their conversation making its way back to Quantico or the brass. She hadn't officially opened a case file. Because as of yet she had no proof any crime had been committed. Just a whole lot of ugly suspicions.

"S'all right. I'm on my cell. Jogging on the beach, in fact. Here, listen to the ocean." Static as he presumably held the phone out. Caitlyn smoothed her palms against her linen slacks, arched her back, and stretched in her seat. Royal's voice soon returned. "Remember the time difference? It's not even six here, way too early for any bosses to be awake."

"Still, this is touchy. You might want to keep a low profile, not let anyone know you've been asking questions about Diamontes." Bad enough she was risking her career looking into this, no sense ruining Royal's as well.

"No worries. All anyone is talking about around here is Korsakov. You wouldn't believe some of the things that guy has done. I worked Organized Crime out of Jersey and it still makes my stomach turn. This is one seriously whacked-out dude."

"His only convictions are for money laundering. They couldn't make the murder charges stick." That much Caitlyn had gleaned from her NexisLexis search last night.

"Only because the grand jury wouldn't convict solely on Diamontes' uncorroborated testimony."

"Let me guess. Any other witnesses were dead."

"Or missing. Those whose bodies were found, well, let's just say they didn't go peacefully into the night. The autopsy reports read like a slasher movie script on steroids."

"Forensics?"

"Nope. Our Russian, Korsakov, is smarter than your average bear." He chuckled at his pun.

"Besides the trial transcripts, can you give me any info on Stan Diamontes?"

"I'll e-mail you the only photo I could find. It's almost ten years old. He's thirty-five now, youngest of four kids, father a banker at Chase, mother a homemaker. A few run-ins with local PDs."

"He has a record?"

"Scarface this guy is not. He likes to surf—doesn't care who owns the beach. Half a dozen arrests for trespassing, no convictions. Went to Stanford, mediocre grades, BS in accounting. Oh yeah, he minored in musical composition of all things. I can try to run down former friends, relatives, see if anyone's heard from him if you'd like, but I have to tell you, if I had a freak like Korsakov gunning for me, I don't care how long of a sentence he got, I'd dig a hole to China and stay good and buried."

Caitlyn drummed her fingers along the steering wheel. Her headache was only a low throb today thanks to the double doses of drugs she'd taken. Ounce of prevention seemed a good idea after last night.

"No. E-mail me the list and if need be, I'll follow up with them. I don't want you sticking your neck out more than necessary. And could you keep me posted on Korsakov's hearing?"

"Sure, whatever you want. Promise you'll tell me what this is all about once you're free and clear?"

"I will. Thanks, Royal."

"No prob. And hey, if you ever need a lawyer—"

"You'll be the last one I call. Take it easy."

"Don't I always?"

She hung up and reached for her well-worn Rand Mc-Nally. She hated nav systems always hounding her with their "recalculating" when she veered off their prescribed route. A detour to Hartford would take only a few hours. She shifted into gear. She'd call on Jack Logan in person, try to jar him into revealing something, and still make it to Hopewell by afternoon. As the pavement hummed beneath her tires, her right foot kept pushing down on the accelerator, answering her instincts telling her she was running out of time.

CHAPTER FOURTEEN

Sarah sucked her breath in, rolled onto her back, the sky opening up above her in a dizzying vista of cerulean. She focused on her breathing. It shouldn't be that hard, she'd done it all her life, but suddenly she couldn't force any air past the knot in her throat.

Sam was down there. Which meant he was dead, really dead. And if he was gone, then so was Josh.

She'd known it. But had never actually believed, truly believed, until this moment. She squeezed her eyes shut against the too-cheerful sunlight and the sting of her tears.

Maybe it wasn't Sam. Who could tell from this distance?

Logic told her not to be a fool, to surrender to the truth. Sam was the only adult reported missing on Snakehead and still unaccounted for in recent years. Sarah sat up, her vision clearing. She dropped the binoculars and grabbed the two-way radio Hal had lent her and spoke into the small handset.

"Hal? This is Sarah, does anyone copy?"

Static answered her for a few long moments. Then Hal's

voice cut through it, reassuring and calm. "You okay, Sarah?"

"I'm fine. I, uh, I found something up here you need to know about."

Another long pause. There was a clatter of silverware and men's laughter in the background. He was probably at the Rockslide, having breakfast. "What's up?"

"I'm at the top of Snakebelly. There's a man down below."

"You want I should call search and rescue?" His voice sounded lighthearted, a bit distracted. He hadn't recognized the implications of what she said.

She swallowed hard. This might be Sam they were talking about. She hoped the Colonel was out of earshot. "No. I think you'd better call the coroner."

The speaker stuttered as if he'd started to say something, then removed his finger from the trigger. Finally his voice returned. Slower, grimmer. The background noise vanished. "I'm on my way."

She put the radio down and sat back on her heels. Gerald Merton, the eldest son and reigning heir to the Merton Funeral Home down in Merrill, was the current county coroner. He'd do a preliminary exam at his funeral home and package the remains for the State Police to take to their lab, where a real medical examiner would perform a complete autopsy.

It would take Hal a good hour or more to pick up Gerald and drive up Snakehead. From there it would be another hour or so before they would reach her location if they hiked up the trail. Faster if Hal pulled off Rattlesnake Pike and left his truck on the side of the road. Then it would be a mere ten-minute hike in, but it would mean bushwhacking through some dense forest and undergrowth.

No problem for Hal, he was used to it. But Gerald was a pasty-faced, overweight forty-something with a beer belly that made him look more like Santa Claus than an undertaker. And they'd have their hands full of gear—a stretcher, ropes, body bags, et cetera.

Either way, she had a wait on her hands. Sarah never was very good at waiting. Especially not now. Not with the answers she'd been yearning for so close at hand.

She sidled to the edge of the gorge and craned her head over it, assessing the damage the spring thaw and rock-slides had done to the rock face. Not too bad. Definitely doable. She could rappel down, get the body—or what was left of it—ready to move, save them some time.

She'd done it before. Most every able-bodied adult in Hopewell was a member of the search and rescue team. Too many uncharted trails, inviting granite walls, and un-mapped caves on Snakehead. They were called out a few times every year to search for lost hunters, hikers, climbers, and spelunkers.

Last time she'd done a body recovery had been right here. Last body she'd helped to bring out of Snakebelly was Lily, Hal's wife. Two years ago, almost to the day, Lily had plummeted to her death from the Upper Falls. Her body and mind ravaged by cancer, in constant pain, most had called it a blessing, but her death had left Hal devastated.

That made up her mind for her. Better to do everything she could to keep Hal's time in the gorge to a minimum. Spare him those painful memories, at least.

Besides, she needed to know if it was Sam down there or not.

Sarah quickly secured her climbing rope, an 11mm dry rope, to a boulder and stepped into her harness. She didn't have her usual SAR gear—no protective gloves or

Vicks to deaden the smell of decay. But from what she'd seen so far, it didn't look like there was a whole lot left to smell on this body.

She emptied her pack, leaving only her camera, ground cloth, duct tape, flashlight, and an assortment of plastic bags. She strapped her knife and climbing gear to her harness. No helmet. The Colonel would have a cow about that; it was against regulations.

The thought made Sarah smile. Breaking regs was one of her favorite pastimes. It was what had brought her and Sam together to start with.

The sun was now bright and warm, radiating off the granite rock face. Sarah positioned herself, double-checked her anchor, and stepped off into space.

CHAPTER FIFTEEN

Less than two hours later, Caitlyn arrived at Jack Logan's new workplace: a shiny high-rise tower that promised a magnificent view of downtown Hartford. Logan's position as a security consultant for a multinational insurance company definitely paid better than a job in the federal government, she decided as she took in his glass-walled corner office adorned with vanity shots of Logan shaking hands or playing golf with a variety of celebrities. Stars whose life he had saved, no doubt.

She gave a small snort. The job suited Logan. As did the office. Big fat bunch of lies. Strip away the façade and Logan was nothing more than a glorified travel agent and hand-holder.

Exactly five minutes after his secretary ushered her into Logan's inner sanctum, he burst through the door, puffed up with self-importance as he rushed to his desk, too harried to spare her a glance.

"Caitlyn, good to see you. Sorry I was tied up. Arab oil sheik wanted a new security review for his family holdings in Paris, Geneva, and Milan." He dumped an ostrich-skin briefcase onto his desk and finally raised his head to look at her. "Well, you're looking good. Guess desk duty suits you. I always figured you weren't cut out for field-work."

Caitlyn wouldn't call her promotion and assignment to teach at Quantico desk duty. Logan might be an ass, but he knew the drill. Get your shots in first, put your mark on the defensive quick, make them react without thinking. Classic old-school style of interview manipulation.

Too bad for Logan, Caitlyn was new-school. Despite his bluster, he couldn't hide the sheen of sweat on his upper lip or the twitch of his eyes when he mentioned Quantico. She strolled over to his immense metal and glass-topped desk and settled herself in one of the uncomfortable tubular steel chairs before it. Stretching her legs out, she crossed them at the ankles. She'd worn her cornflower blue pantsuit—it matched her eyes—and a sleeveless silk blouse that buttoned in the back, allowing the material to fit smoothly against her curves. She'd changed shoes in the car, substituting sling-back heels for her more sensible Rockports. The heels revealed just the right amount of ankle and leg.

Legs Logan now was gazing at, slowly working his way up her body. Caitlyn smiled. Talk about old-school, her distraction was as old as Mata Hari. She remained silent, waiting for him to dig himself in deeper.

He settled on the corner of the desk directly before her, swinging his foot in an arc guaranteed to bring it closer and closer to her calf. "So. What brings you here? Need help with a case? I still do consulting for the Bureau, but it will cost you, of course." He chuckled, straightening his silk tie and twisting his diamond-studded watch to catch the sunlight.

"Just wanted to give you a heads-up." Time to put him

on the defensive. If she knew Logan, he'd be more likely to make a mistake trying to cover his tracks if he thought she was on to something. "I'm reopening the Durandt case."

His ankle twitched, jerked against the desk leg. "Really?" His voice was bland. "I thought we put that one to bed. Didn't they execute someone already, what was his name?"

"Damian Wright," Caitlyn supplied helpfully. "A few things have come up. New evidence. Wright may be innocent of the Hopewell murders."

"What kind of new evidence?" Logan asked, his gaze settled on a point past her shoulder as if he were bored and only asking to be polite.

Caitlyn smiled. "Sorry, Jack. You know the rules."

He focused on her face, mirrored her smile. "You didn't drive all the way up here simply to inform me that an old case was being reopened. You want something from me. What's the game, Caitlyn?"

She remained silent, watching him carefully. His voice had taken on a new edge. The small wrinkles near his eyes that Botox hadn't totally erased deepened. She'd definitely hit a sore spot.

If what she suspected was true, she wasn't surprised.

"I can't help you without more information," he continued in a genial voice. The well-versed mentor showing the newbie the ropes. Roles that suited neither of them anymore.

Hadn't in a long time. Not since two and a half years ago when he'd almost gotten her killed.

He gazed out the window at the late morning sun, his ankle circling once more. "Let's see. Hopewell. Ahh, I remember now. The night you got sick on the drive down. Then you antagonized the local police chief and almost made the vic's mother collapse with a nervous breakdown."

He slanted another smile in her direction. "Not your finest moment, Caitlyn."

Unlike the moment when he'd canceled her backup team, leaving Caitlyn and her partner alone in the fight of their lives. A vision of glass breaking, the look of terror on Santore's face as they both plummeted out the window, the stomach-lurching feeling of free fall, the pain when she'd hit the ground—these all raced through her mind at whiplash speed. She kept her face and her voice neutral, meeting his gaze effortlessly. "Maybe that's why I'm anxious to set the record straight."

"Hmpf. I remember the crime scene. It was raining monkeys and we had to hike halfway up a mountain. The local yokels tried to protect the scene as best they could, but the wind and the rain left us slim pickins. But we had a blood sample from the Unsub."

Caitlyn shook her head. "Wrong again, Jack. The Unsub's blood didn't match Damian Wright."

He jerked up at that, acted startled, his mouth dropping open. But there was no crease in his brow, no other signs of surprise. "Really? You don't say? Whose blood was it, then?"

Caitlyn decided to let him think she knew nothing of Richland's involvement. After all, both he and Logan had worked the Korsakov task force. "Some guy named Stanley Diamontes. Name ring a bell to you?"

He pursed his lips, frowned in thought. "Maybe, maybe."

"He testified against a Russian, name of Korsakov. After that we lost track of him. It was a miracle we matched his DNA at all."

"Korsakov, yes, I definitely remember him. Who could forget? Crazy fucker, had two hobbies: making movies and torturing people. Can't say I'm surprised a witness against him took off, got lost in the mountains with a new name." He straightened up. "So, mystery solved. I can try to find my old case notes on Korsakov if you like. Free of charge for old time's sake."

He slid to his feet, began walking to the door, obviously expecting her to follow him. "Sorry I don't have more time for you, Caitlyn."

She took her time, not moving from her chair until he'd already reached the door and held it open. Only then did she stand and stroll past him, coming to a stop in the doorway. "Thanks, Jack. I knew you'd have the answers I needed. I'd definitely like a look at those files. Especially since Korsakov is getting out of prison today."

His eyes widened and tiny droplets of sweat began to sprout on his forehead before he could hustle her out the door. "Fine. No problem. I'll have Margery fax them down to Quantico by the day's end."

He tried to close the door, but she blocked him. "It'd be better to scan and e-mail them to me, Jack. I'm on my way to Hopewell."

She breezed out the door and through the reception area before he could respond. He banged the glass door shut behind her, his hand mopping his brow. Idiot was so used to the fancy glass walls he'd forgotten they were there. She watched him in the mirror above the elevator call buttons. He lunged for the phone on his desk and began dialing furiously.

The elevator chimed its arrival. Caitlyn entered, looked up for one last glance at her former boss, now huddled over his phone, his face flushed. He met her glance and, startled, stood, cradling the handset between his cheek and shoulder. She smiled sweetly and waved good-bye.

The doors slid shut, and she grabbed her cell phone. "Clemens? . . . Hey, it's Caitlyn. Could you ask one of the guys in the surveillance section to dump a phone for me?"

As Sarah worked her way down the side of the cliff, memories cascaded through her mind. Her and Sam, Sam and her—always breaking the rules, two partners-in-crime.

The first time she'd met him, he'd been trespassing on school property. Tap-dancing down the empty corridor, whistling as he opened classroom doors, peered inside, then shut them once more.

"Can I help you?" Sarah had asked in her best "I've got eyes in the back of my head, so don't try anything" teacher's voice. His nonchalance as he straightened, removed his dark sunglasses, and gave her a slow once-over was annoying.

He stepped closer and flashed her a thousand-watt smile. "I'm looking for the music room. Or the auditorium. I need a piano."

"You need a piano?" she asked, not sure if she'd heard him correctly. "Excuse me, but do you have a child who is a student here, Mr.—"

He stared at her blankly for a moment, then chuckled. "No, ma'am. No child. Is that a problem?"

"The only problem seems to be the fact that you're trespassing."

"Wasn't today the last day of school? Aren't the kids all gone?"

"That's beside the point." Sarah scrutinized him. Very tan, which made his dark hair and dark eyes look exotic. Definitely not from around here. His accent—or lack of one—made her think West Coast. He was trim, well muscled, just shy of six feet, wearing a white polo and jeans that fit like . . . Her gaze trailed down, lingered a moment too long. He twisted his head to peer over one shoulder.

"What's wrong? Did I sit in something?"

Sarah went rigid, felt her face flush with a combination of embarrassment and suppressed laughter. If it had happened anywhere but here at school, she would have acknowledged her ogling, made a joke out of it. Especially as the waggled eyebrow and overdramatic leer he sent her way told her she wasn't fooling him.

"Let's start over. I'm Sarah Godwin." She extended her hand.

He shook it with a firm grasp, didn't push things by lingering too long. Although she did notice the way his smile deepened, wrinkling the corners of his eyes.

"Sam. Sam Durandt."

"Sam Durandt. Who is in desperate need of a piano?"

"Right. See, my keyboard hasn't arrived yet. I've got to," he rapped his knuckles against his temple, "get this song worked out before it drives me nuts."

"Oh. You're a composer, are you?"

"No, not a composer. I mean, not only music. I write songs."

Sarah pursed her lips. Was this guy for real? "Anything I might have heard?"

He rocked on his heels, looked down. "No, not yet. But," he brightened, beaming at her, "maybe this is the one. *If* you could show me to a piano."

She hesitated. She was alone in the building until Mr. Cole arrived to clean. He seemed friendly enough, but . . .

"I'll rent it from you," he blurted into the lengthening silence.

"Rent it?"

"Yeah. I don't have a lot of money, but if you let me work on my song, I'll write one just for you." He glanced up at her, his long, dark eyelashes framing even darker, larger eyes. "Please . . . it's a matter of life or death."

Sarah laughed. He was worse than her students. "All right. Come with me, Sam the Music Man."

Her foot brushed against the granite rock face and Sarah fell, the rope zipping through her hands faster than she had intended. She pulled up, her harness squeezing tight around her hips. She came to a halt a few feet above a large boulder.

She hated thinking about that first day—hated it because the memory invariably led to more memories followed by traitorous thoughts.

If she hadn't met Sam, then she might have met someone else, and he would still be alive, and if he were alive, then so would Josh still be alive, only he wouldn't be Josh because Sam wasn't his father, but she would at least have one of them . . .

She leaned back on her rope, squinted at the bright sunshine, and cursed herself for forgetting her sunglasses. Blinking back tears, she lowered herself to a standing position on the partially submerged rock. Water lapped at her boots, trying to undermine her footing.

A fall here would leave someone beat up pretty good.

Wasn't that what she'd already done? Fallen in love and gotten beat up for it. Battered, bruised, broken.

The words came in a staccato that swirled through her, echoed with the pulse pounding in her temples. Sam would have made a song out of it. Not a funny song or a joke like so many of his songs were.

A ballad, a dirge. A sad, sad song. One that would coax tears from the hardest of hearts.

She blinked rapidly, told herself it was the sun reflecting from the wet mirrorlike granite. She reached for the shiny white lengths of bone visible above the water.

No. She yanked her hand away. *Photos first. Document the scene.*

Everything looked more distant, impersonal, through the camera's viewfinder. Like maybe this wasn't really happening, like maybe it wasn't really Sam and if it wasn't really Sam, then maybe Josh wasn't really—

Her foot slid out from under her. She flung her weight to the opposite side before she impaled herself on the tangled tree branches jutting up against the rock.

Pay attention. As she caught her breath, her pulse racing after the near miss, she sat back and double-checked the photos on the digital screen. A few were blurry—from water spraying up from the rapids a few feet away or from her body shaking? Didn't matter, enough were clear.

With trembling hands, she put the camera away. Then she reached for the bones.

Radius and ulna, she remembered her anatomy. Gently she disentangled a layer of dead leaves and debris to unveil the remnants of three fingers and the bones connecting them to the forearm. They stretched out, now unveiled on a mat of dead hemlock, pointing, accusing her.

Her breath drew shallow as if there wasn't enough air despite the ozone charge of the fast-flowing water spraying around her.

It was a man's right hand. Sam always wore his watch on the left. Didn't he?

Or was she merely trying to talk herself into that?

She took more photos. Up close there were tiny teeth marks on the bones. Gingerly she moved the large, interwoven mat of debris from the other end of the arm.

A man's head, grotesque, swollen, yellow, bobbed up

from the water, breaking the surface, its mouth open in a gaping grimace.

Sarah slipped. Skittering back along the boulder, unable to regain her balance, her feet flew out from under her. Dead leaves and twigs scattered through the air. She slammed back against the rock face, hitting her head. One foot slid into the water, into the grasp of slimy, decomposed vegetation that tried to suck her down.

Her rope stopped her from tumbling completely into the water, where she'd be at the mercy of the current. She lay there, her left leg bent against the boulder, her right one immersed up to her knee, cold water surging in to fill her boot, her head throbbing, her vision flickering with bright lights. At first she couldn't breathe; it was as if all the air had been sucked out and her lungs collapsed.

She made an effort and drew a deep, long draught of sparkling crisp air that burned her lungs. The muscles along her right chest wall voiced their protest and she knew she'd find bruises there by morning. At least she'd live to see morning.

The river cackled at her as the water sprayed into her face, warning her it was always there, ready, waiting for her to screw up again. She took another deep breath and steadied herself on the rope, tugging her waterlogged leg free from the mire. Her boot stayed on, thank goodness.

She flopped back onto the boulder to focus on her gruesome discovery. Her pack had gotten slammed against the rock when she fell, but her camera seemed to be working fine.

The head was misshapen, giving it the appearance of being swollen. The lower jaw hung by one side only. The flesh, eyes, tongue were all gone, as were several of the teeth, leaving a gaping hole behind. The bone was exposed in a few patchy areas, but most of the skull was covered by greasy yellow-brown adipocere tissue and algae interspersed with tangles of hair.

The man's clothes were intact—which explained why his remains hadn't totally disarticulated and scattered at the river's whim. Beneath a black windbreaker, he wore what once had been a light blue shirt with a buttoned-down collar.

Did Sam have a shirt like that? Maybe, probably. It was the kind of shirt every man had hanging in his closet, even a work-at-home dad like Sam.

Her stomach clenched, acid bit the back of her throat as she breathed through her mouth. Not because of the smell, although now there was enough debris stirred up to create a sweetly sick stench. Her vision darkened and she realized she was hyperventilating.

She turned away from the head and forced herself to focus on the river. Down here, right at its surface, it looked deceptively innocent, playful. White water rushed past, breaking against the boulder she had claimed, then moving back out to the center of the current. The side of the chasm blocked her view of the falls, but she could hear them, feel them rumbling.

Her breathing under control, she bent forward, her face mere inches away from the wristwatch bobbing on the water's surface.

It had a dark blue face and Roman numerals. Surely Sam's had had regular numbers and a white face?

Her hand trembled as she slid the hand bones into a plastic bag and sealed it so nothing would be lost during movement. She wasn't sure if she was more afraid this wasn't really Sam or that it was, despite her mind's constant barrage of delusions trying to convince her otherwise.

Had she totally lost it? Finally, after two years of toying

with the idea, had her mind snapped beneath the weight of her grief and despair?

It had to be Sam. There was no doubt. He was the only adult male reported missing on Snakehead.

She licked her lips, but her mouth was too dry for it to do any good. A raven screeched, its call echoing, thundering between the narrow gap in the rock. She slid one finger beneath the silver watchband, freed it from the twig that had snagged it.

Then she turned the watch over. The two bones it encircled ground together with an unnatural clunk that made her jump. They twisted in ways absolutely not human.

The back of the watch was coated with bile green algae. She rubbed it with her fingernail. Indentations of an inscription slowly emerged.

LR. She kept rubbing, hoping to reveal more. But that was it. Just the two letters.

Sarah rocked back onto her haunches, the river bubbling past her as if chuckling at a private joke. She wasn't certain if she should laugh or cry at her discovery.

Good news. She wasn't insane.

Bad news. Sam was still out there somewhere. Which meant Josh was as well.

And who the hell was LR and why hadn't anyone reported him missing?

CHAPTER SIXTEEN

He stopped at the edge of the clearing just as he always did when coming down the mountain. Usually he only risked coming here in the dark. It was strange, coming here in daylight. The place where Sam Durandt had died.

There had been good times here. Once upon a time . . . the sound of a little boy's laughter chased the sunbeams, rustled fresh green leaves before vanishing into his memory. It hurt to remember. Every trip back here, back to her, made him feel as if he was being torn apart, yearning to be with her, yet needing to protect them all by staying away.

Terrified he would fail. If he did, the price would be far greater than his death alone.

"Daddy, don't go. I don't want you to go," Josh told him last night, blinking hard to fight back tears. In two years the kid had had a lot of practice but also discovered how fruitless tears were. That look on his face, Josh trying so hard to be so very brave, was about enough to rip Sam's heart to pieces.

He'd squatted down to place himself level with his five-year-old son. Josh had hit a growth spurt over the spring and was now all lanky elbows and knees as Sam pulled him into a bear hug. He inhaled the fragrance of Johnson's shampoo. No more tears. Josh didn't really need the baby shampoo, not now that he took showers and washed his own hair, but it reminded Sam of Sarah, of the good days when Josh was little, when they were together.

Sam sniffed, struggling to keep his own composure. No more tears. Josh wriggled within his grasp. "Daddy, you're squeezing me."

"Oh, am I?" Sam asked as he stood up, pulling Josh with him so the boy's feet dangled above the ground. "How's this then?" He raised Josh up, planted raspberry kisses on the bare skin above his pajama bottoms, was rewarded with an instant armful of giggling little boy. He bounced Josh onto his bed, allowed Josh to flip him over and pin him down for a full count.

"I win!" Josh cried out. He released his father. Sam sat beside him on the bed.

"You sure do, champ," Sam said as he nestled Josh into the pillows and drew the blankets up over him. He planted a kiss on Josh's forehead. "Now, remember everything we talked about. And you be good for Mrs. Beaucouers."

Josh looked up at him with a solemn expression, one far too old for a little boy to ever wear. He frowned, bit his lower lip, and nodded. "When you come home with Mommy will you sing happy songs again? Ones that make me laugh like the song about Oscar the purple toad with the wart on his tongue?"

"Better yet, we'll get Mommy to sing. She has a voice like an angel."

Josh's eyes crinkled shut as he strained to remember. "Sometimes I think I can hear her, when it's dark and quiet." He opened his eyes wide once more. "But then I wake up and it was only a dream."

Sam rumpled his son's still-wet hair. "I know what you mean, champ. That happens to me too. I think it happens to everyone when someone you love and really care about is far away. It keeps you close to them. I'll bet Mommy hears you when she dreams too."

"But I was just a baby back then. I didn't know any real songs."

"Doesn't matter."

"Do you think she still remembers me? Will she know who I am?" Josh's frown creased his forehead into a deep furrow.

"Of course she will."

"Maybe this will help." Josh slid a wallet-sized school photo from beneath his pillow. Sam took it solemnly, hoping Josh didn't notice the tears he couldn't blink away. Josh had cropped the picture into a heart and glued it onto a red-felt heart with a large pin sewn onto the back. "So you can show her how big I've gotten."

"And how handsome."

"Aw, Dad. Will you give it to her?"

"Of course." Sam pulled him tight once more, using the distraction to swipe his eyes dry on the back of his shirtsleeve, then kissed him again. "That one was from Mommy."

Josh blew his breath out in the saddest sigh a five-year-old ever could produce. "You're going to bring her back, right? You promise?"

Sam locked eyes with his son, holding Josh's keepsake over his chest in the flat of his palm. "Yes, sir. When I come back, I'll have Mommy with me. I promise."

If I come back.

Sam had turned the lights off and shut the door behind him. He shouldered his guitar case—everything else was already in the truck—and walked down the creaky stairs to the first floor of the old farmhouse. Mrs. Beaucouers, their landlady and surrogate grandmother these past two years, waited. A young sixty-seven, she was still tough enough to put the fear of God into anyone who challenged her.

Most important, she was devoted to Josh. Would do anything to keep him safe.

Now she stood straight, her forehead creased with worry. "I don't like this, Samuel. There must be another way."

"I'm sorry, Mrs. B, there's not." He stepped toward the door, but she blocked his way. He pulled up short and took her hands in his. "I've left all the important papers, everything you need in case—" He faltered, tried again. "It's all in the lockbox; you have the key."

She squeezed his hands, her work-worn grip almost as strong as his. "But Josh—"

"You'll take good care of him." She nodded. He leaned forward, kissed both of her cheeks. "Thank you, Mrs. B. You are an angel."

She flushed and pulled her hands away, busying them by wringing the corners of her apron. She was the only woman Sam had ever seen outside of the movies actually wear an apron, but it was part of her uniform. Mrs. B simply would not be Mrs. B without her apron, or her Sunday churchgoing black hat with the discreet widow's veil, or her bright yellow mac and Wellingtons that came out during rainstorms and nor'easters. She was the last of a dying breed of gentlewoman.

If Korsakov ever found her or Josh, he'd kill them both without batting an eye.

"All right then," she said in her crisp, no-nonsense way. "Sooner you get going, sooner you'll be back to your son."

Sam swallowed hard and nodded. He opened the door, but couldn't resist one last look over his shoulder, up the stairwell. "You'll—"

"He'll be fine, Samuel. I promise."

Now it was Sam's turn to sigh. He tried a smile, but it felt tight against his face muscles. He blinked hard, the scene blurring before him. Finally he relinquished his grip on the doorknob and stepped out into the darkness.

It's the only way. He climbed into the rusted Ford Ranger, laid the guitar case behind his seat, and started the engine. It turned over with its usual throaty growl. The Ranger didn't look like much, but since Sam and Josh's life depended on it, Sam kept it in prime running condition. He laid his arm across the bench seat, turned to watch out the rear window as he backed down the familiar curves of the gravel drive.

He pulled out onto the road and paused. There was no other traffic and the only lights were the golden glow of the farmhouse he'd just left. A beacon in the night. He hoped he'd be returning soon.

Keep them safe, Lord, he'd prayed. It still felt awkward, this prayer thing. He'd first started after Josh was born— more one-sided conversations with Whoever Was Up There than actual prayers. With everything that had happened these past two years, he'd begun to do more than simply plead his case or try to bargain with his Higher Power.

It was a miracle any of them were still alive. Now, with Korsakov on the loose, it would take more than a miracle to keep them that way. It would take divine intervention.

That was something Sam would have scoffed at eight years ago when he was still Stan Diamontes, beach bum/ surfer/songwriter and—when the bills needed to be paid— accountant to a Russian indy-film producer/mobster. But a man could change in eight years, could learn to love, to care more for someone else than he did himself, could even find his faith.

He'd driven through the night, arrived at the Colonel's cabin just as dawn unfurled tentative golden tendrils through the starry sky. As soon as he entered the forest, the sunlight vanished again, leaving behind only the hope it shared. One last day. One last chance.

In the dark and silence as he hiked down the mountain he couldn't help but think of the years he'd wasted before he learned the meaning of having real dreams.

Real dreams. Not the fantasies that drove him past the time when he was old enough to know better. Catching the big wave, breaking into the music biz, making a big score. He'd wasted all that time on ideas as wispy as cotton candy, things that were sweet to think and talk about, but nothing to live on. To live for. Or to die for.

Nothing like Sarah and Josh.

A parade of images flooded his mind. Sarah's face the first time they made love, eyes wide, feverish as their bodies collapsed on each other. Sarah looking like an angel on their wedding day, calm, radiant while Sam was certain that he'd lose it, the way his stomach was churning worse than the surf at Point Arguello. Until she took his hand. After that, everything had been fine.

Sarah, her face scarlet with pain, cheeks puffed out as she strained to push-push-push-push. Him holding her hand, standing there as Doc Hedeger and the nurse yelled at her, *Push!* He had felt like the world's biggest dipshit. She was in pain and he was helpless to do anything about it and it was all his fault . . .

Then her face relaxed. A gurgling cry filled the room. He looked down to see this pink mass of arms and legs and slime-covered hair with big blue eyes staring right at him. Sarah's face filled with joy as she laughed so hard she cried. It was the only time he'd ever seen her cry.

Sam cried too, couldn't cut the cord when Doc Hedeger asked him, his hands were shaking so badly.

Sarah pulled their baby to her breast and reached for Sam, guiding his palm to help her cradle their baby. This wonderful, mysterious thing they'd created. Together. As he wrapped his arms around both of them Sam had heard a roaring in his brain, stronger than a wave swamping you, the surf crashing over you, pulling you under, not knowing which way is up and you think . . . *I may never see the sun again, I may never make it to the surface.*

I may die.

The roar Sam felt as he held his family was more powerful than that. It filled his brain, made him hunch his shoulders like a Neanderthal. A primitive protective reflex. He would stand between what was his and the rest of the world. Always. Forever.

He remembered inhaling deeply, smelling Sarah's sweat tinged with pain and fear and joy, smelling blood and innocence. This was his family and he would never, never let anything happen to them.

At least that was what Sam had vowed five years ago. Now he stood in the same spot where it had all begun. Where it had all ended.

His hand brushed against the scar on his side as he reached to touch the gun holstered at the small of his back. He was a cowardly, selfish son of a bitch. He knew that now, had known it for the last two years, only wished it hadn't taken losing the best part of himself to discover. It was past time to pay the devil he'd sold his soul to eight years ago.

Except Sarah and Josh weren't part of the bargain.

He'd like to think he'd changed from the fool he'd been

eight years ago, but as he crossed the clearing, his sigh the only sound, he knew he was no hero.

No hero. Just a fool willing to die for the woman he loved.

More than that. A fool willing to kill.

CHAPTER SEVENTEEN

"Sarah!" Hal's voice echoed between the narrow walls of the chasm. "You all right down there?"

Sarah shielded her eyes from the sun and raised her head. During her wait, she'd been able to uncover the rest of the body's upper torso and had wrapped the head in a garbage bag so it wouldn't separate from the body. It had been slow, meticulous work, but now that she knew it wasn't Sam, somehow the time had sped by.

Hal leaned over the cliff's edge, a rope coiled in his hand.

"I'm fine," Sarah called back. "Come on down."

He vanished. The rope sailed out, uncoiling above her, then fell in an arc to slap against the rock face about four feet away from Sarah. Hal dropped over the side and quickly rappelled down to join her. He wore his wet suit beneath his climbing harness. Always a stickler for the rules, a climbing helmet was strapped to his head. He swayed above her, then finally picked a spot on a boulder on the opposite side of the skeleton to land on.

It'd been a while since they'd worked together like

this. Two years ago . . . When they'd lost Lily, Hal's wife. The memory hit her and she remembered the date. Two years tomorrow. *Shit.* How could she have been so stupid, calling him here for a body recovery?

Hal said nothing, intent on organizing his gear and assessing the situation.

Somehow, Sarah always thought of Lily's death as happening a long time—a year at least—before Sam and Josh's. In her mind, those two months she'd had with Sam and Josh were an eternity she clung to, reliving every second. But in reality, it was only a short span of seventy days that separated the two events.

Funny how she'd never thought of that before. Hal's pack lurched to one side and she steadied him with a hand braced against his back.

"I'm sorry," she said in a voice that barely carried over the sound of the rapids. "I should have called someone else."

He kept his head turned away from her, his shoulders tight, braced against the world. Or against memory. "Who would you have called? There is no one else."

Sarah wished there was some way she could alleviate the resignation and fatigue she heard in his voice. She'd talk to the Colonel; he was president of the village council. Surely they could find funds to hire more help for Hal. Maybe send the Colonel's wife after another of those government grants.

Hal spread a body bag flat across the rock and anchored it beneath his foot. The current lapped at it, trying to yank it away. "You sure you're okay?" he asked in a soft voice, finally making eye contact, assessing her. "I can do this alone."

"It's not Sam."

He glanced up in surprise. "Are you sure?"

"The watch. It's not Sam's."

He pursed his lips in a silent whistle. "Looks like we've got a mystery on our hands then. Any ideas who it might be?"

"Some guy with the initials *LR,* I'm guessing from the inscription on the watch."

He handed her a pair of vinyl gloves and slid a pair on himself. Then he knelt down and leaned forward, grasping the corpse by the shoulders. He gently tugged. The torso raised out of the water a few inches, then stopped.

"I think his foot is wedged beneath one of the rocks," Sarah said. "I was afraid to get too aggressive."

"He feels pretty loose." Hal felt the man's chest without opening the shirt or jacket. "Bag of bones." He released his grip and sat back. "We got everything documented?"

"Everything above the surface. How do you want to work this?"

Despite the cold water, Sarah kept her hands immersed, hoping to keep the slime and decomposed fat covering them minimized. Although regulations required her to wear them, at this point the vinyl gloves would only serve to allow the goo already coating her hands to soak into her skin. It would be days before she'd be able to totally erase the smell of acrid-too-sweet rotting organic material.

Hal's face remained neutral. He tilted his head, examined the angle of the fallen boulders, the depth of the water, the strength of the current. "I'll go under, try to free him. Then we'll keep him as close to one piece as we can, slide him into the bag." He double-checked his safety line and rolled off the rock into the current.

Sarah lay spread-eagle over her boulder, wedging one foot in a crevice, anchoring him. Although the water appeared shallow, no higher than waist deep, the currents were treacherous. Snakebelly's bottom was filled with centuries of decomposing debris, jagged fallen rocks, and snarled tree limbs covered with slick algae and mud. The real danger would be if Hal became trapped down there, wedged in and unable to surface.

He stood for a moment, testing his footing, one hand braced against the rock wall. "It drops off just here," he said, nodding to a spot about two feet before him.

He took one step forward, then another. The water pulled him under, out of sight. Sarah held her breath in tandem, scanning the dark waters anxiously. Visibility was less than a foot. The only sign of Hal was the swirl of debris bobbing up to the surface as he worked it free.

Her chest grew tight, burning with the lack of oxygen. *Twenty seconds,* she told herself, starting an internal countdown. *If he's not back up in twenty seconds, nineteen, eighteen—*

The water parted with a loud splash. Hal hauled himself to his rock and leaned against it, waves crashing against his back, as he gasped for breath. Water sluiced off his helmet and down the sides of his face. "Think I got it. You take the top; I'll take the bottom. We'll float him up, then roll him onto the bag."

"It's a plan." Sarah had to get her other foot wet, balancing on a submerged tree limb to get in position. Icy water filled her boot. Her foot screamed with pins and needles and her balance was precarious at best as she fought the current. Hal drew in several deep breaths, preparing to submerge again when a voice called down from above.

"Hey, Chief!" Gerald Merton's bellow bounced from the cliff walls.

"What?" Hal shouted back.

Gerald held a radio over the edge, waving with it. "There's a lady calling. Says she has to talk to you right away."

"Sonofa—," Hal sputtered, his face tightening. "I'm a little busy here, Gerald."

"I told her. She says it's important."

"It will have to wait," Hal shouted, his voice taking on an angry edge Sarah had never heard before. The Hal she knew never lost his cool. Never. The muscle at his jaw knotted.

"Says she's with the FBI."

Alan Easton dreamed the same dream he'd been dreaming for the past year. Ever since he almost lost her. Sarah, radiant in white, walking down the aisle. The entire population of Hopewell crowded around them, cheering and applauding. Just like the wedding scene from *It's a Wonderful Life*.

Only when they piled into the waiting taxi, Sarah's flowers tickling his nose, her dress billowing in white poufs to fill the backseat, it was Stan driving. The same Stan he'd met freshman year. Hair too long, ruby earring in one ear, ratty Nirvana tee, tie-dyed board shorts, bare feet crusted with sand.

"Where you all off to?" Stan asked merrily as he steered them down the mountain road leading out of Hopewell.

"The Caymans," Sarah sang out. "It's our honeymoon."

"Caymans." Stan nodded thoughtfully. "Funny. That's where I took my wife on our honeymoon. Good place to stash money." He laughed. "So you guys tied the knot. Love, honor, death do you part. How long do you think that will be?"

He stared at Alan in the rearview mirror and suddenly it wasn't Stan driving but Korsakov. The Russian said nothing. He didn't need to. Not with those eyes reflecting red like the devil, drilling into Alan, knowing everything.

Alan sputtered, "I can get you your money back. You don't have to kill her."

Sarah screamed. Alan turned to her, moving in the slow motion of dreams, the movement taking forever even though he sat only inches away from her. Her wedding dress was covered in blood. Stan now sat in the front passenger seat. "You never should have gotten her involved, Alan."

"I only wanted what you had. It all seemed so—" Alan choked back tears, Sarah's blood covering his hands. "Nice. Is that too much to ask for? A nice home, family, town where people respect me, think I'm something special. You had it all—"

"I lost it all." A bullet hole appeared in the center of Stan's forehead. "Thanks to you."

Korsakov the taxi driver said nothing as he drove them all off the side of the mountain. His laughter was the last thing Alan heard.

The vibration of his cell phone startled Alan awake. He groaned and pushed the blonde off his numb arm. Somehow they'd ended up crossways over the bed, his pants balled up into a makeshift pillow.

"Leave it be, baby," she crooned, tracing a finger along his lips.

He ignored her and groped for the phone. It wasn't often that he was able to get away from Hopewell, give himself a break from playing the role that after two years felt more real than his real life. Sometimes when he was alone with Sarah it actually felt better than his life back in L.A. Made him think dangerous thoughts, like maybe Stan had it right, coming here, settling down. Like maybe Alan *could* have it all: Sarah, a family, a home, and the money.

Finally, he untangled the cell from the Italian silk and

checked the caller ID. Logan. What the hell did he want? "This isn't a good time, Jack."

"Time is one thing you don't have, my friend. Tick tock."

"What do you want?" Alan couldn't wait until this deal was done and he could sever all ties to the former FBI agent. Permanently. But, even retired, Jack Logan had the connections Alan needed, so he put up with him as a necessary evil.

"My finder's fee for starters. Wright's been dead two weeks now. Have you made your move yet?"

Alan rolled over, placing his back to the blonde. "No. But I will, soon. It's not as easy as it sounds."

"Why not? The judge signed off on Durandt's being declared dead, didn't he? What's holding you back? I thought you said the wife got access to the account payable on his death. And once you marry the bitch, you get the money after she's dead. Easy as one-two-three."

Alan shoved off the bed and headed into the bathroom. The blonde followed. He shut the door in her face. The room service tray from last night sat on the vanity, a half-eaten plate of fruit and two empty champagne flutes. He grabbed a piece of honeydew and sat on the toilet seat. "Why the rush? You know I can't move on the money until things cool down after the wedding anyway. I haven't even asked her yet."

"Better make that an elopement, lover boy," Logan replied. Alan frowned. He could hear the other man's superior grin over the airwaves. "Korsakov's getting out."

Alan choked on the piece of fruit and jumped to his feet. "What the hell. Are you sure?"

"Certain as the day is long. Seems an appellate court finally ruled in his favor, overturned his conviction on a technicality. Without the government's star witness to testify, he's going to walk."

"When?" Alan gulped, forcing the fruit down, ignoring the burn. He had more important things to worry about than choking to death in some second-rate Albany hotel room.

"Hearing is this morning. Unless the U.S. attorney can pull a rabbit out of his hat, he'll be out by afternoon."

Alan paced the small space, his hand tightening on the phone he clutched to his ear. "Still, no reason to panic. As far as he knows, Stan died on that mountain two years ago."

"Hell, as far as *we* know, that is what happened. Except for the minor fact that Leo Richland vanished as well."

Alan had a sneaking suspicion Logan knew more about Richland's disappearance than he had ever let on. The FBI agent sure had gotten to Hopewell in a hell of a hurry once they found Stan and started the Wright scam. Who's to say Logan hadn't actually been in the area before his official "arrival" with that female feeb, maybe even long enough to ensure their partner-in-crime's silence?

But then what the hell had Logan done with Stan and the kid? He had as much to lose as Alan did if they showed up now. With Richland gone missing, he had to assume they were still alive. Somewhere. Which was why he'd had Logan outfit Sarah's house, computer, and cell phone with the most sophisticated surveillance equipment available. She couldn't sneeze without Alan knowing about it.

Good thing, because she was his ticket to getting his hands on the 42 million Stan had embezzled from Korsakov. Sarah didn't even know that with Stan declared dead, she was now 42 million richer. Once he had her wooed and wedded, the money was as good as Alan's. In fact, the only drawback to their plan was they'd have to kill her to prevent her from betraying them to the Russian.

Unless she was willing to work with him. A true partner. Someone he could trust. No more acting. Remnants of the dream, the way she'd smiled at him as she walked down the aisle, slid through his mind.

"Why would Korsakov come here?" Alan asked, running all the angles in his mind. "He doesn't know about the money." Stan had covered his tracks well—it had only been by accident that Alan discovered the theft after Korsakov went to prison. He never would have guessed Stan had the balls to rip off the Russian like that.

"Maybe to visit an old friend, his former lawyer. Who coincidentally has taken up with the widow of the man who betrayed him, sent him to prison, stole seven years of his life. Or maybe to get revenge on Stan by killing his woman? Who knows, but either way we have to move fast."

"Are you sure he's coming here?"

"He's got a first-class ticket on the red-eye to JFK tonight. I don't think he's headed to visit the family in Brighton Beach."

"Damn. How did he find out where I am? I haven't spoken with him in years." Had Logan squealed? It would be just like the FBI agent to play both ends against the middle, sell out Alan in exchange for more money or other favors from Korsakov.

"Man's connected. Even in prison, no way he could have missed hearing about Stan's death. Not with all that press Wright got. And he has a long memory—you know these Russians. They could teach Machiavelli a thing or two about revenge served cold."

"Yeah, yeah. What are we going to do?"

"You get the wife, make up some kind of excuse. Then I'll pick her up, get her clear of Korsakov."

Alan felt his bullshit meter rev into overdrive. After Alan had hired him to find Stan four years ago, Logan had backtracked, followed the money trail just as he had. Logan was the only other person who knew Sarah was the key to getting the money. Was this a trick so Logan could get to Sarah, use her himself?

He glanced at his reflection in the mirror. Noted the wrinkles and worry lines creasing his forehead, the slump to his shoulders. Immediately he braced himself, pulled in his gut, rolled his shoulders back. He flashed himself a high roller's grin. Logan had brains, but not enough to outsmart Alan.

"I'll meet you in Hopewell, usual place." The abandoned caretaker's shack below the dam was secluded and rarely used—a perfect spot for clandestine meetings. Or murders. Which is what it may come to if Logan tried anything.

"I'll call you when I get close. Bring the wife."

Alan snapped the phone shut without responding. Like hell he would. He wasn't letting Sarah out of his sight until they were safely wed and on a plane to the Caymans.

Damn the timing, though. It was the first day in weeks he'd taken off to have fun. Being so close to Sarah, playing the fool in love when they hadn't even kissed yet, was driving him crazy. Like two days ago when he'd surprised her by taking over a picnic lunch.

He remembered walking up the path, seeing her kneeling in the front garden, that tight ass of hers rocking back and forth as she pulled weeds. He'd wanted nothing more than to lay her down onto the grass and make love to her until she forgot all about Stan.

Then he saw the reason why her body rocked back

and forth was she was crying. Over Stan and the kid. Again.

By the time she turned to him, she'd wiped her tears away. Sarah never showed her tears—at least not to him. She never revealed her real feelings either. He had to read about them in that damn journal of hers. Something else she shared only with Stan, despite the fact that the man was dead. Alan was so damn tired of competing with a corpse.

He closed his eyes, remembering Sarah in the wedding dress of his dreams, and then envisioned carrying her over the threshold and into the bedroom of her house. She never stopped smiling at him as he slid off her clothes, her flesh pressed against his eagerly, until she finally looked up and begged for more, tears of joy in her eyes.

He glanced down, admiring the erection his fantasies wrought. No sense wasting such a good hard piece of wood. Not with a woman bought and paid for outside the door. A woman whose tears he could command.

He glanced at the Rolex on his wrist. Just enough time to finish his fun here, get cleaned up, grab the engagement ring he'd been waiting for the right time to present, and sweet-talk his bride-to-be into eloping to an exotic Caribbean island.

He'd beat both Korsakov and Logan at their own game. If he set it up right, they'd kill each other by the time he returned with the money. And he could keep Sarah for himself. Have it all.

CHAPTER EIGHTEEN

Sam stared through his binoculars down at the house that once had been his. He leaned deeper into the shadows of the pin oak, the tree's bark rough against his skin. Last night he'd debated driving the whole way into town, picking up Sarah, and running as far and fast as they could, but there was no way he could do that, not without being seen.

Even a sleepy town like Hopewell would notice a dead man walking.

He slid his hand across his shaved scalp, slicking away sweat born more of nerves than heat or humidity. Only one chance to get this right—and Lord knew, his track record wasn't in his favor.

No one was home. He returned the binoculars to his pack and brought out his bug detector. He knew that Alan had every room covered except for the attic and the bathrooms. Sam hoped he hadn't decided to invest in more of the motion-sensitive cameras.

Anger balled itself into a fist, making him suck in his breath at the thought of Alan watching Sarah. Of Alan being in her house—their house. The fist of anger lodged

in his throat, making it hard to breathe as he imaginged
Alan trying to seduce Sarah.

At first Sam thought Alan was keeping tabs on Sarah
for the Russian, waiting to see if Sam was still alive or if
she knew anything about the money. It was the only time
he hadn't regretted lying to her, keeping her in the dark.
But then, as weeks turned into months, Sam realized Alan
had bigger ambitions in mind: using Sarah to get the
money for himself.

He had to admit, it was a good, although time-
consuming, plan. Wait until Sam was declared dead, marry
Sarah, take her to the bank in the Caymans where she was
the death beneficiary on Sam's accounts—accounts she
had no idea existed—and then . . . No. Alan was never going to make it to the "and then." Sam was getting Sarah out
of here today.

Besides, if there was one thing he was certain of, it was
Sarah. She gave her trust easily, but not her heart. Alan
would never have been able to convince her to marry him.
Never.

He hoisted his pack onto his shoulders and crept through
the foliage until he was directly behind his house. It was
always so painful, coming home and being unable to speak
with Sarah, leaving her behind. But it was too dangerous.
He'd had to think of Josh.

Now, thanks to Korsakov's release, he no longer had
the luxury of playing it safe.

An expanse of open lawn spread out between the forest and the bathroom window that was his target.

He stood still, listening. No cars approaching. He
sprinted through the grass until he reached the cluster of
lilac bushes outside their bedroom window. Dead blooms
clung to the branches. He rubbed one between his fingers,
inhaling deeply. Sarah always slept with the window

open, loved smelling the lilacs in the spring and the peonies and roses in the summer.

Sam duckwalked along the foundation of the house until he reached the bathroom window. He activated the small palm-sized surveillance detector. The screen glowed green. Good to go.

He pried the screen loose and raised the window. The pack went in first; then Sam followed, swinging his leg over the windowsill. He used his foot to drop the toilet lid down, wincing at the sudden clang of porcelain in the empty house. Nothing happened. No one came. The house was silent. He eased himself the rest of the way inside.

Because of Alan's surveillance cameras Sam was confined to the bathroom. Even in this cramped and crowded room, he still felt Sarah's presence. The cobalt blue tiles they had chosen and laid themselves, the scent of her shampoo—honey and almonds—the way her robe hung from the door, inviting him like an old friend.

He couldn't resist, nuzzling his face deep into the folds of the soft material, pretending it was Sarah who caressed him. *Soon, soon,* he promised himself.

The old railroad clock in the front hall chimed the hour. Three o'clock. Josh would be coming off the bus from day camp, and for the first time in ages Sam wouldn't be there to meet him.

He blew out his breath in frustration. It would be worth it when Josh was reunited with Sarah. He leaned forward, pouring himself a glass of water from the small pedestal sink. His toothbrush still nestled beside hers in the porcelain cup below the mirror. His. Not Alan's.

The gun resting at the small of his back nudged him, a not-so-subtle reminder that the only reason Alan was in Sarah's life was because of Sam's screwups. Mistakes she had paid dearly for.

The crunch of gravel alerted him to a car's arrival. He stood near the window, listening. The carport was on the other side of the house. He strained to hear footsteps on the porch that ended at the kitchen door Sarah always used. Nothing.

"Sarah!" a man's voice bellowed from the front room.

Sam jumped, gagging on the water. He carefully returned his glass to the sink, his hand trembling with fury as he recognized Alan's voice.

He drew his gun, hating the weight of it in his hand, but no longer feeling clumsy with the semiautomatic. It had been a learning process, one that had cost him some blood before he figured out how to work the slide without catching the skin between his thumb and finger, but he'd eventually become a half-decent shot. Nowhere near as good as Sarah or the Colonel, but he sure as hell could shoot the stuffing out of a hay bale from twenty yards.

Edging the door open a crack, he held the gun ready, the acrid smell of gun cleaner replacing Sarah's scent in his nostrils. Alan called Sarah's name again, then pushed open the bedroom door. His footsteps echoed from the oak floorboards. Then Sam saw the man himself.

His teeth ground together and he wondered how Alan could not hear it from where he stood six feet away. Alan looked into Sarah's dresser mirror, combed one hand through his hair, then sat down on the bed. Sam watched, his finger stroking the gun's trigger guard. Alan stretched a hand beneath Sarah's pillow, pulled out a small, velvet-covered journal.

Sarah's innermost thoughts—thoughts Sam never dared trespass upon—and Alan leafed through them like they meant nothing. A thunk sounded as Alan hurled the book across the room, hitting the side of the dresser. It landed on the floor mere inches beyond the bathroom door. "You're meant to be thinking about me. Not Sam. I'm the man right here in front of you! What have you gone and done now?"

To Sam's surprise, Alan slumped forward, risking wrinkling his Italian tailored suit, hands hanging between his knees. Almost as if he cared about Sarah. No. The only person Alan gave a damn about was Alan. He sighed, shook his head, then leaned back and reached for the telephone on the nightstand. "Colonel Godwin? . . . Hi, it's Alan. . . . Yeah, I know I wasn't supposed to get home from my meeting until tomorrow, but I just missed Sarah so much that—"

Sam cringed at the other man's tone of sincerity. Hell, he'd believe him—if he didn't know the real Alan. Sometimes it was hard to remember that once upon a time he and Alan had been best friends, college roommates in fact. Before Alan sent an assassin to kill Sam and his son.

It had to have been Alan. After the damn money. Because the Russian never would have stopped. Not until everything and everyone Sam loved was destroyed.

"She's where? . . . Up on the mountain and she found a body? . . . Who is it?" Alan sat up, sliding off the bed and back onto his feet. "No, don't tell her I called. I want to surprise her. . . . Yeah, maybe tonight's the night. Thanks, sir, I appreciate that."

He hung up and moved toward the bathroom. Sam tensed, held his breath. He knew he should stop looking through the cracked door, turn away to avoid detection. But the desire to confront the man who had destroyed his life, to have an opportunity to maybe even kill him, was too strong.

Alan stepped closer. Sam gripped the doorknob, ready

to explode into action. If Alan took one more step, if he reached for the door, if he looked up and saw Sam's eye in the tiny slit watching him . . .

Scenarios flew through Sam's mind faster than his pulse pounded. A bead of sweat slid from his forehead into his eye, stinging. He blinked hard, his gaze never leaving the tiny sliver that was his view into the bedroom. Just one more step.

Alan saved himself by stopping in front of the mirror, addressing his favorite audience, his own reflection. "Son of a bitch. First I have Korsakov breathing down my neck; now the cops will be crawling all over the place if that's Leo Richland they found."

He banged the bedroom door open and stalked from the room before Sam could hear any more.

Leo Richland was dead? How? When? Sam sat on the toilet and stared at his gun. Probably Alan had killed him. He raised the gun, sighted it on the roses that covered the shower curtain. Could still kill Alan now, one less person to worry about. He'd be picked up on the cameras, but who really cared if it kept Sarah and Josh safe?

He jerked his hand as if a bullet really were zooming through the gun barrel, causing it to recoil. No, he couldn't kill Alan, not until he had Sarah safe. It would raise too many questions, alert Korsakov.

But he had to get a message to her—and he couldn't risk Alan blundering into him while he was stuck here in the bathroom. He glanced around, trying to think of a way to leave a message Alan wouldn't see. Then his gaze settled on the mirror. When he was a kid, he used to leave nasty messages for his sisters to find when they came out of the shower.

Stupid kid's trick, but maybe it was just stupid enough

to work. Sarah always liked to take a shower after a hike, definitely before bed.

He stood and leaned over the sink, exhaling his breath onto the mirror. It wasn't the way he'd planned to reach out to her, but then again nothing about the last two years had gone as planned.

CHAPTER NINETEEN

Sarah helped Hal wrestle the awkward package of decomposed remains through the scrub and back to the road. Gerald Merton lagged behind, wheezing as he carried the rest of their equipment, yelping every time a branch snapped back in his face.

"If you'd hurry it up, you'd catch them," Hal yelled over his shoulder, his tone harsh.

Sarah jerked to a stop, the foot of the vinyl body bag almost slipping from her hands. It wasn't like Hal to lash out like that.

Hal said nothing, merely directed his glare from Gerald to her. His face was red, sweat rolling off his nose and brow. He made a noise of disgust when Gerald stumbled on a root, then started up the trail again, pulling her along as she tried not to disturb their delicate cargo.

Sarah wasn't exactly enjoying the grisly task, even though she was certain the body didn't belong to Sam, but Hal was more upset than she'd ever seen him before. Not just upset. Angry. As if the dead man had chosen an especially inconvenient time to surface. With the anniversary of Lily's death tomorrow, she guessed he had.

They transferred the bag into the back of Gerald's Excursion. He fussed a bit about the smell and water. Hal cut the other man's whining short by stomping away to peel off his wet suit and change back into jeans and uniform shirt.

"Who put a rattler in his cornflakes?" Gerald asked as he and Sarah packed rolled-up blankets around the corpse to keep it from sliding around the rear of the Excursion. "Never seen him so antsy. Not even when . . ." He trailed off, his gaze darting from the body bag to her.

"When we pulled Lily out of Snakebelly," she finished for him, her voice low and solemn. Lily's body had been so battered and bruised, she'd rolled around inside the body bag like a rag doll. They'd lowered one of the search and rescue's wire mesh stretchers down and strapped Lily into it for fear of doing more damage as they hoisted her up. But still, Hal had insisted on zipping open the bag, unwrapping the plastic shroud, and looking for himself.

Shuddering as she remembered the unearthly cry of despair that was the only sound Hal had uttered, Sarah glanced over her shoulder. Hal was behind his GMC Jimmy, one arm rising up in the air as he tugged his T-shirt over his head. She was glad it was her rope they had left behind in case they needed to search Snakebelly further— and she'd do her best to make certain it wasn't Hal who returned to do the searching.

No wonder he was acting so strangely. He might have removed his wedding band, but it was clear he hadn't shaken off the guilt that he'd been busy rescuing some idiot teenagers skinny-dipping in the reservoir, instead of home with Lily, on the night she killed herself.

"Lily. Yeah, right," Gerald muttered, slamming the

door on the anonymous dead man and their conversation. "Tell him I'll get everything ready and meet him down the mountain."

He drove off, giving the large SUV too much gas and fishtailing over the rutted logging road. Sarah watched the cloud of dust in his wake until she heard the chime of Hal opening the Jimmy's door.

"You coming?" he called as the engine kicked over with a low snarl. She grabbed her pack and jumped into the passenger seat. They headed down the narrow, twisting dirt road. "Want me to drop you home?"

"No, the Rockslide will be fine."

"Suit yourself."

They jostled over the road in silence for several minutes. Hal's driving wasn't his usual cautious pace. Instead it was sloppy, careless, overcompensating for curves, almost dropping one wheel off the edge of the road several times. Sarah gripped the side of her seat and pumped an imaginary brake pedal with her foot.

"If you'd taken my advice, you could have been in Montreal with Alan already instead of mucking about with decomposed remains."

She straightened at his tone. He really was upset. With her? "I needed—"

"No." The syllable sliced through the air between them. "No. You need to move on with your life. That's what Sam would have wanted. You know that, Sarah. Don't make the same mistakes I've made."

She stared at him. This was so not like Hal. Telling anyone what to do, how to live their life? "I'm sorry I called you. I should have remembered that tomorrow is the anniversary—"

She choked on her words as he turned to stare at her, ignoring the hairpin curve ahead of them. They almost spun off the road before he corrected their trajectory. Sarah bounced forward, into the dash, bracing both hands against it.

"This has nothing to do with Lily." He took a deep breath. "Okay. Maybe it does. That's why I need you to leave. Tonight. You and Alan take off, get out of here for a long weekend."

"Why tonight?" she asked.

"I'm asking the Colonel for a special town council meeting tomorrow. It's past time they knew how I really feel about how things have been running around here lately." He hunched forward over the steering wheel as if ready to wrestle it from the dash.

"Hal, wait for another day. Not tomorrow."

He shook his head, his gaze riveted on the road ahead. "No. It has to be done. But I don't want you around to get caught in the middle. It might get ugly. Real ugly." His Adam's apple bobbed as he swallowed hard, twice. "Two years ago, after Lily . . . At first I was angry. When Sam came and told me the insurance wouldn't pay up, that I was going to lose the house after all—"

"It wasn't his fault," Sarah protested. "No company will pay on a . . . when someone takes their own life. He tried to help you."

"I don't need charity!"

His words barraged her. This wasn't Hal, the man who never raised his voice, who always shunned the spotlight, simply doing his job without fanfare or complaint. Sarah stared at him in concern. She'd been so buried by her own grief it blinded her to the changes going on in her friend. What else had she missed?

"Never did need charity. Not now, not then. What I need," he drew in a ragged breath and his voice lowered, "is for people to listen to me and let me do what it takes to make this town safe again."

"Again?" He meant after Damian Wright. "Hal, you can't blame yourself—"

"Shut up, Sarah. You don't know what the hell you're talking about."

She blinked at him, stunned. "I don't know? How can you say that?"

"You weren't here. You weren't the one responsible, the one who should have stopped it all."

"Hal—" She measured her words, understanding his guilt and pain. Of course she understood it. She shared it. If she'd only been here when Damian Wright . . . "You're not to blame. But you're right. Maybe this town doesn't appreciate you the way it should. Maybe you should quit." She hated to even suggest it. What would she do without Hal around to lean on? What would the town do?

But it was past time that he put himself first for a change.

"Quit?" He snorted a short-lived laugh. "Maybe that would be best. But I can't do it while I'm worrying about you."

She drew back in her seat, wrapping one hand around the armrest as they bounced onto the paved road leading into town. He braked hard, pulling up with a jerk in front of the Rockslide.

"Hal." She stopped, unsure of what to say to help him. "Remember your promise. About taking some time off." She opened her door and slid free from the passenger seat.

He twisted toward her, leaning over the console to make eye contact through the open passenger door. "Keep your promise and I'll keep mine. You and Alan take off for the weekend. Don't come back until Monday. Deal?"

Hal never asked for anything. The least she could do was give him this. "Deal."

He flashed her a smile that was both hopeful and sad before driving away.

The staccato clacking of a man's boots against linoleum jolted Caitlyn awake. She rubbed her eyes, took a breath, trying to reorient herself. Her heart refused to listen to reason; instead it sped up in excitement at the sound, just as it had every day of her life until she was nine.

That sound meant only one thing: her father was home. Every day, she'd listen for the sound of his footsteps as he'd walk up the path, cross through the kitchen, and enter the living room where she'd be waiting. She'd abandon everything to race across the floor and leap into the air, certain he would catch her no matter how high she flew.

Those few moments in his arms were always the best part of any day. She'd never again feel so safe, so warm, so loved.

Idiot, she cursed her errant memories. *Just meant the chief wore cowboy boots. Like so many of these local yokels.*

She straightened in her seat behind the single desk in the spartan office. After phoning when she stopped for gas outside Albany and being told it would be a few hours before the Hopewell Chief of Police could grant her an audience, she had finished her drive through the twisting mountain roads at a leisurely pace but had still managed to arrive before Chief Waverly.

She'd called ahead to give him fair warning that the FBI was coming, to let him get his house in order, maybe even pull the Durandt case files so she wouldn't be wasting her time. Instead she'd been greeted by a yakky old shrew of a postmistress who refused to allow her entry to the chief's office.

Like that would stop her. She hadn't quite had to go to the extreme of pulling her weapon, but after listening to the lady's yammering, she was more than tempted. Once she convinced the postmistress, Victoria was her name, that yes, she was indeed a bona fide agent of the federal government, Caitlyn proceeded to make herself at home in the chief's chair while the postmistress kept up her monologue about terrorist activity and Homeland Security money and strange goings-on at the dam and it was about time the government sent someone "real" to investigate it.

Finally, customers at the post office pulled the old biddy away. Caitlyn had taken advantage of the relative quiet to open her laptop and review her files.

And drift to sleep. Now she glanced through the open door that separated the post office from the police department. The afternoon sunlight backlit the man. He had a lean, Gary Cooper build, complete with a cowboy hat he hadn't yet removed, shadowing his face. His stride was that of a man accustomed to carrying the weight of responsibility on his shoulders and the weight of a gun on his hip.

He wore jeans and a khaki shirt with a small patch sewn onto the sleeve. No other insignia. A pair of aviator-style sunglasses dangled from the neck of the white T-shirt visible between the unbuttoned top buttons of his uniform shirt. He came to a halt in front of his desk, his head tilting up, finally exposing his face as he raked her with an eagle-sharp gaze. He had high cheekbones, bright blue eyes, a narrow nose that had been broken at least once. A muscle twitched at the corner of his jaw as he stood, staring down at her for a long, silent moment.

"Agent Tierney," he said in a slow drawl, drawing her name out as if he savored it. "Nice to meet you again. You've gained some weight. Looks good on you."

Caitlyn met his gaze, watched as amusement crowded out his annoyance. A smile parted his lips and she gave him one in return. "Chief Waverly. Nice to see you as well. Looks like you've lost weight. Been busy?"

They continued their staring match, neither conceding the contest for several seconds. Usually Caitlyn would have relinquished control of his desk, his environment, back to a local law officer—any little courtesy to convince them to give her full cooperation.

But Waverly struck a chord in her. Unlike the last time they'd met. Back then she'd been fresh off medical leave, her brain fumbling, on overload trying to work the case and fend off Logan's scrutiny, fearful she no longer had what it took to do the job.

When Waverly looked at her just now she saw interest in his eyes, in the way his glance lingered the tiniest bit too long on her lips, her body. Damn if her body didn't respond with an answering spark. She shifted in her seat. No, not a spark, it was more than that.

And it was more than she'd felt in a long time. But she wasn't about to let him know that. Not when she had work to do.

Work that should have her leaping from his chair, spouting off an apology for trespassing in his space, politely thanking him for helping her. Instead, she kept her seat—his seat—and fought him for control in an adolescent staring match.

His chuckle echoed through the tiny space, breaking the silence. He spun on his heel to toss his hat on one of the hooks beside the door, grabbed a metal chair, and slid into it, his long, lean legs stretching out in front of him, ankles crossed. "What brings you back to Hopewell? Does it have anything to do with the corpse I just dragged out of the river?"

"Actually I came about the Durandt case."

His smile slid away as he straightened, one eye twitching at the mention of Sam Durandt.

"I've found some irregularities."

The spark died as his gaze darted to the door. "Guess you'd better come with me, then."

She scrambled from behind the desk, grabbing her bag and hurrying to catch up with him. He marched out the door without holding it for her. *Wow, mention Sam Durandt and look who's got a bee up his butt all of a sudden.* Although, she had to admit, it was a rather cute butt. She caught up with him as he turned onto Main Street. "Where we going?"

"You ate yet? I'm starved."

"Lunch? It's almost four thirty. Yes, I've had lunch."

"Well then, you can talk with Sarah while I eat." He paused before the Rockslide Café and this time he did open the door for her, held it like a proper gentleman. "Seeing as she's the one who found the body this morning."

Caitlyn laid her hand on his arm, stopping him in the doorway. "Sarah Durandt?" she asked in a low voice. "She found a body on the mountain? Today?"

"Yep. From the looks of things, it's been there some time. Two years at least. I'm not sure it will help you much. She's saying it can't be Sam." He nudged past her, calling out to the man behind the counter and asking for a bacon-cheeseburger.

Caitlyn stood there a moment, trying to twist the permutations into a clear picture. When she looked up, all eyes were on her. The man behind the counter, Sarah Durandt's father, she remembered, but couldn't fix on his name, held his spatula aloft as if it were a weapon. Hal Waverly's gaze seemed weary and bemused. He sat beside an older woman, Victoria, the postmistress who'd almost induced her to commit felony assault earlier. Victoria cocked her head and flat out glared at Caitlyn.

Caitlyn stepped inside, the door closing with a bang accompanied by a jingle of bells. Sitting alone at a booth, her face flushed with sun, a full glass of lemonade in front of her, was Sarah Durandt. Sarah met Caitlyn's eyes without flinching although her lips flattened and went pale as recognition hit.

"You all remember Agent Tierney, don't you?" Waverly said by way of introductions. "From the FBI?"

"This isn't the time—," Sarah's father started, leaving his post at the grill despite the smoking slab of bacon behind him.

Sarah held up a hand, silencing him. Caitlyn marveled at the woman's composure. As Sarah's fingers tightened around her glass, Caitlyn caught a hint of what her control cost. Ah, a kindred spirit—keep up appearances to the outside world, even if inside you're ready to shatter into a million pieces.

"Mrs. Durandt," Caitlyn said, taking the two steps she needed to reach Sarah's booth. She ignored the others although she was very aware they listened closely. "I think I owe you an apology."

Sarah looked up, surprise flickering over her face before she replaced it with a fake smile, the kind reserved for strangers stumbling into a private conversation. "An apology?"

"When we met two years ago, I'm afraid I wasn't as sensitive to your needs as I should have been. There were—" Caitlyn broke off, searching for the right words to explain everything that had been battering at her during the time of the Wright investigation. "Extenuating circumstances."

The words sounded flat. Sarah raised an eyebrow, then looked down to concentrate on her fingers wrapped around the sweaty glass of lemonade. "What do you want, Agent Tierney?"

"Just to offer my apology. And a chance to explain. Is there a place we can talk?"

Sarah shot a glance at the others eagerly listening, then stared at Caitlyn for a long, hard moment. For a second, Caitlyn caught a glimpse of the steel she'd seen in Sarah two years ago, the woman who would bend to the horror of her circumstances but who would never, ever break. Sarah's eyes narrowed slightly, she nodded and slid out of the booth.

"Come with me, Agent Tierney."

Sarah left the eager ears at the Rockslide behind and led the FBI agent outside. Two boys zoomed past on skateboards, but otherwise they had the street to themselves. She crossed Main Street to St. Andrew's. The brick church with its peaked roof and squared-off bell tower would be cool and empty at this hour. She tugged on the heavy oak door and held it open for Caitlyn.

The FBI agent appeared very different from the last time Sarah had seen her. Back then, she'd looked gaunt, out of place, with her ill-fitting clothes and pained expression. But now she radiated confidence and strength. Her hair was longer, styled in a shoulder-length bob, her clothes simple but elegant, accentuating her curves without flaunting them.

"I was there," Sarah started, sliding into a pew beneath Josh's favorite stained-glass window. St. George and the Dragon. "When they killed Damian Wright. He wouldn't tell me where he buried them." She looked down at her hands curled in her lap, her nails ragged and torn from her excursion on the mountain. Caitlyn's nails were short but smooth, her fingers slender and tapered like a musician's. She had pale, creamy skin that matched her auburn hair and blue eyes.

To her surprise, Caitlyn reached a hand to cover Sarah's. "I didn't know that. That took a lot of courage. Are you all right?"

No one had asked her that. Not in a long time, not meaning it, not wanting to know the answer. Sarah glanced up. Caitlyn's expression was open, concerned. "You really want to know?"

"I wouldn't have asked if I didn't."

Sarah thought she was telling the truth. She sighed, the whooshing noise quickly devoured by the large, empty space. "I thought I would feel better, knowing he was dead, that he couldn't hurt anyone else. I thought I would be able to move on. Instead, it feels as if everything is moving on without me."

Caitlyn nodded. "Like you're trapped. Like you need to find a path out, some kind of closure."

"Exactly." Color from the stained-glass window played off Caitlyn's pale skin and her blue jacket. Her silk blouse was cream colored with a watercolor splash of pale mauve flowers on it. A distinct contrast to Sarah's dirt-smudged Coolmax tank top. "But no one can give me closure. I have to find it for myself. That's why I went up the mountain. I promised myself I wouldn't stop until I found Sam and Josh."

"Chief Waverly said you found a body."

Sarah shivered. She'd washed her hands about half a dozen times, sanitized them with alcohol wipes, but she still imagined the greasy slick of decomposition coating them. "It wasn't Sam."

"You thought it would be?"

The question surprised her. "Of course. There hasn't been anyone else reported missing on Snakehead. It had to be Sam—I was so certain . . ." Her voice trailed off. "I'm still not sure if I'm relieved or disappointed." She looked up. "Is that why you're here? Because of the body? But how did you know?"

"Did your husband, Sam, did he ever mention anyone by the name of Stan Diamontes? Or Grigor Korsakov?"

Sarah frowned at the unfamiliar names. "No. I've never heard of them before. Why? What's this all about?"

"How about Leo Richland? Does that name ring a bell?"

"No. Please tell me what these people have to do with Sam. Why are you really here?"

Caitlyn's fingers tightened over hers and Sarah pulled her hands away. Caitlyn grimaced, her lips creasing into a frown as she rubbed the base of her thumb with her other hand.

"Sam may not have been alone up there," she finally said, her words emerging hesitantly.

"Of course he wasn't. Damian Wright was with him. And Josh." Sarah stared at the federal agent, trying to puzzle out her meaning. "You mean there was someone else, that Damian Wright had an accomplice? One of those men you mentioned?" Caitlyn said nothing. The silence tightened around them as shadows deepened the colors streaming through the window above them. "Leo Richland. *LR*. Those were the initials on the watch of the man I found today. *LR*."

Caitlyn straightened, poised to spring from the polished

oak of the pew. "Really? Are you sure? Did he have any other identification?"

"I don't know. We packaged him and Gerald, the coroner, took him to the funeral home. The State Police will probably be picking him up tomorrow, take him to their lab."

Caitlyn stood, turned to leave, but Sarah stopped her with a hand on her arm. "If it is Leo Richland, what does that mean? Did he kill Sam instead of Damian Wright? What about Josh? Please, I need to know what happened to my family."

Her voice broke like one of Sam's guitar strings wound too tight. A grating sound, high-pitched, it was too close to pleading for Sarah's comfort. She tightened her grip on Caitlyn's arm and stood to face her. "Please."

Caitlyn didn't move to release herself. She met Sarah's gaze. "As soon as I know anything, I'll let you know. I promise."

Sarah bit her lip before she could beg some more. She gave a small nod and released Caitlyn. The FBI agent walked away, her shadow dancing between the stained-glass reflections like a child playing hopscotch.

The door closed behind her with a solid thud that reverberated into Sarah's bones. She sagged against the end of the pew, her gaze centered on the image of the puny mortal slaying a monster. She thought about Ahweyoh and her Thundergod, about Sam and the way she felt invincible when he wrapped his arms around her, about Josh and the trust he gave them, assuming his parents were omnipotent.

In the color-studded silence of the church, Sarah came close to tears. But what could she cry about? She now knew less than ever. She had no facts, no bodies to bury, no theories, just a bunch of meaningless names and the confession of a madman.

Most of all she had no hope. She couldn't let Caitlyn's questions stir any. That road led only to despair. Hope was her enemy; this she had learned.

Her breath echoed through her, rattling inside her chest like the ticking of a bomb ready to explode. Sarah pursed her lips at the memory. She'd felt this way before and she'd survived.

Just had to take it one day at a time, one step at a time, one breath at a time.

Hal Waverly was working his way through a greasy mound of French fries when Caitlyn returned to the Rockslide. He ate like a man refueling, not a man enjoying himself.

"Has your coroner determined the man's identity yet?" she asked, declining his offer of both a French fry and a seat beside him at the counter.

His laughter made him snort as he choked down a mouthful. The diner was filling with patrons and all eyes were once again on her, the stranger in their midst.

"Now that's the woman I remember," Hal said. "Barking out orders as she kneels in the mud, trying to photograph a crime scene that's turned into a freaking deluge. Thought then you were only trying to impress your boss, but I guess you're always like that."

"Like what?" Caitlyn demanded. Even standing beside him as he sat, he still was tall enough she had to tilt her head to meet his gaze. "Competent? Hardworking? Knowledgeable?"

"Intense. Hyperactive." His gaze traveled the length of her body before coming to a stop on her lips. "Excitable."

"Don't give me any of your 'gee-shucks, we're just a

small town' crap," she said, surprising herself. Usually she was the consummate diplomat, especially with smaller jurisdictions. Something about Waverly brought out the bitch in her. The man exuded sexuality, no problems there. But he also raised all sorts of alarms in her. "Give me directions to this so-called coroner of yours and I'll go myself."

He shook his head, stopped just short of rolling his eyes, and wiped his mouth. "Give me a minute to settle up here and I'll drive you."

The last thing Caitlyn needed was to be chauffeured. But it seemed a small concession after she'd just insulted him and his police force.

"See you tomorrow, Colonel," Waverly said as he handed over a five-dollar bill. "You'll get the rest of the council there?"

"I'll start working on it right away, Hal."

"Sounds like a plan."

He held Caitlyn's elbow as they strolled outside to his GMC Jimmy parked in front of the post office. His touch was casual, not controlling or even flirting. The warm solidity of his hand cut through the fabric of her jacket. Although she wasn't entirely certain if she liked it or not, she didn't shrug it off.

He held the door open for her, offered a hand, which she declined, to help her climb up into the SUV's passenger seat. The car had seen much more use than his office, as evidenced by the multiple travel mugs, ticket books, remnants of fast-food meals, a spare set of clothes hanging from the rear window, wet suit and climbing gear arranged across the rear seat, and shaving mirror attached to the passenger sun visor.

"You got a house, Waverly?" she asked, shoving the detritus aside and fastening her seat belt.

"I vaguely remember one." He adjusted his holster and radio in an automatic movement born of frequent repetition. Nestling into the seat as if it were a well-worn recliner, he stretched his long legs into the wheel well in front of him. After placing his cell phone into the charger, he started the engine.

Caitlyn leaned forward as he placed his arm on the back of her seat, steering the SUV into a tight reverse turn. The police scanner on the dash crackled with chatter from various units. "County-wide dispatcher?"

"Only way we can afford it. Especially during tourist season. I've got three men and myself to cover over a hundred square miles and let's face it." He gave her a self-deprecating shrug. "Superman, I'm not. As you so aptly pointed out. Both times we've met."

Caitlyn sat in silence, staring at the quaint houses and shops they passed. The sun abruptly abandoned them as they entered the forest, the road turning into a corkscrew of twists and turns.

Driving it hadn't been so bad, but riding as a passenger with nothing to focus on the winding road brought with it a wave of nausea that awakened the sleeping giant of her migraine. *Not one like last night,* she prayed, swallowing hard and trying to appear nonchalant as Waverly steered them from one bone-jostling curve into the next.

"It was nice you apologized to Sarah," he said, oblivious to the stomach-roiling roller-coaster ride. "Hope you didn't upset her again during your little talk."

Caitlyn caught the edge to his voice. *Don't mess with my people,* it said, loud and clear. "I don't think so."

"You still working out of the Boston field office with that boss, Logan?"

"No. Logan's retired and I've been promoted to teach at Quantico."

They sat in silence as he digested that. She had the feeling his questions weren't born of a desire to catch up for old time's sake.

"Mind telling me what's brought you all the way up here from Virginia?"

"There's a chance your corpse might be the body of a missing U.S. Marshal," she answered, deciding to trust him with as little of the truth as possible. Not a hard choice given that she knew almost nothing of the truth herself. Everything she discovered, most of which wasn't fact but mere speculation, seemed to make the whole mess more and more complicated.

"Hmpf. You have some kind of psychic premonition Sarah was going to find this guy? That's why you came in a private vehicle instead of one of your official FBI cars?"

She slanted a glance at him. His eyes were on the road, but he wore another of those infuriating smirks. "Yep. Even us small-town cops have eyes in our heads. And," he turned to give her a wide-eyed nod as if imparting news-breaking information, "we can tell time as well. You had to have started out way before Sarah found the body. C'mon, Agent Tierney, fess up. Why are you really here?"

CHAPTER TWENTY

Sarah stopped in front of her house and stood on one foot, rubbing one ankle against the back of the other. While recovering the body she'd scratched herself on some branches in the water and now she was breaking out in a prickly-heat-like reaction.

The Colonel's wife had made the expected disapproving clucks while at the same time pumping her for information after she'd returned to the Rockslide. Hal left to take Caitlyn down to the funeral home while the Colonel was busy organizing the emergency village council meeting for tomorrow. He'd paused between phone calls to come out of the back room and ask if she wanted a ride home, but she'd declined.

She needed to walk, to do something normal, prove to herself that she could. It gave her time to think. Caitlyn had named three men—could there be more bodies on Snakehead? God, what had happened up there?

The mountain loomed over her, its secrets well hidden. Damian Wright's confession had no mention of any accomplices. It was the tale of one man and his dark obsessions. He'd spoken of his fantasies about Josh, described in loving detail what he'd done to him, but had only given a vague admission that he'd killed Sam. The most the Texas Rangers got out of him was that he'd used a knife on Sam and moved the body so he could take his time with Josh.

It had been the stuff of nightmares, the evil Wright sowed with gleeful abandon. The evil he forced others to live with.

Last summer, after reading the transcript of Wright's confession Sarah returned to the motel in Huntsville, showered repeatedly, then stayed in bed the next day, drapes drawn, door barricaded against a world that could have created a man like Wright.

Now, for the first time she wondered if he had told the truth. If he had even known the truth. But why would he lie?

"Sarah." Alan's voice sounded eerily like the Colonel's wife as he called out from her front door. He held an empty saucepan in his hand and wore one of her aprons. She stepped past him, tossing her pack into the corner. "Look at you! You're dehydrated, exhausted, sunburned, and is that poison ivy?"

Sarah glanced down at the welts on her ankle. "Nonsense. I've tramped through these woods all my life and never got poison ivy. Not once."

She reached down to itch the collection of red scratches and almost fell over as the world darkened and spun her around like a whirligig. Alan dropped the pot with a clatter and was immediately at her side.

"The Colonel told me what happened. You promised you'd take better care of yourself," he chided. He wrapped his arms around her, hugging her to him.

"It wasn't my fault," she protested, but she couldn't

resist leaning back into his warmth. For a moment she imagined Sam's arms around her. "I'm not the one who put the body there."

"Or the cliff you jumped off of," he finished in a wry voice that was most definitely not Sam's.

Sarah startled, sat upright. The room swam around her for a moment before her vision cleared. This was the closest she'd been to a man in almost two years. Her heart revved into full throttle as a memory of Sam's hands spread flat against her belly flashed through her, reminding her how good a man could make her feel. How good Sam had made her feel.

Could she find that again with Alan? With any man?

Alan seemed to read her mind as he pulled her tight against him once more, squeezing her. He laid his chin on her shoulder, his breath rustling the sweaty tangles of her hair. "I don't know what I'd do if anything happened to you."

He released her before she could think of a reply or pull away. Some part of her body responded to his touch, his warm whisper of comfort. It was as if part of her had been in a coma and now fought its way back to life. She caught her breath and allowed him to take her hand and pull her upright.

She wobbled slightly, but it was nothing that a few liters of water wouldn't cure. Then she looked at Alan again. Beneath her red-checkered apron, he wore his best suit, the blue one that made him look like he'd just stepped out of *GQ*. He held her hand still, staring at her with an expression of concern and . . . desire?

She wanted to look away, to deny the need in his eyes, the need in her body, but she couldn't. Alan broke the spell, dropping her hand and darting to the kitchen. "Damn! My pasta Arrabbiata!"

A clamor of pots and pans followed. Sarah wandered into the kitchen. "What's going on?"

"It was supposed to be a surprise. I wanted to cook for you. It's a very special recipe I learned from a chef in Florence." He stirred a bubbling pot that threatened to boil over. Sarah inhaled, relishing the scents of garlic, fennel, basil, and tomatoes. When Alan's sauce had simmered down, the crisis averted, he turned to her with a sheepish grin. "I wanted everything to be perfect tonight. For you."

Sarah stared at him, one hand going to her hair, finding a cluster of nettles there. "For me?"

"Why not? You deserve to be happy, don't you?"

Before she could answer, he pressed a large glass of red wine into her hand. "Drink; you'll feel better. Then you take a nice bath, change into your most beautiful dress, and we'll have a proper dinner."

He raised his own glass, clinking it against hers. She drank deeply, the rich, mellow Merlot soothing her nerves like a salve. Before she knew it, she had almost finished the glass. Alan topped it off again. With a laugh, he placed his hand on the small of her back, steering her toward the bathroom.

"After dinner, I have something special I need to ask you," he said as the door shut between them.

Sarah set the glass down on the table beside the bathtub and sagged against the sink. She had a pretty good idea what Alan wanted to ask her and she wasn't ready for it. Not at all.

He was a nice man. A dear, sweet man. A good friend. He'd waited two years for her. Could she disappoint him, hurt him like that? She stared at her reflection in the mirror. Somehow Alan had seen past the grief and the anger and every other excuse she'd cloaked herself in, refusing to return to the outside world. Somehow, despite all that, he still wanted her.

She bent over to start the bath and her vision grew dark again. The wine was already hitting her hard, her toes were tingling, and she felt as if she were floating. She knew better. What she needed was water, not wine.

No, what she needed was courage. She raised the glass to her lips again. For that, wine would do better.

The rush of the water filling the tub echoed the whirling thoughts colliding in her brain. She didn't love Alan. But she did like him. She couldn't bear to hurt him, not after everything he'd done for her. Maybe she should say yes, let him get close, maybe with time . . .

Suddenly, the hair on her arms rose as if a ghost had just walked over her grave. The window was shut, the lace curtains undisturbed; no one was here except her. Yet, she could swear she felt Sam's presence, could smell the familiar tang of his sweat. It was sharper than she remembered, as if he was afraid.

She couldn't help herself. She tugged the curtains aside and stared past the lilac bushes, past the lawn into the dark shadows of Snakehead Mountain. There was no movement in the twilight, not even a stray deer or rabbit. She was alone. Absolutely alone.

Sarah inhaled again, smelled only the lilac bubble bath. She sank down to sit on the edge of the tub. A wave of disappointment washed over her. *Fool, it's you who's afraid, not some figment of your imagination.*

She glanced at the mirror. The steam had formed letters there. She squinted, thinking at first she was mistaken, and looked again.

Our tree, sunset—I'll explain all. I love you forever. Your MM.

Her hands clenched against the side of the tub as she

stared at the words filling her mirror. No, it couldn't be. It just couldn't. Pain stabbed between her eyes and she felt a knot tightening her throat, choking her. Her vision wavered.

She lurched up, anxious to get a closer look at the message, to show it to Alan, to prove to someone else that she wasn't crazy. She broke out in a clammy sweat. Dimly she heard the wineglass shatter on the floor as a thunderous roar overcame her. And then she felt nothing.

CHAPTER TWENTY-ONE

Caitlyn declined to answer Hal's question about her motives. Not only because she was on shaky ground since this wasn't actually official business, but also because all her attention was focused on restraining her migraine and the accompanying nausea. She rolled her window down, sucking in the crisp evening air. After an initial attempt at further conversation, Hal left her in peace.

Finally, they arrived at a large Queen Anne house complete with a turret and wide veranda. Hal pulled around back to where there was a gravel parking lot, a gazebo, and an inviting path into a garden shielded by beech and willow trees. "Serenity Grove," a sign proclaimed.

Hal grabbed his cell phone and jumped out, rocking the SUV as he slammed the door. Caitlyn closed her eyes for a brief moment, composing herself, forcing the headache back into retreat, then joined him at the rear door of the mortuary.

He rang a doorbell and a moonfaced overweight man in his forties appeared a few minutes later. "Hal, didn't know you were coming down tonight."

Hal made introductions.

The man's attention turned to Caitlyn. He wore a T-shirt hidden by a large rubber apron and carried a set of black, extended-length rubber gloves in his hands. "And who's your beautiful companion?"

Caitlyn was surprised by Hal's frown at Merton's leer. She offered her hand and shook his. "I'm Caitlyn Tierney, Mr. Merton. Thank you for allowing me to observe."

Merton kept her hand in his as he glanced at Hal. "Observe?"

"She's FBI," Hal answered tersely. He stepped forward, forcing Merton both to drop Caitlyn's hand and to concede the space. Caitlyn followed the two men through a dark corridor to a windowless room. A stainless steel table with a sink at one end sat under the bright glare of an overhead examination light. A lighted magnification unit was poised over the head of the bed. An unopened body bag lay on the table.

Lined up on the counters were embalming chemicals, surgical instruments, a corkboard with pinups of photographs of the recently deceased when they'd seen better days, several wigs perched on foam heads, and a multi-tiered makeup kit that would rival any Hollywood studio's.

"Sorry about the smell, ma'am." Merton's eyes glinted with a smirk that said he wasn't sorry at all, that he was eager to see how the "lady" reacted to the stench of decomp.

"No problem," she said, meeting his eyes effortlessly. "I've been around much worse."

Which was true. The smell of body decay didn't make her stomach revolt. It was the overwhelming sickly sweet scent of carnations, roses, and a chemical room deodorizer that was meant to smell like apples and cinnamon. Combined with Merton's citrus cologne, which he apparently bathed in, Caitlyn's olfactory senses reeled.

Merton's face tightened with disappointment and he turned to address Hal, ignoring Caitlyn. "Haven't started yet, Chief. No one told me this was a rush job."

"Didn't know myself."

She took shallow breaths through her nose and stubbornly refused to reach in her bag for the jar of Vicks she always carried. Her headache began a drumroll against the back of her eyes and the bright lights didn't help any, but then she noticed Hal looked pretty wretched as well. She had the feeling those zillion or so fries he'd chowed down on weren't sitting so well right about now.

Somehow the thought eased her own discomfort. Petty, she knew, but she'd take comfort where she could find it. Spotting a box of vinyl gloves on the counter, she slid a pair on, shrugged out of her jacket, and set her bag down in a safe corner. Then, as the two men watched, she approached their silent partner, the unknown corpse wrapped in its body bag.

"Mind if I do the honors?" She didn't wait for their answer, but unzipped the bag.

The corpse grinned up at her with a lopsided grimace. She didn't take it personally. Rigor mortis and post-mortem changes often created that rictus. In this case, the effect was amplified by his jaw hanging to one side and his missing teeth.

Remnants of adipocere formed greasy, brown islands of fatty tissue interposed with tufts of light-colored hair and exposed sections of skull. Caitlyn carefully worked the bag to one side, exposing only the skull. She slid a neck support below the head, elevating it so she could examine the entire circumference.

"Ruler?" she asked, holding out a hand without looking.

Merton rummaged through a drawer, eventually pulling

forth a white plastic T square with large numerals on it. He slapped it into her waiting hand and danced back, ready to pounce if she needed anything.

Caitlyn adjusted the ruler. The flash and whirl of a camera told her Hal knew his job. He circled behind her, taking photos from every angle as she positioned the ruler. She carefully combed through the corpse's remaining hair, depositing the remnants of gray algae, dead leaves, and other organic debris into petri dishes Hal held open for her.

Her headache retreated as she concentrated on the corpse. She liked the way Hal anticipated her needs, moving with her in a well-choreographed dance. The only sound in the room was the occasional click of the camera and Merton's nasal wheezing.

Caitlyn parted the clump of hair above the man's left ear and straightened. "Bingo," she said, rolling her shoulders.

"Entrance wound?" Hal took several close-ups of the hole in the skull.

Merton crowded against them, eagerly leaning over the table, blocking the light. Caitlyn used her arm to push him aside. "Excuse me, sir. You don't mind me borrowing this, do you?"

He shook his head silently, stepping back far enough for her to slide the magnifying lamp over. She clicked it on, centered it over the wound. "Entrance wound," she confirmed. "Look at the stellate damage to the bone. That wasn't done by any animal."

"What about a blow to the head?" Hal asked. "He was found at the bottom of the gorge. Lots of chances to hit rocks and such."

Caitlyn considered this. "Maybe. But that doesn't explain this." She grabbed a pipe cleaner from the canister on the counter and probed the wound. "Look now, can you see it?"

Hal's body nestled beside hers as he leaned down and peered through the glass. "Damn. Is that what I think it is?"

"A bullet. Looks fairly large. I'm guessing a forty-caliber."

Hal gave a low whistle. "I'm impressed, Agent Tierney."

"If this is Leo Richland, he could have been shot with his own gun. In which case, we'll have ballistics on file."

Hal cleared his throat, touched her arm. Caitlyn looked up, surprised to see the muscle at his jaw twitching as he stared at her as if she was the one who'd shot Richland.

"Mind telling me just who the hell Leo Richland is?" he asked, his voice booming through the cramped room. "Seems the least you could do, seeing as how all of a sudden I'm in charge of his murder investigation."

CHAPTER TWENTY-TWO

Sarah opened her eyes. She lay on her bed, still fully clothed, a cold washcloth draped over her forehead. Black spots danced in her vision and her head throbbed. The mattress sighed as Alan sat down beside her. His eyes filled with concern, he stroked her cheek with the backs of his fingers.

"Feeling better?"

She nodded and tried to sit up, but the motion made her head spin. Alan reached behind her, propped her up on a stack of pillows.

"You scared the shit out of me," he said. She glanced up at him in surprise. Alan never swore. "I called Dr. Hedeger."

"Call him back," she replied, her voice as wobbly as her vision. "Tell him I'm fine." She swung her legs around and sat upright. He circled an arm around her shoulders to steady her. "Unless he has a cure for stupidity."

"It's my fault. I should have never given you that wine." His fingers drew circles on the bare flesh of her arm.

"That's all it was, right? I mean, you'd tell me if there was something else going on. Wouldn't you, Sarah?"

Her stomach tightened as she remembered the words on the mirror. She felt her breath catch and had to swallow back an ambush of tears. If Sam was alive, then was Josh?

"Sarah? You okay?"

She nodded, her mind barraged by an avalanche of thoughts. Sam alive, Josh alive, how, where, why—or was it all someone's idea of a sick joke? No. No one else knew her nickname for Sam.

She ignored Alan and stared past him, her gaze caught by the bright cobalt and white tiles of the bathroom beyond.

Maybe she had hallucinated it? Maybe the fatigue and wine and everything else had warped her mind, made her see what she wanted to see? She pushed to her feet, staggering a step or two, then moving with steady purpose to the bathroom. Alan followed.

"Sarah, what's wrong?"

The mirror was blank. Of course it was. She turned on the taps, as hot as they would go.

Alan grabbed her waist before she could step onto broken glass. "What are you doing? At least let me clean up this mess first."

Sarah leaned against the sink, her mouth inches away from the mirror, adding her breath to the steam. The mirror fogged over but remained stubbornly blank.

"Nothing." The word emerged against her will, but once it was said aloud she was forced to acknowledge it. "There's nothing."

Alan glanced at her sharply. "Now you're really scaring me. What were you expecting to see?" He tugged her away from the sink, reached past her to turn the water off, and guided her back to the bedroom. He sat her down on the bed once more. "Look at you; you're a mess. Exhausted. You need a good night's sleep. No more climbing alone on the mountain."

She remained silent, staring at the billows of steam escaping from the bathroom. Alan knelt before her, blocking her view. He took her hands in his and finally she looked down, met his eyes. "Promise me. No more. I couldn't bear it if anything happened to you." He squeezed her hands. "Please, Sarah. Promise me."

"All right, Alan. I promise."

JD finished hiding their bikes in a clump of sumac and turned to Julia. She was spreading a blanket out in the center of the clearing. From here they would be able to see anyone approaching the caretaker's shack or traveling on the path down from the ridge to the dam.

"What did you tell your folks?" he asked her, wiping his sweaty palms on the back of his jeans. He was excited and more than a bit nervous about spending the night with her. Did she really think all they were going to do was watch for the strange lights? Was she expecting something more from him—if so, how did he make the first move without looking like a jerk?

"Told them I was spending the night at Beth's house."

Wow. She'd lied to her parents so she could spend the night with him. He stuck his hand in his back pocket, his fingertip tracing the edge of the well-worn condom package. Maybe tonight was the night he'd finally get a chance to use it.

She tossed her hair over her shoulder in that movement he found mesmerizing. It seemed to slow time to a crawl, allowing each strand to fall perfectly in formation. "What did your dad say when you showed him the pictures from last night?"

He shrugged and looked away. "Basically that I was wasting my time and I'd be better off working with him and getting paid off the books. Said they had a shipment of new TVs to take over to a motel in Saranac and he could get his boss to pay me in cash."

She pursed her lips in disappointment, that little crease forming in her chin. God, how he wanted to kiss her, see how she tasted. He knelt beside her on the blanket.

"It doesn't matter. I'm going to find out what's really going on and prove to everyone that—" He faltered. It was hard to find the right words when she was looking at him that way. "That there is something going on," he finished triumphantly.

"The lights we saw last night definitely came from down here," she said, pulling their cameras from her bag. "Maybe we'll get lucky and catch them in the act."

JD wondered who "they" were and what they might be in the act of doing, but the thoughts were quickly cast aside as he thought about the way she'd smiled at him when she said "we'll get lucky."

Oh yeah.

CHAPTER TWENTY-THREE

Caitlyn was saved by the bell. Or rather, by the Dixie Chicks ringtone on her cell phone. She stripped off her gloves, grabbed the phone, and glanced at the number. Royal, calling from California.

"Excuse me," she told the men. "I have to take this."

She stepped out of the room, closing the door behind her as she connected the call. "It's Caitlyn."

"Hi again, sweetheart. You said to update you on the Korsakov thing." He drew the last word out to two syllables, sounding like a gangsta wannabe.

"Yeah. What's up?"

Hal came out of the embalming room, joining her. Pressing the phone to her ear, she crossed the hallway, pushing another door open. She stepped inside the dark room, flicked on the light, and shut the door in Hal's face. A closed casket sat about eight feet in front of her, surrounded by linen-draped folding chairs and bushels of flowers.

"Judge took a long lunch, otherwise I'd have gotten back to you sooner. Right now I'm looking at a free Russian waltzing his way down the courthouse steps."

Caitlyn leaned against the door. Her headache pounded so loud she could barely hear Royal. The smell of carnations was overpowering. "You're right there with him?"

"About ten feet away. You want a picture? Hang on." There was a pause. "Did it come through?"

Caitlyn squinted at her phone's screen. A few moments later a slightly fuzzy picture of a man dressed in a black suit with a black shirt and red tie appeared. "That's Korsakov? The monster you were telling me about? But he's so—"

"Short. Pale. Ordinary. I know. Hey, they can't all be tall, beautiful black men like me. We can't follow him, we don't have probable cause for any surveillance, but I can tell you he's headed your way."

"What's that?"

"He's booked on a red-eye into Kennedy, will be arriving tomorrow morning." Royal's voice grew serious—something that rarely happened in Caitlyn's experience. "Don't you mess with this guy, Cat. He's one sick, twisted bastard. I don't know what the hell you've got yourself into, but you get one whiff that Korsakov's anywhere near and I want you to promise me you'll take off running."

"I can take care of myself," she said. It was difficult to force the words out; her stomach was in such upheaval she had slid halfway down the door. "Bye."

"No, wait! I mean it. Caitlyn, don't you dare hang up—"

His voice died as she fumbled the End button on the phone. Her vision blurred with pain. She debated between simply falling the rest of the way to the floor and trying to force herself up, escape from the room. There were carnations everywhere she looked: lined along the walls, cascading over the closed casket in the center of the room, hemming her in on all sides.

Pain stampeded over her. She was awash in the stench

of carnations, being pulled under, drowning, unable to breathe, to think, to see. Her vision darkened to a too-bright pinhole of stabbing light. Her stomach clenched and the room spun around her.

All she could do was blindly reach out, searching for something, anything to hold on to as she fell into an oblivion of pain.

Her fingers clamped onto a man's arm. *Hal,* the name came from somewhere in the dim recesses of her brain. His face swam before her blurred vision, creased in concern.

Merton's voice stabbed into her brain. "What's wrong with her? Did she faint?" He sounded excited by the prospect.

His voice boomed, then faded as Caitlyn felt her body shrink. Everything around her became monstrously large, towering over her like she was an ant crawling on the ground, looking up at the monsters intent on stamping out its life.

She closed her eyes against the vertigo. The pain pounded against her barriers until she fled to the far recesses of her memory.

Nine, she'd been nine then. Drowning in carnations: white, pink, brilliant red, they surrounded her on all sides, spilling out from buckets as she hid, cowered beneath the table in the rear of the funeral home.

Two pairs of stout, stocking-clad legs blocked her escape. She wanted to scream, to cry, just to be alone, but she was trapped. She clamped her hands over her mouth, breathing through her nose, awash in the sickly sweet scent of funeral flowers.

"Too good for the likes of him, I tell you," one of the women said, green leaves and stems flying below the table-top and into Caitlyn's field of vision as she spoke. "Always knew no good would come of him. She's lucky they're even letting her hold a Christian service. Of course he'll be cremated—can't be buried in consecrated ground."

"No viewing?" The second woman's voice, higher pitched and cruel in its rapacious curiosity, echoed above Caitlyn's hiding place.

"Willa! The man blew half his face off!"

"It was the daughter who found him?"

"She weren't supposed to be there—typical though." The woman clucked in disapproval. "Stubborn, that one. Just like her father, she is. I had her in my Sunday school class and she stood up and argued with me about the miracle of the loaves and fishes. Eight years old and blaspheming to my face!"

"It's that red hair. What did you do?"

"I slapped her, couldn't help myself, she shocked me so. I took her by her hair and dragged her out to Pastor Paul. The girl refused to apologize, insisted she was right; her momma was about in tears with shame. Then the father stormed in, yells at me to take my hands off his child, and gathers her in his arms, carries her out."

"You're kidding."

"Pastor Paul was speechless. And you know the worst? The girl looked back at me and smiled the most evil grin you've ever seen. I tell you, the devil is in that girl."

"Her poor momma."

"Mark my words, she'll come to an evil end. Just like her father."

The witches' voices faded into the past, where they belonged. Replacing them was Hal's soothing tone, coming from a distance, barely audible over the pounding in her brain. "You're all right, now. Just relax."

With the suddenness of a lightning strike, the pain

collapsed, returning Caitlyn to her senses. She was bent double, vomiting into a trash bin, Hal's hands supporting her, holding her hair out of her face.

She blinked. They were outside, behind the mortuary. The early evening sun shimmered off the asphalt drive; there was a small glade of trees and bushes beyond.

"You okay now?" Hal asked. He raised her up, the hinged lid of the trash bin closing with a bang that made her wince.

The headache wasn't vanquished—merely maneuvering to outflank her. It gathered strength at the edge of her mind. She shook her head, instantly regretting the small movement.

"Get me out of here." Each word cost her ground, the headache advancing relentlessly.

Hal straightened, looked past her to his truck, then hugged her against his body, half-carrying her in the other direction. "Come with me," he said, his voice receding into roiling mists of pain. "I know what you need."

He led her past a sign reading: "Serenity Grove." Caitlyn stumbled as her vision blurred with bright flashing lights, laser beams burning holes in her brain. She squeezed her eyes shut against the assault, allowing him to lead her along a mulched path.

The pain grew too much to bear. She stopped, dropped into a fetal position, hands fisted over her eyes, but still the fading sunlight crept in, a sneak attack of scarlet pain. Her face pressed against the ground, the sweet scent of damp earth and grass mixing with the burnt-flesh odor accompanying her migraine.

Her body arched, trying to curl tighter into a smaller target, but the pain only gained in intensity. She reached a hand out blindly.

"My bag," she moaned, the two syllables costing her dearly.

The earth quaked as her purse thudded to the ground beside her. A shadow passed over her and she dared to squint her eyes open, her hand still fumbling, reaching for the salvation hidden within the leather confines. Through a scarlet haze of pain she watched as a man's hands, grown large and spindly as an ogre's in her distorted vision, reached into her purse.

My weapon, he has my weapon. Fear sliced into her, fueling her torment. *It's okay; he's one of us, a brother-in-arms,* a whisper tried to reassure her, but it quickly died away. Caitlyn's hand slapped against the earth as she reached for her weapon and fell short. She couldn't trust him, shouldn't trust him.

Soon her credentials joined the Glock, their leather cover gleaming in the sunlight.

"What have we here?" Hal's voice came from a distant mountaintop, thundering down at her like Zeus hurling a lightning bolt. "Sumatriptan. Phenergan. Toradol. Fiorcet." He paused. She tried to turn her head, to meet his gaze, plead her case, but she didn't have the strength. "I'm going to assume you have a legit prescription for these, seeing as you have enough to kill a horse."

He dropped the purse and walked away, his shadow abandoning her to the cruel sunlight. She cried out, pulling her head down again, trying her best to bury herself beneath the cool soil.

The ground shook as his footsteps returned, each step exploding a land mine in her brain. Sweat poured out of her, smothering her in a sour stench of fear and loathing. Where was her weapon? she thought, her last remnants of sanity cowering beneath the onslaught.

Last chance, last resort.

Like father, like daughter.

Her hand shot out, groping for the familiar, comforting grip of her Glock.

Instead she found a man's hand. He moved behind her, wrapped his arms around her, and lifted her into his lap. Her hands covered her face, shielding them from the cruel sunbeams. Gathering her hair in his hand, he slid a cool, wet cloth over her exposed neck, circling around to her cheeks, easing it between her hands.

"It's okay; just breathe," he whispered. Explosions of pain blew apart the words, almost destroying their meaning, but some primal part of Caitlyn's brain still had the will to fight back. She took a breath.

First one, then another. The stink of burnt flesh receded, replaced by lavender.

His fingers stroked her neck, massaging away the tension there, then moved up to her scalp. She shuddered and cried out when he touched the scar buried beneath the hair on the right side of her scalp.

"Sorry, I'm sorry." The sound of rippling water and his touch returned, now accompanied by cool, soothing tendrils of water he skimmed across her flesh. The flames burning through her consciousness subsided, abandoning Caitlyn in a smoldering wasteland of smoke, a minefield of torment. One wrong step and the pain would blast her to smithereens.

But it was her only chance for escape.

She inched her mind forward, trying to follow the trail he blazed. His fingers, cool, soothing, trailing droplets of water, moved down her shoulders, along her spine. Her sleeveless blouse buttoned in the back. He undid the buttons, unsnapped her bra. A welcome breeze combined with his touch to cool her fevered, sweat-slicked skin. His fingers continued their magic, kneading, massaging, chasing the pain from her tortured muscles, working their way back up to her scalp. This time his touch brought no further onslaught as he smoothed the puckered scar tissue above her ear.

Caitlyn felt as if she were floating, the pain easing, releasing her. Her hands relaxed, she opened her eyes and, when the fading sunlight didn't bring a fresh bout of pain, dared to turn her head. She was lying on a wet bandanna, a cluster of crushed lavender and other herbs in the center of it.

She drew her breath in, relishing the chance to finally fill her lungs. Still, his hands didn't stop. Her blouse and bra fell, exposing her to anyone, but there was no one except her and Hal. The only sound was the cheerful tinkle of a fountain to their left.

"Thank you." Her words came in a strained whisper as if the torrent of pain had shredded her vocal cords.

"Was it a brain tumor?" he asked, his fingers skimming her scar. "My wife—" He cleared his throat. "She had headaches like yours. Medulloblastoma, nothing helped. She's gone now." He wasn't looking at her, his gaze raised up, fixed on a spot far past the treetops. "Been gone a while now."

"I'm sorry. Sorry that either of you had to go through that." She tilted her head, looking at him upside down, and tried her best to give him a comforting smile. "No. Not a tumor. Two years ago . . ." She trailed off, her words interrupted by a memory of vertigo, free fall, then the abrupt deceleration of hitting the pavement. "I fell and hit my head."

He rocked back on his heels, his hands sliding away from her body. Caitlyn missed his soothing touch immediately. She gathered her strength and slowly sat up. Twisting her body, she knelt before him. "Thank you."

His eyes met hers and she was surprised to see him blush. "Sorry. Didn't mean to get so personal." His gaze flicked down her body, to her partially exposed breasts. "Just, that was the only way I could help Lily. Thought it might help you, too."

Caitlyn reached out and took one of his hands. It took both of hers to wrap around his large palm and callused fingers. "It did. You did."

They sat there for a long, sun-drenched minute. His flush deepened. His eyes were blue, the color of stone-washed denim. She hadn't noticed before how attractive he was—too busy sparring with him, trying to prove herself to him. Now she smiled at him, not breaking the contact, felt his palm grow sweaty in her grasp, his pulse throbbing against her fingertips. His gaze trailed down her face, focusing on her mouth as his own lips parted. He pushed himself to his feet, using his hand in hers to help her up.

She wobbled for a heartbeat, but Hal was there to steady her. Caitlyn felt drained from her battle, yet also energized by his touch.

He smiled, slid his hand out from hers. Then he stepped behind her, his fingers skimming over her skin as he reached for her bra and refastened it.

"Not here," he said in a voice so low it thrummed through her veins, a whisper of invitation—one they could both deny and dismiss if need be. His hands lingered before they tugged her blouse shut and began to button it. "Not until you feel up to it, strong enough."

She turned within his embrace, his hands coming to rest on her hips. Raising a fingertip to his lips, she felt a playful grin stretch her face. It felt good. "Don't worry about me, Chief. I'm a fast healer."

CHAPTER TWENTY-FOUR

"Their" tree was a sprawling sugar maple standing beside the creek in a clearing behind the house. This was where she'd taught Sam how to read the night sky, where Sam debuted his songs, where Sarah proposed to him and he declined, where Josh had been conceived, where Sam proposed to her and she accepted.

Sarah remained hidden in the stand of hemlocks about twenty yards from the maple, watching. She'd allowed Alan to feed her, fuss over her, and finally bade him an early, strained good night. They hadn't spoken much during dinner—well, maybe Alan had; she hadn't paid much attention.

As soon as Alan was gone and she had the house to herself, she'd rushed to the bathroom and examined the mirror. As before, it was empty of any hidden messages from beyond the grave. She'd taken a scalding-hot shower, emerged, and it was still empty.

Too empty. Too clean. Where were the dozens of toothpaste splatters speckling the glass? She hadn't cleaned it in over a week. She'd glanced down at her now sparkling-clean floor, no remnants of red wine marred its surface after Alan's efforts.

Alan. She always teased him about his touch of neat freakness. Why would he wipe away the message? Maybe he was trying to protect her from what he thought was a sick joke.

Now, close to the appointed time, Sarah crouched down, peering between the branches that concealed her. Her fingers raked the fallen needles at her side, twirling them into patterns as she tried to make sense of everything.

Maybe Alan knew Sam was alive? *If* Sam was alive.

She shook her head, frowning. How? Alan hadn't arrived in Hopewell until two weeks after Sam and Josh disappeared. The two men had never met.

She stared into the star-bright night, her emotions churning. She could have simply gone to the maple, waited there. After all, it was her tree, her land; she had every right to be there, message or not. Fear held her back. Fear that Sam was alive—if so, then why had he hidden these past two years? Why had he taken Josh from her? Why hadn't he returned or at least sent word that they were safe?

If Sam was alive, how could he have abandoned her to the hell she'd lived with?

Even worse—if he was dead, then Josh was as well. And whoever left that note for her did it because they wanted to hurt her, wanted to drive her back to the abyss of despair that had almost taken her once.

She crouched in the darkness like a thief in the night, refusing to hope, refusing to believe, refusing to move until she had some answers.

A sharp crack disturbed the night, silencing the frogs and crickets. Another followed. A man's form appeared in the edge of her vision, walking through the grass from the direction of the lane. Clouds scudded past the moon and the man turned, looking over his shoulder, revealing his profile.

Alan. He was answering the message. The message left for her. From Sam.

As if in answer to her prayers, a man's silhouette separated itself from the shadows surrounding the maple. Pine needles speared her palm as her fist tightened. It was Sam.

She almost broke cover, rushed into his arms. But she held back, torn between love and rage. The man she loved, who promised to love her for all eternity, could never have taken their son, abandoned her without hope.

If he could betray her so cruelly, then what had he done with Josh?

Sam strode forward, reaching Alan in two steps. Even from this distance Sarah could see the angry way his jaw protruded. He'd shaved his head and now had a short goatee, but it was definitely Sam. No one could mimic that stride, the way his hips rolled as if he waded through shallow water.

Without warning he lashed out with a roundhouse punch. A loud smack sliced through the silence. Alan staggered back, shaking his head, palms up in surrender.

Sam raised his arm, readying another blow.

"I wouldn't, if I were you," Alan said. "Not if you're planning to get out of this alive."

That sounded like two men who knew each other—but Sam and Alan had never met before. Had they?

Sam hesitated, lowered his fist. "Where's Sarah? What the hell have you done with her?"

He actually sounded worried. Sarah strained to catch every word, cursing the open space of the meadow and the cheerful night noises of the stream and insects.

"Nothing. Yet." Alan cocked his head. "You've changed, old friend. You look worried, older. These past few years haven't been kind to you, have they?" Nodding scornfully at Sam's faded jeans, flannel shirt worn over a gray T-shirt, he smoothed the cuffs of his own designer suit. "What, no surfer chicks and killer waves waiting for you wherever you ran to?" Alan laughed, a raw sound that sent shivers down Sarah's neck. This wasn't the man she knew. The man who cared about her, who had taken care of her.

Maybe neither of them were.

"You were better off dead, Stan." Moonlight glinted off a metal object in Alan's hand. A gun. Aimed at Sam.

Sarah's heart thundered against her rib cage. Her fists clenched, she watched them walk across the meadow toward the lane. There was no cover; she couldn't follow. The two men disappeared around the bend, out of sight. Leaving her behind to puzzle out truth and lies.

She swallowed her tears of rage and frustration, almost choking on them. Sam was alive! Was Josh? Where was her son?

CHAPTER TWENTY-FIVE

As Hal led Caitlyn down the path to his truck, the euphoria of being pain free faded. "Guess I've made a mess of things, haven't I?"

"Not so much. Gerald's got the body locked up tight; the Staties are on their way to take it to be examined properly. Unless you're declaring federal jurisdiction?" He looked at her expectantly.

She slouched down on a bench beside the path. "Any way we can get prints?"

He shook his head with a rueful smile. "No, ma'am. No fingers left, just a few bits of bone."

She thought as much. A body in the water for any length of time tended to attract fish. And those soft appendages like the nose, toes, ears, and fingers were usually the first to be nibbled off. She hung her hands between her knees, still feeling a bit clammy. "Then I can't prove it's Leo Richland. Unless we can extract DNA and that will take time."

He sat down beside her, his thigh touching hers. "And again I ask, who is Leo Richland?"

Caitlyn sucked her breath in. The sun had finally set,

leaving them in a twilight blue punctuated by the lights of fireflies. A rich aroma of roses, lavender, and rosemary filled the air. It would have been a perfect summer's night except for one thing: as soon as she finished here, she'd have to resign from her job.

The headache last night had been a mere warning shot. Nothing compared to the head-on collision that bowled her over tonight. There was no way she could carry a gun, do her job.

"Hey, you all right?" Hal took her hand in his. "Maybe I should call an ambulance. Drive you to the hospital in Albany?"

"No. I know all about doctors and their poking and prodding. I've been through it before and I'm not going to do it again." The knot of tension between her shoulders tightened at the thought of more strangers in white coats telling her there wasn't any hope. That the life she'd dreamed of since she was a little girl was forbidden to her.

"What I need is someone I can trust. In case I can't see this through myself. Someone to nail Logan and his crooked ass to the wall, to find the answers Sarah Durandt begged me for." The words came out in a desperate rush, but she felt better once they had been spoken. As if she was taking back control of her life.

Hal sucked in his breath, whistling through his teeth. He squeezed her hand. "All right, then. Why don't you tell me what's really going on?"

And she did. Everything she did know, everything she didn't, everything she suspected but could not prove.

"So you think the Russian, what's his name?"

"Korsakov."

"Korsakov paid your boss, Logan, to send this Richland guy up here to kill Sam—I mean Stan—and frame Damian Wright for it?"

She was silent for a moment. When he said it like that, it sounded preposterous. "Yes. Do you remember who you spoke with when you placed the initial call to the FBI about Wright? Did you find anything in his motel room that looked like there may have been a break-in? Someone could have stolen that camera card, planted it. Did anyone report any strangers besides Wright in the area?"

He held up a hand. "Whoa now. That was almost two years ago. I'll have to dig out the case files."

She stood, wobbled for a moment, then steadied herself with a deep breath. No headache, just a twinge of pressure behind her eyes and a touch of dizziness. "Let's go. We—I—may not have much time."

He stood beside her, one arm wrapping around her waist as she shivered in the night breeze. "You worry me when you talk like that."

Caitlyn turned to him, their faces inches apart, and met his gaze head-on. "I'm no quitter."

He traced her jawline with the tip of his finger and nodded gravely. "My wife used to say that." He broke away from her. "She was a stubborn lady, too. You'd have liked her—hated doctors about as much as you do."

Sam had thought getting gut-shot hurt. But that was nothing compared to the anguish he'd suffered tonight, watching through the binoculars as Alan Easton comforted his wife. The way Alan looked at Sarah, held her hands so tenderly, kissed her good night . . .

The anger kept him warm while he waited behind the maple. A breeze rippling down from the mountain cooled the night air, but Sam still found himself sweating as he tried to think of what he would say to Sarah, how to explain everything.

How to beg for her forgiveness.

When he heard footsteps approaching, he'd almost vomited, he was that nervous. More so than when he'd proposed to her, on this very spot. He rubbed the scar on his right side, the repetitive motion soothing his nerves, and had turned to face his wife.

Only to see Alan Easton approaching instead—Alan, wearing a designer suit and a smirk that made Sam's scar burn as anger surged through him. He didn't think, he couldn't think, as he met his old friend. Words failed him, as they seldom did, so he'd used his fist instead.

The bloody lip only made Alan's smirk more infuriating.

He forced Sam to go first, directing him across the grass back to the lane and a nondescript gray Volvo wagon.

"Hands on the roof, keep them where I can see them," Alan ordered.

Sam complied. It was the only way to get the answers he needed from his former college roommate and business partner. "This your car, Alan? What happened to the Beamer?"

"Had to leave it on the coast when I moved out here to this godforsaken frozen armpit. How did you stand living here for so long, Stan? Must have been hell for a surfer boy like you." Despite his words, Alan's tone sounded forced. Sam glanced over his shoulder, scrutinizing his old friend. Spotted the beads of sweat slipping beneath Alan's shirt collar. Maybe there was hope after all.

When Sam remained silent, Alan crossed around to the other side of the car, resting his gun along the roof, aiming at Sam. "These folks think I'm a goody-two-shoes victims' rights lawyer, so I had to look the part. Of course, when I started I had no idea it would take two fucking years out of my life. But now," he rapped the gun against the rooftop, "you're about to make it worth my while. Give me the account passwords. Tell me and I'll let you live."

"Yeah, right. Just long enough for Korsakov to kill me. Don't try to kid a kidder, Alan. I learned from a master, remember?"

Alan nodded, accepting Sam's backhanded compliment. "Here I thought you were too lazy to pay attention to anything but where your next wave and next lay came from. You set this up from the beginning, didn't you?"

"Most of it," Sam admitted. Best way to get the information he needed was to keep Alan talking. Lord knew, Alan loved nothing more than to hear himself talk.

"Once I figured out what was going on, I went back, retraced your steps. You took your time—maneuvering, pinching a little here and there. Once you had the money, why not just take it and go? Why turn Korsakov in to the Feds? You knew that was signing your death warrant."

Alan would never understand that stopping Korsakov had been Sam's goal. The money was his escape hatch, a way to stay alive and outrun the Russian. That was the hope, anyway. Sam's fingers scratched along the roof, curling with frustration. He needed to get to Sarah, get her out of here, to safety. But he couldn't—not without coming to an accommodation with Alan. Or killing him.

Of course, the 9mm semiautomatic hovering three feet away from him made the last option a bit more difficult. He still had Richland's gun tucked in his waistband beneath his flannel shirt. Every time he touched the weapon he felt the burn of a bullet slamming into his own side. Sam had never killed anyone in his life. He wondered if he had the nerve to do it now.

His scar itched and sweat gathered where his T-shirt

was tucked into his jeans. If the choice came down to Sarah's life or Alan's it would be an easy one to make. Even if it might mean his death as well.

But what he really needed were answers. And time. Time to talk to Sarah, let her know where to go to find Josh, who to trust—and who not to. "It was the cops that led you here, two years ago, wasn't it?"

Alan nodded. "I'm the one who paid off Logan and Richland back when they worked for Korsakov. How do you think we took care of all the witnesses before the trial? But you surprised us—Korsakov never expected you to betray us. Neither did I."

"So when I told Hal about the creep taking pictures of little boys—"

"He called Logan's people; Logan called me. I paid Richland to grab you. Only cost me a hundred thousand. Cheap when you think of the payoff waiting for me. Then Richland went missing and everything fell apart." Alan shrugged. "Nothing went as planned, but things still worked out my way. Just like they always do."

"Why did Damian Wright confess to killing me and Josh?" Sam asked the questions that had been nagging at him ever since that awful, bloody night two years ago. "And how did you get him to waive his appeals, plead guilty?"

Alan's teeth gleamed like a predator's in the moonlight. "That was the easiest part of all. Didn't cost me anything. Turns out Damian always knew he'd be caught someday. Had a fantasy of his life story becoming the next Hollywood blockbuster. Even knew who he wanted to play the lead—Tom Cruise. So all I had to do was dummy up some contracts guaranteeing Tom Cruise as the star of *The Damian Wright Story*, production to begin no later than one year after Damian's death." Alan's laughter sliced through the night. "Suddenly Damian was in a rush to die, couldn't wait to get the needle so Tom could make him immortal."

Darkness gathered around them. Two old friends chatting under a full moon. Except one of them was a heartless killer and the other was running for his life.

"Poor Sarah," Alan continued. "You should have seen her after Wright died without telling her where you and little Josh were buried. It almost broke her. Good thing I'm here to pick up the pieces. We're getting married."

"Like hell you are!"

"Who's going to stop us? A dead husband with a price on his head? You try anything and you put her in Korsakov's sights. You know what Korsakov is capable of; you've seen it firsthand."

Acid burned Sam's throat. He did indeed know what the Russian was capable of. He'd watched and listened for over two hours as a man screamed and begged for mercy. Korsakov's response had been to peel the flesh from the man's face and then burn his eyes out with a plumber's torch.

"You can't let him get to Sarah." He forced the words past his clenched jaws. "Please, if you care anything at all about her—"

Alan's chuckle wasn't the answer he'd hoped for. "You dumb bastard. You really did come back for her, and not the money? Hell must be freezing over, because I would have bet good money no woman would ever make you think about anyone but yourself." He cocked his head, staring at Sam as if he were a zoo specimen. "This place really got to you, didn't it? You fell for the dream. Living a quiet life with a good woman by your side, folks thinking you're something special when really you're a lowlife criminal. And Sarah. What would she think if she knew who you really were, Stan?"

Sam bit back his retort, not wanting to make things worse than they already were. Alan now knew his weakness, and that was dangerous for both him and Sarah. He was tempted to reach for his gun, had never felt more ready to kill a man. But he needed to know what Korsakov had planned, who else knew he was alive. Just taking Sarah wouldn't be enough, even if he were able to get her across the border—not if Korsakov had the Feds in his pocket.

After everything they'd been through, Korsakov was going to win after all. But maybe he could at least save Sarah and Josh. Give Sarah back her son, Josh back his mother, earn a small piece of redemption for himself.

Sam stared into the soulless eyes of his former best friend and knew all too well the price he'd have to pay.

"Is that why you didn't touch the money all this time?" Alan continued. "I thought you were being especially careful, suspicious someone was on to you. But that wasn't it, was it? You were waiting until you could come back for the girl. How deliciously romantic!"

"You want the money, you can have it. All of it." Sam would give Alan what he wanted, if it would buy Sarah and Josh's safety. "Just leave Sarah out of it. Let her go."

"Fool me once, old boy," Alan replied with a shake of his head. "Besides, you've been legally declared dead. Far easier for me to kill you, marry her, arrange a little accident, and then claim the money as her heir. All the Caymans need is proof she was your heir and I'm hers. They don't care that she never even knew about the money, much less who her husband really was." Alan raised the gun, aiming it between Sam's eyes. "A lot less worry and hassle for me that way."

Sam stood his ground, met his oldest friend's gaze. If Alan was ready to kill Sarah for $42 million, how much would it take to convince him to let her live? His scar throbbed as he forced himself to smile at Alan.

"A lot less hassle, but a lot less money." Sam stopped there, dangling the bait. The only time he'd ever seen Alan make a mistake it had been fueled by greed. That was how Alan had gotten in deep with Korsakov to start with.

Alan's eyes narrowed. He licked his lips. "What are you talking about?"

"You found one account—my safety net. How'd you like access to three times as much money?"

The gun didn't waver, but Alan went rigid. "A hundred twenty million? How?"

"Probably a bit more than that by now. The Feds didn't get all of Korsakov's funds. I'm the only one, besides Korsakov, who knows how to access them." He paused, watching as Alan's mouth tightened with greed. *Gotcha.* "Of course, we'll have to hurry. Korsakov's getting out. First thing he'll do is move the money."

"Got out. Today," Alan said absently. He drummed the fingers of his free hand against the Volvo's roof.

Sam weighed the odds of his being able to reach his gun and kill Alan before Alan could fire. Pretty damn poor. And if he was dead, who would save Sarah? Time to push the lie. "I'll make you a bargain. You let me take Sarah to Josh and I'll get you the money, plus I'll make sure Korsakov never knows you have it."

"No way I'm letting you out of my sight."

Sam shrugged. "Fine. Kill me now. Korsakov will find you and kill you long before you have a chance to enjoy a dime."

Alan tapped the gun in annoyance as he considered Sam's offer. A stray wrinkle appeared between his brows, a sign of real concern. The only other time Sam had seen him this worried was before Alan's testimony during

Korsakov's trial. The lawyer had tap-danced his way out of that, protecting both himself and his employer in the process.

The wrinkle quickly disappeared and Alan's customary expression of smug superiority slid back over his features. "No. You go get the kid, bring him here."

Sam wasn't about to bring Josh anywhere near here. Not with Korsakov on the way and Alan on a rampage. "I'm not going anywhere until I talk to Sarah and see her safely out of here. Away from Korsakov."

Alan shook his head sadly. "No can do. That little lady is my ace in the hole." He tapped the gun on the roof, producing a hollow thud that sent a ripple of fear down Sam's spine. "I like Sarah, I really do. But if I don't have the money in twenty-four hours, I'll tell Korsakov where to find her. She can run, but she can't hide, not from him. She'll die cursing your name with her last breath."

Sam swallowed hard. Alan's expression and voice never varied even as he condemned Sarah to an unimaginable death. Sam tried to speak but couldn't force words past the knot in his throat as an image of Sarah, her skin ravaged and raw, her screams shrill with terror, filled his mind.

"Don't even think about trying to kill me," Alan continued. "I'm not in this alone. Anything happens to me, Sarah dies."

Alan opened his car door. "Now that we have an understanding, get in the car. We'll do this together."

If Sam gave Alan control, he was as good as dead. Probably Sarah as well. "No."

Alan jerked up, surprised at Sam's defiance. "Excuse me? Do you really want me to go get Sarah? Shoot her here and now?"

Now it was Sam's turn to smile. It was a fake grin, took

all his willpower to keep his mouth stretched wide. "You can't do that, Alan. She's your ace in the hole. I just need a little time. I'll meet you back here tomorrow night."

"Not good enough. Korsakov could be here by then. Why should I risk letting you out of my sight?"

"What have you got to lose? You still have Sarah. You know I won't let anything happen to her."

"If you're not back here by midnight tomorrow, I swear, money or no money, I'll kill her myself."

Sam's pulse beat in his temples as a red haze of rage swept over him. "Not going to happen, Alan."

"It will if you try anything funny. That's a promise, old friend. One wrong move and Sarah's dead."

CHAPTER TWENTY-SIX

Caitlyn and Hal reached his SUV. Darkness had fallen swiftly, transforming the funeral home into a looming hulk casting a menacing shadow. This time she allowed Hal to hold the door open for her and accepted his hand as she climbed into the passenger's seat. He spread her suit jacket across the rear seat, dwarfed by the folds of his black and blue neoprene wet suit.

"You still look a little queasy," he said, standing in the open door, his hand lingering on her arm.

The raised seat allowed Caitlyn to finally meet his gaze head-on. "A little," she admitted, surprising herself.

"Mind if I try something?" Before she could answer, he reached for her wrist and used his fingers to press down on two areas on either side.

At first all she felt was the pressure against her wrist bones. Then slowly, like a breeze traveling down a mountain ridge, forcing the trees before it to bow to its will, her nausea vanished.

She gasped. It was the first time in two years she hadn't

felt turbulence splashing through her gut. Hal smiled, strolled around to the driver's side, boots crunching the gravel like a gunslinger's.

"How did you do that?" she asked after he climbed in and began to pilot them back up the mountain to Hopewell.

"My wife, Lily, she taught me lots of stuff like that. Holistic healing. We'd go to seminars on yoga, acupressure, tantric sex, herbal medicine. She even had a beehive, used to harvest the queen's jelly, made a special tonic from it." He paused for a moment, the dashboard lights revealing the spasm of his jaw muscle. "When she left, so did the bees."

Caitlyn laid a hand on his leg. Nothing sexual, merely a comforting touch. "I'm sorry."

"Yeah. Well." He gripped the wheel in silence, then abruptly turned to her, his voice bright. "So, where are you from, Agent Tierney?"

She sat back in her seat feeling blissfully free. No headache, no nausea, no motion sickness. She felt almost normal. "Believe it or not, Chief, I'm from a town even smaller than Hopewell."

"No sir."

"Yes. Evergreen, North Carolina. Population three hundred eighteen. We didn't have our own police force. Balsam County Sheriff was the best we had to bring law and order to our mountain."

"You don't sound like a southerner."

She swallowed hard against memories the funeral carnations had resurrected. "When I was nine, we moved up to Chambersburg, Pennsylvania, to live with my father's family."

"Chambersburg. That's right outside of Gettysburg, right?"

"I quickly learned my accent didn't endear me to the

locals. But it was all right. My dad grew up there and he never had a southern accent. So I learned to talk like he did."

"Your dad a lawman?"

"Deputy Sheriff."

"Uh-huh. Thought as much." His hands gracefully steered them around a hairpin curve. "Killed in the line, was he?"

"Something like that." She'd been asked the question so many times that avoiding the truth came natural. But for some reason, this time, she felt a twinge of guilt after lying to him. "How'd you know?"

"Told you, you had the look of someone trying to prove something. Now that I know it wasn't your boss, Logan—"

"Hey, where are we going?" she interrupted as they passed the Hopewell Government Center. He continued through town, ignoring the speed limit on the deserted streets. Seemed Hopewell closed down after dark.

"You said you wanted to see the old case files." He turned onto Lake Road. "They're in storage. Up at my place."

"Why?"

He shrugged, but she noted his grip on the wheel tightened. "Small town, small budget. When the old police station was condemned and torn down after the floods of 2005, we needed some place to keep them. Haven't had a chance to move them back—not that there's a whole lot of room to move them to. Storage was one of the things Victoria Godwin forgot when she designed her government center." His tone made it clear he hadn't been consulted on the new police department's quarters.

He turned onto a gravel road, taking them along the ridge that followed the gorge around the east face of the mountain. Large hemlock trees swayed in the breeze, reaching out with their branches to skim along the sides of the truck. A single-story house with a squared-off tin roof came into view. "So here we are, home sweet home."

The frame house had a wide veranda encircling it. Steps made of river rock and a handicap ramp led up to wide French doors. Caitlyn followed Hal up to the porch.

"My great-grandfather built it," he explained. "Back in the fifties. Probably one of the first people to ever design a fully wheelchair-accessible house. Modeled it on houses he saw in Australia during the war." He held the door open wide. It was oak, lovingly hand-carved with flowing vines and morning glories.

"Was he wounded?" she asked as she stepped inside the foyer.

"No. Not Gramps. His beautiful bride, Eloise, had polio. She was in a wheelchair. But she used to say this house freed her." He led her down a hallway twice as wide as the one in the shotgun cottage she'd grown up in and into a kitchen, flicking lights on as he went.

The decor was distressingly familiar. Single cop. A uniform shirt hung on the back of a chair. The table was strewn with newspapers. On top of them sat a gun-cleaning kit and a dissembled .40-caliber Glock 22. Caitlyn smiled at the familiar scent of gun bluing. On the counter, a scanner nestled between a well-used microwave and a coffee-maker. Several inches of black liquid sat in the bottom of a glass pot more yellowed than a smoker's fingers.

Dishes piled in the sink mirrored the stack of frozen-dinner containers in the waste can beside the back door. She liked that Hal didn't apologize for the clutter or lack of ambiance.

"I'll get the records," he said, hanging his duty belt on a hook beside the door and depositing his pager, radio, and phone into respective chargers before moving into the next room. When he flicked the lights on, Caitlyn saw a paneled den cluttered with cardboard storage boxes. The only furniture was an old-fashioned console TV and a beat-up tweed recliner.

She held back her laughter, rolling her eyes as she thought of her own apartment cramped with crime scene photos, training exercises, workout equipment, and the gun safe she'd inherited from her father. It was the only piece of furniture she kept with her on her travels from one assignment to the next. Everything else she owned was quickly disposed of at the nearest Goodwill and replaced by a quick trip to her new locale's Target or IKEA.

Hal shuffled boxes, trying to unearth the records from the Durandt case. She rinsed out the coffeepot and rummaged through his cupboards until she found a can of Folgers to start a fresh pot brewing. The only sugar she could find was in a dusty covered bowl shoved to the back of the cupboard, but it looked okay and after the migraine she needed the extra boost of energy. She rolled her eyes as she spooned it into her cup—typical guy, he didn't know you weren't supposed to use powdered sugar for coffee. Probably grabbed first box he'd seen at the grocery store.

A tinge of jealousy hit her as she wondered who he'd bought it for. Wife dead two years, she couldn't be the first woman he brought home, could she? She poured a second mug of coffee for him as she heard his footsteps approach on the oak floorboards.

"Hope you don't mind," she said, turning to him with a cup in each hand.

He dropped the document box onto the table and stared at her, his mouth agape. His eyes were wide, but his face had gone pale, as if something had frightened him. Maybe she *was* the first woman he'd brought home since his wife died.

Then he stepped toward her and his expression changed to that bewitching smile she had glimpsed earlier. The one that made him look like Gary Cooper in those old movies her father had loved so much.

"I don't mind," he said, his voice so low it approached a whisper. His hand slid down to rest on her hip. "I don't mind at all."

Caitlyn met his gaze, not moving to free herself from his embrace. He lowered his face to hers, then stopped, hovering a mere inch away, his eyes searching hers. He hesitated, silently asking her permission. He looked so vulnerable, as if he were entrusting her with a precious gift.

She tilted her face and closed the distance between them, accepting his kiss and startling herself with her own reticence. Her usual approach with men was one of brutal competition, forcing them to win her—then just as quickly leaving them when they failed to meet her standards. But not with Hal. He was as wounded as she was. No need for machismo or bravado with him.

Hal feathered his fingers along her jaw, tousling her hair, tucking a stray strand behind her ears, tickling her with his breath as his mouth followed his hand. He returned to her lips, taking his time as he kissed her again.

Caitlyn felt dizzy—but it wasn't the gut-wrenching vertigo born of her migraines. This light-headedness was something that tingled along her nerves, straight down to her toes, curling them until she almost stepped out of her shoes.

The scanner behind them squawked. "Hopewell Two to Dispatch. On scene, three-vehicle TC. Minor casualties, backup, EMS, and fire requested, milepost twenty-four, route three-seventy-four."

Hal straightened, the spell broken. He reached past her for his radio in its charger, then drew his hand back.

"Your guy?" Caitlyn asked, noting the wariness that came to his face. Like a father watching his kid climb across the top of the jungle gym for the first time.

"Yeah. We run short in summer, alternating twelves." His face closed down as the dispatcher responded.

"Hopewell Two, I have County Unit Twelve en route. ETA fourteen minutes. EMS and Fire dispatched, ten minutes out."

Hal tilted his head, listening closely to his officer's reply. "Sounds good. Ten-four, Dispatch."

"I guess Tucker has it covered," he said, his gaze still fixed on the radio, his jaws clenched.

Caitlyn noted the hollows etched below his eyes. "You just finished a long day with that recovery on the mountain and I'll bet you worked a shift before that," she said, recognizing a compulsive overachiever when she saw one. "When's the last time you got a full night's sleep, Chief?"

He tugged his gaze back to her, his index finger rubbing at an eyebrow as if seeking an answer. "Too long to count. But that's why I get paid the big bucks."

"Why don't you hit the sack? I can go through these records myself."

A slight smile curled his lips. "Nah, you've got my curiosity riled up now." His hands came to a rest on her waist. "Besides, I want a chance to see a big-time federal agent in action. Might just learn something." He paused, his hands pressing against her hips with a promise of things to come. "Unless you were considering joining me? In the sack?"

Caitlyn laughed. "Don't push your luck. Let's get to work."

CHAPTER TWENTY-SEVEN

Sarah had watched in frustration as the two men spoke. The nearest cover she'd been able to find was too far away for her to be able to hear Sam at all. Alan faced her, and the wind carried some of his words to her. Enough to stir the cauldron of fear churning in her gut. The sight of Alan raising a gun, looking for all the world ready to use it on Sam, hadn't helped either.

Alan drove off and Sam melted into the forest. She raced through the trees, following Sam, caught sight of him on the trail leading over to Lake Road and the reservoir below the Lower Falls.

Thankful for the full moon and scant cloud cover, she jogged over the trail, dodging tree roots and downed branches with practiced ease. Sam kept up a steady pace himself, although she heard him curse and swear at times as he stumbled and fell once. His lead diminished as she grimly pushed herself. Finally, at the clearing above the dam, she drew close enough to stop him with a shout.

"Sam!"

He lurched to a stop and spun around. His mouth

dropped open at the sight of her and he stepped forward. Sarah raced toward him, launching herself at him, pounding him with her fists as they slammed to the ground.

"You bastard! Where's Josh? What have you done with him?" Tears strangled her words until they were barely audible. Sam did nothing to defend himself other than to ward off her blows before they could inflict too much damage. She was sobbing so hard she couldn't breathe. Blinded by tears and anger, she collapsed onto his chest.

Sam sat up, cradling her against him in a tight embrace. Every breath brought with it his scent—that unique, tangy musk that was his and his alone. Sarah hated herself for it, but she couldn't resist her overwhelming need. She curled her arms around his shoulders, clutching him with all her strength.

God, how many thousands of times over the past two years had she dreamed of him holding her like this, had she wished for this? Now she was terrified to let go, afraid he might break her heart again.

What if Josh was really dead? She couldn't bear it, would rather die than hear it.

Sam's tears mixed with hers, warm against her face and neck. He was trembling, shaking uncontrollably. She caught her breath, wiped her face and nose against his flannel-clad shoulder.

"Josh?" she asked, closing her eyes, bracing herself against his answer.

"He's fine." Sam's voice broke. He laid his palm flat against her cheek, caressing her face. "Safe. Waiting for me to bring you back to him."

Sarah choked on her tears. She slid off his lap, away from his embrace, and caught her breath. Then she slapped him as hard as she could. The crack of flesh striking flesh rang out like a shot.

"You goddamned, pieceofshit sonofabitch!" Her words thundered through the few inches that separated them. "How dare you? Who gave you the right to take my son away? To put me through that?"

Sam sat, one hand covering his cheek, tears still streaming down his face. He looked pale and gaunt. As if all his smooth edges had been filed sharp.

Sarah pushed herself to her feet, standing over him, not bothering to hold back any of her fury. "Get up, you bastard. You're going to take me to my son, right now, this very instant. And then we're leaving you."

He met her gaze. God, his eyes looked ancient. Ancient and overwhelmed with sorrow. With his shaved scalp and the moonlight casting him in an unearthly glow, he looked like a skeleton of the man she'd known and loved.

Slowly, he shook his head. "I can't take you to Josh right now."

Her breath caught in her throat, leaving her speechless. She aimed a kick at his side, but he caught her leg and pulled her down on top of him. Once again she tried to pummel him, bite, scratch, kick, but this time he wrapped his hands around her wrists and held her at bay.

Finally she was reduced to snarling at him like a wounded animal. She would have spit at him, but her mouth was too dry. "Bastard. Let me go."

"Not until you calm down. Listen to me, Sarah. We don't have much time. Does Alan know you're here?"

"What do you care?"

He gave her a shake. "Josh's life may depend on it. And yours."

"Josh? Is Alan going after Josh? I saw his gun—" She struggled anew to free herself from his grip.

"Josh is safe, Alan doesn't know where he is. But he can't know we've spoken. It may be our only hope."

The hated word froze Sarah's blood. How many times had people told her not to give up hope those first few days before Wright confessed? Even as they were bringing in cadaver dogs and calling off the search and rescue crew, replacing them with evidence recovery teams. How many times had she dared to whisper secret hopes in the darkness, muffling them with her pillow, her tears?

"There's no such thing as hope." She practically spit out the words. "Just tell me where Josh is, take me to him." She was begging now, but she didn't care.

Sam pulled her close again, but this time she held herself rigid, an immovable object within his embrace. "Where. Is. My. Son!"

He relaxed his grip and she pulled away from him as if he were toxic. "Promise me you'll listen to everything I have to say." He gazed up at her, his eyes wide with pleading. "Please, Sarah."

She rolled off his lap and onto her knees. "Tell me what I need to know."

He exhaled, his breath a shaky sigh, and rubbed at his right side. "I'll tell you everything. Then," he reached for her hand, but she snatched it away, "you can decide what to do."

His voice was trembling; his entire body shook. She wanted nothing more than to pull him into her arms and offer comfort. Instead, she fisted her hands, held them rigidly at her sides, denying him anything. A single tear slid down his cheek.

"You'll have to decide. I don't know what's right or wrong anymore. It's all up to you, Sarah."

JD hated this feeling. His body tingled with the urge—no, the need—to touch Julia, his mouth was dry, and every time he tried to say anything it came out totally lame.

They sat together on the blanket, watching for the mysterious lights, their jean-clad legs touching. She was so casual, sometimes leaning toward him, brushing his skin with her hair, touching him to emphasize a point as they talked about home, their parents with their hopeless, retro ways, school, their dreams.

God, what was he doing wrong here? He couldn't stop rubbing his sweaty palms along his pant legs when his fingers were itching to stroke her creamy, smooth skin. He wished it were colder so he could wrap his arms around her.

But the night was warm enough that Julia's jean jacket was plenty. They sat in silence for a few minutes, JD thinking of the way the guys would laugh at him not even able to make it to first base, when she turned to him, her neck arched back, exposing a lovely expanse of skin just waiting for him to—do what? Kiss her? What if he did it wrong? Or touch her—an image of her convulsing in laughter at his incompetent fumbling made him yank back the tentative hand he'd stretched out toward her.

It wasn't like this in the movies. Or to hear the guys talk in the locker room. Why couldn't he just be normal? Know what he was supposed to do with a girl?

"Why is this so important to you?" Julia's voice slid through the silence like warm maple syrup, calming his jitters. "It's got to be more than just a chance to win that internship if you're giving up your entire summer. And why the lights? Why not make a film about something easier?"

He slid his gaze up to meet hers and sat up straight. She stared at him with such an earnest expression—like she really cared, like what he said made a difference. To her.

His heart revved up and he licked his lips twice before

he was able to answer. He needed to tell her the truth, not the lies he'd told everyone else. "I wanted to figure out what was going on with the lights because," he looked away, certain that he was probably making a fool out of himself, "I needed to make up for what happened two years ago. See, it was because of me that that guy Damian Wright got away."

CHAPTER TWENTY-EIGHT

Most of the people aboard United flight 803 from LAX to JFK slept. Not Grigor Korsakov. He'd had more than enough time to sleep during the past seven years. He wasn't about to waste another second in dreamland.

Not when he was about to make all his dreams come true.

"You know what really kills people in prison, Dawson?" he asked the gray-suited lawyer beside him, a baby-sitter his uncle had sent. As if even his own family no longer trusted Grigor to play by the rules.

Dawson didn't bother to cover his yawn as he pried his bleary eyes open and focused on Grigor. "Fights?"

"No. Boredom. Sheer boredom."

"Sure. Boredom starts the fights." Typical lawyer, Dawson always had to have the last word.

Korsakov looked out his window into a black emptiness. "Know how I fought the boredom?"

"Directing plays for the prison drama society?" There was no mistaking Dawson's tone of disgust. Evidently, word of Grigor's "entertainments" had made it back to the family.

Even those diversions had grown weary after a while. Nothing to compare with the dramas played out in his mind. Intimate explorations of the human psyche. All starring Stan Diamontes.

Grigor almost wet his pants when Logan told him Stan had a wife and kid. Too bad Stan and the kid were dead. But that still left the wife . . .

His palm grew sweaty as it clenched the armrest. A small noise caught in his throat.

"Grigor, you know what your uncle said. The family doesn't want any more trouble or," Dawson's tone grew sharp, "embarrassment."

"If my father was still alive—"

"Your father's dead; your uncle is in charge now. And he considers you a liability."

"No one felt that way when I was making them money."

"They lost all that money and more when they had to close down operations after your arrest. Business is going well now and your uncle doesn't want anything to jeopardize that."

Grigor slit his eyes, glancing at the lawyer with disdain. He was an artist stranded among money-grubbing pagans. They'd never understood that—no one did.

"Now, what's this town you wanted to buy property in?"

Grigor's smile bared his teeth. "Hopewell? It's up in the mountains. Very peaceful and quiet. I'm going to be able to do some of my best work there."

Julia looked at JD, her mouth open in surprise. JD hung his head, his face flushed with shame. He hadn't told anyone about what happened that day—and now here he was blurting it out to her of all people.

Smooth move, Casanova. Way to get the girl.

"Damian Wright?" she asked, her voice tight. "The guy who killed Mrs. Durandt's little boy?"

"And her husband. And those other kids after he left here." JD drew his knees up to his chest and hugged them. His body shook, but he refused to give in to his tears. Not in front of her. "It's all my fault."

To his surprise, Julia slid closer to him, wrapping her arms around him and pulling his head to rest on her shoulder. "No. JD, you can't think that. How could it possibly be your fault?"

JD's shoulders sagged with the weight of the burden he'd carried for two years. "I saw him. Damian Wright. I saw him that day. Me and Tommy Bowmaster were hanging out at the park, skateboarding, practicing some moves. Tommy fell and banged up his wrist, so he had to leave, but I stayed. I saw this guy, hanging around where the little kids play, taking pictures."

"You couldn't have known who he was or what he was going to do," she protested, defending JD better than he could himself.

"I saw him, Julia. I knew he was doing something creepy. I even saw the car he drove—a white Honda Accord. I watched him leave and I didn't tell anyone. Then he went and killed all those kids, but I could have stopped him. I should have stopped him."

She held him tight as his shoulders heaved with the effort not to break down and cry. "All I can think about is the faces of those kids—it could have been my little brother. The police came by my house a few days later, said Kenny had been in the pictures they found. That creep was taking pictures of my kid brother. What if he'd gone after Kenny? All because I was too lazy to stop him."

"You were only thirteen then; the police probably

wouldn't have listened to you anyway. Besides, what would you have done? Followed him on your skateboard?" Julia's voice was calm, soothing. The voice of reason he'd been searching for for two years.

"I don't know," he admitted. "In my dreams, I clobber him with my board, pin him down, hold him until Hal Waverly or one of his men can come. People cheer and give me a big medal." Not to mention kisses from beautiful girls.

"In my nightmares," he continued, determined to tell her the whole truth, "I watch him drive off and too late I realize Kenny's in the backseat, pounding on the window, trapped. And I run and I run and I can never catch them."

"But those are just dreams. They don't mean anything. In real life, there's no way you could have known he was getting ready to hurt anyone. He was just a creepy grown-up and you were glad to see him leave."

JD blew his breath out and relaxed in her embrace. She smelled so good—how did girls do that? Like fresh rain and vanilla. He raised his face, nuzzled her neck, drinking in her scent.

"So that's why you want to figure out what's making these lights? To make sure no one else gets hurt?" Julia's voice now held a trace of pride.

JD pulled away just far enough to look into her face, to confirm that she wasn't making fun of him. Far from it, she gazed at him with a wide smile accompanied by a look of admiration.

"Something like that," he mumbled, not sure what to make of this girl who didn't call him a fool like the rest of his world did.

"Wow. I mean, everyone else is just wondering about stuff like their music or clothes, stuff that means nothing, but you—wow. You think about what's really important. More than that, you're not afraid to take a chance, act on your ideas. JD, you're like a real hero."

Before JD's stunned brain could formulate an answer, Julia had her arms wrapped around his neck and her lips clamped over his, smothering him in a breathless embrace. She tasted as good as she smelled. He returned her kiss and dared to part his lips against hers, inviting her.

Julia responded eagerly and soon he couldn't remember why he'd been so nervous.

Sam watched as Sarah stared down at him. She'd changed. Lost weight, but somehow it didn't make her look skinny or weak. Rather it defined her muscles, made her look strong, capable of anything. He searched her face, saw the purple circles etched below her eyes, eyes that used to light up whenever they looked at him now narrowed with loathing.

As if the mere sight of him made her sick. "Don't look at me like that," he pleaded.

"Don't look at you?" Her voice took on a brittle edge, ready to splinter into a thousand pieces. "I don't even know who you are. I gave you six years of my life, I gave you a son—"

Her voice broke and so did something inside of him. It was as if a sliver of glass pierced his scar, stabbing and twisting in his gut, leaving wickedly sharp shards in its wake.

Sarah stood, head bowed, arms wide open in surrender—or defeat. Sam couldn't bear to look at her. That wasn't his wife, his Sarah. She never gave up. Never.

Moonlight reflected from her tearstained face, giving her a ghostly glow. She swiped at her eyes with the arm of her fleece jacket. But the tears didn't stop.

Pain spiraled into his heart, making it hard for him to breathe. He'd done this to save her, to save Josh, but his actions had killed the woman he loved. Or at least part of her. He pulled his knees to his chest and looked away.

"Tell me, Sam," she commanded, her voice a strangled whisper barely able to penetrate the empty night air between them. "Tell me everything."

He took a breath, surprised himself by not exploding with the pain that sliced through his body, then took another. Still alive. Couldn't get out of it that easily. That was Stan, always looking for the easy way out.

Not this time.

"My name's not Sam," he started, talking to the shadows before him.

"It's not—" Her exhalation of frustration circled through the clearing. "Then who the hell are you?"

"My real name is Stan Diamontes. I was—I am—a lot of things. I liked to surf. I liked to write songs. I picked up girls on the beach when the waves were slow. I didn't like to work, but my dad wouldn't pay for college unless I majored in something marketable, so I have a degree in accounting."

Her footsteps scuffed through the dirt as she spun around. "You're an accountant? You can't even balance our checkbook."

"I didn't say I enjoyed it. But actually I was—am— pretty good at it. Not the adding-machine bookkeeping stuff, but the computer stuff. Moving money around, making it work for you, hiding it." He almost smiled, remembering his "perfect" crime. A victimless crime since he replaced all the money he borrowed from Korsakov's accounts, just not the interest he earned from it.

Stupid, greedy fool. That was Stan. Ready to try anything for the adrenaline rush of an easy buck, he couldn't resist all those millions sitting around, waiting for his sticky fingers. Convinced himself it was fate, putting him that close to so much money. Fate that introduced him to a madman like Korsakov. An image of what Korsakov would do to Josh and Sarah swamped his vision. Fire lanced along his scar. Turning his head away, he took shallow breaths through his mouth, swallowing bile.

"So who did you make all this money work for?" Sarah asked, her voice closer now.

Sam swallowed once more before he could trust his voice. "A guy named Grigor Korsakov. He wanted to break into the film biz, bad. Was determined to be the next Tarantino. He had money, but he needed it—ah—legitimized before he could use it for his production company."

"Legitimized? You mean laundered. So this guy Korsakov, what was he really? A drug dealer?" She paced across the clearing, her head swinging, scanning the woods surrounding them, a caged animal searching for an escape.

Sam couldn't keep his eyes off her, watching as she regrouped. Her head was high now; there was no air of defeat around her. Instead she seemed to radiate a white-hot fury.

"Drugs, prostitutes, smuggling, gambling." He shrugged. "Any and all of the above."

With a sudden, quick movement, she spun in her tracks and came to a halt a few feet in front of him. Her glare blazed through him like a flash of lightning.

"You worked for a drug dealer and a pimp?"

"No. I worked for a guy whose family happens to be part of the Russian Mafia. They're the drug dealers and pimps. Although Korsakov is the most dangerous of the bunch. I didn't know it at first. By the time I did, it was too late. I was in too deep."

She leaned forward, impaling him with her gaze.

"Excuse me, but it seems you found a way to get in deeper. And to take your son and me down with you."

He flinched at her words. Not because of her sharp tone, a tone he'd never heard from her before, but because of the truth it carried. "It wasn't supposed to be like this."

"It? What it?"

"My life, you, Josh—none of it was meant to happen this way. I had a plan."

"You had a plan?" Her laughter was shrill, a hairbreadth away from hysteria. Sam watched her with concern. She stood rigid, hands curled into white-knuckled fists, her mouth tight with anger. "And just what was this grand plan of yours, *Stan*?"

He hated hearing his old name, hated even more the way she spit it out as if it had a bad taste. Hated that she of all people would ever know the truth about his life.

Kneading his side, fingers probing his scar as if seeking answers from an oracle, he tried to find the words to answer her.

"It all began eight years ago. I was twenty-seven and still living like a kid. No worries, no responsibilities, no plan—no need to plan. And then I watched a man die."

CHAPTER TWENTY-NINE

Sam couldn't sit still any longer. He stood and paced to the edge of the overhang. Moonlight glittered off the dark water of the reservoir nestled in the folds of the mountain. Below the dam, the lights of Hopewell twinkled like beacons surrounded by dark forest.

He gathered his strength and told his story. Speaking to the empty air before him was easier than facing Sarah. "Alan was my roommate in college. He was the ambitious one, made it through law school, worked in corporate law long enough to realize there were easier ways to make money than toadying to partners. He left to set up his own practice—with a very specialized clientele."

"Crooks?"

"Not all of them. More like independent financiers who weren't afraid to gamble if it meant a large return. Power brokers. Producers, agents—the men behind the scenes of Hollywood. He hired me to help skirt any tax issues. At first it was all legit. Questionable maybe, but nothing illegal. It was kind of fun, outwitting Uncle Sam at his own game, using his own rules against him. Then

Alan began to deal with people who liked to play with higher stakes. People with very large sums of money."

"People like your Russian." Sarah's disdain colored her voice.

"Yeah. People like Korsakov. I should have just walked away, but it was kind of . . . intoxicating. Seeing how far I could push the edge. And then, all the sudden I was over the edge and I didn't even know it." He turned to her; she had crossed to the center of the clearing, was closer than he'd expected. The moonlight danced around her and he wondered for a moment if this wasn't all some kind of dream.

Nightmare was more like it.

"When I realized what was going on, I was going to call the cops. But before I could, Korsakov invited me to his house for dinner. Feast, really. Like something out of a movie—caviar and champagne, truffles, vodka, a parade of beautiful women, gold platters. Then he took me to another room for dessert."

He fell silent and turned away once more, gagging as he remembered what that "dessert" had consisted of. The edge of the cliff was so close, he was half-tempted to step over, fly away—except the next stop was the dam five hundred feet below. He cleared his throat and gathered his courage. He had to tell her everything, prepare her for what had to happen next.

"There was a man waiting for us. He was tied to a chair, stripped naked. Bruised up, a wild look in his eyes, his voice hoarse from screaming. He kept asking us who we were, what we wanted, why him. I tried to run, but Korsakov's men held me in place, made me watch as Korsakov ignored the man's pleas for mercy and tortured him. He kept up a running commentary on the history of each technique, who invented it, modifications he'd made, the success rate."

Sarah made a choking noise from behind him. He felt his words tumble out, he was so eager to finish. "I begged Korsakov to stop. He demanded an oath of loyalty to him and I gave it to him. I would have done anything to stop the screaming—well, almost anything. He handed me a gun, told me to go ahead, shoot the poor bastard, put him out of his misery. Held my arm to steady my aim. Told me it was the only way to end the suffering, that I'd be doing the man a favor."

He had to stop, his teeth chattering too hard for the words to come out. He pulled his arms around him, goose bumps lined up along his arms. Then he felt her warmth as she added her arms to his, turning him into her embrace. He let her hold him until his shivering stopped.

"What happened?" she whispered.

He kept his face buried in her neck, refusing to release her. "I couldn't do it. I couldn't shoot him. So Korsakov took a plumber's torch and used it to burn out the guy's eyes. He must have hit an artery or something, because all this blood came gushing out and then he was dead."

His head ached with the memory of the awful silence that had descended over the room. A silence quickly shattered by Korsakov's laughter.

"I asked him who the man was, what he'd done to deserve such punishment. Korsakov told me he had no idea. The guy was someone they pulled off the street. Just to impress me with how seriously they took an oath of loyalty." His mouth was parched; he swallowed, but his throat was dry and scratchy. "So that's when I came up with my plan. I began collecting information about Korsakov's activities and building new identities for myself, here and in

Canada. When I had everything I needed, I went to the FBI. After Korsakov was convicted, they wanted to put me in witness protection, but I knew I'd be safer on my own, so I ran. Stan Diamontes, accountant to the mob and world-class snitch, became Sam Durandt, mediocre songwriter and insurance salesman hidden away in the Adirondacks."

"You never told me." She pulled away from him, her expression clouded. "You let me believe . . . You brought a child into this world, knowing someday we might all be in danger because of your past." Anger edged her voice once more. "Sam, how could you not tell me?"

"I wanted a new life, a new beginning. For us all. I was planning to tell you as soon as I had a new identity set up for you."

A frown wrinkled her forehead. "New identity? Why?"

"I knew sooner or later Korsakov would get out of jail, start looking for me. So I set up an escape route. New passport, place to live, driver's license, even medical card, work history. Meet Samuel Deschamps, Canadian citizen."

"Deschamps?"

"When Josh came, I set up an ID for him too. It's easy for a baby. I used to take him across the border while you were working. He's even had several checkups by a pediatrician in Canada. But, after 9/11, I couldn't get a new passport or anything for you—at least nothing good enough to risk your life on."

"So you planned this? You took Josh and ran, left me behind? Why? How? There was all that blood and Damian Wright confessed. Sam, what the hell happened?"

CHAPTER THIRTY

Caitlyn opened the first box of files, kicked her shoes off, and knelt on her chair to sort the papers into categories.

"I've found the evidence reports and crime scene photos," she told Hal, who stood behind her, sipping his coffee. She took a few swallows of her own. Bitter, needed more sugar. "See those blood smears? Those belong to Richland. Looks like he hit his head on that big rock, rolled around a bit."

"That's what you said happened to Wright. Then he dragged Sam's body away and took Josh. But if Richland was sent to kill Sam, why hide the body? And what did he do with Josh?" He slid into the seat beside her, reaching across her to raise one of the photos.

Caitlyn pursed her lips. "That's the big question, isn't it?" She glanced at him, his eyes bright as they met hers. "Maybe Richland didn't kill Josh? Maybe he and Sam are both still alive?"

"No." Hal dropped the crime scene photo. It skidded across the table, but he didn't retrieve it. "Sam wouldn't do that, not to Sarah. He'd never betray her like that, steal her son away. Besides, look at all that blood. It'd be a miracle for anyone to survive that. Not to mention having enough strength to kill a federal marshal and dispose of his body." He blew out his breath in a sigh of surrender. "No. Sam's dead. Has to be."

"You're right. Sam couldn't have moved Richland, not wounded and alone." She frowned, reaching for the photo, staring at it. It was a hell of a lot of blood, but it was also raining—could have been diluted. Still, there was no way, unless— "Maybe Sam had an accomplice?"

"Couldn't be Sarah. She was in Albany."

Quick to defend Sarah, she noted. And more than a bit prickly about it. "We've been looking at this like a crime of opportunity because we thought Wright did it. What if this was a well-thought-out, orchestrated plan and the only opportune part of it was Wright's arrival to act as fall guy?" She leaned back, sipped at her coffee, enjoying the rush of caffeine and the clarity it provided, cutting through her fatigue.

"I don't understand. You think someone planned to kill Sam and Josh, planned to hide their bodies, then frame Wright?"

"Murder One-oh-one—look to the family first."

He straightened, his jaw muscle spasming again. "I told you, Sarah had an ironclad alibi."

"Doesn't mean she couldn't have hired someone to do it for her. Maybe she hired Richland and an unknown partner to kill Sam and things got out of hand, the partner turning on Richland. Maybe Damian Wright was a lucky break, but it was Sarah who was behind Sam and Josh's murders."

"There are so many things wrong with that idea I don't even know where to start."

"Like what?" she challenged.

"Like why the hell would Sarah *want* to kill Sam? Not to mention her own son?"

For a moment Sam couldn't breathe. It was as if the darkness had entered his lungs, smothering him from the inside out. Surrendering to the flood of memories, he gazed around the clearing. His steps were jerky as he walked to the tree line and squatted, patting the ground.

"Here." The syllable sounded as shaky as the leaves rustling in the night breeze. "This is where it happened."

Sarah rushed to his side, joining him on the ground, her hands encircling his arm. He still trembled, but her touch released the constriction in his chest and he could breathe again. He had to tell her everything; he knew that. At least he wouldn't be reliving it alone.

"There was a man. I saw him taking pictures of the kids, spying. I told Hal about it; he told me he'd call the Feds, keep an eye on him." He shrugged. "I'm not sure what happened next, but somehow the wrong people caught wind of me and the next day a U.S. Marshal named Leo Richland came knocking, said I had to leave immediately.

"You were in Albany, so of course I said no, I couldn't. Then he drew his gun." He slapped his palm against the dirt at his feet, the memory of his helplessness surging through him. "That's when Josh came in, distracting Richland. I tackled him, yelled at Josh to run, run up to our safe place."

"Your safe place?" Her grip tightened painfully on his arm. Anger flooded her voice. Not much he could do about it except keep explaining.

"I was always worried something like this might happen, so Josh and I had a secret hiding spot up the trail a bit. I taught him to go there if anything ever happened— it's a cave stocked with supplies. Just in case."

"Just in case." The words came in a whisper tight with fury. "And you never thought to tell me?"

"I thought about it every second of every day," he protested. "But how could I ask you to accept the risks of a life like that? How could you ever love the man I was? The man I am," he added with regret. "Besides, it was the best way to keep you safe."

Her hands dropped and suddenly he felt light-years away from her. "Just tell me what happened."

"I knocked Richland down, scrambled out the door, figured I'd lose him in the woods. Or at least slow him down, take him in a different direction from Josh."

"Why didn't you go into town? Flag down help?"

"Who was I supposed to trust? I still have no idea how Richland found me. For all I know it could have been Hal who figured out I was Stan—remember, he wasn't exactly happy with me after the company refused to pay off Lily's policy."

"Hal would never—"

"Then who? Someone in the FBI? If Korsakov can buy a U.S. Marshal, he can buy anyone. I had no choice, couldn't trust anyone, so I did the best I could."

"You ran."

"Yeah. But Richland caught up with me here. Shot me." The scar on his side burned with the memory. He rubbed it, tried to silence it, but the pain spiraled into his gut, as vivid as the day it happened.

"The movies have it wrong," he continued, his gaze fixed on the small patch of earth that had almost become his grave. "You don't fly back or crumple to the ground. I didn't even hear the shot at first—it was like my brain was roaring, I couldn't hear anything. Then I felt this burning and I looked down and blood was everywhere."

Her hand covered his, gently tugged it away from his shirt. He sat on the cold ground and allowed her to pull his flannel aside, raise his T-shirt up. The scar tissue glistened an ugly pale silver in the moonlight, the heaped-up edges twining around his side like a viper. He flinched when she reached her hand to it, drew back from anticipated pain.

She traced the area with her fingers, ever so gentle. The area was wider than two widths of her palms. It had taken a skin graft to cover it. Sunken like a crater from the missing band of tissue, it was a misshapen hollow with the rigid muscles of his abdomen defining its boundaries.

"Here," she whispered. To his surprise, her touch soothed the angry burning.

"Yes. Once I got Josh to safety, I collapsed. Was in the hospital almost ten weeks—by the time I got to a doctor, it was infected. Took three surgeries to get it looking this good. I was in a coma for a lot of the time, delirious most of the rest. It was two months before I could walk farther than the bathroom without falling down."

She tilted her face up to meet his gaze, her palm lying flat over the center of the wound. "You're lucky to be alive."

"Luck had nothing to do with it. I had to stay alive. I was Josh's only hope. And yours."

CHAPTER THIRTY-ONE

Sarah snatched her hand away. She rocked up to her feet and looked down at the man sitting on the ground below her. Who was this man she had married and begun a family with? A stranger, a total stranger—yet somewhere inside him was the man she had loved, the man who risked his life to save his son.

But there was no denying he was also the man who had placed her and Josh in danger.

She backed up, anxious to have some breathing room. As the temperature plummeted, the mist the mountain was famous for swirled around her ankles. A cloud covered the moon, plunging them into near-total darkness. With a blink of an eye, Sam vanished.

Her throat tightened and she reached out a hand—her body wanted him back, wanted him near. Not just her body. Her heart.

Leaves rustled nearby and in the darkness the nocturnal stirrings of the forest seemed magnified. Moonlight filtered through the cloud as it passed and Sam's outline came slowly into focus. He remained where she had left him, staring up at her with eyes filled with sorrow and regret.

An owl called out its mournful dirge. Tears welled up behind her eyes. God, how she wanted to take him into her arms, run away with him, forgive him everything. Her heart told her to trust him, to have faith in the man she loved.

She blinked back her tears and held her ground. She'd been fooled before by her heart and its urgings. Never again.

"Richland shot you." The words dried her mouth out. She swallowed and started again. "What happened next?"

Sam climbed to his feet, stared at her a long moment before backing into the shadows, leaning against an oak trunk. "Richland came close, ready to shoot again. I tackled him—well, 'fell on top of him' would be more like it. We struggled and he hit his head on a rock, was knocked out. I grabbed his gun and headed up the mountain to where Josh was waiting." He tilted his head and smiled at her. "He's so much like you. Practical, no-nonsense. Helped me patch up my wound, never panicked. He thought it was an adventure."

The thought of Josh needing to cope with any of this made her stomach heave. She crossed her arms over her chest. "How'd you get over the border?"

"I kept a four-wheeler in the cave. We rode it over the mountain to Merrill where I had a storage locker. There I had all our paperwork, some cash, and a truck ready. Then it was just a question of not passing out before we made it across the border. My landlady found me the next day, burning up with a fever, delirious. The infection was so bad, eating away at the skin and muscles, that the doctors thought it was caused by a burn."

"Who watched over Josh?"

"Mrs. Beaucouer. My landlady. You'd like her. She's a grandmother four times over and loves Josh like he's one of her own." He shuffled his feet as she glared at him, waiting for him to answer her unspoken question.

He said nothing, so she asked it. "Why didn't you call me? Tell me? Let me know you were alive?"

"I did—I tried," he faltered, withdrawing deeper into the shadows. Tendrils of fog swirled between them, forming a ghostly barrier. "I tried calling, but Alan answered, so I hung up. Then when I got out of the hospital, I drove here to see what was going on." He paused. The wind whipped at Sarah's hair and she hugged herself in earnest, shivering. "I snuck up to the house. You and Alan were laughing, having dinner—candles and wine and everything."

Her head snapped up at his wounded tone. "That was November. We were celebrating the first day I was able to go back to work, to start my life again. Alan called it my return to the world."

"Anyway, I couldn't risk your letting Alan know the truth—he'd kill you."

"To hell with Alan. What about telling me the truth? Letting me know my son was still alive?"

"How could I with Alan all over you? He has your house bugged as well as your phone and computer."

"Wait, he what?" Her voice echoed through the fog. Then it hit her. Alan had fooled her just as Sam had. He was only using her to get to Sam. Stan.

Her mind buzzing, she tried to focus as Sam continued. "I went to your school once, was going to reach you there, but then I realized it wouldn't work. If you suddenly disappeared, Alan would immediately know it had something to do with me and he'd come looking. Worse, he might decide to tell the Russian, send his people after us.

"I kept coming back to check on you, I couldn't stay away. Until one night Alan almost spotted me. I realized by coming here I was endangering both you and Josh. A thousand times I thought about trying to get a message to you. But let's face it, Sarah, you're about the world's worst poker player. I couldn't risk Josh's life on that."

Her fingers curled into themselves as his frustration poured over her. He was right; she couldn't act her way out of the proverbial paper bag. If he had told her the truth there was no way she could have kept it hidden from Alan.

"If it was just the two of us," he went on, "I could have figured something out. But not with Josh in the mix. I just couldn't chance it. Then I heard Korsakov was getting out, so I didn't have a choice. We were out of time."

"And here you are, back in my life."

He stepped out from beneath the tree, his strides separating the mist between them. "Here I am." He opened his arms wide, palms up, in surrender. His voice was earnest, honest. "I'm still the man you loved. I'm still the man who loves you. I wish you'd believe me—give me that small comfort before you leave."

Sarah wanted to hate him, but she couldn't. Not after he'd risked everything to save Josh. She rushed forward into his arms, buried her head against his chest, holding him tight. "Before I leave? I'm not going anywhere without you. We need to go get Josh, get away from all this."

His sigh caught in his chest. He wrapped his arms around her and for a moment they stood there, bathed in moonlight and fog, together for the first time in two years. "Josh. No matter the cost, we have to protect him. You need to leave, go get him, and run as far as you can."

She shook her head, his fingers trailed through her hair, and tilted her head back to meet his gaze. "Alan said he would kill you."

"He'll keep me alive long enough to get his money."

"What money?"

"I told him I could get him Korsakov's money. A hundred million."

"Money?" She stepped back, fury simmering through her once again. "That's what this is all about, money? Is that why he came here, why he—" She froze at the thought of how she'd given Alan her trust, her friendship.

"He wanted the forty-two million I stole from Korsakov before I sent him to prison. It's in a Cayman Islands bank and Alan couldn't get to it without you."

"Me? What do I have to do with this?"

"Since I'm legally dead, you inherit it. Once you're dead, your husband—"

Sarah put her hand up to stop his words. Her pulse hammered against her temples and the swirling mist threatened to swallow her whole as her vision blurred. She blinked, drew in a breath of cool, crisp air.

"Sonofabitch!" She whirled, would have raced down the trail, hunted Alan like the animal he was, but Sam's fingers wrapped around her arm, held her in place. Her breath came in short gasps. He pulled her to him, his warmth waking her from her visions of vengeance. *Josh*. She had to get to Josh before any of this ugly mess could touch him.

"It's not Alan I'm worried about." Sam's words penetrated her haze. "It's Korsakov. He won't care about the money. He'll come for revenge. On me and everyone I love."

"So we need to make sure Korsakov never learns you're really alive."

He pressed his lips against hers. Her body responded. She wrapped her hands behind his neck, drawing him into her, devouring him, savoring his taste, his scent, his warmth.

How could she risk losing this again?

When they finally parted, she was shivering. Mist filled the clearing, insinuating its chilly fingers around her heart. When she was a kid they used to make up stories about the ghostly figures formed by the mist, stories about Indian princesses, heroic warriors, lovers betrayed.

Sam held her close, sharing his warmth, banishing the ghosts. At least the ones from her childhood memories. They had something far more dangerous to face here and now. "I left my truck up the mountain, at the Colonel's cabin. If you hurry, you'll be with Josh when he wakes up in the morning."

The thought of seeing the look on Josh's face when she woke him, the feeling of him filling her arms, lanced through her. She stepped out of Sam's embrace, her jaw tightening as she tried to puzzle a way through the labyrinth they had landed in. "What about Alan?"

"He's not getting anywhere near you. Ever again. You're going to leave. Now."

She snapped her head up, glared at him. As if he had any right to give her orders, or even suggestions, after what he'd done. "And you will? Do what?"

"I can't come with you. Once Alan tells him I'm alive, Korsakov won't stop until he hunts me down. There's only one way out of this."

"So you have a plan?"

He ignored the sarcasm in her voice. "I have a plan. It's so simple nothing can go wrong."

"Go on."

He pulled a gun from behind his back. It wasn't shiny like the one Alan had held earlier; this weapon was flat black, squared off, utilitarian. "I kill Alan, Korsakov, and anyone else who comes after me. While you take Josh and run."

Friday, June 22

CHAPTER THIRTY-TWO

Alan drove through town and down into Hopewell's newer—if you could call seventy-odd years being newer—neighborhood where his rented bungalow was situated. He'd chosen this house because of the privacy screen of evergreens on one side and a seven-foot-tall fence on the other. It also had an attached garage with no windows. He hadn't counted on enjoying the cozy jewel box of a house, furnishing it with Sarah's help until it was filled with comfortable, relaxing furniture totally unlike the chrome and leather and glass that in comparison made his L.A. apartment feel staged and vacant.

He left his car in the driveway. By now Logan's would be hidden in the garage. Sure enough, when he entered he found Logan lounging beside the fireplace, a glass of Alan's Johnnie Walker Blue in his hand.

"I've got a job for you," he told the former FBI agent. "Let's go."

Logan took a final sip of his whiskey and climbed to his feet. "What's the rush? Korsakov can't be here already."

"I need you to babysit Sarah."

"Ahhh . . . is the groom getting jitters? Don't tell me she said no."

Alan held the front door open, forcing a smile when what he really wanted to do was to slap the smirk off Logan's face. "I didn't have a chance to ask. Stan is back from the dead."

That got Logan's attention. The former FBI agent did a slow pivot, his eyes narrowed. "Son of a bitch. He must have killed Richland."

"Maybe. What I need now is for you to keep an eye on Sarah so he doesn't get a chance to talk to her or take her away."

Logan followed him through the darkness to his car. They began driving back up the mountain to Sarah's house. "Did Stan say what he did with Leo Richland? Where's his body? How'd he get the drop on him?"

"Your lazy-ass associate is no concern of mine. Except he owes me a hundred grand for my having to clean up after his mess."

"You realize that if Stan is still alive—"

"I know, I know. We're screwed if he tells Korsakov what really happened. That we knew where he was and about the money. Don't worry, I have a plan."

"Yeah, you always do. That's why it's taken us two years to get close to the money. Don't fuck it up now, Easton."

Alan stopped the car in front of Sarah's house and pivoted in his seat to stare at Logan. "Is that a threat? You have just as much to lose in this as I do, so shut up and let's finish the job your associate screwed up two years ago."

He left the car and slammed the door on whatever reply Logan made. Sarah's house was dark. *Good.* He'd fed her enough wine during dinner she should have been out for the night.

"What line are you giving her?" Logan asked as Alan opened the unlocked front door.

Alan paused. Weighing his options. He liked Sarah, liked his life here. But was all that worth giving up a hundred million? Or placing him in Korsakov's sights? He sighed. "I'm not. She's had her chance. You keep her here, out of sight, and off the phone, until I figure a way to get the money from Stan."

"Hope you're not planning to take off and leave me holding the bag. Because that would be a major, major miscalculation on your behalf, counselor."

"Can it." Alan paused outside Sarah's bedroom and listened. Nothing. He turned the knob and pushed the door open. Logan drew his gun. "Put that away," he whispered. "We need her alive."

Logan frowned but reholstered his weapon. Alan crept inside the dark room. The bedcovers were rumpled, drawn up over the pillows. Poor Sarah, must have had another one of her night terrors. Her flailing often activated the camera in here, to the point where he routinely ran out of storage space on its disk.

Alan froze as a floorboard creaked beneath his weight. The huddled mass on the bed didn't stir. He reached out and yanked back the quilt, ready to throw his weight on her if she resisted.

All he found was a pile of blankets.

"Where the hell is she, Easton?" Logan demanded, flicking the light switch on. The room was empty. Alan rushed into the bathroom. Empty as well.

"Search the house. We need to find her before Stan does."

"And what if we're too late? What if your bird has flown the coop?"

* * *

Hal and Caitlyn argued about Sarah's possible involvement in the deaths of her husband and son, finally agreeing to disagree as they waded through the boxes of paperwork and evidence. After several hours and two pots of coffee, Hal excused himself to use the restroom while Caitlyn hauled the box of phone records he'd left with her onto the table.

She finished her coffee as she sifted through the musty reams of paper. These were no good; they were the reports from the tips called into the hotline, not the actual records of Hal's departmental phone conversations.

She stifled a yawn, climbed to her feet, and refilled her coffee cup. The last two cups Hal had given her were black, but she missed the rush of the sugar, so she rummaged in his cupboard and found the dusty sugar bowl once more. This time she added twice as much as usual, the powdered sugar clumping as she spooned it into the mug. It still tasted bitter, so she stirred in one more spoonful.

Sipping at the sugar-dosed-caffeine concoction, she wandered into Hal's living room. More like "storage room." Stacks of boxes were arranged haphazardly on every free inch of floor space, creating a precarious maze between the TV and recliner and doorway. Marked with dates and the occasional hieroglyphic notation as to their contents, they stood higher than her waist.

She finished her coffee, set the cup on the small TV tray beside the recliner, and shuffled the dusty boxes, searching for anything that might contain the records of Hal's initial contact with the FBI. Her eyes began to water and a sneezing fit bent her double as her cell phone rang.

"Tierney," she answered with a sniff, trying to suppress another fit of sneezing.

"Hi, Caitlyn, it's Clemens." The lab tech's voice was

bright and cheery. Caitlyn peered at the cuckoo clock on the wall through bleary eyes. Didn't the man know it was one forty in the morning?

"What've you got for me, Clemens?"

"The guys tracked a number on that dump you wanted."

"Great. Who's it belong to?"

"Actually, Logan made two calls within five minutes of your leaving his office."

"Fine." Caitlyn hoisted a box and tilted it to peer at the one below. "Who to?"

"We used public databases, so we didn't like break the law or anything, so it might be admissible if you need it—"

"Clemens," Caitlyn snapped, her patience frayed. "Forget the legal bullshit. Who did Logan call?"

"Oh. Okay. The first call lasted two minutes and forty-one seconds and went to a Grigor Korsakov."

Caitlyn dropped the box, releasing a fresh wave of dust and triggering a new bout of sneezing. "Man, he worked fast. Korsakov just got released from prison today and already he has his own cell phone?"

"The contract is in his name, but the purchase party was a law firm in Los Angeles," Clemens supplied helpfully. "Do you need their contact info?"

"No, no thank you. Who was the second call to?" Caitlyn brushed the dust from her blouse and slacks. Her skin was itchy, crawling like little dust critters had burrowed under it, and her mouth was parched after her sneezing spells. Clemens said something, but his voice sounded sparkly and far away.

"Caitlyn, did you get that?" The tech's voice finally broke through to her.

She almost dropped the phone, she was so entranced by the dust motes dancing through the air, shimmering gold and silver and red, distracting her.

"Caitlyn?"

"Yeah, sorry. Bad connection." She scratched at her arm, transfixed by the bright colors of the dust specks surrounding her. Everything was so vibrant, vivid. Her head throbbed, but it wasn't a migraine—at least not like any migraine she'd ever had before. "What did you say?"

"I said the second call was to an attorney. Alan Easton. He's there in Hopewell."

"That's nice." *Easton.* She'd heard the name before, hadn't she? She spotted a box in the far corner of the room that had the date she was looking for on it. "Thanks, Clemens. Have a nice night."

She hung up and dropped her phone onto the nearest stack of boxes. Then she climbed over one wall of document boxes to reach the one she was interested in. She had to balance on another stack and lean over, her legs leaving the ground.

"I'm flying," she sang out to no one in particular just as she lost her balance and slipped forward.

A pair of strong hands grabbed her by the waist. "Where I come from, we call that falling," Hal said, pulling her back onto her feet. "What'cha doing down there, anyway?"

She leaned against another stack, almost toppling it, and he pivoted her around, plopping her into the recliner. He stood over her, his features hidden by the kitchen lights behind him, casting him into a tall, gangly shadow. The thin man. She covered her mouth, forcing back a laugh.

"Are you all right? Your face is all flushed," he said, bending down and smoothing his palm over her forehead. His hand rough, calloused against her skin, sent tingles of electricity through her. "You feel warm."

His voice came from far down a tunnel of bright light. She squinted up at him. What was he worried about?

"Never felt better," she told him, pushing herself back onto her feet. It was the truth. Energy surged through her veins. Caitlyn Tierney, superwoman.

A memory of her fall two years ago, the feeling of free fall, flying, tumbling through space, made her gut lurch. Maybe not so super—at least not the flying part. She closed her eyes, but that only made the feeling of vertigo feel worse, like Alice falling down the rabbit hole.

Alice in Wonderland. Aw hell, that explained it. She rubbed her temples, remembering what one of the neurologists at Hopkins had told her about migraines. Specifically a variant that caused sensory distortion, known as the Alice in Wonderland syndrome. He'd called it LSD without the hangover.

"Shit," she muttered, reaching for the coffee cup beside her, her throat parched.

Hal took the empty cup from her. "Caitlyn." His voice sounded echoey, like he stood across the Grand Canyon. "What did you put in this?"

"You really should use real sugar instead of that powdered stuff. It gets all clumpy."

He dipped his finger into the cup, emerging with a coating of coffee-stained sugar. He stared at it, eyes big, as if it was the center of the universe. Caitlyn pouted. She wanted to be the center of his universe. "No one's used that sugar in a long, long time."

She grabbed his hand and raised his finger to her mouth, her tongue licking at his flesh. A shock wave of desire surged through her. She released his hand and leaned forward until his face was inches away from hers.

He smelled of wintergreen—he'd brushed his teeth and used mouthwash while in the bathroom. In a trance, she stroked his smooth cheek. Shaved too. No wonder he was gone for so long.

"This for me?" she asked, sliding her fingers along his jawline.

"Yes, ma'am." He angled his face so that his cheek rested in the palm of her hand.

The touch of his flesh against hers was overwhelming. She wrapped her arms around his neck and drew his mouth down to meet hers. She could feel his heartbeat, the stir of his breath on her skin, his hands as they stroked her back, rustling the silk of her blouse. Every sensation was amplified, more vivid and arousing than anything she'd ever experienced before.

Damn, if this was a new kind of migraine, or even a sign that the scar tissue had broken down, that her brain was even now beginning to leak precious blood, well, all she could say was it wasn't a terrible way to go.

Hal dropped the empty cup onto the recliner, his hands now pressed flat against her back as his mouth devoured her. A small animal noise caught in her throat. She rubbed her body against the chiseled length of his, her hips arching against his pelvis. Ripples of pleasure turned into tidal waves as he began to unbutton her blouse.

"Just tear it," she cried out in a hoarse whisper, reaching her hands behind her to tangle with his in the fight to release her body from the silk. Her clothes, her skin, everything felt too tight; she wanted to burst free.

His teeth clenched together in a grimace as he tore the buttons loose and tugged the blouse away from her. Her bra soon followed and finally, she had her wish, his flesh pressed against hers, his rough palms exciting her even further. He lowered his mouth, trailing whispers down her neck to her breasts.

When he finally captured her, taking her into his mouth, Caitlyn cried out and arched back, her fingers digging into his arms, the only things holding her upright.

* * *

Sarah stared at the semiautomatic in Sam's hand and lost it. A shrill laugh escaped her, accompanied by tears of frustration and amazement.

"Give me that before you hurt someone." She grabbed the gun. "I couldn't even take you hunting with me and the Colonel. As soon as I sighted on a deer you'd start making enough noise to wake the dead."

He stared at her, lips tightening. He wasn't laughing. He reached a hand out, palm up, for the pistol. "A man can change in two years."

She refused to relinquish the gun, instead sliding it into the pocket of her fleece jacket. It looked like a Glock, the same kind Hal and his men used. Glocks had no manual safeties, making them treacherous weapons for amateurs like Sam.

"Not that much, Sam. No one can change that much. You're no killer." She slid her fingers across his jaw, felt it clench beneath her touch. He grabbed her hand, pulled it away.

"I may be a total fuckup," he said, the words emerging in a strangled whisper as his grip tightened around her fingers, "but I'm not going to screw up again. I'll do whatever it takes to protect you and Josh. To make sure you are safe."

"Good, then we're on the same page. Leave. Get Josh. Use your new identities to go some place where no one will ever find you. I'll find a way to join you later." It took every ounce of her willpower to force the words past her lips.

Josh . . . God, how could she sacrifice the chance to see him again? She had no choice. Sam had been Josh's whole world for two years. Josh may not even remember her. She couldn't put her son through the trauma of losing Sam. Even if it meant ripping her heart apart in the process.

"We'll meet." She bit her lip, trying to quiet the quivering in her voice. "We'll meet in Costa Rica."

She turned away from him, wrenching her hand from his grasp. She shoved both hands in her pockets before he could see how desperately she was shaking. Her hand brushed against the semiautomatic. "That will work. Costa Rica on the Fourth of July. In front of the American consulate."

She wasn't even sure if there was an American consulate in Costa Rica, but it sounded good. She curled her fingers around the pistol's grip, caressed its solid, lethal trigger.

Sam circled around her, shaking his head, coming to a stop within an arm's length. "No way. It won't work. Not now that Alan knows I'm alive. Give me the gun. You go get Josh, and I'll take care of everything."

Meaning he'd become a killer. Or die. Either way, she'd really lose him forever. "You'll take care of things. Like you did two years ago?"

He went rigid, a wounded look twisting his features. But Sarah didn't apologize for her words. They were the truth.

"I guess I deserved that," he said in a quiet tone that barely traveled the distance between them. "Sarah, you have to believe I did the best I could—"

"That's exactly what worries me, Sam." He flinched at her words. Sarah stepped closer, unable to control her anger. "Seems to me you've been screwing up your entire life. You'll never understand how you hurt me, what losing you and Josh did to me."

He looked down at the ground as if searching for answers in the tendrils of fog swirling around their feet. "I know what you went through. I read your journal."

Sarah stared at him, stunned. "You bastard. How—"

"Today, when I went into your house to leave you the message. Alan had it, was reading it, laughing at you. I couldn't stand it. After he left, I took it with me. Read it while I was waiting for you."

She opened and closed her mouth twice before she could force any words past the knot in her throat. "You had no right; those were my private thoughts."

"I should have found a way to come back sooner." His voice broke. A single tear slipped down his cheek. "I'm so sorry. I never knew about your trying to kill yourself, I mean I imagined, but you were always so strong, the one taking care of everyone else, I never dreamed . . ."

She raised a hand to silence him, then turned her back, hugging herself. The sharp outline of the gun dug into her belly. Anger, sorrow, fury, bitterness, fear—a cauldron of emotions whipped through her in a frenzy.

He stepped up to her, wrapping her in his arms. Part of her wanted to lunge away from his embrace, pummel him, make him feel a fraction of the pain she'd suffered these past two years.

Another part of her responded instinctively to his touch, wanted to curl up into his arms and never leave again. She indulged herself with a deep breath, reveling in his presence.

Then she pulled away. "If Alan wants this money for himself, he wouldn't risk it by telling Korsakov, would he? So all we need to do is make sure Alan doesn't tell anyone, right?"

He raised his fists to knuckle his temples. Sarah felt a fluttering behind her eyes. How many times had she seen him do that when a lyric frustrated him? Strange emotions stampeded through her, overwhelming her.

Sam looked up at her, his eyes wide and filled with confusion that mirrored her own. His lower lip quivered, just like Josh's did when he was trying to be brave. "I don't know. I guess. But we can't take the chance. It's *me* they're looking for. You go get Josh."

She paced the clearing once more, searching for answers in the shadows that flickered in the moonlight and mist. It would be so easy to do as he asked, to run, be with Josh—and so very hard. She would never see her family again, would never be sure she and Josh were totally safe. Always looking over her shoulder, no one to trust . . .

That was no life. And Sam—she had no doubt he intended to sacrifice himself for her and Josh, but who knew if that would be enough? Who knew if he'd actually be able to do what needed to be done to save them? She'd trusted him once. Could she risk trusting him again?

"No." The single syllable echoed through the darkness like a bullet. "No. There must be another way. We'll go to Hal. He can arrest Alan, call the—"

"No. This all started when I went to Hal in the first place. We can't trust him or the Feds. We have no idea who is working for Korsakov."

She frowned. She'd known Hal most of her life. Had always trusted him. She remembered how strangely he'd acted after she found Leo Richland's body. Upset. Angry. But not surprised. Shouldn't he have been surprised? Asking questions? Instead, it was almost as if he expected it.

Damn. Sam's paranoia was contagious. But he was right. With Josh's life on the line, they couldn't take any chances.

"Okay. Not Hal. What about my dad?" She immediately regretted her words. No way did she want to get the Colonel caught up in this madness.

"Sarah, we can't risk it. Just give me back my gun and go before it's too late."

The sharp crack of a twig snapping ripped through the

night. Sarah whirled. "Someone's coming. Get out of here," she whispered to Sam.

He grabbed her by her waist and pulled her close, kissing her deeply. The footsteps grew closer, drowning out all the other night sounds. But even they faded as Sarah's body responded to Sam's touch. The kiss was brutally quick, but it reawakened feelings she thought long dead and buried.

"Go. Keep Josh safe. I love you." He darted from the shadows and into the clearing where the beam of a flashlight immediately impaled him.

Her chest was so tight she couldn't breathe, couldn't talk. All she could do was hang on to his gaze like a lifeline.

Another flashlight swept through the trees and stopped, aimed at Sam's heart.

"Stop right there or I'll shoot," a man's voice shouted.

CHAPTER THIRTY-THREE

Sarah shrank into the shadows, flanked by two mature hemlocks, her back pressed against an oak. Two men approached Sam. They kept their flashlights aimed so she couldn't see their faces at first. Sam stood, hands over his head, squinting into the light.

The first one rushed forward and kicked Sam's legs out from under him. Sam went down with a grunt. The man followed up with an elbow driven between Sam's shoulder blades. He held Sam down on the ground while the second man stepped closer and lowered his flashlight.

It was Alan. Sarah pressed back against the tree, her fleece jacket snagging on the bark. Alan held a gun on Sam while the first man searched his pockets, taking a cell phone and flashlight. Sam remained silent, his face pale in the light that danced over him.

"Where's Sarah?" Alan shouted at Sam.

Sam opened his eyes, a smile twisting his face. It wasn't any smile she'd ever seen from him before; it was the nasty, fooled-you smirk common to playground bullies. "She's long gone. Gone to get Josh. You're stuck with me."

Alan aimed a kick at Sam's ribs. "Sonofabitch. You'd better make it worth my while or I'll—"

"Got something," the first man interrupted. Alan lowered his light and Sarah got her first look at the other man's face. He looked familiar, but she couldn't quite place him. He was older, midfifties at least, and handled his gun and flashlight effortlessly. Like a professional.

She slid the semiautomatic from her pocket. If they moved away from Sam, she could get a clear shot at one of them.

She froze. What about the other? They both had their weapons aimed at Sam; they couldn't miss at that close range.

"What is it?" Alan asked, squinting over the other man's shoulder.

"A kid's picture." The first man held a small heart-shaped piece of material that he'd taken from Sam's pocket. Sarah had to hold herself back, she wanted so badly to catch a glimpse of Josh.

Sam squirmed. "Give that back. It's nothing to you."

Alan kicked him again. The first man tore the photo from the fabric backing. "School photographer's stamp is on the back. Can't make out the name, but the location is St. Doriat, Quebec."

Alan squatted, taking care not to smudge his slacks, and aimed the flashlight back at Sam's eyes. "You made a big mistake coming back here. Should have just cut your losses and run."

"Our deal's still good," Sam said. Sarah caught the undercurrent of desperation in his voice and was certain Alan did as well. "I get you Korsakov's money, you leave Sarah and Josh alone."

Alan and the other man exchanged glances. "Pick him up, Logan. Let's take him somewhere we can have a nice, long chat."

Logan. Sarah leaned forward, straining for another glimpse of the first man's face. Jack Logan, the FBI agent in charge of Sam and Josh's case.

She clamped her hand over her mouth to stifle her gasp. Sam was right; they couldn't trust the police—not if they'd been involved since the beginning. They couldn't trust anyone.

Which meant it was up to her.

Logan hoisted Sam to his feet, twisting one arm behind his back until Sam had no choice but to bend forward before the bone snapped. Logan marched Sam onto the trail leading down to the reservoir. Alan swept his light around, pivoting with his gun arm crossed over his opposite wrist as if he'd seen too many bad Steven Seagal movies. Then he followed the others.

When she could no longer see their lights reflecting from the fog, Sarah stepped free of her hiding place. She glanced at the path leading up the mountain, to Sam's truck and then to Josh. She stepped forward, following a low-riding trail of mist that beckoned her deeper into the woods.

The weight of Sam's gun pulled at her jacket, bouncing against her hip with her every movement. Alan and that man, Logan, they would kill Sam—or let the Russian, Korsakov, do it, torture him.

She stopped. The mist swirled around her, taunting her. She could go to Josh. Get him to safety.

Or she could save Sam.

Was there a way she could do both?

CHAPTER THIRTY-FOUR

Someone poked JD. Hard. In the ribs. He groaned and burrowed farther into the soft, warm pillow he rested his head on.

"JD. Wake up."

The urgency in Julia's voice jarred him awake. He was lying on her lap—until she pushed him off. He sat up, blinking. Damn, they had fallen asleep. His folks were going to kill him. He smiled, remembering how they'd occupied themselves earlier. She'd only let him kiss her, allowed the merest brush of his hand against her breast, nothing more, but it was still better than anything he'd ever imagined. "What time is it?"

"There's someone out there. Look." Julia placed her hands on both his shoulders, twisting him around so he could see lights emerging from the forest.

A parade of three men. One of them was bent over, being prodded along by another. They were too far for him to see their faces, but when they stopped at the cabin and a man turned on the light inside he saw the guns. Big guns, silhouetted by the stark light, aimed at the first man.

"What should we do?" Julia asked, her fingers clamped around his arm. She pulled herself up close to him. JD liked that she was asking him, trusting him to make the right decisions. He just wished he knew what to do.

"Call nine-one-one. I'm going to go get a closer look."

"No. Don't. What if they see you?"

JD swallowed hard, felt his heart flutter. Too late to back down now, he couldn't let Julia think he was scared or anything. "Don't worry. Nothing's going to happen."

It would have sounded a lot better if his voice hadn't had that squeak in it. He disentangled himself from Julia and belly crawled across the dew-laden grass separating their hiding place from the shed. He stopped, looked over his shoulder, saw Julia's face glowing blue from the light of her cell phone.

Nothing to worry about, all he had to do was keep an eye on things until Hal Waverly or one of his guys got there. Man, he'd forgotten his camera! *Damn, damn, damn!* That was all right; it was still going to be a hell of a story—most excitement this place had ever seen.

His nose itching from brushing against dandelions and wet grass, he finally reached the side of the shack. Inching his way up the cinder-block wall, he knelt at the base of the window.

The men were talking; he could almost but not quite make out their words. Not five feet away from him, the door opened, light spilling out onto the grass. One of the men, the skinny one, came out. JD flattened against the ground, hoping the shed's shadow and the gathering fog concealed him.

The man slammed the door and turned on his flashlight, blinding JD when JD tried to look at his face. He took off at a brisk pace, following the dirt path around to the other side of the shack and up to Lake Road.

JD covered his mouth with his hands, trying to slow and quiet his breathing. Christ, he'd never been so afraid in his life! His heart thudded so loud it drowned out all other noise. He forced himself to creep back up to the window, see if the prisoner was all right. He hadn't heard a gunshot, but . . .

He edged his eyes over the windowsill. The prisoner was Sam Durandt! He sat on the ground, facing JD, alive. How could that be? Sure, the guy had shaved his head and grown a beard, but it was Sam. Mrs. Durandt was going to be so happy. But what about the big guy with the bigger gun?

JD wished there was a way he could let Sam know everything was all right. Wished he could be certain everything would be all right. He lowered himself down, huddled with his back to the wall. He didn't have any weapons; if he tried to rush in, surprise the guy, it was for certain either he or Sam would get shot.

A hand grabbed his arm. He almost jumped out of his skin. He looked over. Julia. She shivered, goose bumps covering her exposed skin as she leaned across and placed her mouth next to his ear. "I called the police. They thought I was joking at first, but finally said they'd send someone."

Her words were so soft he barely caught them. He nodded his understanding. Somehow having her there, beside him, made him feel braver—but also more frightened. What if something happened to Julia because of him?

A man's laughter rattled the window above them. It didn't sound like a funny ha-ha kind of laugh. It sounded like the kind of laugh you heard in the movies right before Hannibal Lecter cut someone's heart out with a spoon and served it with a nice Chianti.

"What should we do?" Julia whispered, her breath stirring the small hairs on his neck.

JD wished like hell he knew.

* * *

Hal backed Caitlyn up against the doorjamb as they continued their dance of passion. She clawed at his shirt, as anxious to touch him as he was her. Intermittent, anonymous voices on the scanner were their audience, occasionally breaking their momentum.

At one point, he lurched up, pulling away, listening.

"What?" she murmured, her teeth gently tugging at his ear, drawing his attention back to her.

"Nothing. Sounds like some kids saw some more lights near the dam. Tucker can handle it."

She finally coaxed him free of his uniform shirt and started in on the T-shirt he wore below it, tantalizing him with her fingers as she drew it over his head. He grabbed it from her, wadded it in a ball, and aimed it at the counter where the scanner sat.

Their lips collided once more. Caitlyn pushed him back a step, came up for air. "Well, this has been real nice, Chief," she said, her fingers twisting in his sparse chest hair, "but maybe we should retire to the comforts of your bed?"

Hal turned his head away from her, his gaze searching the shadows of the hallway beyond the kitchen. As if he were asking the ghost of his dead wife for permission.

"Here's fine," she reassured him, curling one leg around his hips, drawing him back to her.

She enjoyed the cascade of sensations that every touch, every sound, brought. Wished she could have had one of these Alice in Wonderland type of migraines before—there was no pain, just a surge of conflicting feelings. As if she were all-powerful, in charge of the universe but at the same time hopelessly spiraling out of control.

Her depth perception had returned to normal, but everything still seemed too bright, too vivid, colors so intense they burned her eyes. And touch—her skin was sensitive to the slightest brush; the heat of Hal's hands, the whisper of his tongue, had already brought her close to climax several times.

If this was her last night on the job, she sure as hell was going out with a bang. Caitlyn laughed out loud at her pun. Hal didn't notice. He was too busy working her belt free of her slacks.

Sarah scrambled down the path they'd herded Sam along at breakneck speed. She hadn't heard a shot, but that didn't mean Sam was still alive. She came to the edge of the grassy slope below the dam and stopped. Light from the caretaker's cabin cascaded onto the fog like a searchlight.

The cabin only had one window. She approached it quietly, the gun clenched in her hand. The grass was wet, slippery, the fog swirling in the breeze so thick it obscured the building only fifty feet away. She didn't really have a plan, but she couldn't let Sam die. How could she possibly face Josh again, knowing she could have saved his father? Everything Sam had done had been to save Josh; she couldn't let that all go to waste.

Even though she was still angry—no, furious—at Sam for taking Josh from her, it felt so right, so natural, to be back in his arms.

Crouching, she rounded the corner to the side of the shack with the window and door. And almost tripped over someone lying on the ground.

"Ayyy," came a cry that was quickly muffled. Sarah flattened against the wall, holding her breath as she waited to see if anyone inside had heard. A long minute passed and she slid down to crouch beside a boy and a girl.

"Julia, JD—what are you doing here?" she whispered.

JD removed his hand from where it covered Julia's

mouth and opened his own. Sarah held a palm up to stop him and gestured to them to follow her.

Just what she didn't need: two kids in the line of fire. They quietly moved back to the edge of the woods, far enough away that they could talk freely.

"Mrs. Durandt," JD began in a rush, "your husband, he's—"

"You saw Sam?"

He nodded as the words burbled out. "Yes. He's alive. Kind of beat-up. But he's in there." He jerked his head back at the cabin. "Two men—"

"One of them left," Julia put in. "We called the cops."

"They had guns."

Both teens stopped as they locked gazes on the gun in Sarah's hand. "It's all right," she was quick to reassure them. "Everything is going to be all right."

"But, Mrs. D, how did—"

"He was dead, everyone knew—"

Sarah was buffeted by their questions. Questions that she didn't have time for. "You called the police?"

"Yes, but I don't know if they believed me. Everyone knows JD and I have been following the mystery lights."

"Julia thinks the cops thought she was playing a gag, trying to get them to rush out here for my documentary or something. That was about twenty minutes ago and no one's shown up."

"You guys go home. Don't tell anyone about seeing Sam. It's important that no one knows he's alive." The words emerged in a raspy whisper, an echo of all those sleepless nights when she'd cried herself hoarse hoping that somehow Sam and Josh would come back to her.

Beware what you wish for. The gun felt heavy in her hand. Sam was right. The only way to keep Josh safe now that Alan and Logan knew where he was was to silence both men. Permanently.

"But Mrs. D—"

"No buts, Julia. This is really, really important. Do you understand?" The girl nodded her head. Sarah leveled her stare onto JD. He'd be the bigger problem; the boy was a born journalist, questioning everything. "How about you, JD? Can you keep a secret?"

He met her stare, then nodded solemnly. "Yes, ma'am. But will you be all right? That man in there, he still has a gun."

"Don't worry. I'll be fine."

"Still, we're not going anywhere until we're sure you're safe." Julia wrapped her arm in JD's, standing firm with him.

"All right then, but wait here."

"Want me to call Chief Waverly?"

"No, I want you two to get the hell out of here."

Both jumped at her sharp tone, but Sarah didn't have time for apologies. She crept through the heavy layer of fog and returned to the cabin. She sidled up to the window and peered through it. Sam was lying on the ground, eyes closed. Was he dead?

Her heart stuttered. *No, please,* she prayed.

Logan leaned against a tool bench, legs stretched out before him, his gun ready. Sarah crouched down and crawled to the door, then stood again, her hand on the knob. She raised her gun. Now or never.

CHAPTER THIRTY-FIVE

Sam inhaled the wet fragrance of damp earth and fertilizer. The longer he played possum, the more time Sarah would have to escape. Once she was in the clear it wouldn't matter what happened to him. Nothing mattered except Sarah and Josh escaping.

He forced himself to ignore the pain in his shoulder and ribs and tried to melt into the packed-dirt floor as Logan approached.

"C'mon, I didn't hit you that hard." The FBI agent nudged him with his foot. "We have important things to discuss before Easton returns with the car."

Sam debated his options and slowly sat up. Logan lounged against the tool bench across the room from him, between Sam and the door. Fine by Sam, he wasn't looking for a way out, he was looking for a way to stop Logan and Alan before Korsakov found out he was still alive.

"What did you have in mind?" he asked, leaning back against the cinder-block wall, one hand knuckling his temple as he scoured the tiny space for possible weapons.

A rake and a shovel stood in the corner behind the

door. A few hand tools on the bench beside Logan. On Sam's side of the cabin there was nothing but bags of fertilizer stacked to the ceiling and an overturned galvanized-steel bucket. Not a whole lot to work with. He fantasized about throwing the bucket over Logan's head or blinding him with fertilizer, but in the cramped space there was no way Logan would miss him once he began shooting.

"Same as Alan. A way to the Russian's money and a scapegoat for when he finds it missing. Seems to me like you might be the key to both."

Sam thought about that. Alan had given him the impression Logan worked for him, but it seemed Logan had larger ambitions. "You've been in touch with Korsakov?"

"Let's just say that I like to cover my bets. Cut out the middleman. How hard is it to get to the money you hid for Korsakov?"

"Not very." Sam watched as Logan's eyes glittered in the light from the bare bulb overhead. "For someone who knows the pass codes. Like me."

Logan pursed his lips. "You stick with me and I'll let your kid and wife live."

"That's the same deal I made with Alan. Why should I trust you more than him?"

"Alan hired me to track you down two years ago. He didn't care if the kid or the missus got caught in the cross fire, just as long as he got his hands on the money."

Sam had already guessed as much, but it still made his gut twist to hear of his friend's betrayal. "You're the one who sent Richland to kill me?"

Logan shook his head, frowning as if he thought Sam was smarter than that. "Idiot wasn't supposed to kill you. He was supposed to grab you, take you somewhere private until we convinced you to give me the money."

"And then you would have killed me."

"Price of playing in the big leagues. You knew that when you decided to steal from the Russian to start with. So," he pursed his lips, regarding Sam with narrowed eyes, "how'd you do it? How did you kill Richland?"

Sam met the other man's gaze. "You won't believe me, but I didn't. When I left him, he was still alive."

"Don't get smart with me. I'm offering you a fair deal." He stalked over to where Sam sat on the floor. He raised the gun over his head, ready to strike at Sam. "Tell me what happened to Richland."

"Can't tell you what I don't know," Sam replied, his voice calm as he tightened his muscles, preparing to tackle Logan.

The door flew open, banging off the cinder-block wall. Logan's gun went off, the sound deafening in the tiny space. Sam flinched, then realized Logan had been aiming at the ceiling. The only casualty was a bag of fertilizer above his head, now spilling out a steady stream of brown powder.

"Drop it, Logan," Sarah shouted from her position in the doorway. Sam looked over at her in amazement. She held Richland's gun, weight balanced, arms steady as she aimed at Logan's chest. "Now!"

The FBI agent slowly turned to face his new threat. He kept the gun, his grip tight as he held it over his head. Sam climbed to his feet, ignoring the pins and needles that lanced through his leg. Logan still hadn't dropped his gun. Sam lunged forward, grabbing Logan in a choke hold.

Logan struggled, trying to aim at Sarah while clawing at Sam with his free hand. Sam held firm, slowly tightening his grip. "Give it up," he told Logan. "Stan Diamontes might have been an accountant, but Sam Deschamps works in a lumber mill, wrestling uncut timber all day."

Logan made a gurgling noise in reply. The gun clattered to the floor as he turned a dark shade of red and crumpled in Sam's grasp. Sarah rushed forward, grabbing the gun, never losing her aim as Sam slowly lowered the other man to the ground.

"Stand back," Sarah said, her voice low and deadly.

"No. Get me that twine," Sam said. She reached for the ball of twine and tossed it to him, her eyes still on Logan. *You'd think she'd done this a million times*, Sam thought as he quickly tied Logan's hands behind him. Only after Logan was restrained did Sarah relax her guard.

"I thought you were going to get Josh," Sam said, standing once more.

"Right." The bitterness and anger in her voice made him take a step back. "Like I could tell my son his father was dead, after everything Josh has been through." She gave a small shake of her head, her eyes tightening, revealing worry lines that hadn't been there two years ago. "Damn you, Sam. I hate that you've forced me into this. That you brought Josh into it. What the hell are we going to do?"

Caitlyn was about ready to explode with frustration. Every nerve in her body screamed for release, yet Hal persisted in slowly torturing her with pleasure. She'd never before met a man who liked to take his time so much. Part of her wondered if he was avoiding actual sex out of some misguided loyalty to his wife. It was certainly obvious she was the first woman he'd been intimate with since Lily's death.

They had made it as far as the kitchen table. She lay on her back, writhing, ignoring the cold steel of the dismantled Glock digging into her shoulder. Hal was peeling her out of her slacks, his tongue teasing the skin around her belly button.

A squawking noise burst through the room as both his

radio and the scanner erupted with a high-pitched alert. "Dispatch to Hopewell One, do you copy?"

Her fingers fisted in his hair, encouraging him to finish what he'd started. "Don't stop," she urged. He paused, then began stroking her once more, his fingers moving in time with his tongue.

The dispatcher didn't give up so easily. "Chief, you there? We've a report of shots fired in your vicinity. Closest responder is twenty minutes out."

Hal scrambled to his feet, lunging for his radio as Caitlyn slid from the table and tugged her slacks back up.

"Waverly here," he said into the radio, turning the scanner off with his other hand. "What's the twenty?"

Caitlyn grabbed the uniform shirt draped on the chair beside her and slipped it on. She tossed Hal his own shirt. He snagged it one-handed, a frown creasing his face, listening to the dispatcher. She slid into her shoes as she reached for her bag and the special compartment where she carried her Glock.

She snapped her holster on her hip. Hal yanked his duty belt from the peg near the door. "I'll be there in five," he said, grabbing his cell phone and pager as she opened the door for him. Once he had his belt in place, she asked, "What's the story?"

"Probably nothing," he said, jumping into the GMC and starting it. She climbed into the passenger side. "Kids down near the dam saw some strange lights and called in that a shot had been fired."

He sped the SUV down his drive and spun out onto the dirt road, turning in the direction of town. As he steered with one hand, the other checking the equipment on his belt, he spared a glance at her. "Can I just say how damn sexy you looked back there? Gun on your hip, wearing my shirt and not much else, good God, I almost lost it then and there."

Caitlyn snorted a short laugh. Now she knew how to make him finish the job. The adrenaline rush of heading into action multiplied the desire still coursing through her. Hal effortlessly steered them onto another bumpy dirt road. His chiseled jaw, intense expression, even the twitching around his eye and white-knuckled grip on the steering wheel seemed to make him all the more desirable and ruggedly handsome.

Damn, this wasn't her. Almost having sex with a stranger. It was as if she were possessed, having an out-of-body experience. Had she actually been ready to jump him, right there in his kitchen when they should have been working? Impossible. Work always came first.

At least that's what her rational side said. The rest of her body and mind told it to take the night off.

Hal stopped the car. Fog enveloped them in an opaque mass that was claustrophobic. "No sense shooting each other in this pea soup," he drawled, reaching over to hand her a small LED flashlight. "There's a cabin about fifty yards straight ahead. Single door, single window."

"I'll clear it," she told him. "You know the terrain better, you secure the perimeter."

He chewed on his lower lip, considering. She could see he didn't like it, but with this blinding fog there was no other way. Not with only two people.

"Maybe we should wait for backup."

"The dispatcher said they were twenty minutes out," she argued. "Besides, the more people running around with guns in this," she gestured to the white cloud smothering them, "the more chance someone's going to get hurt."

He nodded, then surprised her by squeezing her hand.

"All right, but be careful out there. I've got big plans for you."

Caitlyn slid from her seat, leaving the car door open to avoid any sound. She took two steps forward and looked to her left, where Hal should be. He and the car had vanished, swallowed whole by the fog.

Blind leading the blind. She jogged forward toward the unseen cabin. Her feet found a smooth, well-worn path, so she followed it, alone in the whiteout. Then she froze. Voices carried through the night air, too faint for her to pinpoint their location.

She had no way to communicate with Hal. *Rookie mistake,* she chided herself. That's what rushing in got her. She held her gun at the ready and took one step, then another, toward the voices and presumably whoever had fired the shot.

Her palms were sweaty. Damn fog was so clammy it stuck to her like a second skin, coating her with drops of moisture. She alternated her grip on the Glock, wiping one hand on her shirt, then the other.

Her foot hit a concrete wall. Still blinded by swirls of mist, she reached out. There was a short stoop and, above it, a wooden door. She squinted, thankful her migraine had subsided and her vision was restored to normal. As she strained to decipher the murmuring voices beyond the door, the handle rattled.

Caitlyn jumped off the stoop and took up position on the blind side of the door. Her heartbeat pounded through her head, fueled by adrenaline.

She raised her gun and waited.

CHAPTER THIRTY-SIX

Sarah tried to reason with him. "Sam, get out of here. The police are on their way." One of them had to get Josh to safety. He wouldn't be safe now that Alan and Logan knew where he was.

"No. Not without you." She'd forgotten how damned stubborn he could be. He reached a hand out, palm up. "Give me the gun. I'll take care of him."

His lips were white and his hand trembled, but conviction filled his voice. She hesitated, ashamed she actually thought twice about pulling the trigger and silencing Logan herself. Different from rushing in, facing an armed man. This would be an execution.

Damian Wright's face filled her vision. "No. I'm not going to kill an unarmed man and you can't either. You know that as well as I do, Sam Durandt."

He looked up at the sound of his name. Well, *her* name for him, Sarah thought wryly. "It's not who you are," she continued. "I don't care what name you go by."

"You don't know me," he persisted, emphasizing with

his outstretched hand. "I can do it. I have to. To save you and Josh."

"Don't be an idiot," Logan said from his position on the floor between them. "You can't do it. That would make you as bad as Korsakov. Isn't that why you went through all this? To prove you're nothing like him, that you're not a killer."

"Shut up," Sam snapped. Sarah watched as he rubbed his hand along his side where his scar was.

"He's right, Sam." She laid a hand on his arm. His muscles bunched beneath her touch.

"Listen to the pretty lady. Besides, you need me. If you both want to get out of this alive, that is."

"And how do you intend to do that?" Sarah asked.

"Simple. Alan and I aren't your real problem. The Russian is. You let me go, get me the money, and I'll kill him for you. No fuss, no muss. You two ride into the sunset with little Josh and live happily ever after."

Sam frowned. "What about Alan?"

Logan shrugged as if Alan were of no consequence. "No problem. I'll take care of him for free."

Sarah tightened her fingers around Sam's arm, trying to pull him back to reality. "Sam. We're talking about killing people here. Cold-blooded murder."

"Is it murder if they'd kill us without thinking twice?" he argued. "Or if they've already tried?"

The sound of tires crunching on gravel and the growl of an engine echoed through the night. Sarah glanced out the window, but it was obscured by droplets of mist and the impenetrable fog. All she could see were her and Sam's reflections. Hers clutched a large gun, more scared and worried than she ever remembered, while Sam looked absolutely desperate and lost.

Some pair they made.

"No time to bargain," Logan interrupted her thoughts. "Sam, you get out of here and meet me later today, take me to the money."

"Not here," Sam said, obviously not liking his bargain with the devil. "Up at the Colonel's cabin." He locked his fingers around Sarah's hand.

"No. She stays here," Logan ordered, an edge to his voice. "How else can I guarantee you'll hold up your side of the deal?"

Sam started forward, fists raised, but Sarah stepped between the two men, placing her hand flat on Sam's chest. "He's right. I need to stay." She whipped her head around to stare down at Logan. "To make sure he and Alan don't tell anyone where Josh is."

Logan nodded, a superior smirk forming on his face. She raised her gun, aiming it directly between his eyes. "Sam might not be able to kill a man in cold blood, Agent Logan. But don't you dare think you can gamble with my son's life. If you try to double-cross us, I will pull this trigger without hesitation."

The steel in her voice surprised even her. The Colonel would have been proud, but it made her ill to think of the possibility of being forced to end a life. Logan swallowed hard, the muscles edging his eyes tightening.

Then he nodded. "Deal."

"Go, Sam. Now."

He glared at Logan, shaking his head stubbornly, but finally relented. "Tonight," he promised her, planting a quick kiss on her forehead. He yanked the door open and raced out into the night.

Sarah hesitated, then ran after him. She needed to tell him—just in case—needed to say the words one last time.

He was already lost in the fog. Gone.

A rustling sounded beyond her. The beam of a flashlight danced through the mist.

"Drop the gun. Now!" A woman appeared beside her, a ghost conjured from the shadows and fog. When Sarah didn't immediately obey, the woman stepped closer, revealing a gun aimed at Sarah's chest. It was Caitlyn Tierney. Wearing one of Hal's khaki uniform shirts. "Drop it, Mrs. Durandt."

Sarah couldn't stall any longer. Hal Waverly emerged from the fog in front of her, his gun drawn as well. "Sarah, give me the gun."

Hal slowly walked toward her, approaching her from the side opposite from Caitlyn. Staying out of her line of fire, Sarah realized. Good God, did they actually think she might be dangerous?

She crouched down and placed Sam's gun on the damp earth, jerking back from it as if it were a viper. Hal stretched out with his leg and kicked it toward Caitlyn.

"Hold still, hands up," Caitlyn shouted, keeping her gun aimed at Sarah's heart.

Sarah jumped at her tone, then stood stock-still, her hand hovering in midair. Hal circled behind her and patted her down. She winced as he removed Logan's gun from her waistband. "I can explain all this."

"That'll be fine," he said. His voice was distant, held none of the warmth that she was used to from him. "But in the meantime, for everyone's safety, I'm going to put these handcuffs on you. You really shouldn't say anything more until you get a lawyer."

Sarah felt all the energy and fight drain from her. He tugged her arms behind her. Her throat went dry. There had to be a way out of this. She flinched at the bite of the cold steel handcuffs as they ratcheted around her wrists. Only then did Caitlyn relax her guard and come closer.

"Who else is with you?" Hal asked.

"No one. It's just me." She couldn't let them know about Sam. Had to buy him time any way she could.

Caitlyn stepped forward, peering around the edge of the doorway, her gun raised as she scanned the cabin. "Just you, huh?"

"Hi, Caitlyn," Logan called out in a cheerful voice. "You mind untying me, sweetheart? My arms are getting cramped."

CHAPTER THIRTY-SEVEN

Grigor parted company with the lawyer at JFK. He came very close to killing the man, sending his uncle a message, but he didn't have the time before his flight to do it right. An artist should never compromise. So Dawson left to take a limo into the city while Grigor headed toward the early shuttle to Albany.

"Good luck with your house hunting," Dawson said in lieu of a farewell.

Grigor hadn't bothered with an answer. He fidgeted throughout the short flight to Albany, enjoying the bucolic view from his window. He had no luggage; he didn't need any. Waiting for him in the terminal were two hulking men dressed in identical black suits and white shirts.

"Grigor," the first said, embracing him European style. "It is good to have you back with us."

"Thanks, Max. Were you able to get everything I require?"

"Yes. I believe you'll be pleased."

The second man remained silent. Alexi never spoke, but in Grigor's mind that was a plus. Both men were distant cousins from his mother's side and had joined in on his entertainments since they were teens cruising the seedier and more interesting neighborhoods of L.A.

They strolled out into the morning light where a black Chevy Tahoe waited. Alexi drove them ten miles out of town and pulled over at a vacant parking lot of a scenic overlook. Max took obvious pleasure in demonstrating the new toys they had collected for Grigor. He sprang out of the Tahoe after flipping a switch on the dash.

"Flashing lights, hidden behind the grille," he said. "Just like the police." He vaulted around to the back of the SUV and lowered the rear cargo door. From the hidden compartments surrounding the spare tire he pulled out a small arsenal, handing two .45-caliber semiautomatics to Alexi and taking one for himself. Then he unveiled a bundle wrapped in black silk. "Your favorite, Grigor. Walther PPK, just like James Bond. A complete set of surgical scalpels, German steel of course. And," he gestured with a flourish to the small golden object remaining, "voila."

Grigor frowned at first, handling the lightweight handgrip. Then he fired it up. A brilliant blue flame blazed from the end of the blowtorch. "Magnificent. Where did you find it?"

"Martha Stewart makes it. It's designed for cooks. So much nicer than the plumber's torch, yes?"

Grigor laughed, a gleeful noise that bubbled forth as he twirled the lightweight blowtorch like a holiday sparkler. "It's brilliant. Excellent work."

Max gave a small nod and Grigor could tell he was pleased by the praise. "What have you discovered about our target?"

"Everything," Max assured him as they resumed their positions in the Tahoe and continued north to the mountains. "Hopewell, New York. Population four hundred sixty-eight. Police department consists of three officers and a chief, only two vehicles. They do have a mutual aid pact with the county sheriff department. No fire department. No major highways, only a single county road leading in and out. Our target, Sarah Durandt, lives at Three-Twelve Lake Road and teaches English in the local middle school—"

Grigor pivoted in his seat, interrupting Max's litany. "Pictures. I need to see."

Another beaming smile from Max. "But of course." He opened his laptop and swiveled it to face Grigor. "Welcome to the Hopewell Chamber of Commerce website. The county sheriff has their own site as well. We have maps, building plans, satellite imagery. And for real-time data, we've spent the last few weeks installing cameras targeting our areas of interest. You have everything you need right here at your fingertips."

Grigor scanned the photos and reams of information scrolling down the screen. He despised computers; they were for peons like Diamontes to use, not an artist like himself. But now he saw perhaps there was something more to the machines and cyberspace. Nothing close to the level of artistic achievement he had attained, but poetic. In an ironic way.

"We have everything in place. Including," Max smirked at Alexi, "enough Semtex to destroy the dam above the town. The resulting flood will take out the only bridge and road connecting it to the rest of the world as well as the only cell tower. Once we cut off communication, the entire town of Hopewell is our playground."

Cold fire burned through Grigor's gut at the image of five hundred souls, huddled together for his enjoyment. His mother's father claimed a distant relationship to Stalin, had bounced Grigor on his knee, extolling the dictator's virtues and whispering tales of his "diversions." Ever since he was a child, Grigor had been fascinated by torture and mass murderers, had studied the masters back to the days of ancient Persia and Sparta.

Now he would surpass them all. Five hundred lives, his to command. His masterpiece—bigger, bolder than Picasso's *Guernica*. A living, breathing, bleeding testament to his genius.

"I want to see this place for myself. Then we'll pay Miss Sarah a visit. Get a look at the lovely lady up close and personal." He thought for a moment. Best to personally demonstrate the consequences of betrayal to his inside man. "Just one quick stop along the way."

"Since I only have the one holding cell," Hal said as he escorted Sarah inside the police department's cramped office, "I'm afraid I'll have to handcuff you to a chair. Until we get this all straightened out."

Sarah didn't argue; she was still too stunned by the turn of events. Josh and Sam alive, Alan a crook who wanted to kill her, Sam a crook who had other crooks trying to kill him, the FBI in on it all, maybe Hal as well, Sam lying to her, hiding her son from her, stealing two years of her life from her. Not to mention the biggest shock of all: the realization that Sam was the only one she could trust to save Josh.

Her body felt heavy and she was glad to sit in the chair Hal guided her to. Thank goodness he'd returned to his usual self after finding Logan. Hal seemed to assume Logan was to blame for this mess.

"Hey, that's not right," Logan protested as Caitlyn opened the door to the holding cell and motioned him inside. "I'm the victim here. She was holding the gun on me. If anyone gets locked up, it should be her, not me."

"Go on, Jack," Caitlyn said, giving him a small shove.

Logan dug in his heels. "C'mon, cut me some slack here, Caitlyn. I'm a federal agent, just like you."

"*Former* federal agent. Get in."

Hal finished restraining Sarah's left wrist to the chair arm and strode over to confront Logan. He stood, hands on his hips, leaning forward so that his face was mere inches from Logan's. "My house, my rules. If I want you locked up, you get locked up. Now!"

The last came out as a bark that made even Sarah jump.

Hal placed his hand on the small of Logan's back, and before Sarah could blink the former FBI agent was locked in the cell. Caitlyn crooked her finger at Logan, who thrust his hands through the bars and waited impatiently while she removed his cuffs.

"Terroristic threats, false imprisonment, assault," he said in a petulant tone, shaking his head at Caitlyn. "This isn't going to end well. You can kiss your career good-bye, Caitlyn."

Sarah was surprised to see Caitlyn grin at that. "Already have, Jack. Already have. Shut up while I talk with Mrs. Durandt, will you?"

"You're wasting time, Caitlyn. I'm the one you should be talking with. After you do, you'll be wishing you'd cooperated with me, shown me some respect."

Sarah ignored Logan as she watched Hal unclip his gun and lock it in his bottom desk drawer. He took the wallet he'd taken from Logan and quickly looked through it. Her heart did a flip-flop when he pulled out Josh's picture. Hal jerked his chin toward her, but he said nothing, merely pocketed it, leaving Logan's wallet on the desk in plain sight for Caitlyn to examine. Then he gave her a small nod.

She released the breath she'd been holding and mouthed the words, *Thank you.* Doubt and uncertainty twisted through her mind. Should she trust Hal? All he had to do was look at the back of the photo and he'd know where Josh was . . . She swallowed, her mouth parched by fear. What if Hal was working for Korsakov? How could she save Josh?

When Caitlyn joined them at the desk, Hal was thumbing through Logan's credentials. "He does have a permit for the HK. But not for the Glock."

Caitlyn cleared the magazine and rounds from both guns. Her hands floated effortlessly over the weapons, as if she could perform the maneuver in her sleep.

"Expensive," she said as she sighted down the Heckler & Koch's barrel, breaking every rule of gun safety by aiming it at Logan. "And it's been fired recently. Hope those insurance folks give you a nice severance package, because I don't think you'll be working much in the future, Jack."

"Caitlyn, we need to talk," Logan replied, exasperation coloring his tone.

"I'm all ears," Hal answered. Logan curled his lips in a frown and turned his back on the police officer. "Agent Tierney has no jurisdiction in this matter, so until you decide to speak with me, I'm afraid that cell will be your home."

"We'll see about that, you shit-kicking redneck," Logan muttered.

Hal's face flushed. He scooped Logan's gun and ammunition into an evidence bag. Caitlyn examined Richland's gun, frowning as she traced a fingernail along the bottom of the grip. "This one hasn't been fired, but it looks like government issue. I can have our guys at Quantico run it through the system."

Hal reached for the gun and took it from her, dropping it into a separate evidence bag. "It's four in the morning. It can wait."

Sarah saw the narrowed look Caitlyn shot him. Hal had turned around while he locked all the evidence in the small safe that sat behind his desk. "Matter of fact," he said, his back still to her, "why don't you head down the mountain to your motel, get some rest? We can straighten all this out by the light of day."

Caitlyn settled into the other chair, stretched her legs out before her. "Sorry. I never had a chance to check into a motel. You're stuck with me." She turned to Sarah. "So, Mrs. Durandt. Do you want to exercise your right to an attorney or would you like to clear this all up right here and now?"

"Don't say anything, Sarah," Logan called out. "Call Alan. He'll straighten this out."

Caitlyn swiveled to stare at him. "A minute ago you were calling her a desperate criminal who kidnapped you at gunpoint. Now you're helping her with her legal rights?"

Logan shrugged and smiled. "You know the Bureau's motto, Caitlyn. 'Truth, justice, and the American way.'"

"Bullshit. What in hell is going on here?"

Hal intervened. "Calm down, everyone. If Sarah wants a lawyer, she has every right to call one. And she deserves some privacy while she does. Agent Tierney, would you mind joining me out in the hallway?"

Sarah was grateful for his help, but the look of suspicion that settled onto Caitlyn's face made her nervous. Hal pushed the phone over to where she could reach it and tapped Caitlyn on the shoulder, nodding toward the door leading into the post office.

"We can't leave prisoners unattended," Caitlyn protested.

"They're not going anywhere. Besides, I'd like to have a word with you. Now."

Sarah hesitated, her hand on the phone receiver. Caitlyn stood, but her eyes were narrowed and her brow creased as she stalked from the room. Hal followed her and closed the door behind them.

"Alone at last," Logan sang out. "That police chief of yours is a real rube. He must have a soft spot for you, though. So, here's how we play this. You saw lights on in the cabin, found me there. When you saw the gun in my hand, you jumped me, took me by surprise, and tied me up. You were just getting ready to call the police when Chief Bozo and the girl-wonder showed up all hot and bothered."

Sarah listened, hating to lie to Hal, but accepting the necessity. The less Hal knew, the safer Josh and Sam would be. Logan's eyes glittered as he craned his head to look through the small window in the door Caitlyn and Hal had passed through.

"Your chief does have good taste, though. I tried for years to get Caitlyn in the sack and all I got for my troubles were threats of reporting me for harassment. I wonder if she was worth it. I'd expect her to be a ballbuster. Maybe that's why he's willing to serve her up now."

Logan's stare raked over Sarah. She felt dirty, clammy as if he'd had his hands on her. "Or do you two have something going? Has Chief Bozo been knocking on your door, comforting the poor widow lady?"

"Go to hell."

He laughed. "Just don't forget our deal. Call Alan, play it like Sam jumped me. You heard the gunshot, stumbled in on everything. Act all sweet and innocent. I'm sure you know the routine." He leered at her, one eyebrow arched. "Our favorite lawyer still has ideas about getting you in the sack, he'll forget everything else if you play along.

Promise him the world. Play to his male ego. Tell him you don't care about Sam. Tell him all you care about is getting your son back, you'll do anything if he helps you."

Sarah swallowed hard. She would do anything to get Josh back, but pretending she cared about Alan made her skin crawl. He'd see right through her, she was certain.

No. She'd have to get it right. She raised the receiver and dialed Alan's number. Sam and Josh's lives depended on it.

"What the hell is wrong with you?" Caitlyn wheeled on Hal as soon as the door shut behind him. "You can't leave prisoners unattended."

"Maybe you haven't noticed, Agent Tierney, but this isn't the FBI. You get me a budget that lets me do everything by the book and I'll be happy to. My only other option is to drive them down to the county lockup in Plattsburgh and I'm not ready to do that. In fact, I'm betting there won't even be any charges brought on all this."

He leaned against the wall beside the bulletin board with the Wanted posters as if this were a normal day's work. His face was relaxed, but she saw his hand working, opening and closing into a tight fist.

"You're betting on your friend, Sarah Durandt," she said. "Look, Hal. I like her too. But there's something going on here. And I think she's in on it, up to her pretty little eyeballs."

"I've known Sarah practically all her life. Trust me, she wasn't involved in what happened to Sam and Josh."

"What about Logan? I told you what I'd found at Quantico—"

"Which is why he's the one behind bars." He pushed off the wall and raised both hands, placing them on her shoulders, squeezing lightly. "You sure this isn't about what happened earlier? I'm sorry if I put you in a compromising position." He flicked the collar of her shirt, lowered his head, and kissed her. "It was worth it, Caitlyn. Every minute. It was a precious gift, and my only regret is that we don't have more time."

Caitlyn hated the way his touch made her blood surge, almost causing her to forget the reason why she'd come to Hopewell to start with. She turned her face away from his without returning his passion. He stepped back, arms spread wide in surrender.

"All right, if that's how it's going to be. But I meant every word of what I said."

"I'm more worried about what you're not saying. What's going on here, Hal?"

He hung his head, shaking it slightly. "I only wish I knew. But you have to trust me. Your heavy-handed FBI ways aren't going to work around here—just like they didn't two years ago. Leave it to me and I promise, I'll take care of everything."

She frowned, felt the pressure begin to build behind her eyes. Damn, she'd been pain free for hours and now she'd pay the price. If this headache was anywhere near as bad or disorienting as the last ones, then she would have no choice but to trust Hal to finish what she started.

Hal brushed his hand along her forehead, soothing the furrows there as if he could sense her headache as well. "Guess we gave Sarah enough time."

"You mean gave *them* enough time to get their stories straight."

He strode to the door, his boots clacking on the linoleum. She had no choice but to follow.

Sam stumbled through the fog, thoroughly lost. He was searching for the fork in the trail that would take him back to Sarah's, but instead found himself on the main trail leading to Lake Road.

"Sam, over here!" a strange voice called out his name, and he wondered if he was hallucinating. Then two figures walking bicycles appeared from the mist, beckoning to him. "This way!"

He wasn't sure if he should run and hide or trust them. Then he drew close enough to see who they were. "JD and—" He faltered, searching for the girl's name.

"Julia, Mr. Durandt. Julia Petrino." She held her hand out as if they were meeting in a receiving line.

He took it in both of his. "Julia, of course. You wrote that beautiful sonnet about the Indian princess and her Thundergod. Won the middle-school writing contest two years ago. My wife was very proud of you."

Even in the thinning fog he could see the blush creep over her face. "It's my favorite story, Ahweyoh flying into the air, so sure of their love that she knows her Thundergod will save her," she said with a shy smile.

Sam knew the legend well. "Sarah loves that story too."

He remembered the first time Sarah had told him about the two Indian lovers. The first time they had made love, on top of the mountain where it felt as if they had owned the world, that anything was possible. He had promised himself he would tell her the truth that night, but after falling under her spell he convinced himself that a woman like Sarah would never have fallen in love with a stupid, selfish idiot like Stan Diamontes.

Surrounded by her arms, comforted in the warm embrace of the mountain and the stars above them, he had decided that he was now a different man, a new man. And the next morning as the sun seduced the mountains with its golden glow he had risen and retrieved the last piece of Stan still remaining. A photo of him surfing after he'd chased the big waves to Oahu that he kept in his wallet. Until then, he'd thought that was the happiest day of his life.

Sam breathed life back into the fading embers of their campfire. He held the photo out to the dancing flames, watching as they licked its edges, turning from yellow to red to blue, before greedily devouring Stan's image. Small curlicues of ash had risen into the air, flying out over the gorge until they vanished.

Stan Diamontes was dead. And Sam Durandt had the rest of his life to look forward to.

After the photo finished burning he woke Sarah. The rising sun bathed her in streams of ruby and gold. They made love again and as they clung together, shivering in the morning breeze, tears had warmed Sam's face.

Sam choked back the memory and returned his focus to the two kids in front of him.

"Are you all right?" Julia asked.

Sam didn't trust his voice yet, so he merely nodded.

JD grabbed Sam by the arm, squeezing his biceps. "Wow," he said breathlessly. "What happened to you? Skinhead and all bulked up—were you in jail?"

Sam said nothing. What could he say? It didn't matter, because JD and Julia filled in all the gaps in conversation.

"Was it you causing all the lights? We've been following them for days; they've been spotted down by the dam and two spots up on the ridge."

"Near the Upper Falls and just past Hal Waverly's house. Where'd you go, Mr. D? Why'd you come back? Who were those men with the guns?"

"Do you need a doctor?" Julia asked.

"Yeah. Looks like they beat the crap out of you."

Sam had to admit he was limping a bit, and he was certain he'd cracked a rib. "No doctor, thanks." He stopped and turned to the two teens. "You two can't tell anyone you saw me or that I'm still alive."

JD waved him off. "Sure, we know that. Mrs. D said the same thing. I'm thinking those guys with the guns are holding your son for ransom. So what are they making you and Mrs. D do? Blow up the dam or something?"

"Are they terrorists? Al-Qaeda?" Julia asked breathlessly. Sam noted the way JD's arm wrapped around her waist protectively. Guess he didn't need to ask what these two were doing out all night while watching for their mysterious lights.

"They are very dangerous men, that's all you need to know. All right?"

They nodded in unison, their eyes wide with excitement. Good Lord, was he going to have to lock them up somewhere to keep them out of trouble? "Do you know what happened to my wife?"

"Hal Waverly and the FBI lady took her and the man to the police station."

Sam blew his breath out in exasperation. There was no way he could show his face anywhere near town. Now that both Alan and Logan knew where Josh was, he couldn't waste any time. "Do either of you have a cell phone?"

Julia pulled one from her pocket. "The reception up here isn't very good," she cautioned him.

He flipped it open and dialed Mrs. B's number. She answered after the second ring, her voice crackling with static. "It's me," he said. "Everything all right there?"

"Speak up, Sam. I can barely hear you."

"Josh, is he all right?" He was practically shouting, pacing up and down the path in search of a reliable signal.

"Up all night with one of his bad dreams, he just fell asleep a short while ago. Are you okay?"

"No. Things are," he darted a glance at the two teens,

eagerly listening to his side of the conversation, "more complicated than I thought. I need you to take Josh and leave. Go to that place I told you about. There's money in the lockbox."

"The motel outside of Montreal? I have to tell you, Sam, I don't like this. Not one bit. That boy needs his parents, both of them."

Sam raised his head, beseeching the heavens. The fog was lifting and the sky lightening, but he still was no closer to saving Sarah and Josh than he had been yesterday. If anything, he'd made things worse. "I know, I know. Please, Mrs. B, I need you to do this. I need you to keep Josh safe."

Her sigh was punctuated by static. "All right. We'll go this morning."

"Thank you. Tell him I love him—" The line went dead before he could finish. He stared at the phone for a moment, then flipped it shut.

Julia gave him a halfhearted smile. "Your boy, Josh, he's all right?"

"He is for now," Sam muttered, trying to think of a way out of this mess. His brain was fried with lack of sleep and every thought he had seemed fuzzy and out of focus. Mrs. B would keep Josh safe. All he had to do was save Sarah, and stop Alan, Logan, and Korsakov from going after her. A bitter laugh escaped him. Alone, unarmed, how was he going to stop three killers? "Could you guys keep an eye on Sarah? Call me on Julia's phone when she leaves the police station, let me know where she goes?"

JD's eyes went wide. "You mean tail her? Sure."

"You couldn't let anyone know what you're doing. Not even Chief Waverly. Don't try to talk to her. Just let me know where she is."

"My dad would kill me if I lost my phone," Julia said.

"I just want to borrow it," Sam reassured her. "Just for

today." He considered his options. "Can you get a message to the Colonel for me?"

"The Rockslide will be open in a little bit; he's probably already there. What do you want us to tell him?"

"Don't tell him it's from me. Ask him to come to," he thought for a moment, "the caretaker's cabin below the dam."

"That's no good," JD put in. "What if the cops come back to search it or something?"

"Or maybe the terrorists have been using it as a base of operations," Julia added. "You'd be walking into a trap."

"All right. You tell me where. I can't be seen in town."

They exchanged glances. "How about the clearing above the dam?" JD suggested. "You know, the one where—"

"The one where I almost died. Yeah, think I remember it." An expression of chagrin clouded JD's face and Sam regretted his harsh tone. "Good idea. Okay, the clearing above the dam after the lunch rush is done." He paused, knuckling his temple, trying to force a coherent thought into his frazzled brain. Much as he hated the damned thing, he felt naked without the gun. "Ask him to bring a gun—a pistol, not a rifle. Got it?"

"Sure thing, Mr. D." They swung onto their bikes, balancing as they turned to look at him. "You going to be all right until then?"

"We have some leftover sandwiches if you want them." Julia rummaged around in her backpack and handed over a brown paper bag.

Sam had to smile at their combination of youthful enthusiasm and heartwarming naivete. He'd just risen from the dead, been beaten up, had his wife and child threatened at gunpoint, and they thought a few bologna sandwiches would make everything all right.

"Thanks, kids. Don't let anyone hear you when you talk with the Colonel."

"Not even his wife?" JD said with a grin.

Sam rolled his eyes and both kids smiled. "Lordamighty. Especially not the Colonel's wife."

They pedaled down the trail. He began his lonely tramp through the woods and back to his hidey-hole of a cave. It was warm and dry and safe enough that he'd be able to catch a few hours of sleep before meeting the Colonel. To Sam that made it worth more than any five-star hotel.

He just wished he knew what the hell he was going to do afterward.

CHAPTER THIRTY-EIGHT

The sun was rising as Alan steered his Volvo onto the interstate. He headed south. A guy like him could find plenty of places to hide in a big city like New York. And plenty of opportunities.

It wasn't a setback, he'd told himself after almost running into the police when he'd returned to pick up Sam and Logan. No, rather an opportunity.

Because there was no way in hell Korsakov would let Sam or Logan live. Having seen the Russian when he worked himself into a frenzy, he wouldn't be surprised if Korsakov torched the entire town in retribution for Hopewell giving sanctuary to Sam all these years.

But Alan still had a chance. He'd hightailed it back to his house, tossed everything of value into the car, and headed off into the fog. Alive without a hundred million was better than being a dead man with it.

Still, all that money . . . The things he could do with it cascaded through his mind, torturing him with could-have-been scenarios. And Sarah. He was surprised how much he regretted not being able to take her with him.

The things the Russian would do to her . . . he shuddered, imagining her screams. She didn't deserve to die, not like that.

His cell phone rang, breaking his reverie. He looked at it in its perch on the dashboard and narrowed his eyes in suspicion. What if it was Korsakov? Or what if Logan rolled on him? The cops could track those phones.

It rang again. What if it was Sam? Maybe he'd gotten clear of the cops and still wanted to deal? After all, as far as he knew, Alan was on his way to Bumfuck, Quebec, right now, ready to kill his kid.

His hand hovered over the phone. The safest bet was to ignore it, toss it out the window, and buy a new one at the next Walmart. But one hundred million dollars, that was a helluva payoff. Least he deserved after spending two years setting this up.

He grabbed the phone and flipped it open. "Yeah."

"Alan?"

Christ, it was Sarah. Maybe he could save her after all. His foot eased on the accelerator. "Where are you, baby?" he asked. "I stopped by your place to check on you and you were gone. I was worried."

"I'm in jail. With your friend, Logan." Her voice was clipped, rushed. "At least he says he's your friend. Says you knew him back when he worked for the FBI."

"Logan?" What the fuck had gone wrong? How had Logan and Sarah ended up together, much less in jail? And where the hell was Sam? "What else has he told you? What happened?"

"It's a long story. I can't talk here. Not with him listening." Her voice dropped to a hush. "I don't trust him, Alan. I need your help. Can you come down to the station? Please?"

He couldn't resist a smile when he heard her pleading.

In two years, she had never asked anything of him, had always been the one taking care of everything herself. But now Miss Self-sufficiency needed him. In more ways than she could imagine.

He weighed the risk of Logan telling her everything—no, wouldn't happen. The former FBI agent had as much to lose in this as he did. And if they were both in jail, neither of them was going anywhere near the money anytime soon.

But Sam. They had to get to Sam before he emptied the accounts. Sarah was the best leverage he had. Then he and Sarah could escape together, leave Logan and Sam to the Russian.

There was an emergency vehicle turnaround ahead. He slowed the Volvo and pulled onto the gravel path that connected both sides of the interstate.

There was a long pause before she answered. Her breathing sounded panicked.

He stepped on the accelerator, now anxious to return to Hopewell.

"I'm scared, so much is going on. I can't trust anyone but you, Alan," she said. "Please, Alan. Please come and get me out of this."

"I'm on my way, sweetheart. Don't worry, I'll take care of everything."

Sarah hung up the phone feeling as if she needed a long, hot shower. Even then she might never feel clean again.

Sam had said Alan planned to kill her. She hugged herself with her free arm. To kill her after the marriage—after she shared his bed, vowed to love, honor, and cherish.

"What happened to my life?" she whispered.

Her only answer was Logan's cackle coming from behind her. She covered her face with her hand and rested her elbow on the edge of the desk.

Hal knocked and came in. "All done?" he asked in a too-bright voice.

Sarah raised her head and nodded. "Alan's coming. I don't know how long he'll be."

Caitlyn appeared behind Hal, hands on her hips in a defiant posture reminding Sarah of the first time she'd seen her two years ago. She and Hal had clashed then as well. Caitlyn remained at the door, standing apart from the rest.

Hal plopped down in his desk chair. "This is how we're going to work this. Mr. Logan, do you still want to press charges?"

"I'm not sure. I'm going to wait until the lawyer gets here and see what my options are."

"Uh-huh," Hal said as if expecting this. "In the meantime, as soon as the government offices are open at nine, I'll check out your permit and gun registration. If that's all clear, you'll be free to go."

"That's not for hours," Logan protested.

"I know. So, I'd suggest you get comfortable." Hal looked across his cluttered desk at Sarah. "You all right? I can move the cuffs, if you'd like."

She noticed that he didn't say "remove" the cuffs. Caitlyn tensed, watching. "I'm fine."

"All right, then." He settled back, propping his feet on the desk, and crossed his arms behind his head. "So we wait."

Sarah looked up as Caitlyn made a disgusted snort and left, banging the door behind her.

"Nicely done, Chief," Logan said, applauding. "Now you want to let me out of here?"

"Shut up," Hal snapped. He dropped his feet to the floor with a thump and came around to Sarah's chair. "Sarah, I've covered all I can for you. What the hell is going on?"

"Don't say a word, Sarah," Logan warned. "Not if you don't want to lose everything. Again."

Caitlyn turned on the lights to the post office section of the building and considered her options. She glanced back through the window into the police department. Hal was crouched down on the floor, head-to-head with Sarah Durandt.

There was definitely something fishy going on here. She wished she hadn't left her cell phone behind at Hal's house. Ahh, there was a phone jack right beside the computer on the service counter. Even better, there was a phone attached to it, cleverly hidden on a shelf behind the counter. Sitting on top of the thinnest municipal phone book Caitlyn had ever seen.

She'd written field reports that took more pages than the Clinton county directory. Within minutes she had Gerald Merton on the line.

"The bullet?" he asked, his voice groggy. "It's gone."

"I know," Caitlyn repeated for what felt like the tenth time. "I need the name and contact information on the officer who signed for it."

"No one signed for it."

"Sure they did. When the State Police came to collect the evidence and the body."

"They haven't. They won't—not until Chief Waverly calls them."

Her grip on the receiver tightened. "They haven't been called yet?"

"Nope. And I'd know because as county coroner I have to release the body to them."

"What happened to the bullet?"

"The chief's got it." He sounded exasperated, as if he were explaining the obvious. "He dug it out while you were on the phone. Took it with him. Guess you were so sick, he didn't want to bother you."

She could almost hear Merton's sneer through the phone. A junior Jack Logan in the making. "You're sure about that? The bullet isn't there?"

"Of course I'm sure. Saw him button it into his pocket, didn't I?"

She hung up and patted the breast pockets of Hal's shirt that she had appropriated. No, couldn't be that lucky. She'd grabbed one from a kitchen chair; he'd ended up with the same one he'd had on last night.

Caitlyn pursed her lips, glared at the closed door to the police office. She called Clemens. His voice was muffled and she could hear someone snoring in the background when he answered. The fiancée, no doubt.

"It's Caitlyn," she said, pacing as far as the phone cord would allow her. She couldn't sit still, felt as jittery as if she'd devoured a gallon of espresso. "I need another favor."

"Sure." His voice emerged in a sleep-choked rasp. He cleared his throat. "What do you need?"

"A trace on a gun's serial number." She dug out the scrap of paper she'd scrawled the Glock's registration onto before Hal whisked the gun out of sight. "How long will it take you?"

"A few days or so."

"Sooner would be better."

"I could put a rush on it if you have a priority case number."

She was silent. She should have contacted the nearest field office as soon as she suspected the body Sarah found might be Leo Richland. But she hadn't and now she was screwed until she had his identity confirmed.

"I take it you're still off the books," he said when she didn't answer. "On that camping trip up in the mountains."

"More like a fishing expedition. And I'm hooking some whoppers, just nothing concrete yet."

His sigh resonated over the phone line. "I'll get it as fast as I can."

"Thanks, Clemens."

"Just be careful. All right?"

"Always." She hung up. If Hal was stuck in the office waiting with his prisoners, it gave her a chance to go to his house—she needed to pick up her phone, of course. And maybe get a look at those files he'd distracted her from last night.

CHAPTER THIRTY-NINE

JD flew down Main Street, screeching to a halt in front of the Rockslide, feeling like James Bond. Julia pulled up alongside him, looking prettier than any Bond girl he'd ever seen—even Halle Berry in her skimpy bikini.

"What are you going to say?" she asked, her cheeks flushed with the wind and excitement.

"I'll tell him I need his help with the documentary."

"All right. I'll go check and see if Sarah is still at the police station."

JD leaned his bike against the lamppost and sauntered inside the café. Once he was out of Julia's sight, he wiped his palms on the legs of his jeans. *Even James Bond got nervous,* he thought. The trick was to never let 'em see you sweat.

"Hey, kid," his dad called from his usual place at the counter. "Come to have breakfast with your old man?"

JD nodded and smiled, taking a seat beside his dad. The Colonel was manning the grill, running his spatula through a mound of hash browns.

"You want the same as your dad?"

"Yes, please."

"How's the movie coming?" the Colonel asked. "You figure out where those lights come from yet?"

"Maybe." JD nodded his thanks as the Colonel poured him a glass of orange juice. He hadn't realized how dry his mouth was until he had finished it in three quick gulps.

"Don't encourage him," his dad put in between bites of sausage and French toast. "Kid's wasting his whole summer tramping through the woods when he could be making decent money working with me."

"Dad—"

"Don't you 'Dad' me. I told you—"

The Colonel raised an eyebrow and they both fell silent. "Seems to me that your dad and I wasted a lot of our summers tramping through these woods when we were kids. Didn't hurt us any."

"That was different. We didn't have big dreams of going to some fancy college. College costs money. Lots of it."

"I know what I'm doing, Dad," JD said, exasperated that these old guys just didn't get it. "I'll find the money. My way."

His dad threw his hands up in the air. "Your way. Running through the woods, chasing ghosts and thinking anyone would want to buy a movie of it."

"Excuse me, Dad. Ever hear of *The Blair Witch Project*? Anyway, I'm not trying to sell my movie. It's to help me get a job next summer. If I can get that internship Mrs. Durandt told me about—"

He stopped, suddenly remembering why he was there. Grown-ups, why couldn't they stay on track?

The Colonel set his plate down in front of him.

"Actually, that's why I came in this morning. Do you think you could spare a few hours this afternoon to help me out? No one knows these woods better than you do."

The Colonel actually smiled at the suggestion. Gee, maybe he should think about acting or something instead of journalism. "Of course I can. That all right with you, George?"

His dad speared a piece of French toast and dunked it into his coffee. "Sure, why not? Sooner the kid's finished with this crazy movie of his, sooner he'll be ready to see reality."

"Dad—"

George Dolan spun off his stool and threw a five-dollar bill on the countertop. "I've got to get to work."

He stalked out, his back rigid. The Colonel stared down at JD, making him feel like a cockroach under a microscope.

"I asked him for help first," JD muttered, his head hung low. "He said no."

"Yeah, well, you gotta remember he just wants what's best for you."

"Then why won't he ever listen to me?"

The Colonel laughed. "You figure that one out, you let me know. My kid's all grown up and she still never listens to me. Finish your breakfast. I'll meet you after lunch."

"Up in the clearing above the dam. At two?"

"Deal. Then tomorrow you help your dad out with his deliveries. Maybe he can knock off early and you guys can go fishing or something."

JD shoveled his food in. He was starving. Then he remembered the second part of Sam's request. How the heck was he going to get the Colonel to bring a gun with him?

Before he could think of anything, the door opened and a short man with a full head of dark hair entered. He didn't just walk in; he made an entrance as if he owned the place. With his black suit, black shirt, and ruby-red tie, he looked rich enough to plunk down enough cash on the counter to buy the café here and now. Hell, buy the whole damn town.

The Colonel straightened and approached the man, placing himself between the stranger and JD as if he sensed something wrong with the guy.

Was this one of the terrorists? The hash browns and sausage JD had devoured now threatened to come back up. A lump formed in his throat and he couldn't swallow, leaving him gulping.

"Can I help you?" the Colonel asked.

The stranger smiled. Perfect white teeth. He looked like he'd stepped out of a movie: James Cagney meets *Jaws*.

"I seem to be lost," he said with a deprecating shrug of one shoulder. "Can you tell me what town this is? I was following the road and it just," he shrugged again, but his eyes remained lasered on the Colonel's, "dead-ended here."

The Colonel laughed at that and seemed to relax. "People often miss the turn at the base of the mountain. This is the Village of Hopewell and you're right, the road stops here. Only one way in and one way out. Unless you're a mountain goat. Why don't you pull up a stool, have some breakfast before you head back down?"

"That sounds good." The man eased himself onto a stool at the end of the counter and perused a menu. His voice had a slight accent, one that JD couldn't place. He seemed in no rush. Didn't act like a terrorist, just another dumb, lost tourist from the city.

But those eyes, deader than a fish's left in the sun for too long. The stranger's glance slid over to examine JD, lingering longer than need be, taking in the sweat that had broken out on JD's brow, the quiver of his pulse along the sides of his neck, the sound of his heartbeat ratcheting into overdrive.

The guy opened his mouth in another one of those wide and blinding smiles and a horrifying thought struck JD. Had the terrorists already gotten Julia?

He bolted from his stool.

"Hey," the Colonel called out. JD froze, didn't turn for fear his eyes would betray him if he faced the stranger again. "Don't forget. Two o'clock."

"No, sir," JD stuttered. "Thank you, sir."

He ran out, banging the door behind him.

Caitlyn told herself she had every right to be inside Hal's house. After all, she was retrieving her property. And the door was unlocked. Still, the house seemed creepier than it had last night. No longer warm and welcoming, it vibrated with a hostile presence.

"Scared of ghosts, Tierney?" she chided herself as she walked through the main hallway to the living room. She grabbed her cell phone and pocketed it. Her blouse lay on the floor in a wrinkled heap, surrounded by small pearl buttons.

It had been one of her favorites, but she made no move to retrieve it. The cuckoo clock chimed the hour and she jumped. The house fell into eerie silence.

Not silence. An undercurrent radiated through the foundation, setting her teeth on edge. She detected a noise below the threshold of her hearing but loud enough to raise the hairs on the back of her neck.

"The waterfall." Talking aloud helped to dispel the gloom. "It's so close it makes the entire mountainside tremble. Imagine living with that all the time. You'd go crazy."

Satisfied she'd solved one mystery, she proceeded to

work on the next. She climbed over the boxes that stood between her and the one she wanted in the far corner. As she suspected, the departmental phone records were nestled inside, gathered in a logbook. She quickly flipped through it, searching for the days preceding Sam and Josh's murders.

And came up blank. The dates in question had been neatly razored out of the ledger.

She sat back on her haunches. Sometimes she hated when she was right. No one except Hal Waverly could have tampered with the phone records and expected to get away with it.

Had Logan bribed him? She reached for her cell phone.

"Clemens here." the lab tech sounded resigned, as if he knew it was her before he answered the phone.

"Me again." She ignored his tone. "Any hits on the gun registration?"

"Caitlyn, I just walked in the door."

"Right. Well, this one is easy. Got your computer on?"

"Yes."

"Run a quick financial on Hal Waverly, Hopewell's Chief of Police. If you need his Social and date of birth—"

"No, I have them. Aren't that many Hallenforth Waverlys in Hopewell, New York."

"Hallenforth? Really?" God, she'd almost slept with the guy and she didn't even know his real name. Maybe there was a lot she didn't know about Chief Waverly. She held the phone between her ear and shoulder as she restacked the boxes, leaving them just as she had found them. Except for the tampered logbook shoved into her bag.

"Got it," Clemens' voice broke into the silence. "What

did you want? Everything current looks clean. Except he must've gotten a major raise two months ago. He's depositing ten grand the first of each month."

She frowned at that. Hal said the town was broke. No way he'd have gotten a raise from them. So who the hell was paying him? And for what?

"Go back two years." She wove her way through the boxes, heading toward the front door. "To the time Sam Durandt was killed."

"Okay. Wow, you're right. The guy was in debt up to his eyeballs. Hospital and medical companies threatening to sue, bank ready to foreclose on the house, major-league problems."

"And?" She paused in the main hallway near the front door, waiting for his answer, even though the sinking feeling in her stomach told her she already knew what he would say.

"And it all vanished. Paid about one hundred thousand dollars in cash, cleared it all except the second mortgage and he's kept up with that."

"When did he pay the cash?"

"Two years ago, end of August. Good thing too. The bank was ready to seize his house September first. Made it in the nick of time, lucky guy."

"Luck had nothing to do with it. Thanks, Clemens."

"You're welcome. Hey, after all this is done, think you could help me apply to the academy? Don't get me wrong, I love working here in the lab, but I want to get out in the field like you do."

Caitlyn almost laughed. Tried to picture the lab tech out in the field where you never knew who you could trust. "Careful what you wish for. Call me with those results."

She hung up and stepped outside onto the porch. The sun was now high enough to cast a bright swath of brilliance on the yard and the drive but left the porch cloaked in shadows. She squared her shoulders and headed back to her car.

Time to get some answers.

CHAPTER FORTY

Sarah's mind spun in circles as the second hand on the clock over Hal's desk swept the minutes aside.

All she could think was that each passing minute brought Josh closer to safety and this nightmare closer to ending. Although she was beginning to doubt the ending would be a happy one. Logan would kill Sam once he got the money. If Alan didn't kill him first.

Not to mention the Russian.

She shuddered, remembering Sam's expression when he'd told her the horror story of how Korsakov tortured and killed a man for the sheer pleasure of it. She understood why he'd felt compelled to keep Josh safely hidden.

Finally she couldn't stand it any longer. She had to try something.

"I need to use the restroom."

Hal had been typing on his computer, the screen turned so neither Sarah nor Logan could see what he was working on. He could have been running a search for Josh in St. Doriat or looking up Logan's new employer or playing solitaire. Whatever he was doing, his expression never changed.

Sarah took that as a bad omen. Even worse, once he uncuffed her from the chair and escorted her to the public restroom in the other half of the building, out of earshot from Logan, he still treated her like a stranger.

"Want to tell me how a Canadian boy who looks just like Josh, only a few years older, ends up with his picture in Logan's pocket?" he ambushed her as she emerged from the restroom. He replaced the cuffs back on her wrists, although this time in front. Less of a threat, but still not trustworthy. "Tell me everything, Sarah. It's the only way I can help you."

She turned to him, placed both her hands on his arm as if depending on him for support. "Please. You have to let me go."

"Sarah. I want to help. I've been trying to help. But you need to be honest with me." An unfamiliar emotion choked his words, surprising her. "Is Josh alive?"

"Yes."

His breath escaped him so fast he fell back against the wall. "I thought, I was certain, how—Sam?"

"He's safe. For now. But there's a very bad man coming and he wants Sam dead. Please, Hal. You can't tell anyone Sam's alive. It's the only way to buy us enough time to get to Josh and save him." She didn't ask him to release her. It wouldn't do any good anyway. She couldn't run—not without risking Alan or Logan telling the Russian that Sam was alive.

He pressed Josh's picture into her hands. Sarah couldn't stop staring at it. Two years. He'd gotten so big. But those eyes. And that smile. They hadn't changed, not at all.

"I don't understand any of this. What happened?" Hal asked.

"The man whose body I found yesterday. His name is

Leo Richland. Logan sent him to kill Sam two years ago." She watched his face closely. No surprise. No emotion at all.

Had she just signed Sam's death warrant? Telling Hal he was still alive? No. Hal would never work for someone like the Russian. And if he was working with Logan, then Logan would have told him.

But his posture, so stiff, the way he wouldn't meet her eyes. There was something going on, something he wasn't telling her.

The door burst open and Alan breezed in, a smile creasing his face. "So what's all this about then?" he asked. He approached Sarah and clucked his tongue when he saw her handcuffs. "False imprisonment, Chief? Please, you know my client is innocent."

Hal shrugged. Whether at Sarah or Alan she wasn't sure. They followed Alan into the police side of the building, where Hal cuffed Sarah to the chair once again. He surprised her by whispering as he leaned over her, "Trust no one."

Did he mean Alan? Or Logan? Maybe he meant Caitlyn. After all, she'd been there right beside Logan when they supposedly investigated Sam and Josh's deaths. Before she could react Hal straightened and turned to Alan. "Want to hear what the charges are before you go making any decisions, counselor?"

Alan waved aside such technicalities. "Just give me a few minutes alone with my client and we'll have this all sorted out."

"He means me," Logan called from where he lounged across the cot in the holding cell. "I'm the innocent party in all this."

"It was your weapon that was discharged," Hal reminded him.

"Accident. I was startled. That's no crime."

"So you keep saying."

"They're both my clients," Alan stepped into the fray, radiating calm and competence. "If you just give me a minute, I'm sure I can have this all straightened out, Chief."

Hal leveled his gaze onto Alan. "I'm tired of this bullshit. You talk to your clients as long as you want. No one's going anywhere until I make sure Logan has a license to carry those guns and someone gives me a reasonable explanation. Understand?"

"Of course, Chief Waverly. Mind if we use the room?"

Hal rolled his eyes and shrugged his shoulders. So unlike Hal, breaking all the rules like this. Again, Sarah wondered if he knew more about what was really going on than she'd thought.

"I need some fresh air anyway. I'm leaving the door open, so don't get any stupid ideas." Hal bent down, unlocked his gun from his desk drawer, and walked outside, propping the door open on his way. A fresh breeze rushed in, stirring the papers on his desk and clearing the stuffy atmosphere.

Alan quickly turned Sarah's chair around to face Logan and scooted his own close to hers. "What the hell happened?"

Sarah listened as Logan spun the tale he'd prepared for the two of them. Alan narrowed his eyes at one point, then faced her head-on, his hands covering both of hers, squeezing them against the arms of her chair.

"Is this true? Sam was already gone when you got there?"

She nodded, forcing herself to meet his gaze.

"Sam tackled Logan and just ran away? He didn't try to find you or kill Logan or anything?"

She heard the disbelief in his voice and knew this was her only chance. "We'd argued. In the woods before you came. I told him I never wanted to see him again, that all I wanted was Josh. I made him promise he'd go get Josh, bring him to me."

Alan tilted his head, one eye squinting as if he saw the lies she'd woven between her truths. "Why didn't he just send you to Josh? He knows Korsakov is coming, why risk him finding you?"

"He did," Sarah stuttered. "He was. But you came and took him before he could tell me where Josh was."

"So you followed us down to the cabin?"

She nodded and looked down, not trusting her voice.

"You heard a gunshot and rushed in, found Logan lying there?"

She nodded again, found herself biting her lip, and forced herself to relax.

"Where was Sam?"

"It was foggy," Logan put in. "You couldn't see your hand in front of your face."

"I'm asking her," Alan said, his voice level but his hands squeezing her wrists so hard the bones ground together. "Sarah, where is Sam?"

That she could answer truthfully. She choked back a sob of pain and frustration and raised her head to meet his gaze. "I don't know."

Caitlyn was surprised to find Hal slouched against his SUV, watching the open door of the police station.

"Did they escape?" she asked, trying to keep her tone light.

He glanced over at her. God, he looked wrecked. Dark hollows had formed below his eyes, his lips were pinched, and a tremor shook one hand as he drummed it on the hood of the GMC. What happened to the vibrant man who had literally swept her off her feet last night?

Maybe that Alice in Wonderland migraine had clouded her judgment in more ways than one. Something sure as hell had.

"Alan's here," he said, jerking his chin at the open door.

She waited, but he didn't follow up with any explanation. "Alan?"

"Alan Easton. He came to town after you were here last time. Big-shot victims' right lawyer, tried to help Sarah get in to see Damian Wright so she could find out where Sam and Josh were buried."

She leaned against her still-warm car. A victims' rights lawyer out here in the middle of nowhere, helping Sarah interview the man who most likely did not kill her husband and child? This was getting stranger and stranger.

"Did you say Alan Easton?" she asked, her memory finally putting two and two together.

"Yeah. You heard of him?"

"Sure. He's supposed to be really good," Caitlyn lied. Really good at talking his way out of a grand jury indictment while simultaneously not adding to the evidence against his Russian boss, that was. "I'd love to meet him."

She strolled into the station, startling the three people huddled together near the holding cell. "Don't let me interrupt anything," she said, drawing on every ounce of southern charm she'd learned from her mother. She held her hand out to the stranger in the group. "You must be Alan Easton. It's nice to meet you."

The lawyer looked up in surprise, ready to expel her from his private client conference, but she beamed at him and his expression changed. He took her hand and rose to his feet. "And you are?"

"Supervisory Special Agent Caitlyn Tierney," she said, holding his hand a moment too long. "I used to work with Jack."

Easton nodded. "I recognize your name from the case files, Agent Tierney."

"It's 'Caitlyn,' please. I understand you actually interviewed Damian Wright?"

"Briefly. I was trying to convince him to meet with Sarah, give her some closure." He shook his head mournfully. "I'm afraid I failed."

"Still, I'd love to hear about it sometime. I mean," she smiled again, "you had a chance to see firsthand how the mind of a predator works. Any insight you could offer would be most valuable."

She felt Jack's BS meter rev up as he leaned his weight against the bars of the holding cell. She turned to him. "I'm sorry this is taking so long, Jack. I did call Quantico, asked them to expedite the records search." Now she favored him with a long, lingering glance, was rewarded when he relaxed and nodded. "Least I could do after giving you such a hard time earlier. You know how slow things can go in these small-town jurisdictions."

"Thanks, Caitlyn. I appreciate it."

"Now, Mrs. Durandt, it seems I owe you another apology." Caitlyn fished out her handcuff key and unsnapped the bracelet on Sarah's arm. "The gun they found you with was reported as being lost during the search for your husband and son two years ago. The deputy who dropped it is thankful you recovered it, but I'm afraid he'll be facing disciplinary action for being so careless."

"Wait a minute," Alan protested as she held a hand out to Sarah, helping her to her feet. "She needs to stay here. There's paperwork to sort out, I might file a cross-complaint—"

Caitlyn wrapped her arm around Sarah's waist and waved off Alan's objections. "Chief Waverly will help you with all that. But I have a favor to ask Mrs. Durandt. Do you think it would be possible for me to transport you home and make use of your shower? I'm in desperate need of a place to clean up."

She watched, holding her breath to see if Sarah would take the bait. Sarah's glance darted from Logan to Easton and back again. Ahh, it was Logan she was most afraid of. She'd have to see what hold he had over Sarah. She gave a gentle tug on Sarah's waist, aiming her toward the door.

"Sure, I guess," Sarah said, almost stumbling. "That would be fine. Ah, thank you."

"No, thank you."

Now came the hard part. Caitlyn kept her hand on Sarah's elbow as she escorted her out to the Subaru. Hal stepped forward when he saw them emerge from the station.

"What the hell you doing? That's my prisoner!"

"Not anymore," she said, opening Sarah's door and helping her into the car as if she were in custody. Caitlyn quickly jogged around to the other side of the car. "Federal jurisdiction. Sorry, Hal."

She started the car and spun out of the gravel parking lot before he could say anything. As she glanced in the rearview mirror she saw him standing gape mouthed, an expression of twisted anger and distrust on his face.

The man she'd been attracted to last night had totally vanished. Had he ever truly existed?

"Was that true?" Sarah asked. "What you said in there about the gun being lost?"

Caitlyn heard an undercurrent of hope in the woman's voice. "That gun was lost by a law enforcement officer, yes, ma'am. It's the truth."

Sarah's lips tightened and she crossed her arms over her chest as she sat back and considered Caitlyn's words.

"So the officer, he wasn't hurt?" she persisted.

Caitlyn twisted the wheel, turning onto Lake Road. Sarah obviously knew more than she'd let on, but not everything.

"I think he's down in Merrill right now," she answered truthfully. Only she left out the part about him being zipped up tight in a body bag.

CHAPTER FORTY-ONE

Despite her initial request and her true need for one, Caitlyn didn't actually take a shower once she reached Sarah's house. Instead she roamed the living area, Sarah watching nervously, and asked Sarah about each memory the photos on the mantle represented, where she'd found the antique railroad clock that chimed the hour, how her school year had gone . . . anything to keep the woman talking.

The one thing Caitlyn retained after her accident two years ago was her people-reading skill. But for some reason, ever since she'd arrived in Hopewell it had been on the fritz.

Sarah, the one person she'd thought innocent in this mess, was acting more guilty than ever. Shifting her posture, feet pointed toward the door, gaze hovering somewhere past Caitlyn's shoulder, not meeting her eyes.

Had could Caitlyn have been so blind?

And Hal. It was so obvious he was hiding something. Could he and Sarah be in this together?

Then where did Logan fit? Last night she had broached the possibility that Sam's death was a contract killing. An

Assistant Special Agent in Charge of the Federal Bureau of Investigation would never get their hands dirty with a simple killing for hire.

But they might send someone else to do their dirty work. Someone like a mediocre, low-level Deputy U.S. Marshal.

It would explain why Logan suddenly came down from his executive suite to take over her investigation of Damian Wright—he'd used it as a cover to come check on why Leo Richland went missing.

Had Damian Wright even been in Hopewell? If Hal and Sarah were in it together with Logan, they could have made it up, planted the photo card. No, Damian's reflection was on the photos of Josh.

"Oh, I love your kitchen," Caitlyn continued her mindless prattle, her focus on Sarah's reactions. "It's so bright and cheery." And, just like the living room, still filled with reminders of Josh and Sam. What mother could kill her son and live surrounded by his memory like this?

"The bathroom is right here." Sarah opened a door opposite the kitchen entrance. "Take your time." She ushered Caitlyn inside the bath, which was painted daffodil yellow and white just like the kitchen.

Caitlyn had no intention of taking her time. She cracked the door to keep an ear on Sarah as she quickly changed clothes, exchanging her more formal linen slacks and Hal's uniform shirt for jeans and a button-down top. As she changed she noticed bright colors behind the simple white cotton shower curtain.

She edged the curtain aside. Bright rainbow fish decals covered the inside of the tub along with two mesh hammocks filled to the brim with a child's tub toys.

Caitlyn touched one of the fish decals. Easily removed, as were the hammocks. Yet two years later they were here, clean and waiting for their young owner to return.

If Sarah had her husband and son killed, then who were the toys for? If she was guilty, had it sent her over the edge into some kind of psychotic breakdown? Maybe that explained her extreme mourning, her obsession with finding their graves. She wanted to undo the horrible thing she'd done.

Caitlyn gathered her stuff and shoved it back into her travel pack. No matter what theory she came up with, nothing felt right. She was missing something.

She emerged and heard the shower running in the master bath. Took the opportunity to take a quick look at Sarah's bedroom. Nothing except for a queen-sized bed obviously slept in by one person on one side. The side that was Sam's was plain to see—the notepad with half-written song lyrics and a jar of colored pens sat by the lamp. Waiting for him just like Josh's toys.

Caitlyn didn't risk the wooden steps up to the attic that Sarah had told her they'd converted into Josh's room, but she did go through Sam's office. Nothing there except evidence that Sarah was searching the mountain for something. Sam and Josh? Or Leo Richland?

Maybe she'd found exactly what she'd been looking for.

Caitlyn returned to the kitchen just in time to find Sarah, dressed in jeans and a long-sleeved T-shirt, hair still wet, cooking eggs. She still seemed nervous, but a bit calmer after her shower, as if she'd made a decision.

Or talked to someone. Maybe the shower had been a cover for a quick phone call out of Caitlyn's hearing?

The microwave dinged. Both women startled. Sarah turned away from the eggs to remove two mugs of steaming tea.

"This smells delicious," Caitlyn said, taking the mug from Sarah. "It doesn't smell like tea, but like," she sniffed, "I don't know, my grandmother's kitchen."

"It's called Good Earth. Supposed to be calming, soothing. The Colonel's wife brought it after . . ." Sarah gave a brittle laugh as she sipped from her own cup. Caitlyn looked up, caught a strange expression race over the other woman's face. Amusement mixed with anger.

"Thanks for letting me clean up here." She sipped the steaming tea while Sarah finished cooking the eggs. It tasted of cinnamon and spices. "Do you mind if I ask you a few questions about Chief Waverly?"

Sarah straightened, leaned against the counter, one hand holding a spatula. "Guess not, since that was his shirt you were wearing this morning. But shouldn't you be asking him?" She paused, giving Caitlyn a discerning look. "If you're that interested, I mean."

Last thing Caitlyn was about to explain was her interest in the police chief. Or how she came to be wearing his uniform shirt. Somehow Hal had played a role in Sarah's tragedy. She just wished she could figure out exactly what. "He said his wife died of cancer. Right before you lost your husband and son."

Sarah's spatula clanked against the cast-iron skillet as she stirred the eggs furiously. Finally she turned the burner off, scooped the eggs onto waiting plates, and brought them to the table. Her eyes were clear, but her lips were pinched. "I shouldn't say—it's none of my business—it couldn't be connected to Sam and Josh, but . . ."

Caitlyn waited. Sarah's words had rushed out in a single breath, then drifted away. The clock ticked, the refrigerator hummed, and a stray rose branch scratched against the window over the kitchen sink. Caitlyn dug into her eggs, surprised by how famished she was. Sarah played with hers but never took a bite. Finally, Sarah gave a small nod, as if giving herself permission to think unforgivable thoughts.

"Hal and I grew up here. Me since I was eight, he's lived here all his life. We've been friends forever. I should have seen it—"

"Seen what, Sarah? How did Hal's wife really die?"

Sarah abandoned her fork in her untouched eggs. "She drove up to the Upper Falls, stripped naked, and jumped."

Caitlyn pushed her mug aside and leaned forward, elbows on the table. "She killed herself? And Hal? Where was he?"

"He would have stopped her if he could. See, those last weeks, he was taking care of her full-time. Oh, the rest of us, we stopped in, brought him food, tried our best to help. But Lily, she was—" She gave a little shrug, her lips blanching as they pressed together. "Toward the end there, she wasn't the woman we knew. She was out of control from the pain. It was like she was possessed. Hal was the only one who could soothe her, keep her from hurting herself or someone else."

Caitlyn knew firsthand Hal's soothing touch. Wondered if she'd allowed his healing talents to cloud her judgment. "Couldn't the doctors?"

"Hal's insurance had long since run out. Besides, the doctors said the only hope was to give her enough morphine that she'd probably die from it. Hal couldn't bring himself to let them do that—even if he could afford to take her back to the hospital. They set up hospice workers to visit, but they just made Lily worse. She was out of her mind, said they were trying to kill her, to poison the entire town, that she was the only one who could save us."

"Save you from what?"

"Somehow she'd gotten convinced that the Indian legend of the Thundergods was true. In it an Indian maiden sacrifices herself by leaping into the falls and her Thundergod lover saves her."

"And thus saves the town?"

Sarah nodded, was silent for another long moment. "Hal's never forgiven himself for answering the call that night. He couldn't afford any more sick leave, the village had already given him an extension on his pay so he could keep the bank from foreclosing, so he tried his best to work from home. By that time, Lily would go crazy at the sight of anyone else, so we couldn't even really help.

"Some kids went skinny-dipping in the reservoir. Got stuck naked in the water, forgot that the way the bank is sloped there'd be no way for them to climb out again from the other side. Hal answered the call, went to rescue them. That was two years ago tonight."

"And Lily?"

"She must have left right after Hal did. I don't know how she made it up the Pike without driving off the side of the mountain. The autopsy showed enough painkillers and sedatives in her system to kill a grizzly. When Hal found her missing, he went nuts. Then we found the truck and realized what happened." She raised her now cold tea to her lips, her fingers white as they gripped the cup.

"We found her body two days later. In Snakebelly— same place I found that body yesterday."

Caitlyn sat back, her own drink forgotten as she plucked at an itchy patch of skin on her arm. Her veins buzzed— with fatigue or sexual excitement left over from last night she wasn't sure. But her skin felt so tight she wanted to claw her way out of it.

"Must be long hours for a police chief around here," she said, shifting in her seat. "Especially one as committed as Hal."

"It's nonstop when the tourists are here in the summer and fall. I've tried to get Hal to take a break, but he's a stubborn man. Just loves this town too much to trust it to anyone else, I guess."

Caitlyn looked down, her fingers still worrying at her forearm. There was no rash or signs of a bug bite, but she couldn't stop. It was as if angry gnats had crawled under her skin and were now trying to burrow farther. The same gnats kept buzzing through her mind with a suspicious and ugly thought of how Sarah's loss and Hal's might be connected. Maybe they both had reasons to want their spouses gone. She wondered if Sarah had an alibi for the night Lily died. But where did all that money in Hal's account come from? "I guess the insurance must have still paid off? That's how he kept his house, right?"

There was a knock of porcelain hitting the wood too hard. Caitlyn looked up, saw the blood had drained from Sarah's face.

"No," she said, stumbling over the single syllable. "Sam said it was the worst thing he'd ever had to do, telling Hal that the company wouldn't pay. Sam even offered to give Hal money to tide him over, help him with the mortgage. He knew how much that house meant to Hal."

"When was this, Sarah?"

"August, just a few days before Sam and Josh . . ." She looked past Caitlyn, her gaze focused on the refrigerator festooned with its colorful finger paintings, their edges yellowed and curling with age. She made a choking sound, cleared her throat. "Sam said he talked to Hal about Damian Wright, that he warned him—it would have been the same time."

"Sam said?" Caitlyn leaned forward, engaging the woman's attention. It was the second time Sarah Durandt had referred to her husband as if she'd just spoken with him. "Sarah, what do you mean, Sam said?"

* * *

Grigor left the diner and sauntered up Main Street, enjoying the summer morning quiet. No screams, no men cursing, no bulls shouting orders. He could see why Stan had been attracted to this place. The streets were clean; the people nodded and smiled even at strangers. A man could do some serious thinking in a place like this.

Then he reached a hideous orange brick building. The government center was even worse than the photos on the computer. Looking at it offended his sensibilities. The picturesque scenery surrounding it only increased its ugliness.

For now it was a necessary evil. But not for long.

Smiling, he strolled to the door leading to police headquarters. A cheerful bell announced his entrance. Inside he found a single cramped room with a single desk, two chairs, one cell, one cot. All empty.

The interior door from the post office opened. No bell there. Just a middle-aged woman with hair that wept henna.

"Chief Waverly's out," she announced, her gaze taking in everything from his shoes up until it hit his eyes and ricocheted away. The postmistress. Max said she and her husband were the biggest gossips in town. "You just missed him. He was working all morning, most of the night, not sure when he'll be back."

He inclined his head in thanks. Widened his smile as he imagined her blood, fresh, bright red, mixing with all that orange hair. "Thanks. I'm Gregory." He handed her a business card with his professional name. Black gloss with gold lettering. Just the one name. It was the only name anyone needed. "We're scouting locations for a film. Of course I wanted to let the chief know in advance. Matter of courtesy, you understand."

"Oh my." She fluttered the card before her. "A movie? Here in Hopewell? How exciting." Then she paused and looked at him. "Do you think you'll be needing any extras?"

"Well now, Miss—"

"Mrs. Victoria Godwin. My husband, the Colonel, he owns the Rockslide Café. In case you need any catering done while you're in town."

"Mrs. Godwin." He took her hand, turned it palm down, shook it, didn't let go. "You'll be the first person I think of when it comes to extras. Believe me."

She melted beneath his touch. "Thank you. What kind of movie is it?"

This time his smile was genuine. "A horror film. The likes that has never been seen before." He chuckled. "You're going to love it."

Sarah stared at Caitlyn for a long moment. Her chest tightened as sweat broke out all over her. Sam managed to keep Josh and his secret safe for almost two years. She'd known for only a few hours and first Alan and now Caitlyn had been able to read her like a neon sign flashing in Times Square.

She closed her eyes, utterly exhausted. Physically, mentally, emotionally exhausted. No, that wasn't the right word. What came after exhaustion? Breakdown.

Not a bad idea. Sarah slumped forward, resting her head on the kitchen table, and allowed her emotions to swarm over her like a nest of angry timber rattlers. Tears she'd held back for so very long, a torrent of fear and anger and more fear, arrived with a vengeance. Her body shook; her shoulders heaved; her head rocked against the tabletop.

Caitlyn's chair scraped back and the FBI agent crouched beside Sarah, wrapping her arm around her. "Jesus, I'm so sorry. I did it again. Mrs. Durandt, Sarah, I'm sorry. Just take a deep breath. That's it, you'll be all right."

Sarah almost felt guilty about tricking Caitlyn into a show of sympathy. Or was it just a show? Caitlyn had arrived that night with Jack Logan—who obviously knew more about Sam than he was telling anyone. Except Alan.

If Caitlyn's suspicions about Hal were correct, Sarah couldn't even trust the man she'd known for over twenty years. Could Hal have betrayed Sam? And her? Just for money?

Now her breath came in ragged gasps for real. Sam was right. There was no one they could trust.

It was all up to her. And so far she'd failed miserably. How the hell had Sam managed to keep his sanity while living in this world of deceit and treachery?

The enormity of what he had sacrificed, what doing the right thing had cost him, finally hit her. What would she have done if faced with the same choice?

"I talk to Sam every day," Sarah said, finally raising her head. Caitlyn grabbed a dish towel from the oven door and Sarah used it to wipe her tears and blow her nose. "I'm sorry. I've never lost it like that before. It must have been finding the body yesterday. I really thought it would be Sam. That maybe if I had found him and Josh, I could finally find some peace."

Sarah stared into the yellow daisies that covered the cotton towel, hoping Caitlyn bought her performance. The FBI agent was silent for a long moment before resuming her seat at the table.

"Sam told you he'd spoken with Chief Waverly about Damian Wright. When exactly did you speak with him, Mrs. Durandt?"

Sarah noticed the way Caitlyn lowered her voice and

raised her inflection, to soften any hint of accusation in her question. She could feel Caitlyn's eyes on her as she left the table and busied herself by clearing the cups and plates.

"Whenever either one of us traveled, we talked every night. On the phone. So it must have been whatever night Sam told Hal. Surely it's in the files somewhere. I must have told you this before. After all, a father would tell his wife a pervert was trying to take photos of their child, wouldn't he?"

Caitlyn was silent. Sarah realized she was allowing her to incriminate herself. The strident tone she'd fallen into, the bitterness she'd revealed with her last statement, was all too obvious. No, Sam hadn't told her about Damian Wright. She wasn't sure if that was because Hal asked him not to or because Sam really hadn't believed there was a threat to Josh after all.

Or maybe because that last time they'd spoken that summer, she'd spent all their time ranting about the educational system and the dunderheads in the government who were wasting her time, and had threatened to walk out of the mandatory seminar and quit her job. She'd been so upset that it had taken Sam twenty minutes to calm her down, convince her to stay in Albany.

Oh God, was this all her fault? If she'd given him a chance, would he have told her? Would she have raced home, been able to prevent all this?

Sarah banged the ceramic mug onto the countertop. It exploded in her hand. "Damn it!"

Caitlyn rushed to her side, but Sarah waved her away.

"I don't think this is a good time to talk," Sarah said, trying to sound calm. "I need to pull myself together." She knew she sounded demented, a raving lunatic trying to hold the beast within her in check. More tears burned at the back of her throat, as if once started it would take a lifetime to drain them all.

"So I see," Caitlyn said, her tone now neutral and professional. "But it really would be best if we spoke now. Cleared everything up." She paused and Sarah focused on the broken bits in the sink, looking anywhere but into Caitlyn's all-knowing eyes. "Once and for all."

Caitlyn's cell phone trilled. Sarah was grateful for the reprieve. She cleaned out the sink, dumping the shards of glass into the garbage. Grabbed a sponge to take care of the puddle on the floor. Before she could start, she looked up to see Caitlyn hanging up. She'd only said three words during the entire conversation: "Are you sure?"

Now Caitlyn stared at Sarah the same way she had glared at Logan earlier. "Mrs. Durandt, I'm afraid we definitely do need to question you further."

"Why? I haven't done anything wrong."

"That was Quantico. The gun you had in your possession belonged to Deputy U.S. Marshal Leo Richland."

Sarah shrank back against the counter. "You think I killed him?"

"I think we need to talk further." Caitlyn took a step toward Sarah. "To be safe, I'd like to take you down to the sheriff's office in Plattsburgh, where we can document everything."

Sarah couldn't tell them how Sam had come by the gun, not without exposing him and Josh. Her vision began to darken with red spots as her head throbbed.

"You mean you want to arrest me." She couldn't be arrested. Not now, not today. She had to keep Alan and Logan from going after Sam or telling Korsakov where to find Josh. She couldn't do that if she was in jail, deflecting questions she had no answers for.

Sam had been right. Her only choice was to run.

She dried her hands on the dish towel and turned her back to Caitlyn as she hung it on the oven door. Then, faster than a whipsnake, she grabbed the cast-iron skillet and swung it at Caitlyn's head.

CHAPTER FORTY-TWO

Hal Waverly's house was easy to find if hard to get to, bouncing over a dirt road that continued up the mountain after they turned onto his drive. Grigor liked the looks of the place. Well-proportioned, there were sturdy but elegant architectural touches in the curves above the shutters, the gingerbread on the veranda, the hand-carved doors. A house that had been loved.

He walked through it, shaking his head at the interior and its lack of decor. Disrespectful. Crap furniture surrounded by boxes of crap. One of the bedrooms had no furniture at all except a twin bed and dresser. This was the room that fascinated Grigor.

Madness and despair lived here. The wall above the bed was covered with sketches traced in blood. Images of a woman soaring, a waterfall and snake below her, a man poised to either save her or condemn her.

The windows were boarded over with plywood, gouges along the edges where someone had tried to claw their way out. More scratches appeared on the door, with its shiny, sturdy lock, and behind the headboard. Soft leather restraints lined with lambs' wool dangled below the chenille bedspread.

He stood in the center of the room, absorbing its dark energy, enjoying the sensations and images it wrought. Yes, a good house.

The bathroom across the hall was littered with prescription bottles. Decadron, Ativan, Trazodone, Darvon, Ambien, OxyContin. A cornucopia of anti-psychotics, pain medications, sedatives, tranquilizers. All dated two years ago. Lily Waverly. Ah, the dead wife. Without her and Damian Wright he might never have found Stan's hiding place.

Two twisted minds who never met yet brought him here. Kismet.

Finally he looked in on the chief whose snoring accompanied the subliminal roar of the waterfall just downriver. Max had showed him the dock and scenic viewpoint across the road where the river bend created an eddy of calm water upstream from the treacherous rapids and the Lower Falls with their precipitous hundred-foot drop into the gorge.

He watched Chief Waverly sleep, oblivious to his presence or the fact that his life was about to change forever.

The room was almost monastic. The double bed had an intricately carved headboard that matched the dresser, but other than that there were no personal items except for a single framed photograph. A wedding photo. Two lives, starting their journey, the rest of the world shut out as a man and woman gazed at each other.

"Wake him. Bring him to the clearing," Grigor ordered Max.

While Max followed orders, Grigor strolled outside, inhaling the sunlight-tinted air. After Alexi got into position, they'd parked the SUV and the Toyota they'd acquired on their way to Hopewell at the trailhead that led to the clearing where Stan had been killed.

The clearing was a short hike down from Chief Waverly's house and, aside from its sentimental value as the site of Stan's death, was perfectly situated for Grigor's next performance. It had a clear view down to the dam and the fire tower, yet was private and hidden far from view and out of earshot.

He arrived before Waverly and Max. The couple from the Toyota still struggled with their bonds, as if they had any hope of escaping. Fools. He shook his head, but he was smiling. Fools with hope—the best kind of entertainment.

They were young, midtwenties, drenched in the sweat of terror. Bound to trees facing each other, they communicated with grunts muffled by their gags and eyes wide with panic. Yet they never stopped looking at each other. Just like the couple in the wedding photo.

He wondered at that. Max had found them at a gas station off the highway from Albany. No wedding bands, different last names on their IDs, but they acted as if they were bonded.

Grigor had no idea what love was. The word was used so carelessly he wasn't sure it had any true meaning at all. But he did understand the intensity of the emotion—he'd never had the chance to fully explore it. Had Stan died trying to save his child? Would he have died for his wife?

One thing for certain. The wife would die screaming Stan's name. In love or hate Grigor had yet to decide.

Footsteps behind him broke his admiration of the way the light cast jagged shadows over the couple's faces. Fracturing them into pieces of a puzzle. Light and dark in perfect balance.

"So nice to meet you, Chief Waverly," he said without turning around. "I'm Grigor Korsakov."

"Who are these people? You need to let them go."

Grigor couldn't believe Waverly had the audacity to make demands. As rude and crude as his furnishings. Did the man not see this was a situation that called for finesse? Could he not realize he was no longer chief of anything around here?

Grigor pivoted to face Waverly. "No. *You* need to free them. Pick one."

The Hopewell police chief's face was creased with sleep marks, but his confusion added new twists to his expression. Pride, outrage, anger, followed by the emotion Grigor sought: fear.

"What do you mean, I need to pick one? Let them go. Now." A cop's voice of command. Grigor ignored it. Waverly's hand dropped to where his gun would be if he had been wearing more than jeans and a T-shirt. But he didn't back down. Grigor had to give him credit for that.

"I thought it only fair to give you a little demonstration of what happens if you don't follow my instructions to the letter," Grigor said.

Waverly whirled, ready to tackle Max, but Max had his gun drawn and aimed at the back of the bound woman's head.

"You're part of my family now, Chief Waverly. Until now money's been enough to cement our partnership, but I require loyalty from my family. Your choice. He dies and she lives. Or vice versa."

The man and woman became frantic at his words, fighting their bonds and attempting to scream past their gags. Grigor ignored them, focusing on the chief.

"I've done everything you asked. Looked the other way while your men prowled the town, let them review the case file of Sam's death. There's no need to involve innocent civilians."

The chief's tone grew desperate. Grigor remained silent, enjoying the emotions playing across Waverly's face. Frustration mingled with despair.

"I'm not going to do it," he continued his pleading. "Release them both and I'll do what I promised I would. If you hurt either of them, we're finished."

Grigor tsked. Max grinned. He knew what was coming. "That won't do, Chief Waverly. Not at all. You see, I own you. I own this town. If anyone tries to leave, they will die. If anyone resists, they die. If you don't follow orders, one of your townsfolk, the innocent people you've sworn to protect and serve, will die."

"You can't do that."

"Of course I can. I can do anything I want." Grigor waved a hand at the couple. "Now choose."

"No. I won't. Look, the FBI is here. They took Sarah. So you might as well leave while you can. I won't say a word to anyone, I promise."

Grigor laid a gentle palm on Waverly's arm, steering him to face the young couple. "The FBI doesn't worry me. But that's beside the point. This is about you and me. Choose."

Waverly said nothing, his jaw working hard, eyes narrowed as he fought to find a way out of the dilemma. Another optimistic fool.

"Very well. I'll choose for you." Grigor cocked his finger as if it were a pistol, aiming it at the girl. "Eeny, meeny, miny." He swung his aim back and forth from the girl to the boy and back again. "Moe."

As he pointed to the boy, the boy's eyes went so wide white showed all around. Suddenly his head jerked back, hitting the tree, a perfect circle drilled into the center of his forehead like a third eye. The only sound was the crack of the high-velocity round snapping the tree bark.

"The same will happen to anyone, anywhere, anytime you step out of line," he told Waverly. "Tell me you understand."

The boy's body slumped forward, a smear of blood and brain matter painting the tree trunk, surrounding the wound the bullet had gouged.

The chief's chin bobbed as he swallowed hard. Fear and anger tangled in his gaze. "I understand."

"I'm not sure that you do, but it's a start. Now, I'm off to visit an old friend's wife."

"I told you, Sarah's gone."

"Then it won't matter if I see for myself."

"Wait. What about the girl? You said you'd let her go."

"No. I said I'd let her live." Grigor nodded to Max. "Take her to Alexi. He deserves a little entertainment for a job well done." Waverly looked like he might intervene, but Grigor took his arm and led him away. "Poor thing. By the time Alexi is done with her, she'll wish you'd had the courage to make the choice and let her die."

He didn't add that by the end of the day the entire town would feel that way, would blame Waverly for their misery and pain.

Caitlyn saw the skillet coming at her an instant too late. She blocked the blow with her arm, but lost her balance. Her feet slipped on the wet floor in a banana peel slide, landing her on her back with a thud.

She thumped her head against the table edge going down, but didn't black out. As she reached for her weapon, Sarah threw the skillet down, a look of horror on her face, and raced out the back door. By the time Caitlyn regained her feet and followed, she was a distant blur at the forest's edge, vanishing into the trees.

Caitlyn ran a few steps, then stopped in disgust. No

way in hell she'd ever catch Sarah. The woman was like a deer or some kind of wild creature. She rubbed her forearm where the skillet hit her. Sarah hadn't meant it as a killing blow, more like a diversion. No major damage except to her pride.

She squinted at the sun. High noon. Just like Gary Cooper she was on her own. In a town where nobody could be trusted and everybody lied.

She stared at the spot where Sarah had disappeared. Sarah had been telling the truth during most of their interview; Caitlyn was sure of it. Right up to the point where Caitlyn had practically accused Hal Waverly of being involved in her husband's disappearance.

Caitlyn bounced on her heels, pacing the wooden floorboards of Sarah's veranda. She listened to the way her footsteps echoed, liking the *tap-tap-ratta-tap*. She sped up, then slowed again. Her skin had stopped crawling and itching; now she felt energized, jazzed . . .

Actually, she had been pretty edgy, hyper since last night. But it wasn't the sex—or almost sex. What the hell had she been thinking, considering having unprotected sex with a total stranger? The way she'd practically attacked Waverly—that wasn't her. She kept her feelings under control, just like she kept her migraines under control . . .

Oh shit. She stopped before a planter bustling with snapdragons. The breeze swept through them, blurring their vibrant colors. Were these strange feelings, her recent irrational behavior, caused by residual effects from her traumatic brain injury, like her migraines? Maybe she couldn't even trust herself.

She pursed her lips and turned back into the kitchen. Grabbing her bag, she strode through the house, ignoring the photos of Sarah, Sam, and Josh, the lovingly balanced, comfortable decor, or the sweet scent of cinnamon. She needed the bullet Hal had taken from Richland's body. If it matched Richland's gun, she'd charge Sarah Durandt with the murder of a federal agent.

CHAPTER FORTY-THREE

Sam pressed the binoculars into the flesh of his face as if they could provide some way for him to be miraculously transported from his hiding place down to the drive. He wished he had kept his gun. If he had, this would all be over now.

A blur of motion from the back of Sarah's house caught his eye. He moved his binoculars to spot her racing across the yard and up into the woods. No one followed, although another woman appeared on the back porch a few moments later.

What the hell was going on? He pivoted and aimed his focus back toward the drive. Korsakov hadn't moved, didn't act as if he had heard or seen anything.

Sam cursed silently. He grabbed his pack and sprinted through the trees to catch Sarah.

He intercepted her just as she hit the trail leading down to the dam. "Sarah! Stop!"

She spun around, her sides heaving with effort. She carried nothing with her, wore only regular sneakers, not her hiking boots.

"Where are you going? Why are you running?" He drew close and wrapped his arms around her. "What happened?"

She shoved him back. "They think I killed Leo Richland."

"Who does?"

"The FBI. They were going to arrest me. That would have messed up everything, so I hit her and ran." She began jogging down the trail.

"Wait, where are you going?"

"To find Logan. If we don't keep our end of the bargain, he'll kill Josh."

"We've got worse problems than Logan. Come with me." He led her back to the ridge where he'd been spying on her house. "Look there."

She took the binoculars. "There's a man standing by my car. He's talking with Caitlyn." She paused. "Caitlyn looks angry—no, scared. She's backing away."

He wanted to wrench the binoculars from her, to watch for himself, but he didn't.

She lowered the binoculars and turned to Sam. "Who is that? What does he want?"

"That's Grigor Korsakov. He wants to kill me. And you."

Caitlyn spotted the lone man standing near her car as soon as she turned down the path leading from the house. Who could miss him? Even if it weren't for the black suit and flashy red tie, energy radiated from him, flashing a neon warning sign: BEWARE.

As she drew near, he stopped his quick-jerk pacing to lounge against Sarah's Ford Explorer. His stare as he watched her approach was palpable, intensely compelling. The hairs on the back of her neck tingled.

So this was the infamous Grigor Korsakov.

How could she have thought him ordinary when she'd seen his picture? A short man, no more than an inch taller than her own five-six, he was anything but ordinary. Energy danced from him, swirling like storm clouds before a bolt of lightning. He smiled, drawing back rich, full lips to reveal a perfect set of brilliant white teeth.

Not bad for a guy who'd just spent seven years in the pen. She wondered how much it had cost to protect that perfect smile and face while he was inside. Using her peripheral vision, she scanned the area. No signs of another vehicle, no signs of other men. She kept her focus on Korsakov. Definitely not ordinary. He was as mesmerizing as a hooded cobra and just as deadly.

"Are you Sarah Durandt?" he asked in a richly mellow voice sounding of fine wine and caviar.

"Sorry, no." She stopped an arm's length away from him, sliding her hand inside the outer compartment of her bag to rest on her gun.

He cocked his head, his smile growing wider as if she'd made a joke. "Are you sure? I was told that she lived here alone."

"She's not at home right now." A fleeting frown creased his features and Caitlyn saw the only flaw in his facade. His eyes were leaden, flat, with irises so dark it was impossible to tell where the pupils stopped and the color began. She'd faced off with gangbangers, sociopaths, psychopaths, even a serial killer—but none of them had eyes as dead as Grigor Korsakov's.

Eyes that penetrated to your very soul, then with a flicker condemned you to the depths of hell.

Caitlyn suppressed a shudder, forced her smile to remain plastered on her face. She edged to one side and headed for her car. Korsakov moved with her, blocking her path.

"You must understand. It's extremely important I find Mrs. Durandt."

He hadn't touched her, his hands still slouched in his jacket pockets, but Caitlyn's muscles tightened in anticipation of an attack. "I'm sorry I can't help you," she said, keeping her voice level and her gaze even with his. "The door's open. I'm sure she wouldn't mind if you waited inside."

He nodded at that and almost turned away, then smiled even more charmingly as he spun back to her. "I'm so sorry. I don't mean to be a pest. But you see, I've never met Mrs. Durandt. I don't suppose you could show me some proof that you're not her?"

Caitlyn was half-tempted to pull her weapon as evidence of who she was. Instead, she kept her hand firmly wrapped around the Glock's handle as she slid her wallet from the inside pocket of her bag. She held up her driver's license, glad there was no mention of her being a federal agent on it.

" 'Caitlyn Tierney, Manassas, Virginia,' " he leaned close to her and read. Without moving back, their faces mere inches away from each other, he looked into her eyes, his smile now rigid. "That's a long way from home. You're quite certain Mrs. Durandt isn't at home?"

"Quite," Caitlyn said, snapping her wallet shut and dropping it back into her purse. "I'm running late, so you'll please excuse me."

He blinked slowly, like a reptile, and she knew he was considering restraining her. She tensed, half-hoping he would make a move. As she looked into his dead, dark eyes a flutter of fear spun through her and she realized she wasn't certain, gun or no gun, that she could take him down.

Finally he touched the Bluetooth device on his ear and

gave a small nod as if he'd received verification of her identity. Creepy. A sociopath augmented by technology. And unseen accomplices. She needed to find backup, someone she could trust in this damn town.

He stepped back, granting his permission for her to leave with a flourish of his hand. "Good day, Miss Tierney," he called as she slammed her car door shut and started the engine. "I'm sure I'll be seeing you later."

Caitlyn hoped that next meeting happened with an inch of bulletproof glass between the two of them and stainless steel handcuffs on his wrists. She barely looked at the road as she sped away, her attention riveted by Korsakov's reflection in the rearview mirror. She gripped the wheel tight, her breathing rapid, heart pounding as if she'd just had a close escape from death.

CHAPTER FORTY-FOUR

"How did you find me?" Sarah asked as Sam led her to his cave.

"I ran into those kids—JD and Julia. They gave me a cell phone and called me when you left the police station. I've been watching for Alan and Logan, thought we could settle things before Korsakov got here."

"Too late now."

"Yeah. Look on the bright side. If he thinks Alan and Logan have betrayed him, he'll kill them for us."

"Great, we'll have one psychopathic killer on our trail instead of three."

"Maybe they'll all kill each other."

They stopped at a large boulder angled away from a limestone outcropping. Sam threw his pack into the crevice behind the boulder.

"I showed you this place," Sarah said

"It's come in handy over the years." His voice was grim.

"What are we going to do?"

He looked past her, down the mountain toward the town. "We can't go through town. Korsakov is sure to have the road blocked." He paused. "You go up to the Colonel's cabin, get my truck, and go get Josh. I called my landlady; she's taking him to a motel outside of Montreal."

"And you'll be?"

He rubbed at his side, turned away from her. "I'll create a distraction. Give you time. Go down there and give them what they want. Me."

She was shaking her head before he had a chance to finish. "No. We've already covered this. I'm not going to tell Josh his father is dead. I can't put him through that."

"So we're back to square one."

"We can try the Colonel." She really didn't like the idea of putting her father in the line of fire. "Maybe he can round up some men—"

"And take on trained killers? If Korsakov is here, his men are as well. And they'll be armed with a helluva lot more than hunting rifles."

"We can't call Hal. Caitlyn thinks he was bribed to frame Damian Wright for your murder. Thinks maybe he was involved from the start."

Sam tensed. "It would explain a lot. But where does that leave us?"

She raised her head, nodded up the mountain. "Looks like the only way out is up. We'll climb the mountain, get your truck, go after Josh."

"We can't. Not with three killers and their hired guns trailing us."

"What do you want to do? Meet Logan like we agreed, let him take care of the rest?"

"I don't trust him, but it would get you and Josh out of the line of fire." He wouldn't meet her gaze.

She considered that, then took his hand. "I'd rather take my chances trusting you."

He blinked rapidly and squeezed her hand tight. As if

he understood how much trusting him again, after what he did, cost her. "But—"

"There's no time to argue. Grab your stuff and let's go."

Grigor inhaled deeply. Sarah Durandt's house smelled like a woman. Soft and comfortable, no sharp edges. He ran his fingertips across the chenille blanket draped over the back of an overstuffed chair and imagined how the house would smell when he was done with her. That delicious scent of terror.

Not solely a visual artist, he enjoyed evoking all of the senses during his entertainments.

The mess in the kitchen puzzled him. Two mugs, one shattered in the sink, two plates . . . Manassas Red hadn't been here alone. She'd lied to him.

He took his time wandering through the house, peering into private nooks and crannies, absorbing the essence of the woman who lived here. By the time Max returned, he was lounging on Sarah Durandt's couch, leafing through a family photo album. Happy people, laughing people, beautiful people trapped in time.

Once he got his hands on Sarah Durandt, she'd never be happy, laughing, or beautiful again. Not when he was through with her.

"The lady went down the road a mile or so, headed to Waverly's house." Max clumped through the front door, destroying the blissful silence.

Grigor merely nodded at Max's words. "The fascinating lady from Virginia lied to me. She wasn't afraid, yet she also asked no questions. As if she already had the answers."

"Not like she can go far if we want her back again. Not with Alexi blocking the road."

That coaxed a smile from Grigor. Alexi was a wizard with a sniper rifle, would stop anyone trying to flee.

The pale redhead with the creamy smooth skin and the husky voice . . . he imagined her screams intertwined with Sarah's. A symphony of horror.

Max's cell rang and a minute later he returned. "That was Logan. Turns out he's not the only FBI agent interested in Hopewell and Sarah Durandt."

"Former agent," Grigor corrected.

"The redhead, she's FBI as well. Maybe she and Waverly are working together?"

Interesting. Max was good at getting things done, but sometimes he missed the big picture. An FBI agent arriving the same day Grigor did? Why would the FBI be interested in Sarah Durandt now, two years after her husband died?

Grigor held his hands up as if composing a portrait. The big picture was what he was all about. Most people never realized they were mere points of light on the universe's canvas, but Grigor understood. More, he knew he had the power to indelibly change that canvas, to draw his own portrait by pulling enough anonymous dots into his realm of control.

Grigor was destined for great things, to leave his mark on the world, on history. Just as his grandfather had. Just as Stalin had. A mark the color of blood and terror, a mark forever etched into the stories passed from one generation to the next. Grigor's story would be his ticket to immortality.

Max fidgeted, uncomfortable as Grigor's thumbs and index fingers framed him. "You okay, boss?"

A lazy smile widened Grigor's mouth. "I'm fine. Fine and dandy. I think I understand why I'm here, what I'm meant to do."

"Uh, I thought you wanted to grab the girl, and find out

where Stan hid the money he stole from you," Max said as if uncertain of Grigor's mental capacity. Then he jerked his body away from Grigor's piercing stare and gestured at an array of photos lining the walls and fireplace mantle. "Cute kid, though."

"Very cute," Grigor allowed, stroking one finger along the image of Stan holding a bright-eyed toddler. "You remember that night we went driving on Mulholland? When Alexi clipped the dog and Stan jumped out, trying to save it?"

"Yeah. Pouring rain, mud sliding all around, cars skidding—Stan almost got killed. All for a mutt who ended up dying anyway."

"All for a mutt." Grigor inspected the other photos of the happy family. Noted the gleam in Stan's eyes, the way he never looked at the camera, instead remained constantly focused on his family. The center of his universe. "Logan said Alan came here right after Stan and the kid were killed."

"Guess he wanted to see if the missus knew anything about the money Stan stole."

"What if Stan isn't dead? What if he knew Alan was getting close, tracking the money, and so he took the kid and ran?"

"Gutsy move. But that guy in Texas confessed."

"Confessions can be bought." By his so-called associates, Logan and Easton, no doubt. Traitors.

"Why leave the wife behind? They sure do look happy."

"Maybe he had no choice, no time." Grigor tapped his finger on the glass right over Sarah Durandt's pretty, heart-shaped face. "And now his luck has run out."

"You think he'll come back? Now that he knows you're looking for him—it would be suicide."

"The man already died once, what's he care?" Grigor

laughed at the thought, the noise scraping past his throat. It'd been a long time since he'd laughed, a longer time since he saw anything as humorous. "First Logan tells me he found where Stan was hiding all those years I was in jail, then he and Alan both conveniently let me know they're doing their best to find the money Stan stole from me—do they think I'm stupid? That I don't know betrayal when I hear it? They knew about Stan and the money long before they bothered to tell me."

Max flinched at the sharp edge in Grigor's voice. "We'll get them too. Don't worry, we'll get everyone."

"My family has disowned me; my people have betrayed me—everyone in this town is guilty; they all hid what was rightfully mine! She," he swept his arm across the mantle, dashing the photos to the floor, where they shattered, Sarah's face smiling up at him through glass shards, mocking him, "she married the bastard who did this to me; she bore him a son."

"Grigor, calm down. You know me and Alexi are here for you, man. Just tell us what you need us to do and we'll do it."

"I need," his breath snagged in his throat, burning, "my cameras. We're going to start a new project. I'm going to title it: Death of a Treacherous Town."

"All right then, JD," the Colonel said as they climbed the path to the clearing, "what did you need help with?"

Instead of answering, JD rushed ahead. "Sam?" he called quietly, his voice echoing through the trees. "Sam, you there?"

The Colonel caught up with him at the edge of the clearing and grabbed him by the arm. "What's going on? You know this is the place where Sam and my grandson . . . What kind of game is this? Answer me!"

The old man's face was scarlet with fury and his voice made JD jump. "No game. Honest, Colonel. Sam's alive and so is your grandson. I saw Sam this morning."

The Colonel's grip tightened like a tourniquet. As he stared into JD's eyes, JD knew what it would be like to face a firing squad. Then the Colonel let go. His face went slack and he took a step past JD.

"What the hell—"

JD spun around to see what had scared the Colonel. At the far edge of the clearing a man was tied to a tree, his head down, face hidden. The tree had a hole splintered through its bark. Something dark stained the edges.

"Sam," the Colonel cried. He touched the man's neck and wrist, searching for a pulse. Then closed his eyes for a long moment before raising the man's face.

His exhalation swirled through the trees. JD remained frozen, watching. "He's dead, isn't he?"

As if that hole in the middle of the guy's forehead was Halloween makeup. Somehow he hoped the Colonel would say "no" or, even better, the guy would open his eyes and give him a wink, let him in on the joke. Because until now all this was just stuff for a movie, make-believe, not real. Not even seeing Mrs. Durandt with a gun last night or those other men or Sam all beat-up had made it seem real.

But this . . . this was as real as it got.

The Colonel said nothing. Gently, he lowered the man's head. Then he turned to JD. "Tell me everything."

JD gave him a quick rundown of what he and Julia had seen. "Julia's watching Mrs. D at her house, just like Sam asked us to."

"So Sarah knows Sam is alive?"

"Yes, sir."

"And Sam was alone when you met him?"

JD nodded.

"Then who is this man? And who killed him?" The Colonel frowned, then began to jog down the path toward Mrs. Durandt's house. JD raced after him, his mind filled with questions.

"But, sir. What about Sam?"

"Face it, boy. He's not coming. Which means either they got Sam or they got to him. Maybe through Sarah."

"But Julia, she's at Mrs. Durandt's house." JD broke into a panicked sprint, passing the Colonel as he ran down the mountain. He stayed on the path, past Mrs. D's house until he hit Lake Road. Then he turned and ran to the clearing across from Mrs. D's driveway where he'd left Julia eating the lunch he'd brought her from the Rockslide.

Their bikes were still both there. His cell phone, which he'd lent to Julia, lay on the ground, open and on. The towel she'd been using as a tablecloth was crumpled up and muddy as if someone had dragged it and the food on it through the bushes. On one edge a muddy footprint was imprinted. Much too large to be Julia's.

JD's heart slammed into his throat, threatening to choke him. Pounding footsteps down the gravel drive signaled the Colonel's arrival. "Sarah's gone."

"They got Julia," JD said, his voice cracking. "They took her."

"C'mon. We need to get Hal and his men working on this."

JD shook his head. "Sam said not to tell Chief Waverly. Said the bad guys would know." His eyes burned with tears. He blinked furiously, refusing to give in to the feeling that this was all his fault.

"We can't handle this alone. We need to get the police involved. Now."

The Colonel's barked order broke through JD's shock.

He glanced around the clearing one final time, hoping he'd see Julia, her familiar, beautiful smile in place, returning with a great story of how she'd outwitted the bad guys.

But the clearing remained empty. No Julia. No one except one frightened teenager and one scared old man, both trying to pretend everything was going to be all right.

CHAPTER FORTY-FIVE

"Hal?" Caitlyn shouted, her voice echoing through his house as she walked through the open front door. No answer. The postmistress said after Hal released Logan he'd gone home to get some sleep.

She walked down the hallway, gun drawn and ready, feeling dirty for suspecting him, dirty for allowing him to get so close to her. God, she'd almost slept with a man she now believed was involved with a murder.

The kitchen and living room were empty. The hallway had three doors. One opened to an empty bathroom. At the far end, another door was closed, but the second door in the hallway was ajar. Hal's bedroom, empty. After clearing it, she stepped into the final room, her gun sweeping from one side to the other. No one.

Thick curtains pulled tight over the only window. There were dark smudges on the wall forming drawings and some sort of words in a strange language. She turned on the light and stepped closer. The words had been drawn in blood.

The only furniture in the room was a bureau and an old brass frame twin bed. On top of the bureau lay an antique gilded hand mirror. *Odd for a man to have,* she thought as she traced a finger across its surface. A fine, white powder coated her fingertip.

Shit. That explained a lot. Like why she'd been jittery, irritable all day, the way she'd jumped him last night, her inability to concentrate or stay still. She brushed the finger onto her jeans. Not heroin, probably not cocaine—the effects had lasted too long. Meth. He'd dumped methamphetamine into her drink last night.

No, she'd done it to herself. The powder he used instead of sugar.

She knew the statistics. Over a third of meth addicts held down steady jobs, quite a few of them in law enforcement. Hell, how could she have been so blind?

Hal's voice came from the door. "I tried to tell you."

Caitlyn jumped, her hand going to her weapon. But she didn't draw it. Hal kept his hands spread open, empty, away from his duty belt. He stepped over the threshold gingerly, as if he might break something by crossing the invisible barrier.

"How long have you been using?" She nodded to the mirror.

"I started when Lily got bad. Was working doubles to keep up with the bills but still fell behind, with the doctors and all. I didn't have a choice. I couldn't quit my job. And no one else could take care of Lily. I needed help. Then one day I pulled a trucker over, found his stash of amphetamines. His magic wake-me-ups, he called them. Did the trick. When I ran out, I tried some meth from the evidence locker. Saved it for the really bad nights, didn't use it every day, but it got to the point where I was actually hoping Lily would have one of her spells. That I'd have an excuse to use some more."

"Is that your wife's blood?" Caitlyn asked, nodding to the wall with the paintings.

"Her final message to me. Two years ago. Tonight. I should have known. She was so quiet that night. As if the pain had burnt itself out." He sank onto the bed, stroking the pillow with his fingers, a gentle touch.

"I failed her," he whispered, his voice rough as if choking on something. "I wasn't there to save her." He glanced up. "Now I need your help. To save Sarah. I can't fail again. Not after what I did to her and Sam."

"What did you do?" Caitlyn kept her hand on her Glock. She liked Hal, she really did, but if he killed Sam, she had no choice but to take him in. "Hal, were you there on that mountain when Sam died?"

To her surprise, he looked away, a snort of laughter shaking his shoulders. "I thought I was. Just goes to show how screwed up I was after Lily died. That was the last day I used. I quit. Cold turkey. Couldn't stand the thought of what I'd done, not when I saw the price Sarah paid. God, I was so stupid." He bowed his head, snagged his hair between his fingers.

He quit meth cold turkey? Not many people had the strength to do that. If he was telling the truth. But she thought he was. Finally. "Tell me everything."

"It was Richland's fault—no, I take that back. It was nobody's fault but mine. I'd been up two nights working and had a meeting with the bank that morning, my last chance to save the house, to save the only thing left of Lily, so I used. Just to stay awake. My last time, I promised myself." He snorted in derision, both of them knowing an addict's promises were worth less than nothing.

"The bank turned me down and I knew I would lose the house. I was heading home—the last night I would have in my home, with Lily and everything I'd grown up with, before the sheriff came to serve the papers. Then Sam flagged me down. Told me about the guy he saw taking pictures of Josh."

"So that part was true. Damian Wright did target Josh."

He nodded. "I knew about the kids he'd killed up north, so I called the Albany FBI field office right away. They put me through to the task force tip line, where I left Sam's info, but no one would talk to me or tell me anything. Just another hick cop trying to grab some attention, it seemed to them."

Caitlyn filled in the blanks. "That's how Logan knew about Sam. The task force had hundreds of tips coming in a day. The only way to keep track of them was to tag them each with the tipster's DMV record. When he reviewed them, he must have seen Sam's DMV photo and recognized him."

Hal shrugged, his shoulders sagging. "All I knew was it was already a shitty day and the idea of some sick pervert coming into my town and thinking he could get away with it—I can't remember ever feeling that angry."

He shifted on the bed, pulling Lily's pillow into his chest, hugging it tight. "I used again. Stayed up all night and managed to track Damian Wright, but he wasn't in his motel room when I got there. All I could envision was that monster out there, his hands around the neck of some little boy. It was out of my jurisdiction and I had no warrant, but I needed to find him, so I searched his room. All I found was that camera card; he must have dropped it or something. Tiny little thing, but when I got back to Hopewell and put it into the computer it made me sick. Filled with stolen moments of happiness. With Sam's kid front and center."

"You went after him on your own?"

"No. I was ready to call in the sheriff and State Police,

but before I could Leo Richland arrived, flashing his federal badge and insisting he was in charge of the manhunt. He made me take him to Sam's house, left me in the car like I was some lackey while he went in to interview Sam.

"Sitting there in the car, the sun so warm, I crashed. First time in three nights, four days, I slept. Slept hard. It was hours later—almost dusk—when Leo came pounding on the car door, face covered with blood. Yelling and screaming. Said Wright shot Sam, had killed Josh and taken him, and hit Leo on the head, left him for dead."

"Shit," Caitlyn exhaled, slumping against the dresser. Hal's voice filled with pain, but she didn't go to him. She believed him . . . but she didn't trust him.

"Leo dragged me out of the car before I even thought of calling for backup—I was still crashing, my brain fuzzy and crowded with the need for more sleep. He led me to the spot where Sam was shot. All that blood, no way anyone could have lived, I thought. He said we needed to follow, but the trail he led me on was Sam's. I told him we needed to find Damian and Josh, so I circled back and when I found Josh's Tigger I wanted to go that way.

"I'm ashamed to say it, but he got the drop on me. Took my weapon, insisted we follow Sam's trail even though it went in the opposite direction. I told him Sam was probably crazy with blood loss, didn't know where he was going, that our priority had to be to save Josh."

He blew out his breath, his gaze searching the shadows gathering in the far corner of the room. "That's when he told me Josh was already dead. So we followed Sam's trail, but by this time the rain had started and I lost the trail. Leo went crazy, threatening to kill me, saying he had to get Sam, even offering me ten thousand dollars, and I knew something was going on, more than a U.S. Marshal chasing a fugitive.

"I took him up to Snakebelly because I figured that might be where Wright would take Josh. It's the best place on the mountain to dispose of a body. When we didn't find anyone there, Leo tried to kill me, said he had to erase all evidence that he was here. I tackled him, grabbed my gun back. Tried to get him to tell me what was really going on, but he rushed me, tried to shove me over the edge, and I shot him."

"You killed Leo Richland?" Damn, she was going to have to arrest him.

He nodded slowly as if the weight of his actions dragged him down. "It was self-defense, but yes. I killed him."

She drew her weapon, motioned for him to stand. "I'm sorry, Hal."

"I understand." He stood still as she removed his service weapon and handcuffed him with his own cuffs. She pocketed the key and put his Glock on the dresser, out of reach.

"You know your rights. Want me to read them to you?"

"No, no. I waive them. Caitlyn, please hear me out. You're the only one who can save Sarah."

Once he was restrained, she motioned for him to continue. "Okay, tell me what happened next. Then you covered your tracks? Called us?"

"No. I think that was Logan, checking up on Leo. I searched Leo's pockets, found even more cash and figured that was just the start, so I tossed his body, and went back down the mountain. It was useless trying to track Sam and by now I figured he'd bled out somewhere in the woods. If I'd called for backup maybe things would have been different, but instead I went to Leo's car. Found the hundred thousand and knew I could save my house, my future. Keep Lily's memory alive.

"That's when I found the burner phone with a number

I finally traced to Korsakov's organization. Along with Logan's private number. From there it wasn't hard to realize Logan was working with Korsakov and he was the one who had sent Leo to grab Sam."

She knew Logan was dirty, but working with Korsakov? Probably also working against the Russian. The only person Logan was loyal to was Logan. "It was just Logan's bad luck Damian Wright got to Sam first."

"That's what I thought at the time. I dumped Leo's car in the quarry down at Merrill, and by the time I got back here you and Logan had arrived. I pretended to find the crime scene for the first time—by now it was pouring rain, so forensics were hopeless, but I couldn't stand the thought of Wright getting off, so I planted the camera card."

"And we fell for it."

He grimaced. "You know the rest. I haven't touched meth or any drugs since. Not that that helps Sarah any. Once I figured out who Korsakov was and who Sam really was, I figured he might come looking for Sarah someday, so I've been trying to keep her safe." He looked up at her, his gaze wounded. "But I failed again. Korsakov is here. And he wants Sarah."

"Sarah's gone."

He jumped to his feet, off balance with his hands restrained behind him. She drew her weapon. He backed off, eyes wide. "Where? Does Korsakov have her?"

"She ran. Last I saw her she was headed up the mountain."

He thought a moment, nodded. "Sam. She must have run to Sam."

Caitlyn stared. "Sam's dead."

"No. He's alive. And somewhere on Snakehead Mountain."

CHAPTER FORTY-SIX

Sam allowed Sarah to lead the way. Instead of following the winding trail, she set off on a trajectory that seemed to lead straight up the side of the mountain. As they climbed, alternating between traveling through dense forest, shrouded in darkness, and scrambling over exposed ledges, the sun beating down on them, Sam decided Sarah took this route so he'd be so out of breath that they couldn't speak with each other.

Pain speared his side with each step and his legs had gone past pain to a rubbery numbness as he forced them to keep moving. Finally he simply stopped, sank down onto a wind-scoured ledge, gasping for breath. Sarah didn't even notice until she was halfway around the next bend in the trail; then she returned, standing over him, her hands on her hips.

"Thought you said you were a lumberjack or something."

"I work in a lumberyard," he corrected her. He pulled out his CamelBak and took a deep drink, then handed it to her. "But Superman couldn't keep up with you when you're in a mood like this."

Her eyes grew dark and stormy as she glowered at him. "Superman wouldn't have left me fighting for the life of my son."

Not a whole helluva lot he could say to that. He kicked life back into his legs, letting them dangle over the cliff edge. For the first time, his fear of heights didn't bother him. There were so many other fears overwhelming him right now that it was crowded out.

She was silent for a moment before joining him on the ledge. She unbuttoned her shirt pocket and slipped Josh's photo from it. Wordlessly, she held it out in front of both of them.

"Hal took it from Logan," she said, her voice barely a whisper. "Gave it to me. He's so, so happy." Her entire body began to shake. He circled an arm around her shoulders and was surprised when she tolerated his touch, allowed him to pull her close.

"We'll make it." The words were meaningless and they both knew it, but he felt better for having said them aloud.

Before she could respond, Julia's cell phone vibrated in his pocket. He grabbed it. "Hello?"

"Sam the man, how the hell are you? Where the hell are you?" Alan's chipper tones smacked him like a sucker punch.

"How'd you get this number?" Sam asked cautiously.

"From the fair maiden, Miss Julia. She's currently enjoying our hospitality up at the Colonel's cabin. Logan says hello, by the way."

"Don't you dare hurt her—"

Sarah yanked at his hand, pulling the phone away from his ear so she could listen as well.

"That's up to you, now isn't it? I'm figuring Sarah is with you, so don't try anything stupid. I want to see both of you here by nightfall. Leave everything behind except the clothes on your backs. Then you and Logan will take a ride down the mountain while I entertain the ladies."

"No. I'm not going anywhere until you let Julia and Sarah go."

Alan's laughter was his only answer.

JD and the Colonel were passing the Rockslide on their way to the government center when JD's dad came out of the café. "Where you two headed in such a hurry?"

"Got to talk to Hal," the Colonel huffed. "No one's answering at the police station or the post office."

JD said nothing, just sped up to a jog, leaving the two older men behind.

"Wait," his dad called. "JD, I came to say sorry about earlier." To JD's surprise, his dad caught up to him, matched him stride for stride. "Why do you need the police? What's wrong?"

"They have Julia," JD panted.

"Who?"

"Whoever killed the dead guy up the mountain."

George Dolan stumbled on the curb to the post office. JD burst inside, his lungs burning, grabbed the door to the police station, and yanked it open.

Empty.

Except for the Colonel's wife locked in the cell.

CHAPTER FORTY-SEVEN

Grigor licked his lips after finishing a delicious dinner of leftover pasta courtesy of Sarah Durandt. She kept a well-stocked kitchen, had an admirable set of well-used but sharply honed cutlery and a cache of climbing equipment that created a myriad of interesting possibilities.

Alexi and Max kept him apprised of everyone's movements via the cameras they'd placed throughout the town and Alexi's high-powered sniper's scope. They'd seen no sign of Sarah or Stan—*if* Stan was still alive, but Grigor suspected he might be; it just felt right, like it was meant to be, him and Stan meeting again. The universe aligning, back in balance with Grigor free and Stan in his grasp.

Manassas Red was still with Chief Waverly. Their anonymous dead man on the mountain had been discovered, but no matter. Max had the government center secured. They controlled all routes in and out of town. As soon as he gave the order, they'd take down communications.

Other than that the town was quiet. *Not for long*, he thought as he put Sarah's maps to good use. Fire, flood, famine . . . he might not be able to create the last, but he sure as hell could orchestrate the first two.

He used a bright red crayon taken from a child's toy box to mark four more spots on the map. Satisfied with his work, he folded the map and slid it into his pocket.

Just in time for Max to return.

"Done?"

Max nodded and handed Grigor a small radio. "Power's off. I sent an emergency broadcast to the entire town, set a curfew. The streets are quiet."

Grigor chuckled. "Won't be for long. Let's go have another chat with Chief Waverly and our redhead. I have a feeling they might have some interesting answers for us."

"We have to do what he wants," Sam insisted as they hiked the last hundred yards to the Colonel's cabin.

Sarah ignored him, trying to puzzle out alternative options. She wanted so badly to stop Alan and Logan that she dreamed up scenarios more fanciful than any Hollywood director could ever devise.

For once, Sam had been the voice of reason, pointing out the flaws in each of her plans.

"How can you be so calm?" she snapped.

"Josh is safe. If I get them their money, you and Julia will be safe too," he said in a confident tone. "That's all I care about anymore."

She stopped short, grabbed his arm. "You'd better care about more than that. You'd sure as hell better care about getting out of this alive." She swiped away unbidden tears as he stared down at her with a sorrowful expression. "Damn you, Sam Durandt, don't you give up on me, not after all the shit you've put me through. It's going to take me a lifetime to pay you back for the hell I've gone through and I want you to suffer every minute!"

He threw his head back and laughed. "That's my Sarah. You sure know how to make me an offer I can't refuse."

"If you won't fight for me, then fight for your son. To see Josh again."

"I am fighting for Josh," he said, one finger tracing her cheekbone, wiping the single tear that escaped her eye. "And you. No matter what happens, promise me you'll remember that? Maybe tell Josh his old man wasn't as bad as everyone says."

He left her, walking past the two cars and his truck to the cabin. Sarah ran after him. "Sam, no! Wait."

The cabin door opened and Alan emerged, aiming a gun at them. "Just in time. Come on in."

CHAPTER FORTY-EIGHT

"Get me out of here," the Colonel's wife screamed at JD.

"What happened?" JD's dad asked as he ran through the door, followed by the Colonel.

"Some man, I've never seen him before, he came into the post office, pointed a gun at me, locked me in here."

"Where is he?" the Colonel asked.

"I don't know. Gone. Probably robbed the post office. And here I thought we'd be safe with the police station right beside us."

"Don't worry, we'll get you out." The Colonel grabbed a set of keys from a hook hanging behind Hal's desk. A minute later Victoria was free.

"I'm going to get Hal." JD pulled against the door to the post office, anxious to get help for Julia. It rattled but didn't move more than a quarter of an inch or so. "It's stuck."

"What's the problem, son?" the Colonel asked.

"The door. It's locked or something." JD shook it to demonstrate.

"Nonsense," the Colonel's wife said. "There's no lock on that door. Fire code." She marched over, the men moving aside for her four-foot-ten frame, and reached for the door handle. The door didn't open for her either.

"We'll just go out the other way," his dad said, walking to the outside door. He pushed against it. "It's locked as well."

"No. It locks from the inside," the Colonel pointed out. He added his weight and the two men heaved against the door. No luck.

There was no window in the outside door, so the men joined JD and Victoria at the inside door, craning to peer through its window. "Looks like a bar or something. One of those police locks that push against a door."

"Like a traffic boot?" JD asked.

The Colonel nodded. "Who the hell would want to lock us in here?"

"That man. He must still be out there. Call Hal. That's what he's paid for," Victoria ordered.

JD's father was nearest the phone. He raised the receiver. "Dead." He grabbed the radio, pressed the button. "Nothing." His words came fast, like they were under pressure. He sat down in Hal's seat and turned on the computer. "It's dead as well."

Then the lights went out.

"Don't panic," Victoria said. "The building has an emergency generator. It should kick in any minute."

They stood still, the only sound their breathing in the small, cave-like room. For the first time JD noticed there were no outside windows. How could Hal stand working in here?

"The generator should have kicked in by now," the Colonel said. JD felt him brush past as he fumbled his way across the room. "Hell," he muttered as there was a slam of flesh striking a hard object. One of the chairs skidded across the room; then a beam of light circled around the room from a flashlight, spotlighting their faces in a high-powered glare.

"Anyone have a cell phone?" JD asked. He'd given his to Julia; it was still sitting at their picnic area where he'd left her. Julia. It'd been hours since he last saw her; anything could have happened. "We need to call the State Police. The FBI. Someone."

Both older men looked at him like he was crazy. His father refused to carry one except in his delivery truck for emergencies. And who was the Colonel going to call when everyone in town came to him to gossip?

They turned to look at Victoria. A frown furrowed her face. "It's in my purse," she said, pressing her face against the window, staring out into the darkened post office. "Behind the counter."

"That's all right," JD's dad said, bending over the bottom desk drawer. "I think I found—"

"Get away from that!" the Colonel barked.

"What the hell is it? That looks like," JD's dad backed away from the desk in horror, "like, but it can't be—"

"It can. It's a bomb."

Caitlyn blinked at Hal. "Sam's alive? And Josh?"

"He's fine. I don't have all the details, but I'm guessing Sam is the one who hit Leo on the head and then ran with Josh. Must've realized Leo was there to kill him and that Korsakov sent him."

"So Damian Wright was never on that mountain."

"Nope. I think he realized I'd stolen one of his camera cards and took off. Doesn't matter. What's important is that we stop Korsakov."

"Stop him from what?" she asked, still reeling from the knowledge that Sam and Josh were alive.

"Nothing much," Korsakov said as he entered the room accompanied by a man carrying an MP5 machine gun aimed at Caitlyn's chest. "Blowing up the dam, burning down the town, flaying a few folks alive." The Russian grinned at her, raising his own weapon, a semiautomatic. "Maybe starting with you, Red. I don't tolerate liars."

"Don't you touch her." Hal lunged at the Russian, but the second man swiveled to aim at him.

"Drop your weapon," Korsakov ordered Caitlyn. Neither Hal nor Caitlyn moved. Unfortunately, the room was small enough that the second man could easily cover them both from where he stood in the doorway.

"Okay, we do it the hard way." Korsakov sidled between Hal and Caitlyn, taking care to stay out of his man's line of fire, took Caitlyn's Glock. She thought about shooting him, but he never gave her the chance—not without ensuring Hal's death as well. The Russian patted each of them down, taking his time with Caitlyn. Hal was practically snarling by the time he'd finished with her.

"You could have told me you were a Fed, Red," Korsakov said as he flipped through Caitlyn's credentials. "Supervisory Special Agent. Out of Quantico. Guess I should be impressed."

"My backup will be here soon," Caitlyn ad-libbed, hoping she wasn't signing their death warrants by pushing him. "You might have time to escape if you leave now."

The Russian laughed. It was a noise that, although strangely melodic, made her flesh jump. Or maybe it wasn't the laugh. Maybe it was the dark, lifeless look in his eyes as he leveled the full weight of his stare on her.

"Leave? Now why would I want to do that? The fun is only just beginning."

* * *

Sarah followed the men into the cabin. There was no light except what came from the single Coleman lantern and the setting sun. Julia huddled in a corner, crying.

"Are you all right?" Sarah crouched down to the teenager's eye level. Julia nodded tearfully and threw her arms around Sarah, clutching her so hard she could barely catch her breath.

"Did you hurt her?" Sam demanded.

"Relax, we didn't touch her. Good thing it was us who found her and not the Russian," Logan answered.

Sarah looked over Julia's shoulder as Logan clamped his fingers around Sam's arm and began to muscle him out the door. Sam dug in his heels, his fists tight.

"I'm not going anywhere until you let them go. They're no threat to you. It'll take them all night to get down the mountain."

Alan moved to stand beside Sarah, patting her hair as if she were a pet. If it wasn't for Julia holding her tight, Sarah would have gladly broken his hand for him. Followed by a nice eye-gouge and a knee to the groin.

"I'm not risking any double crosses," Alan said. "Go on, get out of here. If the money isn't in my account by morning, I'll kill them both."

His voice was normal; that was the amazing thing about it. They all sounded so normal, so rational, as if they were discussing the day's stock quotes.

"Leave them and come with us," Sam tried one last time, his gaze locking with Sarah's. "How can you be sure Logan won't take the money and run?"

Alan laughed and Logan's face turned dark with fury. "He thought he could, but no worries. Logan isn't going to betray me. Not unless he wants to be running from Korsakov for the rest of his life. Or rot in prison. If he doesn't return, all the evidence I've gathered will be put to good use."

He pulled Sarah to her feet. Julia reluctantly let go, remaining on the floor. "Go on. Sarah and I have a lot to," he smiled at Sarah and her stomach clenched in disgust, "discuss. Privately."

Sarah drew her breath in, forced herself to remain calm. "Go on, Sam. Remember what I said."

Sam gave her a sad half smile. "Your lips promise me a chance at life."

The song he'd left unfinished two years ago. She opened her mouth, wanting to say more, but it was too late. He was gone.

CHAPTER FORTY-NINE

Grigor studied the two law enforcement officers before him, noted the way Hal Waverly shifted his body to protect Caitlyn, despite being handcuffed. He wished he had more time, but the next few steps of his plan had to go on schedule. Still, no reason not to have a little fun.

It wouldn't take long to break the chief. Especially not here, in this room.

"So you killed Leo Richland," he said. Waverly straightened in surprise. "Please, Chief. I told you I'd be watching and listening. You didn't think I would simply trust you to follow orders, did you?"

Ah, that got a rise out of Caitlyn. "Hal. What's he talking about?"

"Tell her, Hal. You already told her the hardest part, about how you betrayed your wife to do your duty and then how you betrayed your best friend for money. Surely betraying your town was a logical progression?"

"I didn't—I haven't." Waverly's face went red as he tried to stammer out a defense. He hauled a breath in, focused on Caitlyn. "I did it to protect Sarah. A few months ago they came to me, asked me to keep an eye on Sarah, report her movements. Then the last few weeks they've been looking around town at night—"

"Those lights the kids were talking about."

"Right. I knew they had something big planned—you don't do reconnaissance just to grab a woman. I learned he was getting out." Waverly jerked his chin in Grigor's direction. Grigor merely smiled, happy the chief was too intimidated to say his name. "I read his file, the things he was accused of. I wasn't going to let that happen, not here, not to people I care about. I was going to give the town council my resignation, kill the Russians myself if I had to. After Sarah was safe. So I arranged for her to leave."

"And once again you failed."

"She's gone. You'll never find her."

"Right. You said. Up the mountain. To join Stan." That was the part Grigor had liked most of all. Of course Stan was still alive. It was fate that they meet again. And Grigor couldn't wait. Once he had the town under his control, he would have all the time in the world to teach Stan and his wife exactly how much pain the human body could endure before the mind snapped. "My Stan. Still alive after all these years. Just waiting for me."

"But they're gone," Caitlyn protested. Still some fight left in her. Not so much in the chief. "You might as well leave before things get worse."

"Don't underestimate me," he snapped. "Both Stan and Sarah will pay. But first, there are a few things I need the chief to help me with. Let's get comfortable." He eyed the restraints on the bed. "Caitlyn, on the bed. Hal, you sit on the floor."

Both resisted, but the choice between complying and a bullet in the brain was an easy one. There was one moment when he thought Caitlyn might prefer death if she could take Grigor with her. But Max knew what he was doing and quickly had her faceup on the bed, wrists bound by the leather restraints before she could make her move.

"Remind you of anyone, Hal?" Grigor asked. Waverly went pale, finally realizing Grigor's plan. "Your poor Lily. Out of her mind with pain, yet you left her. Abandoned her to do your duty."

Grigor tsked as he moved to the head of the bed and flipped open his knife, placing it on Caitlyn's cheek, the point aimed at her eye. He was close enough that he could count the freckles on her creamy skin, feel the quiver of her pulse. She didn't flinch. Instead she slowed her breathing, focused on his gaze. Not many had the courage to do that.

He remembered the way she'd stood up to him when he'd first met her outside of Sarah's house. She would be fun to break.

But right now, he was rushed for time. He edged his gaze back to Hal. "Show him our toys, Max."

Max grabbed the small duffel bag and pulled out one of the Semtex charges. "Max and Alexi have distributed these to a variety of local landmarks. Including four at the base of the dam, your government center, and a few others." Grigor pulled up his sleeve to reveal the wires leading to a heart rate monitor on his wrist. "Anything happens to me, they all blow."

He shook his sleeve back into place. "But in the meantime we can have some fun. Hal, you remember the price you pay if you don't play. You didn't make a choice earlier today, but now you're going to have to. Do we blow one of the charges or do we make lovely Caitlyn scream in pain, just like your darling Lily?"

"Don't, Hal," Caitlyn said. Grigor slid his knife to her lips, pressing hard enough that he'd draw blood if she tried to speak.

"Shhh . . . it's Hal's turn to play. Don't worry, yours will come soon enough."

"I don't—I can't—" Hal's gaze circled the room like a crazed animal pacing its cage.

"Of course you can. You just need to decide. Who are you going to betray? Your town or your woman?"

Sweat beaded on Hal's forehead. As much as Grigor would have loved to prolong the man's misery, he had a schedule to keep.

"How about if I make her scream?" With a flick of his knife he sliced a line down the middle of Caitlyn's chest. He avoided her face—that would come later, much later. If there was time.

She tried to choke back her cry of pain, but still jerked hard enough to rattle the small brass bed. Grigor ran his finger along the blood welling from the cut. He raised it to the wall above the bed, drawing a heart below Lily's sketches of the leaping woman and the snake.

"Are you going to let her die? For what? A town that doesn't appreciate anything you do for them, a town that stole your final moments with your wife, that's stolen your life? Face it, Hal. You're going to die here, but the only thing they'll remember about you is you betrayed them."

"No, I never—"

"Yes. Yes, you did. If it wasn't for you, I'd never have come to Hopewell. You made the call to the FBI two years ago. You let my men in two months ago. You're the one responsible for all the death and destruction yet to come. You, Hal. Are you going to let Caitlyn die as well?"

"You'll just kill her anyway."

Ah, the last line of resistance.

"Of course I will. But there are good ways to die. And there are very, very bad ways to die." He sliced Caitlyn's skin once more, adding two more lines to the vertical one. A letter *K*.

This time a small moan emerged from between Caitlyn's gritted teeth. Not loud, but enough to bring Hal to his knees.

"Do it. Blow the town up. Just let her go." The man was practically sobbing.

"Good choice, Hal." Grigor nodded to Max, who radioed Alexi. Seconds later a thunderous explosion shook the house.

Sam wanted to walk out the door without looking back. It would be easier for everyone that way. He couldn't do it. His feet tripped on the threshold and he turned his head, glanced back.

He froze in place, unable to break free of the sight of Sarah. Her eyes blazed out in defiance until she locked eyes with Sam.

His pulse beat in his throat; he would have screamed if he could have gotten a breath. The heartbreak in her eyes told him she knew as well as he that they both wouldn't survive this day. But then she smiled. Not one of her brighter-than-the-sun grins that had first made him fall in love with her. No, one of her twisted, "hey, this is the real world, deal with it" half smiles to let him know she had faith in him. That she knew if there was a way for him to make sure she and Julia made it out of this hell alive, he would find it.

The blood drained from his face. How could she place her hope in him? A fucked-up loser who should have been washed up on some Santa Monica beach years ago?

He gave her a tiny nod. Let her know he understood. He stepped out the door and out of her sight.

As soon as his foot hit the hard-packed dirt of the

parking area, a plan began forming. He pursed his lips, whistled a little ditty he'd called "The Idiot's Guide to Driving Drunk," and strolled toward Logan's Taurus, his plan shaping up.

It was a suicide mission, but it would buy Sarah the time she needed. From the gleam in her eye, he was certain she had her own plan cooking. That was his girl. She never stopped thinking about ways to make things better and she never, ever gave up. Not even on a hopeless beach bum like him.

He reached a hand for Logan's driver's door.

"No," Logan said, waving his gun. "We'll take the truck. You drive."

Sure thing. Sam forced himself to hang his head so that Logan wouldn't see the grin he couldn't suppress. He slumped his shoulders, his ditty still swirling through his head as he opened the truck's door and climbed up onto the seat, springs squeaking and groaning beneath his weight.

Sorry, old friend, he thought to the Ford Ranger. *We've had some good times together, but now those good times are about to come to an end.*

For one of us at least. Logan yanked open the passenger door and tore Josh's booster seat from the truck, hurling it to the ground. "What's that?" he asked, craning a look into the small compartment behind the seats.

"My guitar. Want me to open it for you?"

"Leave it," he said as he hoisted himself up into the passenger seat and slammed the door. He didn't bother with the seat belt, instead turned to keep his gun trained on Sam. "You pretending to be a cowboy with your truck and guitar? Hide the truth of what you really are to the world? A liar and a thief."

When Sam was silent, Logan gestured for him to start

the truck. Sam made a three-point turn, narrowly avoiding the tree trunks clustered around the tiny clearing, and bumped the Ford over the rutted dirt track.

"What's Alan got on you?" Sam asked as he began to accelerate.

"Easton's going to get himself a bullet if he's not careful." Logan craned his head, looking through the windshield at the thick foliage whipping against the sides of the truck surrounding them. "The man's a fool. He sees a hundred million dollars and thinks of the shit he can buy with it. A new car. A boat. Idiot. Money is power. Control. With money you can own anything—or anyone."

"You couldn't buy me," Sam argued.

"Which is why we can't let you live. Otherwise you might blab to Korsakov. But," he turned to Sam with a grin revealing teeth as crooked as the logging road they were driving on, "I'll let you decide where you want to be buried and how you want to die."

Sam shifted down, the truck growling in response. He pressed on the accelerator, taking the first curve so fast the rear tires nearly spun off the side of the road. The only thing on that side of the road was a whole lot of nothing. That was the point, right?

"You're not really going to let Sarah and Julia go, are you?" Sam asked. "They know too much."

"Oh, we'll let them go," Logan said. "Promise. Just no guarantees Korsakov won't pick them up and make an example of them." He shifted in his seat, leaning toward Sam. "So, what's it gonna be? A bullet in the head? Or one to the heart?"

One more turn and Sam saw the spot he wanted. He gunned the engine, slamming down on the accelerator until he thought his foot would break through the floorboard and find empty air. Logan was flung back in his seat as they careered over the edge of the road and off the side of the mountain.

"How about none of the above?"

CHAPTER FIFTY

Alan turned to them, gun aimed in front of him. Julia. Sarah had to focus on her, do whatever it took to get her out of here alive. No matter the cost.

Alan crowded close to Sarah, his expression more serious than she'd ever seen. If she was reading his expression correctly. Seemed like she'd been blind to so many things these past two years. She backed up, leaving Julia in the corner, until she was pinned against the wall beside the fireplace.

The only light was the flickering of the lantern, casting the mounted antlers hanging just beside the mantle next to her into ghostly shadows. She remembered how proud the Colonel was. That buck had been her first kill, a four-pointer. She had polished and sharpened those antlers herself, mounting them to a sturdy piece of oak and hanging them with pride as the Colonel watched. Now she was the one as trapped as a deer in a hunter's sights.

A chill wind blew in through the still-open door, taunting her with freedom.

To her surprise, Alan pulled out a small radio transmitter. "They're coming your way," he reported. "I've got the wife."

She couldn't hear the reply, but didn't have to. "You're double-crossing Logan. You're working with the Russian."

"I am now. Realized Sam was right, there was no way in hell Korsakov wouldn't come after anyone standing between him and the money or your husband. This way I'll at least get some cash out of the deal and I'll get to live without looking over my shoulder." He sidled closer, eyes wide in anticipation.

"Stay away from me." She focused all her fury into her voice.

"Listen to me, Sarah. This is our last chance."

"You lied to me. For two years you let me think Sam and Josh were dead."

"I thought they *were* dead."

"It was always about the money, wasn't it? I never meant anything to you except a big fat paycheck."

"Baby, that's not true. I admit, at first, maybe. But you have to believe me. I came back for you. You and me. We're going to drive off this mountain, get our money, and live happily ever after. Together." He stopped inches away from her, his gaze dropping from her eyes to her lips, then down to her breasts. She shifted her weight, one hand behind her, gripping the wall.

"What about Sam?"

"Sam's a dead man. You know that." Alan slid the gun barrel across her stomach. Her muscles clenched, trying to pull away from his noxious touch. His smile widened and now his eyes fastened on hers as the gun inched below her shirt, caressing her bare skin. The metal was cold, rough as it crept up, coming to a rest between her breasts.

"And Julia," she persisted. "You'll let her go?"

He sighed but never looked in Julia's direction. "Sure. Of course. Anything you say."

Liar. He couldn't afford to leave witnesses. He thought she was fool enough not to realize that. That he could seduce her with the promise of money and freedom. He raised his free hand to smooth her hair back from her face and Sarah saw her opening.

She kept her eyes locked on his, parted her lips, teasing him as she ran her tongue across them. His body tensed in anticipation. She held her breath as he leaned forward, angling his mouth to meet hers.

Then she plunged the razor-sharp antlers into his side, twisting them up, gutting him.

His scream split the air.

"Run, Julia," she shouted, keeping her grip on the antlers. The gun clattered to the floor as he tried to push her away. She didn't see where it landed, only had eyes for the sight of Julia racing to safety.

Alan slumped, his weight wrenching the antlers from her grasp. "You—bitch—" The words emerged in a harsh groan as he clutched his side.

Sarah didn't wait. She ran to the door. She had to get to Julia. And find Sam.

"What did you do?" Caitlyn asked as the tremor shook the house. It took everything she had not to fight against the bonds restraining her to the bed, but she knew struggling was useless. Physical strength wouldn't win this fight.

"Relax, Red." Korsakov swept her hair back from her face. Gently as if she were a child. It took everything she had not to cringe beneath his touch. "It was only the cell tower. Don't want folks calling out, spoiling our fun. We'll get to the dam soon enough."

"This is your idea of fun? Pushing a button and blowing a dam, killing hundreds of people?" She rolled her eyes, slowly, dismissing him. "I thought you were more inventive than that, Korsakov."

His expression never changed as he squeezed her cheeks in one hand, leveraging his wrist against her throat, choking her. "I'm an artist. I don't expect someone like you to appreciate the scope of what I can invent."

She jerked her head free, her face burning with pain. "I read your file. I think you went soft in prison. All those years locked away, relying on other people to do your work, pushing little buttons from a distance. Don't you want to get your hands dirty again, Korsakov?"

"This," he sat up, arms flung out to both sides, "is my masterpiece. Captured on film for all eternity to see my genius."

She persisted, trying to find a crack in his psychotic delusion. "But even after you blow the dam, it won't last. Not as long as you want it to. You'll get at most a day or two before the helicopters start flying in with State Police or the National Guard. Even if you cut off the power and cell coverage, word will get out. And you'll either be caught or killed before you have a chance to enjoy yourself. To create a real work of art. A visionary piece."

He angled his head, attention focused solely on her words. "What are you proposing?"

She drew in her breath. "Leave now. Take me with you. We can go somewhere private. Somewhere safe. Where you'll have all the time in the world."

He looked away. Had she lost him?

"Think of all those fantasies that filled your head during those seven long years you were in prison, Grigor. You had dreams, plans. Surely you don't want to waste your one chance to make them come true? If you stay here, you'll be caught or killed and your vision will die with you." She dropped her voice to a seductive whisper. "You know I'm right. Let's go. Now. Before it's too late."

He leaned back, his gaze bright with anticipation. She had him.

"Release her, Max. We're going."

Caitlyn focused on breathing deep as Korsakov moved away to allow Max room to remove her restraints. He unfastened her left hand, then reached down for her right. As soon as she felt the last buckle loosen, she swung her weight into his back, driving her fist into his exposed kidney area, and leapt to her feet.

Hal took advantage of her diversion to head butt Korsakov, knocking him to the floor. Caitlyn leapt for the Glocks on the dresser, grabbing one and spinning to aim at the Russian. His partner had rolled to his knees, ready to launch himself at Caitlyn, but Korsakov waved him back.

Then he began laughing. "Nice try, Special Agent. But you forgot one thing." He pulled up his sleeve. "All I need to do is push this button and this town and everyone in it dies."

She froze. Hell, he was right. She'd hoped to knock him out, give Hal time to run for help, but no way that was going to happen.

His smile mocked her with his too-bright teeth and dead eyes. "Give Max the gun."

She had no choice but to comply. Killing him would kill everyone in town. Not that she still wasn't tempted. Max climbed to his feet and yanked the gun from her hand.

"I think you were right about one thing, Caitlyn," Korsakov said as he stood up and shook the wrinkles from his suit. "I might need to leave town sooner than I anticipated. But I won't be taking you with me. You're far too dangerous. Probably the most dangerous person in town. Next to me."

He nodded to Max, who prodded her through the doorway and down the hall. Korsakov followed with Hal.

"Where are you taking us?" Hal asked.

"Not far. Just across the road to the river. I thought we'd reenact your wife's favorite Indian legend."

Just before the last tire left the ground, Sam twisted the wheel furiously and the truck spun sideways, flying into the air.

"Sonofabitch!" Logan's gun went off, the bullet crashing through the windshield. The front passenger corner of the truck smashed into the trunk of a two-hundred-year-old hemlock. The seat belt grabbed Sam so hard he thought it was about to cut him in two. His vision went white as the air bag exploded in his face, pushing him back.

Logan blasted through the windshield as they came to an abrupt halt. His foot caught on the dash, torquing his body sideways and propelling him headfirst into the tree.

The wheels of the truck hit the ground. It landed, resting at a thirty-degree angle on its side. The tree stood in the middle of the engine compartment like an ungainly hood ornament with Logan pinned between two hundred years of wood and two thousand pounds of steel.

The pounding in Sam's ears made him dizzy. Conking his head against the steering wheel after the air bag deflated didn't help any. He blinked hard. Blood was running into his eyes, but his vision was clear. Clear enough to see Logan's body twisted like a rag doll in unearthly directions that had literally torn the leg with the foot caught in the dash from his body.

Sam swallowed hard against the wave of nausea

accompanying that sight. Thank God Logan's slacks were still relatively intact, there was little blood on the surface. It was knowing what lay beneath that made Sam's stomach heave.

He turned his head away and took stock. His hands were wrapped around the steering wheel in a death grip. He focused on releasing them. When he opened his hands, his fingers stubbornly remained curled and pain rumbled through his wrists. The air was curiously still and quiet, as if the forest held its breath, waiting to see what would happen next.

His chest hurt like he'd been kicked by a mule and he couldn't feel his right foot at all. Had it gone through the floorboard like he'd imagined? Maybe it was lying a hundred feet above them on the side of the road?

Aw hell, maybe this wasn't such a good idea after all.

He wasn't sure how long he lay there, trying to remember how to breathe, but it was long enough for the last remnants of the setting sun to fade. Dim sparkles of moonlight filtered through the tree branches, just enough to convince him he really was still alive.

Focus, Sam. Alan still has Sarah.

That thought cleared his mind. He heaved his weight against the door. At first it wouldn't budge; then slowly, with a groan of metal scraping against metal, it gave an inch. He slumped back, panting, sweat pouring from him. He still couldn't feel his right foot, but the pain cascading over the rest of his body more than made up for that.

He took a deep breath and tried again. This time the door popped open. He fell sideways, almost all the way out of the truck. Until his foot caught.

"Mother of God!" His yell tore through the night. No one seemed to care. As loud as his shout was, his foot was screaming louder. God, he'd rather cut it off than feel this.

Bone scraped against bone, sending shock waves through his body.

Now he really was going to vomit. He caught the door frame with his hands, hauled his weight back onto the seat, releasing the pressure from his trapped leg. But once woken, the pain wouldn't stop its clamoring. He wrapped his fingers around his calf trying in vain to stabilize the leg, to free it, or yank it totally off—anything to stop the pain.

A searing light stabbed into his eyes. He held up his hands to block it.

"Sam? Are you all right?"

Sarah. It was Sarah. Sam didn't try to fight the tears of joy that overwhelmed him. He cleared his throat, wiped a hand over his face, and caught his breath as she maneuvered through the brush to his side of the truck. Her flashlight bobbed through the darkness, flashing on Logan—or what remained of him—then on Sam, then over his head and back again.

"Are you okay?" he asked as she joined him.

"I'm fine. Julia's in the car, waiting. I stole Logan's car," she said with a trace of pride in her voice. Then a shadow covered her face.

"And Alan?"

She leaned across him to examine the situation more closely. "Hold this." She handed him the flashlight. She leaned forward, her fingers gently probing his leg. "I think maybe I killed him."

Her tone was flat and he didn't ask any questions. She wiggled something and he bit his lip against a shriek of pain. She turned her head to look up at him. "Your foot is wedged under the gas pedal. It's bleeding, probably broken. I can slide it out if I can twist it to one side—but it's gonna hurt."

He sucked in his breath. "Do it."

CHAPTER FIFTY-ONE

Korsakov and Max led them out of the house and down the drive to where it intersected with the dirt road leading up the mountain. The sun had set, but ribbons of red and orange still colored the sky over the mountains to the west. The sound of the falls downstream drowned out any other night noises.

Max prodded Caitlyn and Hal onto the dock overlooking the calmer water of the eddy. From here it was easy to see the white water dancing over the rocks above the falls.

"Hal had his chance to make a choice," Korsakov said. He pressed his body against Caitlyn's from behind, pushing her into Hal so they were face-to-face. "Now it's yours."

He slid his hands down her hips, then raised them, directing her arms forward, wrapping them around Hal's chest. "Duct tape them below his back," he told Max. Soon she and Hal were restrained together, her wrists taped at the small of his back, his still handcuffed behind his back. "Now tape his ankles."

Hal bowed his head, his mouth close to her ear. "I'm so sorry," he whispered. "This is all my fault."

She had no answer. He'd done all the wrong things for all the right reasons. Trying to remain loyal to both his wife and his job; trying to save his home; trying to protect Sarah.

Shoving her emotions aside, she concentrated on their current dilemma. It was easy to see what Korsakov meant by her choice: He'd turned Hal into a deadweight. If she freed herself, he'd drown. If she didn't, they'd both die.

Unless she could figure out a way to free them both. She still had the handcuff key in her pocket. Maybe she could free herself, then rescue Hal.

She heaved in one deep breath after another as Max finished his work and stood back.

"Throw them in," the Russian ordered.

Max took a few steps back to get a running start, then plowed into Hal and Caitlyn, sending them off the end of the dock and into the water.

Caitlyn almost lost the breath she was desperately trying to keep inside as they flew through the air and hit the water. It was cold, shockingly cold. The dark water swallowed them fast, the faintest gleam of ruby-red sunset visible overhead.

Despite the lack of white water, the current was still strong, tossing them about even as she tried to worm her way free of Hal's body. He didn't resist; in fact, he did his best to help her, as if he'd accepted his fate.

She wished she had a way to tell him to hang on, that she had a plan. She stretched her arms as far as they could go, over the top of his, and brought them over his head even as the water pulled him down. They tumbled against some rocks and a submerged tree limb, slowing their movement as the river tried to pull them out of the eddy and toward the falls. She hooked her leg around Hal's armpit, knowing she'd never find him again in the dark water.

The key was in her front pocket, but the denim was wet and hard to maneuver with her wrists taped together. She crashed into a rock, hitting her hip, almost losing Hal. Then her fingers snagged the key.

Lungs burning, vision dancing with tiny starbursts as her brain screamed for oxygen, she clutched the key and felt for Hal's arm. His weight pulled against her as if he was trying to push her away.

They reached the rapids. Hal careened into a rock, but it wedged him in place even as the current battered her. She pressed her face against his, could just barely make him out as she raised the key to show him. All she needed was for him to turn enough for her to reach his wrists.

Her lungs were heaving with the effort as she fought against gulping down the water. She wasn't going to make it, a voice whispered treason. No. She would save him. She had to.

She tugged at his arm, fighting the current. Felt the metal of the bracelet. Almost there . . .

The key slid against the handcuff and fell from her numb fingers. Hal's gaze met hers, his eyes the only thing she could see in the dark water tugging at them.

He pressed his lips against hers, forcing what was left of his air into her. Then he shook his head sorrowfully and jerked away from her, pushing off the rock with his legs, propelling her to the surface even as the water pulled him down.

Her face broke free of the water, gulping in air. The rapids pulled her back down, but she fought free, took in another breath. Hal, where was he? She twisted and turned, fighting to find him.

He was gone. He'd sacrificed himself to save her.

She wasn't about to let his death be in vain. The roar of the falls was louder now, drowning out everything, even the panicked pounding of her heart.

The current tumbled her upside down once more. Another snarl of tree limbs grabbed her. A red sheen glimmered below her—was that the surface? Or her vision dimming from lack of oxygen?

She was overwhelmed by the impulse to exhale, to release her remaining oxygen, surrender to the water.

The idea brought with it a sensation of peace, of calm.

Caitlyn kicked away from the tree's embrace, fought to gain the darkening red gleam. Her legs could barely move as they fought against the current, her arms flailed through the churning water, and her chest felt ready to explode.

The smudge of red was dimming, growing farther away. Panic seized her and she kicked harder, one last try.

Her mind grew hazy; she couldn't feel her arms or legs. She was floating, floating through space. Was this what her father had felt in that instant before his brain shut down?

Her body slammed into a rock bed, scraping her back raw. She pulled away, gasped for air, drew in water, and began to choke and sputter. As she heaved her chest forward, her face broke through the water and she sucked in fresh air.

After several deep breaths, she was able to focus, to look around. Her leg was caught under a rock outcropping, trapping her. Good thing too, because she was in another eddy just above the falls. The spray from the angry water filled the air with starry sparkles caught in the moonlight.

She raised her head, looked to the riverbank. Empty. Korsakov and his man gone. No signs of Hal. She blinked water from her eyes and looked into the face of the blue moon hanging so low that she was certain she could reach out and touch it.

It was up to her, now. Alone, unarmed, half-drowned. But there was no one else to stop the Russian and save the town.

CHAPTER FIFTY-TWO

Sarah craned her head to look up at her husband. The bright light of the flashlight etched his face into crevices of pain. And she was about to cause him more.

She realized for the first time that her anger was gone. Sam had made mistakes. Many of them. But he was a different man now and everything he'd done in the past two years had been done in the hopes of keeping her and Josh safe. She hadn't totally forgiven him—she might never—but she was beginning to understand.

Reaching a hand out, she took his and gave it a strong squeeze. "I love you, Music Man."

His eyes widened as he looked down at her in surprise. She took that opportunity to wrench his leg out in one quick, firm movement.

His scream echoed through the small space. The color drained from his face and his hand gripped hers so tight she couldn't feel it. Then he released her and slumped back. "You've got some bedside manner there."

"It worked, didn't it?" She turned back to examine his ankle. It was already swollen, purple and scraped raw, oozing blood from several areas. But it was in one piece. "Let's get you out of here."

Together they maneuvered him out of the truck. Sam couldn't put any pressure on his leg, so he leaned on her.

"Wait," she said, handing him the flashlight. She reached back into the truck and grabbed his guitar case, hauling it over the seat and then slinging it over her free arm.

In response, he grabbed her waist, pulling her close, and planted a wide-open kiss on her mouth.

"C'mon. Julia is waiting." She guided him down the mountain to where she'd parked the car. The truck had flown off the topside of a switchback and landed close to the straightaway on the downhill side, saving them the need to climb back up the mountain.

Julia was waiting, hiding in some bushes off the edge of the road. She leapt out to help Sarah wrangle Sam the rest of the way to the car.

Sarah lowered the guitar, ready to toss it into the back, when the glitter of headlights on a curve above them came into view. Alan. Coming for them. "Julia, can you drive?"

"No, ma'am."

"All right, get into the back," she ordered, trying to ignore the knot of fear in her throat. "Sam, take the wheel."

Sam tensed beside her, craned his head to stare up at the lights. "No. It's me he wants."

"Listen to me. You can drive. Get Julia out of here." She firmly pushed him down into the driver's seat. "I'll take care of Alan."

"How?" Sam asked as he maneuvered his injured leg to the side and slid into place behind the wheel.

Sarah propped the guitar case against the side of the car and unsnapped the small pouch attached to its lid. "With a little help from the dark and the woods." She pulled out a package of wire guitar strings. "And these. Now go. If this works, I'll meet you down at the Rockslide."

"No. I'm not leaving you again. I'll wait for you."

The lights above them were moving slowly but steadily in their direction. As if the man behind the wheel was having a hard time maneuvering the car. She hoped he'd have a harder time walking.

Sam snagged her waistband, pulling her forward into the car for a quick kiss. "Did you mean what you said?"

"I'll always love you; you're the father of my son," she said. "That doesn't mean I always like you. Or that I've totally forgiven you. Yet."

She slammed the door shut before he could wrench any more confessions from her. "Keep your lights off so he doesn't see you. Now go!"

The Taurus slid past her, lights off, engine purring as Sam eased it down the road. She wanted to race after them, jump in, tell him to just drive as fast as he could.

Instead she tore open the package of wire guitar strings and found the longest length. She coiled it around her palm. The bite of metal against her flesh took her mind off Sam and Josh as she considered her plan. She had to finish this, now, tonight.

No more running, no more hiding. She couldn't let Alan off this mountain alive.

The glare of headlights impaled her. She feinted, running along the road as the car behind her sped up, aiming for her. She turned to look over her shoulder, saw Alan, hunched over the wheel of his Volvo, his face filled with hate.

Good. He was focused on her. Not Sam or Julia.

She could smell the fumes, felt the rumble of the engine hurtling toward her. At the last possible moment, she leapt off the road and into the shrubs. The car braked and fishtailed, spinning sideways to land with two wheels off the road fifty feet away from her.

Alan opened his door, staggered out. He'd removed his jacket. His white shirt was drenched in blood, but she'd obviously not wounded him as seriously as she'd hoped. Damn silk suit. The extra layers of fabric must have blunted her blow. His tie was missing as well and his hair stuck out from his head as if he'd turned into a wild man.

"Sarah!" he called into the night, brandishing the gun. "Come out, Sarah! I won't hurt you if you give me what I want."

His voice was cajoling, but the gleam in his eyes was murderous. Her fingers tightened on the guitar string. She'd finally found something more important to Alan Easton than money.

Killing her.

She broke cover, rustling through the bushes with enough noise to wake the dead. *Sorry, Colonel*, she thought as she continued to break a trail that a blind grandmother could follow. Or a city-slicker lawyer.

She knew exactly where she needed to go. Snakebelly. Was it really only two nights ago that she'd camped on this ledge, dreaming of Indian princesses and Sam? Alan's footsteps broke through the night, following her trail.

She quickened her pace until she reached the spot where she'd anchored her climbing rope after they'd removed Leo Richland's body from Snakebelly. Good, it was still there. She drew the rope through her fingers until she had a good length coiled and ready to go. Quickly she fastened a makeshift harness around her hips.

Spinning the length of wire before her, she wrapped one end of wire around a sapling at ground level and kept hold of the other end. She crouched down in the shadow of a boulder and waited.

"Sarah! Don't make this harder than it has to be. Come out now like a good girl. You know I'll find you. Or if not you, I'll find Julia." He stepped into the small clearing. "Now you've nowhere to go." He swept his hand with the gun from one side to the other, squinting in the moonlight as he scanned the shadows. There was only one hiding place large enough. He aimed the gun directly at her.

"Come out, Sarah. It's over." He stepped forward, now only five paces from the ledge.

He took another step, raised the gun. And fired.

Sarah jumped at the crack of noise that shattered the night. The bullet struck the rock above her, splintering her with shards of granite.

"Now, Sarah!" he commanded, his tone one of victory as he took another step closer to her.

She stood, keeping her hand behind her. He leered at her, the gun centered on her chest. "That's a good girl."

He took one last step. Now he stood before her, almost touching her. His breath came in gasps; his chest heaved with adrenaline and exertion. "Now I know why people hunt. The thrill of the chase. It's exhilarating."

The whites of his eyes gleamed in the moonlight. Sarah stood still, waiting for her opening. The abyss waited less than a foot away from them both.

He prodded at her with the gun. "You've been a bad girl," he whispered. "You're going to pay for what you've done."

Sarah forced herself to meet his gaze. "Like hell I will."

His slap rocked her back against the edge of the boulder, but it gave her the momentum she needed to overcome his greater weight. She grabbed his belt and pivoted against him, yanking the wire tight with her other hand. At first he allowed her to use his weight to get up.

Too late he realized she was leveraging him over the edge. His foot caught in the wire, his hand with the gun jumped up, slamming against her jaw.

The wire sliced into her palm, but she refused to release it. She rammed her body against his, pushing him over the edge. He stutter-stepped, still trying to catch his balance. For one frozen moment her face was a mere inch away from his. His mouth was open wide, but no sound came. Just a rush of breath as he reached out for her.

She toppled over the edge with him, the wire finally slipping from her grasp.

CHAPTER FIFTY-THREE

It was awkward driving with one leg stretched out beside the other, using his left foot. Every time he jostled his right foot a fresh explosion of pain would crash over him. But the worst part was when he lost sight of Sarah in the rearview mirror. It was as if he'd lost part of himself.

Daddy? He imagined Josh's voice if he returned without Sarah. *Why couldn't Mommy stay with us? Didn't she want to come home?*

Okay, he was wrong. Now he really knew what pain was—the thought of shattering his son's heart.

Sam couldn't really blame Josh if he never forgave him. Just as he couldn't blame Sarah. He'd made a complete mess of things.

But if Sarah came back, they could start over. No Korsakov, no Alan—just her and Josh and Sam. A family. Again.

"You okay back there, Julia?" he asked, more to try to distract himself from his morbid fears of Sarah's death than anything.

"Y-yes, sir." Her voice was muffled by tears.

"We're going to get out of this. All right?" Then he remembered that he still had her cell phone. He pulled it from his pocket and handed it to her over the backseat. "Why don't you call your parents, let them know you're all right?"

She took the phone. He slowed the car as they approached a hairpin turn, dared to turn the lights on. Not much farther.

"Can't. There's no signal," Julia said leaning over the backseat, her voice more normal now.

"It's all right. We're almost there."

Together Sarah and Alan hurtled through the darkness. Her stomach lurched with the feeling of free fall. Then, after an agonizing moment, her rope yanked her to a stop.

Alan plummeted past her, his screams fading into the darkness long after his body vanished from her sight.

Sarah hung at the end of her rope for a long moment before she could catch her breath. Then she rocked her weight forward, nudging the rock face, until she found purchase for her feet. She placed her weight back against the rope and climbed out.

Sarah made it back to the Volvo and started down the mountain. Her hands could barely grip the steering wheel, they were so torn up from holding the wire and the rope. But other than that, she was pretty much in one piece.

She rolled her shoulders, daring to relax for the first time in days. Sam was safe, Josh was safe, they were going to make it—

A woman's form jumped out from the shadows. Sarah stomped on the brakes, the car spinning out on the dirt road. She felt the brake pedal pump against her foot as she wrestled the steering wheel, trying to keep the car from plummeting over the side of the mountain.

The car came to a stop mere inches away from the woman. She didn't seem to notice, was already sprinting to the driver's side, pounding on the door with one hand.

It was Caitlyn. The car rocked with the force of her blows. She looked like a madwoman, her hair wet, shoved in all directions, clothing soaked and clinging to her. Her face was white in the moonlight, one eye almost swollen shut, blood smeared over her cheek and chest.

"Let me in! Federal agent!"

Sarah rolled down her window. "Caitlyn, it's me. What happened?"

Caitlyn fell against the car, her chest heaving as she gasped for air. "Hal Waverly. He's dead. The Russian—we have to stop him."

"Korsakov?"

"We've got to get to town. He's got bombs. He's planning to blow up the dam!"

CHAPTER FIFTY-FOUR

Sam pulled up to the curb in front of the Rockslide. Julia hopped out, obviously anxious to be free of today's adventures. He debated sitting here, waiting for Sarah, rather than leaving the car. His foot hurt so much he'd almost bitten his tongue in half to keep from crying out.

The dome light came on when Julia opened the door. He was surprised by the puddle of blood his leg sat in. Every time he moved, more blood squished out from beneath his sock.

"Sam, I think you need Doc Hedeger," Julia said, leaning in to peer at him and his leg. "I'll go get him."

"Help me inside the café first," Sam said. "The Colonel can help me wrap it up, stop the bleeding until the doc gets here."

She nodded and sprinted around to his side of the car, letting him lean his weight against her as he slid out. As soon as his leg left the seat and swung to the ground, pain catapulted through him. His stomach reeled and he felt like he was going to black out. He leaned heavily against Julia, thankful for her youthful strength, as she half-dragged him to the café door.

The entire town was dark, he realized. But inside the Rockslide there was light—not as much as normal, only the few hooked up to the emergency generator. The Colonel was a stickler for being prepared for anything. He swayed as Julia loosened her grip long enough to hold the door open for him.

"Just a little farther," she said.

Sam nodded, his entire being focused on the black and white linoleum beneath his feet. Smears of blood splattered the gleaming surface below his foot.

"Good evening, Stan," came the voice from his darkest nightmares. Sam jerked his head up as Julia came to an abrupt halt. "I knew if I waited patiently, sooner or later you'd catch up with me."

Grigor Korsakov slid out from the booth where he sat in the farthest corner of the café. Sam could barely keep his head held high enough to meet the Russian's gaze. His body swayed; if it wasn't for Julia, he would have fallen. Still, he unwrapped his arms from her body.

"Go," he whispered to her. "Run. Now."

Sarah rocketed the car down the dirt road. They came to the intersection with Lake Road. To the right was Hopewell, to the left the road to the dam.

One way led to Sam. The other to probable death—and the chance to save the lives of everyone in town.

"What are you waiting for?" Caitlyn asked, tugging at the wheel with her good hand. "Go."

Sarah spun the wheel, heading toward the dam. For the first time she appreciated the awful decision Sam had to make that night two years ago. Injured, almost dead, he'd still found the strength to get off the mountain and take Josh to a safe place.

She pushed down on the accelerator, gravel spraying the road behind her, pinging against the undercarriage. Caitlyn kept talking, repeating the instructions about how to dismantle the bombs for the fourth time, as if the more she talked, the less likely they were to die tonight.

A fact they both knew was a lie.

"He's using radio-controlled detonators. Called someone else who I'm guessing has line of sight. All it takes is one spark of electricity to the blasting cap and—" She threw up her hand for emphasis.

"The southeast corner of the dam," Sarah said. "There's a fire tower. From the top you can see the entire reservoir and most of town. He could see everything."

"Perfect location. That's where he'll be," Caitlyn said grimly. "You get to those bombs; there were four on the map. I'll keep Korsakov's man busy as long as I can. He won't blow the dam—not unless he's on a suicide mission. So that will buy you time."

Sarah bounced the Volvo onto the dirt track leading down to the dam. "Stop here," Caitlyn ordered. "Kill the lights." They cruised to a stop behind the caretaker's cabin, hidden by the thick foliage.

Caitlyn reached up to turn the dome light off. "Open the trunk."

Sarah pulled the latch, wincing at the noise. Caitlyn left the car, reappearing a moment later armed with a short crowbar with two sharp, notched edges.

"Wait for me to get clear of the car, then you sneak over to the dam wall, start on the bombs."

The FBI agent slipped past the sumac and hugged the shadows below the dam as she maneuvered over to the fire tower on the opposite end. Once she reached the base of the tower Sarah slipped out of the car and followed. She started at the far end of the dam, searching through the dark shadows until she found the first bomb.

They hadn't even tried to conceal it. It was a mound of clay-colored bricks with several wires leading to an electronic receiver and two blasting caps. Sarah reached out her hand, then yanked it back when she realized it was trembling.

Her breath left her in a whoosh and she felt light-headed. All she had to do was to pull the blasting caps away from the C4. If Korsakov triggered the bomb, the blasting caps would still explode, but it wouldn't do any serious damage. As long as Sarah wasn't holding one when it went off.

She squinted her eyes, double-checking where the blasting caps were inserted into the puttylike explosive. *Piece of cake. Just a little tug and . . .* She sat back, suddenly holding the detonator in her hand.

It was easier than she had dreamed. Able to breathe again, she threw the blasting cap as far away from her as she could. It landed in the grass with a soft thud. She did the same with the second one.

She crawled through the darkness searching for the next bomb. One down, three to go.

CHAPTER FIFTY-FIVE

Sam lurched forward, trying to block Korsakov's aim at Julia. The Russian merely smiled and sidled to his left, the gun in his hand pointed directly at the girl. She'd started for the door, stopped when she realized she couldn't make it without getting shot.

"Smart girl," Korsakov said. "Friend of yours?"

"She was just helping me out of a jam," Sam said, keeping his voice casual as he slumped against the countertop near the cash register. "Let her go."

He realized his mistake as soon as the words left his mouth. Korsakov raised an eyebrow. "You giving me orders now, Stan?" He crooked his little finger at Julia. "Come here, little girl. Get comfortable. We'll be here a little while."

"Why?" Sam said, as Julia took a hesitant step forward, then stopped again. "Don't you want to get out of town before the cops come? Anyone could pass by these windows, see you with a gun, and call them."

"Sorry, no. The power is out for the entire town. Except for the generator here. Oh, and the Chief of Police imposed a curfew, told everyone to stay off the roads during the emergency. At least that's what the good citizens of Hopewell think." He shivered in delight. "All snug in their beds, not knowing that they probably won't see the light of day again. After I blow the dam, that is." He held up a small radio. "But we have time." He smiled at Julia. "Long enough for us to get acquainted."

Julia crossed her arms over her chest, hiding her breasts from the Russian's rapacious leer. While Korsakov ogled her, Sam closed his fist around a napkin dispenser.

"Julia, run!" He hurled it at Korsakov.

The Russian fired, hitting Sam in his injured leg. He pivoted to fire again, but Julia was too fast; she'd darted out the door and vanished in the night.

Sam grabbed onto the counter, fighting to remain upright. He didn't feel anything—the pain from his broken ankle had already overwhelmed him. Blood spread out over the lower thigh of his jeans. Suddenly he wasn't sure which way was up and he slowly toppled to the ground.

"That was stupid, Stan," Korsakov said, approaching him and placing an Italian-clad foot on his wound, pressing down to both stop the blood flow and inflict as much pain as possible. "As always, you were trying to take the easy way out. You thought I would kill you quickly, that you would die an easy death."

He crouched down until his face filled Sam's vision. "Sorry, old friend. That's not what I have in mind for you." He paused, glanced out the door as if expecting someone else to appear there. "Or your lovely wife. She should be joining us soon. If Alan's good to his word. And then we'll blow this pizza joint." He chuckled. "Literally."

Caitlyn was sore from head to toe, the pain radiating through her body all consuming as she hauled herself up the steps leading to the top of the three-story-tall tower. Every breath hurt, so she was guessing she'd cracked a few ribs. And she couldn't raise her left arm above her waist, so add in a broken collarbone or shoulder separation.

The only part of her body that didn't hurt was her head. A few lumps and bumps, but no headache and certainly no steamroller of a migraine. In the past exertion and fatigue had been prime triggers, but she'd been relatively pain free all day.

Go figure. She grabbed the splintery wooden railing and climbed another step up, her bare feet pressed against the rough wood. She tried not to look down where the darkness swallowed everything except for the cascade of moonlight on the reservoir waters. The sound of the falls was louder up here and the ancient fire tower swayed with their vibration.

She wondered if Hal's body would end up caught in the screens filtering the reservoir. Closed her eyes for a moment, unable to cast aside the last image of his face turned to hers. He'd seemed at peace. For the first time since she'd met him.

She rounded the last landing and took the final steps leading to the top landing, moving quietly. A girl was huddled against the corner, her wrists and ankles bound by duct tape, a gag caught in her mouth. She looked up at Caitlyn and pushed back as if trying to get through the rough-hewn wood wall.

Caitlyn shook her head and raised a finger to her lips. The girl nodded, then jerked her head to the observation deck beyond the roofed portion of the tower. Caitlyn crouched to remain below the windows and duckwalked to the opposite door. It stood open. Beyond it a man had arranged a chair and table where he had a sniper's rifle, spotting scope, and radio. He peered through the scope, aiming it across the ridge to where the police station was.

"Start the countdown," Korsakov's voice came over the radio.

The man was too far away for Caitlyn to stop him from changing channels on the radio and pressing a button. But his movement turned his back to her for a precious moment. Long enough for her to stand up, sprint forward, and take a solid swing at his head with the crowbar.

The steel bar bounced off his head with a satisfying thud. To her surprise, it didn't knock him out. Instead he swung his head in her direction and stood, shoving the chair aside. He had a pistol holstered in a shoulder harness on his left side but didn't reach for it. From his expression he didn't see her as much of a threat.

She'd see about that. Caitlyn swung again, this time aiming at his knee. She felt bone crunch and he staggered, dropping against the railing, but he reached out and grabbed her as he fell, pinning her beneath his weight. Something popped in her ankle and she cried out in pain.

She lurched against the railing, almost slipping through it. He reared forward, slapping her hard enough to knock her teeth together. The movement gave her the opening she needed to grab his gun.

Caitlyn fired point-blank, the blast deafening at such close range. He raised his arm, ready to push her over the railing. She fired again, twice more, hitting center mass each time. He swayed, mere inches away from her and the edge of the platform.

She kept firing and he toppled backward over the railing.

A bright light filled the sky, a thousand fireworks exploding. A rush of wind blasted them, followed by a noise louder than a banshee's howl. The tower jerked violently. Caitlyn reached out and grabbed for the railing as the night splintered into fire.

CHAPTER FIFTY-SIX

After the nearby explosion rocked the building JD's dad and the Colonel went into a quiet panic. It took them twenty minutes to pry open the gun cabinet, only to find it empty.

"What blew up?" JD asked, frustrated that he couldn't get out to help Julia. Was she near the explosion? Maybe the terrorists used her as a human bomb like in the movies.

"Not the dam or we'd still be feeling and hearing it," JD's dad said.

"Probably either the cell tower or the road out of town," the Colonel said. "Those are the weak areas in our defenses."

The Colonel's wife kept hitting the window of the inside door with a riot baton, but all she got for her efforts was a noise as if they were trapped inside a drum.

"Probably bulletproof," the Colonel said. But that didn't stop him and JD's dad from smashing a chair and trying to punch out the window with the legs.

JD backed up out of their way. The only place to go was near the desk. He glanced down at the bomb in the drawer. It had a complicated nest of wires and components that looked like the inside of a video game. Suddenly one of the displays lit up.

"Dad?" he called out, shouting to make himself heard over the noise of their pounding. "Hey!"

The grown-ups all stopped and stared at him.

"It's doing some kind of countdown," JD said, the calmness in his voice surprising him. He knew he was scared, but somehow he couldn't feel it any longer. It was as if he were floating, ready to accept whatever happened next.

"Let me see," Victoria said. "Oh Lord. It's counting down seconds."

"How many?" the Colonel asked.

"Ninety-two, ninety-one—"

"JD, get away from there," his dad said, pulling him away. "Here, get under the bunk; it will shield you."

"What about you, Dad?"

"Never mind me, just get under there. I'll cover you with the mattress."

"You too, Victoria," the Colonel ordered.

"No. Whither thou goest, so do I."

"Victoria!"

It was plain to see that no measly two-inch mattress was going to stop a bomb and no way JD was going out hiding under a bed like a baby. He stood beside his father, reaching for his hand. "I'm fine right here, Dad."

"I never told you how proud I was of you, Son."

JD looked up to see tears glittering on his father's cheeks. Before he could say anything, there was a pounding on the door.

The door opened and Julia stood there. "What's the deal?" she asked holding the pressure lock in her hand.

JD grabbed her arm and pulled her away. "Just run."

Together they raced down the hill followed closely by the three adults.

Sarah looked numbly at the detonator in her hand. Had she done that? she wondered as the sky rained dirt and gravel down on her. In front of her, the dam trembled but did not break. Light blazed through the sky farther north.

Town. Something in town had exploded.

She shook her head, images of Sam and Julia and the Colonel at the café filling her mind. Her vision darkened and she felt faint for a moment, as if all the blood had been drained from her. She shook herself hard. No time for that. She still had one more bomb to find and disarm.

Before the same thing happened here.

Sam felt the floor heave below him and his head explode. No, not his head, he realized as cutlery and glass flew to the floor around him, peppering him with shards of glass. Korsakov was thrown off balance, landing on his back, slamming his head against one of the booths. Sam barely had time to roll over and cover his head before the plate-glass window blew out. A howling wind blasted through the café, toppling stools. Crashes ricocheted from the rear room and several tables overturned. Sam couldn't hear anything over the roaring in his head.

The wind subsided and silence ensued. He raised his head. One of the pedestal tables in the booth had flipped over onto Korsakov. It wouldn't slow him down for long, but maybe long enough.

Sam ignored the pain lancing through his leg and dragged himself across the debris-strewn floor. Korsakov's gun lay just a few feet away. The Russian was already moving, struggling to haul the table off his chest. He saw what Sam was doing and a ghastly smile played over his face, lit in flickering half shadows by the single remaining fluorescent light dangling overhead.

"Whoops. Guess we miscalculated that one." Korsakov gave a grunt and heaved the table away from him. He rolled and darted a hand out for the gun that Sam struggled to reach. Sam pushed himself as hard as he could, sliding on his own blood, and grabbed the gun first.

Korsakov's laughter echoed through the pounding in Sam's brain. "Go ahead," he taunted. "Shoot me. If you have the guts."

Sam leveraged himself up to a sitting position. "No problem," he said, raising the gun.

Korsakov's smile only widened. "Well, actually there're two very big problems." He sat up. "That was just one bomb. Anything happens to me, the entire town goes up."

Sam ignored the Russian's words, curling his finger around the trigger. "You're bluffing."

Korsakov laughed. "Well then, there's always reason number two."

A large shadow fell over Sam. The cold, hard muzzle of a gun pressed against the side of his head.

"What's it going to be, Stan? Both of us dead or both of us alive?"

CHAPTER FIFTY-SEVEN

Sarah yanked the detonator out of the last bomb and ran to the foot of the tower. "Are you all right?" she called up to Caitlyn.

"I'm fine," came the breathless reply.

"Sam is in town; I need to go to him, get help."

Caitlyn appeared on the top landing, limping and holding her one arm. She sank onto the steps as if her leg wouldn't hold her weight. "You go. I'll just slow you down."

Sarah hesitated. "You sure?"

"Go. Get your husband. I'll be right behind you. Here." A dull thud as Caitlyn tossed a semiautomatic pistol down, followed by the magazine of bullets. "Be careful."

Sarah scooped the gun up, rammed the magazine home, and ran to the Volvo. "I'll send help," she called over her shoulder. Caitlyn merely gave a weak wave.

The blast hadn't hurt the car, Sarah was pleased to see. The engine turned over smoothly. She gunned it and headed back up the dirt road into town. To her surprise, the streets were empty and relatively clear. A few mailboxes and trash cans were overturned amid broken glass, but even most of the streetlights were still working. Some shingles had blown off the church across from the Rockslide. Other than missing its window, the café appeared intact.

She blew out a sigh of relief. Her headlights revealed a wall of smoke farther down the street where the government center stood. Or used to stand.

The sheriff had been quick to respond. A Tahoe with grille lights flashing red and blue stood in front of the café. She pulled up alongside it. A man was helping someone inside the Rockslide while another man staggered to his feet under his own power.

The man slumped against the burly deputy was Sam. She left the car and ran over the broken glass to the doorway. Then she saw the guns.

Neither of the men wore uniforms; rather they wore dark suits. One held a gun against the back of Sam's neck while the other, the one on the floor, had a pistol aimed at his body. Sam lost his footing, almost falling to the floor, and the first man lowered his gun to grab him and haul him onto his feet. His cry of pain wrenched at her, but the other man in the café simply laughed.

Sarah had never shot at a person, never been in combat, but it was as if she heard all the Colonel's war stories rush through her head. *It's like you're in a trance,* he'd told her the one time they'd seriously discussed it when she was a girl. *You don't even realize you're shooting at men; you're just trying hard to stay alive and protect your own.*

She raised and fired at the man holding Sam, hitting him square in the chest as he pivoted to face her.

"Drop it!" she shouted to the second man. He aimed at her, had a clear shot.

Sam lurched forward, throwing himself at the man. They fell to the ground. The man fired his gun. Sarah felt a rush of air as the bullet passed her.

Sam tried to roll his weight onto the man. Blood was smeared everywhere, both men sliding in it as they fought to gain the upper hand. The man with the gun tried to aim it at Sam, blocking any shot Sarah might take.

"Sam, move!" she shouted. "I've got him."

Instead of rolling off the man, Sam grabbed the stranger's shirt collar and used it to bash the guy's head on the edge of the bench behind them. At first the man flailed, trying to break Sam's hold on him. Sam didn't let go; he kept banging and banging the other man's head against the bench until the gun clattered to the floor and the man's eyes rolled back into his head.

Sarah ran forward, kicking the gun clear. "It's all right, Sam. Stop."

Sam gasped, his breath rattling through him in a sick wheeze as he leveraged his weight back, still trying to knock the other man against the bench.

"He's got a bomb. Detonator on his wrist."

Sarah knelt beside Sam, placed her arms around him. "Sshhh," she whispered into his ear. "It's okay. You can let go now."

He dropped the man, who fell to the floor, lifeless. Then Sam slumped into her arms. She held him tight, supporting him.

"I tried," he sobbed. "I tried so hard . . ."

His eyes closed and he collapsed.

December 24, 2007

Six months later

CHAPTER FIFTY-EIGHT

DECEMBER 24TH

I still hear Alan's screams, sometimes I'm not even asleep. When I do, I go up to Josh's room and watch him as he lays sleeping. He hasn't had any nightmares in months, sleeps so deep and peacefully that his own snoring doesn't wake him.

Just like his father.

When I do dream, I often see Damian Wright's face, that ghastly smile he gave me right before he died. As if he pitied me, knew what was coming. He opens his mouth and it's Alan's scream I hear. What scares me the most is I don't feel guilty about killing Alan or the other man—I took two lives that night, shouldn't I feel something more than relief? Than joy at the sight of Josh and Sam alive and whole?

I tell myself I'm not the monster Damian was, that I'm nothing like Alan. The Colonel and I have been taking long walks now that hunting season has begun. We've yet to shoot anything or even draw a

bead on our prey, instead we've been content to
merely track and watch them. Sometimes we'll talk—
for the first time he's told me the truth about his war.
Maybe someday I'll be ready to tell him about mine.
    Sam says I'm spoiling Josh but—

Sarah dropped her pen and the journal as the phone rang again. She looked to her bedroom door. Sam and Josh were in the kitchen decorating sugar cookies. It rang a third time. She rolled her eyes and grabbed the receiver.

"Sarah? It's Caitlyn. Sorry to disturb you on the holiday."

Sarah tensed but Caitlyn's voice was lighthearted. She forced herself to take a deep breath and eased her grip on the phone. "Hi, Caitlyn. Merry Christmas. Have you gotten any snow down there?"

"No, but I heard you got dumped on. Listen, I just wanted to let you know. Korsakov is dead."

"What? How?"

"His own family took a hit out on him. Heard he was going to make a deal now that he was facing the death penalty for Hal's death. They'd pretty much already disowned him after he lost all that money seven years ago, but I guess this was the last straw."

Sarah's gaze darted around the room. Nothing had changed. But everything had changed. "So, we don't have to worry—I mean, they're not going to—"

"No. You all are safe and in the clear."

Sarah slumped on the edge of the bed. Blew her breath out. "Wow. Thanks, Caitlyn. That's about the best Christmas present anyone could ever give us."

"You're quite welcome."

There was a pause as Sarah gathered her thoughts. "Caitlyn, do you ever dream? About that night? About Hal?"

Caitlyn's breath rasped across the phone line.

"I'm sorry, I shouldn't have asked—"

"Yeah, I do," came Caitlyn's quiet reply. "They're getting better. It's not exactly something you forget about overnight."

Sarah paced the length of the room and closed her door. "That's what I thought. But Sam, he doesn't dream, not since he got home from the hospital."

"You and Sam are sleeping together now?" Caitlyn's tone held a note of surprise.

"No, he's still sleeping in the office. But some nights I just need to know he's there, so I go in and I watch him." She leaned against her dresser scrutinizing her face in the mirror. "Am I crazy?"

"You're not crazy, Sarah. For you the nightmare began last summer. For Sam and Josh it was finally over. They're home again, safe and sound. Well, except for the pins in Sam's ankle, that is. Plus, I think it's different for guys. They don't worry as much about the could-haves or should-haves as we do."

"I was such a fool, trusting Alan."

"No. You were human. So," her voice took on a note of jocularity, "when you gonna cut Sam a break, forgive him? After all, the guy risked his life and almost died for you and Josh how many times?"

"You don't have kids, you can't understand. To do what he did . . ." Sarah trailed off. It was the same argument she'd been using for six months now. The words no longer had the impact they once did. She changed the subject. "I still can't believe I didn't see what was going on with Hal. How could I have missed that?"

"Don't beat yourself up. Over a third of meth addicts are professionals holding down steady jobs. Including teachers, lawyers, doctors, and law enforcement officers."

"Speaking of doctors, what's up with you and the neurosurgeon?"

"Neuroradiologist," Caitlyn corrected. "Things are good."

Sarah could hear the smile in her voice and guessed the doctor who saved Caitlyn's life by diagnosing the leaking blood vessel that had caused her migraines must be close by.

"How's Sam like teaching music?" Caitlyn asked.

"He's a natural." Sarah brightened. "You should see him with those kids. And he's loving playing Santa Claus, dividing up the finder's fee the government gave him among Katrina victims, the National Center for Missing and Exploited Children, and more. He's like a kid again. And guess what? He finally sold a song!"

"No kidding. Which one?"

"The one he was working on when he left. Sold it to a daytime soap opera of all places."

"I don't want to hold you up. Give him and Josh a kiss and hug for me, all right?"

"Thanks, Caitlyn. Merry Christmas."

Sarah hung up and glanced into the mirror again. A broad smile creased her face. She stared at her reflection, realizing it wasn't the news of Korsakov's death that had brought that gleam of joy to her eyes. It had happened while she was telling Caitlyn about Sam—it was the same light, floaty feeling she'd felt seven years ago when she'd first fallen in love with him.

Nonsense. She grabbed her hairbrush, pulled her hair back, and set it back down on the dresser. And realized something was missing. Puzzled, she left the bedroom and joined Sam and Josh in the kitchen. As usual, they'd managed to get more of the icing and candy sprinkles on the floor and themselves than on the cookies. Josh's mouth was ringed with pink as he licked frosting from his finger.

"Josh, were you in my room?" she asked. "Did you take the ring box from my dresser?"

He giggled and shook his head back and forth.

"I did," Sam said. Josh's laughter grew as Sam turned to him and placed a finger over his lips. Obviously they shared a secret. "I didn't think you'd notice so quickly. Here." He reached into his pocket and pulled out the small black velvet box.

Sarah looked from one of them to the other, both grinning like idiots. They were so much alike with their dark hair and dark eyes crinkled with delight.

"What's going on?" she asked as she took the box. Then she opened it. Nestled inside was a gleaming diamond engagement ring. Sarah felt her mouth drop open in surprise.

"I promised you I'd get you a real one as soon as I sold a song," Sam said, startling her further by dropping to one knee and reaching for her hand. "The only question is, will you wear it? Sarah Godwin, will you be my bride? Again?"

His voice cracked and Sarah saw fear in his eyes. She stared at him for a long moment, trying to settle her own emotions.

Josh broke the solemn spell.

Laughing, he ran and threw himself into both their arms. Sam stood, taking Josh with him, sandwiching him in his favorite kind of hug. A calming warmth settled over Sarah as she clutched both her men. Never again would she take this for granted, neglect this.

Josh giggled from between them as Sarah leaned forward and kissed Sam. "I already am your wife," she answered Sam. "For always."

But it's not over for Caitlyn Tierney . . .

Read the first chapter from
C. J. Lyons' next utterly gripping
thriller right here.

BLACK SHEEP

And buy it now:

Available in ebook on 26th February 2013

CHAPTER ONE

"Drop the gun!" Caitlyn Tierney shouted to the FBI agent.

The agent hesitated, chin bobbing as she tried to decide the correct move to make. Tough choice since Caitlyn held the agent's male partner against her chest as a shield. She'd grabbed his weapon and now used his greater height as an advantage. The only portion of Caitlyn's five-six frame visible to the female agent was Caitlyn's hand holding his own weapon to his head.

The female agent held her weapon steady, aiming at her partner and Caitlyn behind him. Fat lot of good that was going to do her, but it was standard procedure.

Caitlyn braced herself against the larger agent. He smelled minty fresh, as if he'd chewed gum or used mouthwash before following his partner into this squalid dump of an apartment. Sweat trickled down from his hair-line, beading at the back of his collar. His hair had been freshly trimmed; his skin still held tiny nicks from the razor.

She glanced around. He was her only cover. The rest of

the apartment was bare of furniture except for a sagging tweed couch shoved against the far wall and a coffee table made of cheap two-by-fours. Back to the wall, Caitlyn's only exit was the door to the right of the female agent across from her.

"Let's talk about this." The female agent's voice quavered, but her aim didn't falter. "Let him go and we'll talk."

"Shut up or I shoot him!" Caitlyn responded, effectively removing the agent's best weapon: her command authority. Hard to negotiate or intimidate when you can't speak. "Drop your gun. Now!"

Make a choice, make a choice, Caitlyn thought. The overhead ceiling fan swooshed, barely stirring the air with its listless movements. The place stank of mold and sweat, of windows that didn't open, shag carpet decades out of date, and too many years of too many people making too many bad decisions. The FBI agent was just one more, standing in the weak light of a naked sixty-watt bulb, her mind stuttering through a minefield of options.

Don't make me do it. Choose. Just choose.

The agent didn't choose. Her aim faltered, dropped down, then raised halfway up in indecision.

Caitlyn shot her in the forehead, followed by a double tap to the chest.

Then Caitlyn touched the muzzle of her weapon to the male agent's temple. "Bang. You're dead."

"Tierney!" The scenario leader yelled her name from his observation post. "What the hell you doing?"

Trying to teach them how to stay alive in the real world, Caitlyn thought. She'd been where these New Agents in Training were: forced to choose between following procedure and taking a chance on her instincts.

Six months ago when she'd had a gun to her head and another pointed at her partner, Caitlyn surrendered her weapon. If she hadn't, she'd be dead—and so would five hundred innocent civilians. But she'd done it consciously, knowing her Glock wasn't her only weapon. That it wasn't even her best weapon.

These NATs needed to learn to think like that. It might save their lives someday.

The scenario leader, Mike LaSovage, one of the FBI Hostage Rescue Team members, clomped over to her, aiming his clipboard as if it were a weapon. "Supervisory Special Agent Tierney, a word, please."

Caitlyn removed her helmet and rubbed her right temple, lifting her short red hair, matted by the training gear, away from the itchy scar. She glanced at the female NAT she'd shot. The woman trembled. Her hand touched her face shield, coming away with neon green paint on her fingers—the color of Caitlyn's Simunition.

"She needed to make a decision," Caitlyn muttered, wiping her own sweaty palms against her black cargo pants. Simulation or not, the scenario hit close to home, awakening memories as well as a surge of adrenaline.

"The purpose of this exercise is to allow agents in training a chance to follow proper arrest procedure, not to throw them into a hostage negotiation." LaSovage turned so his back was to the NATs. Didn't want them to see

Mommy and Daddy fighting. The Bureau was above that. Follow the bible—a four-inch binder crammed full of rules, regulations, and standard operating procedures—and you'd go home at night, was the catechism the kids were meant to learn from these exercises.

Despite the fact that a few were close to Caitlyn's age, they were just kids. No idea what the real world held for them. Decisions made in a heartbeat, bullets fired that could never be unfired, good people lost because of your actions—or inaction.

"You saw the way they entered," Caitlyn argued, feeling older than her thirty-five years as she spied the crushed expressions on the NATs' faces. Nine years carrying a loaded weapon, almost dying twice, killing a man in close-quarters combat, watching a good man sacrifice his life to save hers: Permanent scars crisscrossed her body and her soul. She couldn't remember ever being as young as these new agents. "He was more concerned about following her lead than the threat I posed. Totally opened his weapon side to me. How could I resist? No real suspect would have."

LaSovage looked over his shoulder to where the two dead agents huddled together commiserating and hopefully dissecting their mistakes. "It was a sloppy entrance. But this is their first exercise outside of FATS video training. First real-life scenario. You didn't need to push it that far."

"I'll bet they don't make the same mistakes next time."

He grimaced in agreement. "Maybe. But let's play the rest of these by the book, okay?"

Caitlyn had never done "by the book" well. Used to be she could fake her way through it, pretend her actions were guided by rules and regulations, but after returning from an extended medical leave for emergency brain surgery that saved her life, she'd given up the pretense. Which was why the powers-that-be had left her in limbo, on temporary assignment here at Quantico.

"You doing okay?" LaSovage asked, trying not to stare at her hair, still not fully grown back after her operation. "Can't be easy after—"

"I'm fine." How many times a day did she have to tell people that? Or pretend she didn't notice their stares as she walked through the halls at the academy.

Six months ago she'd have embraced the idea of continuing on as a permanent instructor—she enjoyed teaching and loved challenging her students. But to be stranded here as temporary duty, merely so she could remain under the scrutiny of the bosses without becoming a PR risk? Suddenly her office in Jefferson Hall felt as cramped as a prison cell.

Her last case had earned her an unofficial reprimand from the Office of Professional Responsibility and an official, but grudgingly given, commendation for uncovering corruption in the FBI's higher ranks, the US Marshal Service, and even the sacrosanct FBI National Laboratory.

The brass would have preferred if she'd taken their offer of a medical pension and left the Bureau quietly, but no way was she going to let them bully her into quitting. Given that she knew of several embarrassing skeletons hidden in the FBI's closet, they couldn't fire her, not without risking another blot on the Bureau's public image.

Which left Caitlyn and her career in limbo.

"You sure?" LaSovage persisted. "We could grab a beer or something after we're done here. If you want to talk."

His glance dropped to the top part of the scar that ran vertically up her chest, visible above her tactical vest. The rest of the scar formed a letter K with the crossbars slashing above and below her left breast. If it weren't for her fair skin the scars would have been less noticeable, but after six months they were still reddish and she'd given up trying to hide beneath turtlenecks. Just like her attitude, they were now part of her, take it or leave it.

His concern seemed more genuine than the morbid curiosity most of her colleagues had exhibited. Interesting since, although LaSovage was a four-year veteran of the Hostage Rescue Team, the FBI's vaunted equivalent to an elite SWAT unit, he'd never actually had to kill anyone.

During the course of their careers it was rare for FBI agents to draw their weapons outside the range. Which made Caitlyn, so young, yet already almost dying a violent death twice and killing a man up close and personal, a distinct anomaly. She heard the whispers: Was she reckless? Stupid? Or just plain unlucky?

She wished she had an answer. "Thanks, but I need to be somewhere tonight," she told LaSovage. "Maybe next time."

He nodded, gave her an uncertain smile as if wondering if she was trying to protect him or herself, then turned to usher the next group into position.

They finished out the remaining training for the day, and she returned to her office in Jefferson Hall to grab her laptop and car keys. She was surprised when the female agent in training from the earlier scenario appeared at her doorway, now wearing clean regulation khakis and a blue polo shirt.

"What would you have done?" the NAT blurted out, ignoring the strict protocol that usually guided NATs' interactions with their instructors. Belatedly she added, "Ma'am."

"What's your name?" Caitlyn took the seat behind her desk, but left the NAT standing at attention. This group was new, hadn't taken any of her classes yet, so she didn't know them personally; she'd merely been playing a bad guy in today's scenarios to help with evaluations.

"Garman, ma'am. Mary Agnes Garman."

Mary Agnes? Sounded like a nun's name. She was only a year or two younger than Caitlyn, in good shape but not as fit as the recruits coming from the military or law enforcement, with an hourglass figure that did not fit her name. Although who knew what nuns looked like under those habits?

Caitlyn filled her mind with an image of a mother superior holding a compass—a mnemonic technique she'd cultivated after her brain trauma made remembering things like names a struggle. Not that she'd ever share that secret with anyone.

"What did you see as your options, Garman?"

Mary Agnes hesitated, not in indecision as she had earlier, but in thought. "You didn't give me any."

"Exactly. What's wrong with that statement?"

Her rigid posture sagged. Caitlyn nodded to the chair across from her, and Mary Agnes slumped into it. "I gave you the power. But—" She scowled in thought, her gaze drifting past Caitlyn to the window, already dark with the early-January sunset. "But I still had no options."

"Tunnel vision. The adrenaline makes you focus on what's in front of you, the direct threat. It does that to your mind as well. But there are always possibilities. Don't ever forget that."

"I could have lowered my weapon, but regulations—"

"Do the bad guys play by the rules?"

"No, but—"

"In here"—Caitlyn gestured to the cement-block walls surrounding them—"you have to know the rules, live by them. And that's not a bad thing. Nine times out of ten they'll save your butt."

"And the tenth time?"

"Look for options. You never considered any other options today. Instead you hesitated, couldn't commit to a course."

"I froze. I got my partner killed." The remorse and fear in Mary Agnes's voice was real. Good. Better she learn the hard lessons now before the gun pointed at her shot something more lethal than a paintball.

"You did. Next time you won't."

"What would you have done?"

"You still controlled the exit."

"It was too far away."

Caitlyn shook her head. "No. It was only three steps to

your right. Adrenaline. It distorts everything. Good thing is, the bad guys are affected as well, have the same limitations."

"I could never abandon my partner." Her voice made it sound like sacrilege, reinforcing the mother superior image in Caitlyn's mind. As if what Caitlyn suggested was as bad as betraying a family member. Which, in a sense, it was. Unless you imagined past the knee-jerk blind obedience to ethics and codes of conduct.

"Yes. You could. Three steps and you would have been behind cover, able to observe, negotiate, call for backup, or shoot if the hostage taker took further action."

"Further action. You mean kill my partner."

Caitlyn stood. Stretched her arms wide. "Look at me, Garman. I'm all of five-six, can bench one thirty, maybe one fifty on a good day. What good would a six-foot, two-hundred-pound deadweight do me?"

"You wouldn't have shot him?"

"Not unless he was no longer useful. And that would only happen if—" She arched an eyebrow, waiting for Mary Agnes to put the pieces together.

It took a moment, but the frown faded as the answers fell into place for the agent in training. "I blocked your escape. If I was out of the picture, dead, you could make a run for it. By standing there, I gave you more reason to kill us both."

"Exactly. You were thinking about what you wanted, but you should have been focused on what the hostage taker wanted. Embrace the possibilities, decide how you can control the outcome."

Mary Agnes took a deep breath, chin bobbing in agreement. She stood with renewed energy. "Thank you. Supervisory Special Agent Tierney. You gave me a lot to think about."

Caitlyn smiled, remembered why she enjoyed teaching so much. "No problem, Garman. Have a good night."

Mary Agnes headed back to the dormitory while Caitlyn took the steps down to the lobby, waved to the guard there, and jogged through the cold, her coat flapping open, to her Subaru Impreza WRX parked in front of Jefferson Hall. A thin coating of frost crackled across the Subaru's windshield, but she didn't waste time scraping it clear. She still had thirty-six miles to drive to Paul's place in DC.

She took back roads, avoiding 95 and the constant snarl of traffic on the interstate. Usually she enjoyed the hour-long drive. It provided needed breathing space.

As extroverted as she was introverted, Paul often joked that if it weren't for him, she'd be living the life of a hermit. She never let him know how close to the truth that was. She'd yet to invite him to her place in Manassas for a night, was more than willing to let him think it was because as a neuroradiologist he had to stay close to GW.

In reality, she simply didn't do entertaining. Or strangers in her space. So much easier to make the drive, enjoy Paul's company, and leave when she wanted. She liked the freedom, needed the control—another thing Paul teased her about.

Only lately he wasn't teasing. He was hinting. Emptying a dresser drawer and shelf in the bathroom for her.

Talking about how much her drive took away from the time they had together.

He was ready to settle down. With her. For the long term. And it scared the shit out of her. Caitlyn didn't do relationships, never had. She did longer-than-average flings that ended in shouting matches, bruised egos, guys storming away, and her sighing in relief at another bullet dodged.

Paul didn't shout. He wasn't an alpha male, not like her usual guys, and his ego didn't bruise. He cuddled. Comforted. And actually enjoyed it.

Worse, so did she. Being taken care of was a foreign experience to Caitlyn. Paul wrapping his arms around her, sharing his strength, putting her first—it was sweet and sexy and so very addictive. Another thing that scared her. Ever since she was nine and lost her dad, Caitlyn had lived her life and guarded her heart with one rule: Trust no one.

Paul had snuck past that barbed-wire rule and now she was at a loss how to handle things. Part of her wanted to embrace the life he offered: a normal, stable, caring, trusting relationship.

The child in her screamed to run, run, run before she exposed herself too much.

She'd loved every moment of their six months together. Paul had reminded her that there was more to life than just her work. After almost dying, she'd needed that, needed a little of what everyone else seemed to have: someone to come home to, a connection with the world outside the FBI.

Despite the fact that Paul had given her more than any other man she'd ever been with, she knew she didn't have the feelings for him that she should have. It worried her. What was wrong with her that a normal relationship with a terrific guy terrified her more than facing an armed felon? Paul had saved her life six months ago when he diagnosed her brain aneurysm. If she couldn't bring herself to trust him, would she ever be able to trust anyone?

Caitlyn hesitated before pulling into the underground garage at his building. She could call, make an excuse about the training going late, drive back to Manassas and the peaceful solitude of her apartment. He'd never know she was lying—she was pretty good at it. Her chest tightened. Mouth went dry. She didn't want to lie. Not to Paul.

But she was afraid of what she might be facing when she went inside. Afraid of what she'd do when he forced her to make the choice. She didn't want to lose him, wasn't ready to return to her solitary ways.

Not a ring, please nor a ring, she thought as she left the Impreza and waited for the elevator. Her cell rang and she grabbed it like a drowning woman lunging for a lifeline.

"Tierney."

"Excuse me, Supervisory Special Agent, this is the operator at the Washington Field Office. 1 have an urgent call for you from the prison chaplain at Butner Federal Correctional Institution. Will you accept the call?"

The elevator came and she entered, hit the button for Paul's floor. Who the hell did she have behind bars at Butner? Maybe one of the convictions from her time in Boston had turned and they moved him to the facility in

North Carolina? After all, Bernie Madoff and Jonathan Pollard were doing time there, as well as a smattering of mobsters turned witnesses for the prosecution.

As always, her curiosity got the better of her. Not to mention an excuse to delay seeing Paul—the thought felt strange, as if she were betraying Paul, but it also gave her a weird sense of relief. Why did relationships have to be so damn confusing? Give her a felon to take down any day of the week. "Sure, put him through."

"Caitlyn Tierney?" The man's voice was unfamiliar. "I'm Pastor Vince Whitford, one of the chaplains at Butner."

She left the elevator and stopped outside Paul's door. No sense knocking if this was something that was going to take her back to work. "Yes. Why are you calling, Pastor?"

He cleared his throat, obviously uncomfortable. "I've been counseling a prisoner here at Butner Medium who tried to kill himself a few days ago. Eli Hale."

Hale, she'd never arrested anyone—oh, hell. She did know that name. Hadn't heard it in twenty-six years. The image of a man, taller and broader than her father, as black as Sean Tierney was pale, his voice low and husky and shaking with laughter as he chased after his daughter and Caitlyn, playing the scary monster to their damsels in distress, a game that always ended with Caitlyn and Vonnie gathered under Eli's massive arms, giggling as he twirled them around until they were dizzy with delight.

"Eli Hale?" It was her turn to clear her throat as childhood memories flooded through her. Vonnie, her best friend in the whole world—until they'd been yanked apart after Caitlyn's dad was forced to arrest his own best friend, Eli Hale. For murder. "Is he okay?"

"He is now. The doctors are releasing him from the medical unit tomorrow, but I convinced him to agree to meet with you. I think you're the only person who can help him."

Anger and confusion twisted through her, tossing her childhood memories aside. Except the one that never left her: the image of her father lying dead, killed with his own gun, by his own hand. Unable to stand the guilt of seeing his best friend convicted of murder.

She swallowed bile. "I think you have the wrong person. There's no reason on earth why I'd want to talk to Eli Hale. Or him to me."

"Please, Agent Tierney. Don't hang up. A girl's life is at stake."

Caitlyn's fingers closed around the cell phone, almost but not quite touching the end-call icon. She wanted to hang up, to end this painful trip down memory lane. But . . ."What girl?"

"Eli's youngest, Lena."